WE
ARE
BLOOD
AND
THUNDER

WE ARE BLOOD AND THUNDER

KESIA LUPO

BLOOMSBURY

NEW YORK LONDON OXFORD NEW DELHI SYDNEY

BLOOMSBURY YA
Bloomsbury Publishing Inc., part of Bloomsbury Publishing Plc
1385 Broadway, New York, NY 10018

BLOOMSBURY and the Diana logo are trademarks of Bloomsbury Publishing Plc

First published in Great Britain in April 2019 by Bloomsbury Publishing Plc
Published in the United States of America in March 2020 by Bloomsbury YA

Bloomsbury books may be purchased for business or promotional use. For information on bulk purchases
please contact Macmillan Corporate and Premium Sales Department at specialmarkets@macmillan.com

Library of Congress Cataloging-in-Publication Data
Names: Lupo, Kesia, author.
Title: We are blood and thunder / by Kesia Lupo.
Description: New York : Bloomsbury, 2020.
Summary: Lena, a cryptling, and Constance, the duke's banished daughter, must use their forbidden magic
to discover who cast a spell over their homeland, shrouding it in deadly clouds and sealing it off.
Identifiers: LCCN 2019020785 (print) | LCCN 2019022123 (e-book)
ISBN 978-1-5476-0305-3 (hardcover) • ISBN 978-1-5476-0306-0 (e-book)
Subjects: CYAC: Magic—Fiction. | Fantasy.
Classification: LCC PZ7.1.L86 We 2020 (print) | LCC PZ7.1.L86 (e-book) | DDC [Fic]—dc23
LC record available at https://lccn.loc.gov/2019020785
LC e-book record available at https://lccn.loc.gov/2019022123

Typeset by RefineCatch Limited, Bungay, Suffolk
Printed and bound in the U.S.A. by Berryville Graphics Inc., Berryville, Virginia
2 4 6 8 10 9 7 5 3 1

All papers used by Bloomsbury Publishing Plc are natural, recyclable products made from wood
grown in well-managed forests. The manufacturing processes conform to the environmental
regulations of the country of origin.

To find out more about our authors and books visit www.bloomsbury.com and sign up for our newsletters.

To Jeff

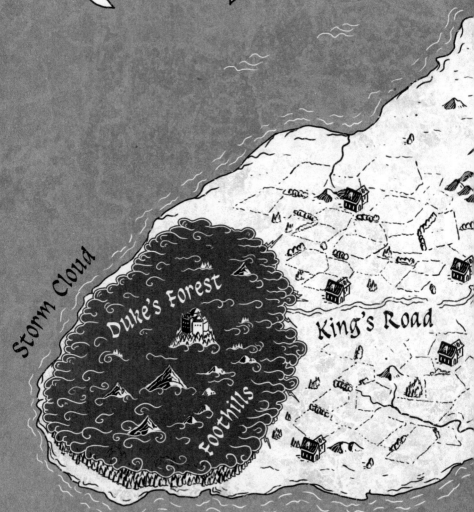

HOLY COUNCIL OF THE NINE GODS

FAUL
THE HUNTSMAN GOD
Color of disciples' magic: **SILVER**

Disciples of Faul are responsible for policing the magical population. They are tasked with finding and bringing in Rogues, dispatching Radicals, and capturing magical criminals. Few are suited to the magic of Faul, and the life-threatening demands exacted upon disciples are sure to dissuade some potential candidates.

MYTHRIS
THE MASKED GOD
Color of disciples' magic: **PURPLE**

Disciples of Mythris are known as spies and assassins, often employed by the state, sometimes by private individuals for the right price. Little is known about the specific content of their work, and their temples tend to be hidden away.

JOK
THE WARRIOR GOD
Color of disciples' magic: **RED**

Disciples of Jok are combat specialists, learned in the arts of fighting and military tactics. This temple is one of the most populous—few major wars have been fought in recent times and disciples are instead well compensated as general peacekeepers and guards.

NOMI
THE EXPLORER GOD
Color of disciples' magic: **GREEN**

Disciples of Nomi are skilled in spells of navigation and, particularly, scrying (the finding of lost things). Very few people are suited to this set of skills despite the lure of the exotic locations to which disciples are posted.

IMRIS
THE HEALER GOD
Color of disciples' magic: **BLUE**

Disciples of Imris are specialist healers and physicians. Although priests of other temples may be physicians, the disciples of Imris are multifaceted and incredibly delicate in their expertise. Imris has many disciples.

REGIS
THE RULER GOD
Color of disciples' magic: **WHITE**

Disciples of Regis are cut out for leadership and politics. They have truth-seeing and divinatory abilities, useful in both these professions. Regis is a popular temple, attracting academically gifted mages.

TURAH
THE LAND GODDESS
One of the twins
Color of disciples' magic: **OCHER**

Disciples of Turah are skilled in agricultural magics, sensing and encouraging growth in the soil, and even (for her most powerful disciples) controlling the weather. Turah was once a most revered goddess, but these days few are attracted to this temple.

JURAH
THE JUSTICE GODDESS
The second twin
Color of disciples' magic: **BLACK**

Disciples of Jurah are rare in Valorian, although in the past they were among the most esteemed, their powers allowing them to null and manipulate the abilities of other mages. Nowadays the few remaining disciples of Jurah play a largely ceremonial role as the king's executioners.

AMORIS
THE GOLDEN GODDESS
Color of disciples' magic: **GOLD**

Disciples of Amoris study the magics of good fortune and seduction. They are the financiers of Valorian, with their temples (which operate variably as bathhouses or the only legitimate brothels on the continent) by far the most profitable of the nine. An enduringly popular temple.

In the Year of Kings 554, the mountain city-state of Duke's Forest was beset by a mysterious vapor. It started out as little more than a few wisps of gray cloud, emanating bafflingly from the earth of the lower town, ruining the townsfolk's garden crops. But gradually, month by month, it grew—vapor became mist, and mist became fog, and the fog, eventually, became a storm cloud.

Inside the cloud, a traveler could expect to encounter flashes of light and rumbling noises, sudden gusts and squalls of thin, poisonous rain that stung bare skin. And sometimes, like the eye of a storm, the cloud appeared to sleep—as still and immutable as the mountain itself.

In the first two years, trade was crippled, domestic animals sickened, the rose gardens of the upper town were ruined—yet the cloud, insatiable, crept uphill toward the castle at the mountain's summit. By the start of the third year, the mountain was swallowed up entirely . . . and that's when the Pestilence came.

At the start of the fourth year, the Duke shut and chained the city gates, declaring a state of quarantine. After six years, the people of Duke's Forest, ravaged by disease, cut off from the outside world, and shrouded from the sky, had sunk into isolation and despair.

Duke's Forest: A History

PROLOGUE
A Cryptling

Before the storm cloud

Lena swept the last of the dust into her sack and stood up tall, wiping a grimy hand across her forehead. Her brass lantern flickered across the crypt's rough-hewn walls as Hunter slunk past, a twitching rat hanging from his jaws. He dropped it and purred at her, before savaging the poor creature's torso. The largest mouser prowling the crypts, Hunter was vicious, ginger, and apparently immortal. For the hundredth time, Lena wondered why he'd picked her bed in which to sleep, leaving dubious gifts of rodents and birds at its foot.

Lena tied the dust sack shut and hoisted it over her shoulder, casting one last look at the empty, fresh-polished sarcophagus where the body would be laid in the morning for its last rites, the Descent. Her stomach twisted, and she swallowed hard as bile rose in her throat. Earlier in the afternoon, she'd been allowed to watch while Mortician Vigo prepared the body in one of the special rooms beneath the gardens. She had managed—but only by digging her nails hard into her palms—to stop herself from fainting.

The dead man's Ancestors lay all around, stretching into darkness. Now attuned to the scent of the morticians' special preserving ointments, Lena picked out sharp herbal smells beneath the ever-present musk of her world. The tomb itself was relatively small, and while noble families had the luxury of individual sarcophagi, the stonemason's family—like most others—had cut long, body-shaped niches into the walls, one over another, or shared two bodies to a resting place. Husband with wife. Sister with brother. Baby with mother.

Each body's empty eye sockets had been sewn open, their eyes replaced with smooth rocks painted as eyes, or sometimes glittering gemstones. Mortician Vigo said that the Ancestors were sleeping, but Lena didn't think so. They were staring at the ceiling, at the floors of the living world above. Waiting.

Waiting for what?

A chill ran down her spine. She touched her forehead, lips, and heart in the old sign of reverence. When she'd been very little, the Ancestors had frightened her—she'd had nightmares about the staring stone eyes, about the way the older corpses' flesh and skin were shrunken and leathery but their hair as thick and lustrous as the day of death. How, from certain angles, even the oldest of the Ancestors looked like living people lying in the dark. But now she was eleven, almost a grown-up, and she wasn't afraid of anything.

Hunter mewed, and Lena nearly jumped out of her skin. *I'm not afraid of anything*, she reminded herself firmly, calming her racing heart.

"All right—let's go," she whispered to the cat, after a deep breath. "It's a long walk back."

She tried not to hurry as she started down the passages under the upper town, leading to the network of small cellars beneath the castle that the cryptlings called home. You weren't meant to hurry—it wasn't respectful, Mortician Vigo said. Hunter weaved through her legs, in and out of the lantern light, very nearly tripping her up.

For a time, everything was quiet and ordinary, the only sounds the occasional scuttle of a rat, or the snap of one of the mousetraps Lena had set out on her way down—the cryptlings and the cats were supposed to keep the vermin at bay. But as she drew farther through the cobwebbed passages, she started to hear something strange . . . a voice. It grew louder gradually: a low, rhythmic murmur, drifting from somewhere up ahead.

Lena frowned and stopped. Who else might be down here in the dead of night? As far as she knew, the stonemason's was the only funeral tomorrow, and she was the only cryptling on duty. No one else was allowed down here.

Suddenly she was frightened. She flicked off her lantern and stood in the dark for a few moments. She didn't like the thought of being seen—didn't like the way people's eyes settled on her, on the black mark on her cheek. She felt

Hunter slide past her legs, hurrying ahead impatiently, as she stood listening in the quiet. The voice carried on—distant and musical. A sad song, perhaps . . . or a poem. But Lena couldn't make out the words. She wondered if they were in another language.

She continued down the familiar passages in darkness, trailing her fingers along the wall, her feet silent in the padded canvas slippers they had to wear in the crypts. The voice grew closer, louder, as she neared the passages she knew were directly beneath the castle itself, where the noble Ancestors and their households were interred. But she saw nothing—and after a time, the voice stopped.

Her heart beat faster. Somehow the silence and darkness were more unnerving now that she knew someone, somewhere, was sharing them with her. And that's when she saw it: the flicker of light. She clutched tightly the iron handle of her lantern and her dust sack, half convincing herself to run. Cold sweat broke out across the back of her neck.

At first, she wondered if it was a trick of her eyes in the dark—she'd known it to happen before, green-purple shapes blooming like strange flowers, disappearing, and re-forming at a blink. But this was real, she saw, as it grew closer—a clumsy, winding speck of light, fluttering on and off, bright, then dim. A . . . butterfly?

She watched, her heart hammering. She'd never felt so terribly alert, every sense sharp, nearly painful.

The creature was made of metal—filigree wings, a smooth brass body. It landed on the edge of a sarcophagus nearby, its wings gently rising and falling, rising and falling, like the breath of a tiny animal.

It was beautiful.

Lena set down her things and stepped closer. The light emanating from the creature's body was flickering, like a sputtering candle. She reached out to touch it . . . but hesitated, fingers outstretched.

All the rules Vigo had ever told her ran through her mind at once, like a flock of startled birds. *Don't reveal your face aboveground. Don't touch anybody, especially anybody who's not a cryptling. Don't touch the Ancestors, except as your duties demand. Don't touch the grave goods. Don't touch anything. To other people, Lena, you are dirty. Everything you touch is sullied.*

And yet . . . she'd never seen anything so beautiful. Lena stopped thinking. She reached out and cupped the butterfly in her hands. She felt its delicate legs like feathers on her palms. It was incredibly light and made a faint whirring sound like a watch as its wings fluttered weakly.

Suddenly its little light extinguished and the crypt was plunged into darkness. Lena shivered. The creature was silent and still, the slight warmth quickly fading from its body, as if it had never been.

Is it broken?

She waited a few moments more, her heart in her mouth. Somewhere she could hear hurried footsteps, a voice calling—but if they were searching for the butterfly, they were moving in the wrong direction, some way off to her left. Lena opened her palms and ran her fingers along the butterfly's body. Its wings were fully outstretched, and she liked the feel of the filigree patterns against her fingertips. It was strangely soothing.

But the butterfly didn't belong to her. She should drop it here and go home.

Even though her mind had decided, her body didn't move. She shouldn't take it, should she? She couldn't. If anyone found out she had removed anything from the crypts, she'd be in trouble. Even if she hadn't found it on a body, it was still grave goods. Who would believe her when she said it had been flying toward her, as if it had chosen her, as if it had *wanted* her to take it?

Somehow it didn't matter: the determination was already hardening in her heart. She wasn't allowed to have things of her own: even her clothes were shared hand-me-downs, her soft shoes worn thin by other cryptlings' feet. And aboveground, she knew, the un-Marked children of the upper town had rooms filled with toys and trinkets—and even clothes that only they had worn. Except for the dark birthmark on her cheek, she wasn't any different from them. So why shouldn't she have the butterfly? She felt her breath quicken. It was only one thing. Such a small thing. She'd keep it secret, of course. She'd never tell a soul. It would be something hers and hers alone—her only possession. Was that so much to ask?

Lena slipped the metal creature into the inside pocket of her habit, picked up her lantern and sack, and continued on through the tunnels.

ONE
The Hounds

Sixth year of the storm cloud

Lena ran until her lungs felt close to bursting, her feet thumping, sliding on the steep cobblestone road, down the peak of the city toward the walls and the forest beyond.

The Justice's words rang loud in her ears.

You have been found guilty of magecraft.

The storm cloud was all-encompassing, a thick, poisonous gauze clinging to her clothes, obscuring her path.

I sentence you to die.

Islands of muffled light trembled in the gloom—a lit window here, a patch of fading sunlight there. Her feet thumped into grayness, invisible.

The hounds will eat your flesh.

She could hear them—howling, growling. Had they finished off Vigo? Or had they grown tired of his old body, and were they now lusting after hers? He'd bought her time, but it was all for nothing. Tears stung her eyes as she pushed herself faster.

Your bones will lie bare under the sky, banished from the sacred crypts.

She could never outrun them. Nobody could. At seventeen, she would be far from the youngest to fall under the hounds' vicious teeth; you only had to see the chewed-up remains at the foot of the city walls to know that. But there was a chance—just a chance. She had to try.

Your soul will never join the Ancestors, will never feast on the glories of ages past, will never guide the fates.

Lena found herself down in the lowest tier of the city. The fog was thicker here. She stumbled to a halt, suddenly unable to breathe, a crushing pain in her side. Pulling up the neck of her habit to cover her mouth and nose, she felt tears welling behind the glass of her shield-eyes.

You will be dead, in this world and the next.

A howl broke the gloom, then a chorus of howls, swiftly followed by frenzied barking; the hounds were gaining. No time to cry. She turned and ran, harder than ever, hobnailed boots clacking against the pavement.

Soon the city walls loomed above, and a small bone crunched under her foot. She felt sick, but pressed on around the curve of the wall, desperately scanning the base where the dark stone met the bone-littered ground. The gates had been locked for two years, bolted with broad beams of oak, ivy grown over the rusted locks—but nearby . . . Vigo had told her . . .

Lena scanned the rotted undergrowth for the outline of the old rosebush—and found it, her heart no more than a hollow, fluttering thing in the back of her throat. She could so easily have missed it altogether, a tangle of bare thorns almost lost among the skeletal remains of its neighbors. Parting the branches with her thick leather gloves, she spotted a slight dip in the earth. So small.

I used it as a child, he'd said, in the few moments they'd had together before the hounds. *I would slip out into the forest to play when I was supposed to be at my lessons. It was before my . . . deformity.*

She'd shaken her head wordlessly, clutching at his old arthritic hands, the hands that had first picked her up from the steps down to the cryptling cellars when she was a baby, wailing into the dawn. She'd been crying again then.

Lena, I cannot run. But you might just be fast and small enough to escape.

It was her only chance.

Lena threw herself to the ground as the howls behind her grew in intensity—along with the clink and scratch of claws on the cobblestones. She pressed herself under the bush, the old thorny stems snagging at her habit and showering her with rot, and scrabbled into the musty darkness beneath the wall. Curling her fingers as best she could into the damp soil, Lena pulled herself forward, wriggling until her feet were almost concealed under the rosebush, the weight of the great thick wall, dark and cold and ancient, bearing down over her head.

The gap was tight, her lungs constricting as she forced her shoulders farther, her arms outstretched. She thought she could feel a wisp of air from the other side—but it was then that a bark came from close quarters, followed by a frenzy of growls, a snapping of teeth. Something closed around the tough leather heel of her boot; a surprising strength pulled her backward. Panic fueled her. Reaching up, she gripped the wall's slick underside with clawed hands. Her shield-eyes snagged on a root, the leather strap snapping. She let them fall, kicked out hard, and redoubled her efforts, squirming frantically under the wall until she could see the light filtering through the other side. She squeezed her shoulders forward and, with more difficulty, her hips, ripping the coarse material of her habit. By this time, she had begun to sob—but somehow she forced her way out.

Lena staggered to her feet, half falling into the forest. Her heart plummeted as she absorbed the sight confronting her. The forest was a picture of decay, the trees visibly withering. A gray residue veiled their bark and occasionally bumped outward in a strange fungus. The storm cloud was as thick as it was within the walls of the city, flashing and rumbling between the trees. She thought of her shield-eyes, fallen under the wall—but where she had crawled, the hounds could surely follow; she couldn't risk retrieving them. She ran instead, stumbling over roots, slipping on wet leaves. Here and there, a rotted trunk had fallen across the path, or a branch half snapped from a larger tree threatened her head.

Gradually, the howls and barks faded altogether, but it was a long time before Lena allowed herself to be certain she had not been followed—perhaps the dogs, penned for so long within the city walls, had been spooked by the alien scents and noises of the forest. Or perhaps the houndmaster had assumed her dead and called them off, or perhaps he'd feared losing them forever among the trees, as so many travelers had been lost before. In any case, she was painfully grateful. She slowed down, rubbed her stinging eyes, and caught her breath. She rested her hands on her knees for a moment, her heartbeat slowing—and then she reached for the brass butterfly she kept in the pocket of her robe. It was as big as the palm of her hand, warm from her body. Tracing the delicate filigree of its wings, she felt her breathing slow.

Whenever she held the butterfly, she remembered how she had felt the night she'd found it—or rather, the night it had found her. She had felt wanted. Calm. Secure in the knowledge that she was worth something, because she had something of worth.

Out of the corner of her eye she saw a shape—a human shape, hunched at the foot of a tree. Her stomach convulsed and she ducked behind a rotten tangle of undergrowth, pressing her hand against her mouth to stifle a rising scream. But the figure didn't appear to have noticed her. The cloud shifted, alternately revealing and concealing a long cloak, brown boots, large leather gloves. So still, so quiet, his hooded head resting on his chest. Sleeping? But she saw no movement, not a twitch, no rise and fall of breath. Slowly, Lena realized the man was dead.

She slipped the butterfly into her pocket, stood up, and walked toward him, her whole body still trembling—but gradually calming as she approached the corpse. She wasn't afraid of the dead—not unless they . . . She shook her head, not wanting to think about it. No, it was the living who frightened her.

She crouched, examined a blade dropped near the body glinting in the faint evening light filtering through cloud and trees. It was a short dagger, the hilt twined with a dragon motif in silver, its eye set with a green gem. Hardly thinking, she picked it up, slid it carefully into her belt. As she moved on, she realized the man had been resting at the edge of a small clearing. And she saw another body. A woman, her back turned to Lena, marked by her perfectly preserved, long red hair, splayed in the mud. And another—a man curled up under his cloak by the blackened remains of a fire. Without meaning to, she glimpsed his face, decayed and ghastly.

These bodies had been here for a long time. Had they been trying to reach the city? They were strangers, surely. What had killed them?

She didn't want to wait to find out.

She returned to the narrow path and carried on at a stumbling run.

After a time, it grew so late that she could barely distinguish the trees from the darknesses in between—but soon she began to see other things, shapes in the fog twisting into suggestions of hands, eyes, mouths. She blinked, rubbing her face and cursing the loss of her shield-eyes. No one in Duke's Forest would step outside with their eyes unprotected—the toxic storm cloud caused visions if they were exposed for too long. Every now and then, larger shapes loomed from between the trees, and she could not prevent herself from starting backward before they dissipated, even though she knew they weren't real.

She imagined the strangers' bodies in the clearing moving, rising up, following her. *Don't. Think.* But despite her stern thoughts, and the exhaustion screaming at her to stop, she quickened her pace.

Eventually, Lena could continue no longer. Her legs gave out, and she felt her fingers burrow into the mossy mulch of the forest floor. The hallucinations were worsening. She knew she was vulnerable out here—to *real* threats— if she wasn't able to run. She remembered Vigo's tales of the giant snakes and wild boar that infested the wood and screwed her eyes shut against a wave of terror. She took a deep breath. She needed her wits now more than ever.

But the forest stretched in all directions, and she had long lost the road—how would she escape? And even if she were to find her way out, what fate could a girl like her expect in the wider world? She felt for the birthmark on her cheek, several shades darker than the brown of her skin. Even the people of Duke's Forest had regarded cryptlings—marked out by their various deformities—with a mixture of disgust and begrudging respect for their duties. Vigo had said the gods were cruel, their followers toying with dangerous magic. What would they make of her? What did they do to Marked people outside Duke's Forest?

Would *they* try to execute her too?

Lena felt a sickly chill spread from her throat to her stomach as she considered the most terrible possibility of all: What if the storm cloud had swallowed everything, leaving the city of Duke's Forest the lonely center of the universe? What if those people had been trying to reach Duke's Forest to save themselves?

No—she could not give up. Lena opened her eyes and dragged her exhausted body upright once more, determined to continue, but now she was surrounded, not by trees but by a mass of people, each one of them turning toward her—each one of them familiar. These were the dead of Duke's Forest, the dead the Pestilence had taken, the dead she had helped to undress, wash, and embalm, replacing their eyes with the painted stones and glittering gems that now bore into her.

She was a convicted mage and an outcast, and the Ancestors were angry.

She stumbled back against a tree, touched her forehead, lips, and chest in a silent prayer, her hand shaking. "Please . . . ," she managed, but the Ancestors' hearts were hollowed out. The world turned black.

Lena had been sixteen the first time it had happened, a year before the Justice had condemned her to die. She'd been helping Vigo embalm an old guardsman, dead of the Pestilence, in one of the special preparatory chambers beneath the castle's gardens. Thick glass bricks had been set in the ceiling, allowing weak light—and the occasional flash of the storm cloud's blue-green lightning—to filter down on their delicate work.

She had pulled up the guardsman's left eyelid to sew it in place with the curved needle and special white thread. Eyes were something of a specialty of Lena's, with her slender, accurate fingers—and although she had once hated the feel of the cold gems slotting into empty sockets, in time she had come to find it satisfying.

"Have you thought about what you're going to do?" Master Vigo had said, in the manner of one who had asked the question a hundred times. He was in the process of removing and potting the organs, a special stoneware jar for each one. The smell of spoiling flesh filled the air, but Lena had grown used to it long ago. "You ought to. You have barely a year until you come of age." He deftly pulled the liver through the small incision he had cut in the body's side and slipped it into the waiting vessel, already packed with the sharp-smelling preservative oils and herbs.

"I haven't thought about it," Lena lied, trying to sound dismissive. "A year is a long time." In fact, she'd been thinking about it a lot recently. She'd never chosen this life. The birthmark on her face had chosen it for her—or rather, her parents had, whoever they were, when they decided to abandon her to the fate of a cryptling rather than raise a Marked child.

"It's not, and you're a fool to pretend you can put it off for much longer."

Lena shrugged as she pulled the fourth stitch neatly through the thin skin of the lid. Vigo was a miserable old goat, but she'd come to love him, and she knew he was right. As she leaned forward to make her fifth and last stitch, she felt the weight of the brass butterfly in her pocket. Her secret, ever since she had found it fluttering in the catacombs. She knew if anyone saw it, she'd be accused of stealing grave goods, a terrible crime for a cryptling—but somehow she couldn't bear to let it go. It was the only thing she had.

"You'd make a good mortician," said Vigo, limping around the body to inspect her work as she tied the thread and snipped it with a pair of small, sharp scissors. "You've got a steady hand, Lena—and you're quiet, respectful." She glanced up at him. She could tell his leg was hurting him today—the tension around his eyes and mouth showed itself in hard lines through his pale, papery skin. He had a wooden peg from the knee down, to replace the limb they'd had to amputate, but no matter how hard Lena tried to find him the right kind of padding, and the right sort of salve, the place where it met the stub was nearly always sore.

She smiled at him weakly and shook her head, setting down her needle. She couldn't tell him the truth. She couldn't admit that because every option involved working in the crypts for the rest of her life, she didn't feel like she had a choice at all. Subconsciously, she touched the mark on her face, a black stain as big as a child's clenched fist. If it weren't for the mark, she'd be ordinary. Imagine. Where would she be now? *Maybe with my parents in a mansion in the upper town, eating sweets and laughing . . .* Lena pictured strong sunlight spilling through tall windows, no cowl to shadow her face. She tilted her head slightly toward the glass roof, imagining how the warmth would feel against her skin.

"Lena?" Master Vigo shot her a concerned glance. "Are you all right?"

"Sorry," she said, returning her attention to her task, slotting more of the white thread through her needle. It was stupid to fantasize as she had when she was younger. Life was difficult for everyone now: for a year, the city had been under quarantine. Instead of eating sweets in sunny rooms, half the people of the city were dead, rich and poor alike, and the other half lived in fear. As the cloud had deepened and darkened, strange flashes and rumbles disturbing its noxious peace, the Pestilence raged through the population, spreading its fever of hallucinations and shivers that left each victim dead in a matter of hours. The disease had visited three times—always in the warmest months, as if it thrived on the meager heat of a mountain summer. It was September, and the latest flurry of deaths was drawing to an end.

"Why not be a mortician?" Vigo went on, warming to his subject as he pulled out the intestines. "People need us more than ever. We are busier than we've ever been. And the Justice knows he won't find any mages among our number. You'll be safe here."

"The Justice," Lena whispered. "Yes . . . I am glad to be safe from him." Ever since the Duke had fallen ill, the Justice had ruled the city with a cold, hard grip. Like most of his citizens, the Justice knew the unnatural storm and Pestilence could have but one cause: magic. Unlike most of his citizens, the Justice had dedicated his attention to searching for the mage or mages responsible. He was obsessed, the other cryptlings whispered, ordering his guards to search for evidence of magic, burning the few magical books and toys in the city, his vicious hounds chasing suspect after suspect to an early, gruesome grave at the city walls. Lena could hear the dogs sometimes, howling in the kennels at dawn, and the sound chilled her to the core. But the cryptlings, dedicated to serving the Ancestors, had never suffered under his rule. The Justice *loved* the Ancestors. Since he'd accepted the reins of power, the ceremonies and rituals dedicated to their honor had grown threefold—old prayers and rites resurrected, new ones invented.

Vigo slid the remains of food from the intestines onto the floor, a system of flowing drains transporting the waste out of the city. "But what do you say, Lena? Would you like to be a mortician?"

Lena wasn't listening. All right, so she was safe down here—but it still wasn't enough, was it? What if she wasn't meant to be here at all? What if this was all some big mistake—like her parents had left her little basket on the steps just for a moment, and returned to find it gone? Or she'd been swapped with another child by accident? What if there was some other life she should be living, some other place where she would belong? She didn't feel like she belonged here, that was for sure—and yet this was where she was trapped. She found her vision blurring, frustration trembling her fingers.

"Why aren't you answering?" Vigo snapped. Quickly he tried to soften his voice, though he still sounded irritated as he packed the intestines into their stoneware grave. "If you want to try something else, you only need say."

He'd misunderstood her silence completely. Lena felt instantly sorry: it wasn't his fault she felt this way. She gathered herself together and spoke at last. "I would like to stay with you, Vigo, of course I would. I just wish . . . I just wish there were more options to choose from. Before the quarantine . . ." She looked down at the corpse. One eye sewn open, one eye shut, his face was frozen in a grotesque wink.

Vigo sighed, sealing the intestine jar with a deft twist of his swollen-knuckled hand. "Before the quarantine, you would have had the option to leave Duke's Forest altogether, is that what you're saying?" As he set the jar down and wiped his hands, he looked very old and tired, and Lena knew he understood.

"No, I just . . ." She shook her head. "This is my home, Vigo. But it sometimes feels like a prison too."

He sighed. "People like us are marked out for the life we lead, Lena—marked out by the Ancestors themselves. I understand your frustration. When I was your age, I wanted to see the world too—but what was I to do, as a cripple? It is cruel, in a way, the fate that we are handed. My parents abandoned me after my accident. I was a child of six, old enough to remember who they were, to remember their love, our home, my brothers and sisters, my name." Lena said a silent prayer of thanks that she had been so young when she was abandoned. It was easier not quite knowing what you had lost—and although Vigo spoke briskly, in his usual matter-of-fact tone, she could hear the pain beneath his words. "It is cruel," he carried on, his voice quickening, "to give it all up. But it is also an honor. Our families abandon us, divest us of our names, and sever our ties to our own blood Ancestors—but it's only in order that we might serve *all* the Ancestors. Think on it."

Lena thought on it, but found herself wondering which of the corpses under the mountain were related to her by blood—and whether she'd prepared a body for a grave that was an aunt, or a cousin, or a brother, without ever realizing. Had Vigo ever prepared one of his parents or siblings, recognizing their faces but unable to acknowledge them for who they were?

"Ordinary people *never* see the Ancestors," Vigo continued, "except at funerals. Are we not blessed to be around them constantly? The work we do is the most sacred of all work. I have been here seventy years, Lena, and I feel my life has had purpose, and joy, and sorrow, as much as any other life. I had a wife for many years." His eyes grew suddenly watery, and he turned aside. "I had a child."

Despite the sincerity in his voice, the suppressed tears, she wasn't in the mood to play along. Not today. "Seventy years in darkness," Lena said, setting down her needle and picking up the green-painted eye-stone, not caring if she hurt the old man's feelings. "A wife and child who lived and died in darkness. Sounds bad enough to me."

"It is not as if we never go outside, Lena," he snapped.

"Hidden under a cowl!" she protested, grasping the eye-stone tightly, feeling it cold and hard in her palm. "We might as well be underground. It's like *they*"—she gestured at the frosted-glass ceiling, at the city above—"can't bear to see us. Like we shame them. I don't feel chosen at all. I don't feel special. I feel the opposite of special." She turned to the opened eye, scooped out the eyeball with a spoon, and slotted the gem in its place. She sullenly plopped the eyeball into a copper dish.

Vigo went quiet for a moment, studiously tending the herbal mixture with which he would pack the dead man's cavities, the whisper and rattle of the pestle and mortar the only sounds in the preparatory chamber. In the silence, Lena grew to regret her words about his wife and son, who had died years before she was born, but she wasn't sure how to say sorry. Eventually, Vigo apologized instead, his voice slightly unsteady. "I am sorry you feel this way. If not for the quarantine, you would have had the opportunity to leave forever. But now . . ."

"I never said I wanted to leave forever." Lena hung her head, feeling shame burn tight and hot in her chest. "I don't. No one should have to face such a stark choice—to stay forever or leave forever. What kind of a choice is that? I just . . . I just want a *real* choice. I want to feel like I'm in control for once."

21

She picked up her needle again and started to pull back the second eyelid to sew it into place.

That's when it happened.

That's when the dead man's eye turned to her face and looked right at her, accusingly. She felt the swivel of it under her touch.

She leaped backward, dropping her needle and thread and knocking an urn of priceless embalming oil with her elbow. It toppled and shattered.

Vigo looked at her as if she'd gone mad.

"He ..." Even as the words started to leave her lips, she swallowed them. The man's eye was dead and sightless once more. "I ... I'm not feeling well."

It was true: she felt sick. She had imagined it. She *must* have imagined it. Vigo sent her back to her cell and cleaned up the mess—despite his infirmities—insisting that she rest. Lying on her bed like a corpse herself, staring at the ceiling, she had felt terrible. She played the moment over and over in her mind. Even when Hunter had sat on her chest, purring like a furnace, she'd felt somehow detached from the world, trapped in that moment of horror. *Was* she going mad?

Later, in the refectory at dinner, she'd asked the other cryptlings if they had any stories—Ancestors moving or twitching as they were prepared. . . . But it was the usual stuff. The hunchbacked boy who sat opposite Lena told her he'd prepared a corpse that farted. The deaf girl next to her mimed how she'd watched as a dead man's arm had risen up like a balloon, and everyone laughed. Lena nodded, smiling, pretending her experience had been similar. It was true: the contents of bellies could sometimes flood the body with gas, and that could make a corpse move. She told herself that was what had happened. But deep down she knew it was different. Who had ever heard of gas moving eyes? And besides, the man's eye had fixed on her like he knew what she was doing—what she was *thinking*. Gas couldn't do that.

Next thing Lena knew there were footsteps, and she started from the forest floor, spitting dead leaves from her open mouth, scrambling back toward the protection of the tree trunk behind her. A shadow began to emerge from the fog. Lena tried to raise herself to her feet, tried to run, but she could not; her legs cramped with cold.

The shadow solidified into a darker mass holding a bulb of purple light. The figure stopped before her, as if Lena had been its destination all along. She recoiled. There was something wrong with the face of this creature—a smooth brass surface with glassy black eyes and a gaping mouth. A faint *tick-tick-tick* noise appeared to emanate from the face, a cog turning somewhere at its jaw. Lena's hands scrambled at the sides of the tree as she pulled herself upright, shivering, and she hurriedly drew the knife from her belt.

"Get back!" she managed shakily, swiping the blade through the air.

The purple light sped toward her, and Lena saw it was attached to the end of a long cane, which rapped the back of her hand sharply. Her silver knife went spinning to the ground. She snatched her hand to her chest, her knuckles burning.

This was no monster, she realized, raising her eyes. The strange face was a mask, and the figure was a young woman's—a rich woman's, at that. This she could tell by the velvet dress cinched in at a tiny waist, the round golden talisman hanging almost to her stomach, the gold-tipped cane at her side, and the slim kid-leather boots. Long fair hair had been wound into a tight coil at the top of her head. But this wasn't just any young woman. The light on her cane was no ordinary lantern. How could it be? The light glowed not yellow, like fire, but an unnatural purple.

She's a mage. Lena's stomach twisted in terror.

Lena watched as the mage observed her in turn: her faded black habit, the cowl shadowing her face. The mage reached forward with her cane and pushed back Lena's hood; the bright purple light made Lena's eyes smart. The woman put the bulb of the cane under Lena's chin and turned it one way, then the other. Lena could feel a strange, mild heat burning inside the glass. Her heart hammered in her chest. The mask's gaze seemed to linger on the dark birthmark on her smooth cheek—perhaps with disgust, perhaps with curiosity.

And then, through the grille over the mouth of the mask, a metallic rasp said, "So you're a cryptling. What are you doing here?"

Lena was silent.

"I said, what are you doing here? What of the quarantine?"

said the mage. "Speak now and tell me the truth or I shall lose my patience." She had an authority to her voice that made Lena afraid *not* to answer.

She shook her head, trying to steady her senses. "I . . . was convicted of magecraft and sentenced to death. I escaped. The Justice . . ." She trailed off, clenching her fists as grief and anger overwhelmed her.

"The Justice? What of the Justice?"

"He's been hunting mages since the quarantine. He thinks there are mages in the city causing the storm cloud. And he convicted . . . me. He killed my . . ." What had he been to her? A parent? A teacher? A grandfather? "He killed my master. For trying to protect me. But before he was murdered, Vigo told me a way out."

"I see." The masked mage regarded her coolly, offering no sympathy, no apology. But she lowered her cane, and somehow Lena felt she understood.

After a few moments, she found the courage to speak again. "I . . . please, I don't know the way out of the forest. Can you help me?"

The young woman nodded slowly. "I will . . . but you must do something for me too."

Lena waited. What could she possibly do to help?

"A man has been pursuing me—you will find him at the forest edge. His name is Emris. You are to tell him that I helped you. Tell him that I said he is mistaken, that I am innocent." She rapped the side of Lena's head with the cane. "Do you understand me, girl? Repeat it."

Lena stammered and flushed with indignation. If she weren't so reliant on this stranger's help, she'd have told her where to stick her cane. "I . . . I am to tell the man at the forest edge that you helped me, that he is mistaken and you are innocent." *Innocent of what?* she wondered.

"Good." The mage lowered her cane. "Now go. There are those in the world who do not come from Duke's Forest, nor believe in its superstitions." Her voice was heavy with a cold kind of pity. And as she walked past, she added, "Keep walking, mage, and follow the footsteps I have left behind. You will soon find your way out."

Lena watched her slender figure fade into the shifting air, the unnatural purple light on her cane gradually swallowed by the cloud. *Mage.* A shiver ran through her and she clenched her fists tight to stop her hands from trembling.

She took a deep breath, swallowed, and tried to relax a little. When she felt steady enough, she picked up the silver dragon-knife from the forest floor and slid it into her belt. Then she turned her eyes in the direction from which the masked lady had emerged. *Follow the footsteps.* Lena had wondered how; in the darkness, in the fog, she could barely see her hand in front of her face. But gradually, as she watched, the masked mage's footsteps began to *burn*.

A twisting path illuminated the underbelly of the storm cloud in purple imprints, winding into the distance. And Lena knew she would never have found her way without it. The forest's trick paths looped and disappeared and reappeared without rhythm or pattern, and the storm cloud flickered blue and green between the trees, casting crazed shadows. But the footsteps were steady, trailing far ahead until the thickening vapor reduced them to a blur, then a faint smudge of light.

Lena followed the path.

TWO
Constancy

As the masked mage glimpsed the tall wooden gates of Duke's Forest, dawn lit the storm cloud a ghostly white. She heaved a sigh of relief. The journey had felt like an endless nightmare. The hem of her cloak and long trailing dress were smeared and spattered with mud, her left hand trembling as it gripped the pommel of her cane. She had a gash on her ankle where she'd slipped against the loose rock of the foothills.

At least she'd lost Emris somehow at the forest edge. She'd long since felt his pursuit fall behind, his presence slipping from her senses. Sadness tugged at her throat. Would she ever see him again? Either way, she hoped the girl would deliver her message.

She stopped a few paces on, her heart sinking as quickly as it had risen. An enormous wooden gate loomed out of the storm cloud, fifteen feet tall, the mossy stone walls slick and sturdy on either side. Ivy twisted its fingers over the old wood, the leaves sickened and gray, but the stems strong, damp, and snakelike. The gates had been locked for two years, but it looked like longer. A worn sign had been nailed to the gatepost, white paint stark against dark wood. She stepped closer to read it through the dense cloud: *UNDER QUARANTINE BY ORDER OF THE DUKE.*

She drew up to the gate, laid her gloved hand against the chains threaded again and again through the central beams, and wondered what she'd find on the other side. Quarantine. She remembered the articles in the papers two years ago, the shock on the streets as a whole city shut itself off from the world. But yesterday's papers were trampled in the gutters, and people had soon forgotten. Who really cared about a place like this, anyway? A city on a mountain, in a forest, in the middle of nowhere?

To her surprise, the metal of the chains felt tingling-warm to the touch, even through the fine silken material of her gloves. The chains were thrumming with magic.

She adjusted the wheel on the side of her mask. Her view of the world shifted: the physical world faded and blurred, the wood of the gates softening into a waterfall of brown. Instead, the spell-scape came into focus, lending a different kind of sharpness to her surroundings. The storm spell fizzed in the air, encompassing her completely. If she glanced over her shoulder, she knew she would find the shining, lightning-like paths—the spell's veins and arteries—that had allowed her to trace her way through the forest. If she glanced down at herself, she'd find not a mere body but a weave of shining purple magic running in tandem with her blood, albeit flickering and weak after her long journey. But there was something else here. Another kind of magic.

She gazed at the lock and chains, confused. A red glittering magic protected the metal. She reached out to touch the lock with her hands, her magical senses following, examining the work. It felt like armor—hard and unyielding. A protection spell. The faded color suggested the spell was old—perhaps it had been cast when the gates were locked—but it was clearly the work of an experienced mage. The spell was simple but bold and unusually strong. The color also suggested a disciple of Jok—the warrior's god. Whoever it was, they'd wandered a long way from home.

She frowned. The girl in the forest had told her the Justice was executing mages—and besides, Duke's Forest was famously anti-magic. The masked lady knew that better than anyone. And yet, it seemed a spell had been used to prevent the citizens of Duke's Forest from escaping.

Or, perhaps, anyone else from getting in.

Who had cast this spell to keep the chains from rusting, to keep the lock jammed tight? And had it been cast from the inside or the outside? How had the mage-girl escaped? A weakness in the wall somewhere?

You don't have time for this. Not now. Just focus on getting inside.

She drew on her dwindling reserves to unpick the spell, the tremor in her left hand growing more pronounced as she laid her cane against the chains and burned the red magic to frays. "Gods' balls," she cursed, clenching her fist harder to steady the shaking. The old rusted metal shuddered and glowed purple, the lock on the other side clicking open and falling to the ground with a *thunk*. The lady pulled the chain loose with her steadier right hand, breathing heavily behind her brass grille, and slipped through the slender gap she'd created.

Home sweet home, she thought bitterly.

Her ruined kid boots crunched on a pile of bones. She glanced around, turning the mechanism on her mask to bring the scene into focus, the spell-scape shimmering into the background. A human skull stared back at her from a pile of detritus. And then she spotted a thighbone. A rib cage still ragged with the remnants of flesh.

She crouched, picked up a medium-size bone that must have been the upper part of an arm. Holding it up to the eyeholes of her mask, she spied tiny serrations in the white. Chew marks. She peered through the shifting gloom again, anger sharpening her vision. The mess of human remains pressed up against the gates as if they were still trying to escape. She glimpsed the tiny hand of a child.

A mage hunt? The girl had told her the Justice had been convicting mages, but she could never have imagined anything on this scale. On top of the Pestilence. She remembered what the mage-girl had said: this was the Justice's doing. How had the Duke let this happen?

Dropping the arm bone, she stood straight, suddenly reinvigorated.

She shut the gates—resealed them seamlessly by twisting together the old magic. It was better this way. If anyone checked, they'd never guess how she'd gotten in, or that she'd used magic to do so.

The lower town was almost unrecognizable. Six years ago the shops had been busy, and bright market stalls were set up in the square. Now it was nearly empty, black windows gazing out over slick cobblestones, the noxious cloud crawling in between. It flashed and flickered intermittently, blue and light green, and a rumble sounded close to her ear, startling her. The storm cloud—yes, that's what they were calling it. Peering at the inhabited houses with their windows glowing softly, she glimpsed ragged curtains, dirty blinds, gaps in doorframes stuffed with old rags. *Homes under siege.*

The road to the top of the mountain, to the castle crouching on its summit, was steep and ill-maintained—she stumbled several times, leaning heavily on her cane for support, relying on the *tick-tick* of the clockwork in her mask to filter out the vapor and its effects. She passed through the upper town, whose mansions and grand houses appeared to be entirely abandoned. All the way up the mountainside, the storm cloud lay like a slumbering beast stirring in its dreams. Only as she neared the summit did it start to thin, the castle towering overhead. By now she knew she was close to spent, a bead of cold sweat trickling down her brow.

"Who goes there?" Two figures stood on either side of the wrought-iron portcullis at the top of the narrow path, designed for defense. As she drew nearer, she heard the ring of two swords pulled from their scabbards, glimpsed a dull flash in the semidarkness. "Stop, in the name of the Duke!"

She obeyed, a few paces short of the portcullis. "Is this how you treat all your visitors?" she remarked drily.

Hurried footsteps approached, another figure emerging from the gloom. The masked lady saw the hulk of a thick fur cloak, a sword hilt peeking from a shoulder-bound scabbard. "What's going on here?"

"An intruder, my lord," said one of the guards.

"I'm no intruder," she said, surprised at the strength and clarity of her own voice. She drew yet closer, and as a bank of fog passed by, clearing the space between, the guards gasped.

"What kind of creature—"

"Stay back!"

Both raised their swords across their torsos, unbalanced in their haste. Beneath their peaked iron helmets, the masked lady saw the whites of their eyes. She hesitated in confusion, but quickly realized their mistake. She could imagine how her clockwork mask appeared to them: an expressionless metallic facade, a grimacing mouth, and wide circular eyeholes, demonic in the gray daylight.

"Relax," she said. "It's a mask. Here." Slowly, she undid the leather fastenings and exposed her face, her skin tingling as it met the damp, cool air. In an instant, she felt her power weaken further. She tried to disguise the growing tremor in her hand, gripping the mask tightly as the shaking passed, then slipping it into the special concealed pocket in her cloak. She focused on the wide courtyard beyond the gate. The cloud was thin enough up here not to be an immediate danger to her eyes, thin enough even to see some of the buildings around the courtyard she'd raced across as a child, spinning her hoop. She felt an unexpected stab of sadness and guilt. Now a washerwoman was hurrying into a narrow doorway with a basket of laundry, casting a curious glance over her shoulder at the commotion.

The third fur-cloaked figure stepped closer, right up to the iron gate, his face framed by the bars. She recognized him instantly: his black curly hair the picture of his mother's; his alabaster skin, now shadowed by the beginnings of a beard; his tired eyes a warm dark brown.

She shook her head in disbelief. He'd been a gangly boy of nine when she'd left, but he'd grown into a handsome young man.

"Winton," she said softly.

At first, he gazed at her, uncomprehending. But as he studied her face, she watched shock and suspicion pass over his features, replaced by a kind of delight. "Is it really you, Constance?"

She smiled. "It's really me. I'm home."

As Winton shouted an order to open the portcullis, Constance realized her arrival had begun to draw a crowd: a few servants gathered nearby, a black-liveried valet loitered in a doorway, a lady leaned from her upstairs chambers in curiosity. The big iron wheel creaked and popped as it drew the gate up into the walls—others arrived, drawn by the sound. Visitors were clearly an uncommon occurrence at the castle. Constance had never seen the courtyard so busy with people and yet so still: everyone was watching, waiting.

Once the gate was raised, she stepped into the courtyard. Winton stood in front of her, gazing at her face, his eyes shining. "For Ancestors' sake, what happened to you?" he cried. "I thought you were dead!" And without waiting for her reply, he enveloped her in a tight embrace—so quickly she barely had time to tuck her left arm behind her back, out of the way. He was a half inch shorter than her, but as she circled her right arm around his shoulders, she felt how broad and strong he had grown.

Across the courtyard, a loud *bang* sounded, echoing strangely across the stones. Winton released her and turned around. Constance quickly spotted the source of the noise: a door had opened violently, thumping against the wall. A man stood on the doorstep of the tall, round tower to the right of the gates—the north tower, she remembered—his rich velvet robes disheveled; his eyes wild; his beard long, gray, and tangled; his wrists painfully thin. And he met Constance's eyes with a wild gaze, hurrying forward through the shifting fog as if he knew her, his black cloak whipping around his legs.

She squinted. Did she know him too?

"My daughter! My daughter!" he cried.

And suddenly Constance recognized the stranger, her heart convulsing.

It was her father. It was the Duke.

She had to stop herself from fleeing him—and the shocking truth.

My father is crazy.

Six years ago, her father had been the sanest, most practical person she knew—sane to a fault. She remembered his level, determined gaze and couldn't match the father she had known then with the specter now rushing at her through the storm cloud.

Before he reached her, Constance glimpsed another tall man emerging from the north tower as if in pursuit, his brown coat—the many-pocketed outfit of a physician—flapping in his wake.

The Duke gazed at her—and for a second his dark eyes cleared. She felt confusion drain from her body, replaced by pity and horror. And then his head bowed down, as if with the weight of heavy thoughts, and he buried his face in her neck, clutching her close, shaken by sobs. She felt the wet of his tears on her collarbone. *Is it really Father?* Constance suppressed a shudder as the Duke's bony arms encircled her tightly, and she held her breath: his white hair was greasy and foul-smelling. What did the Duchess think of this? Why had she not ensured he was properly cared for?

Gradually, she forced herself to return the embrace, meeting Winton's eyes over her father's shoulder. Her half brother lowered his gaze.

After a time, she gently pried the Duke from her and turned to her brother. "Winton, where is your mother?" she asked quietly.

He shook his head, and for the first time she realized he

was dressed head to toe in black. "She . . . she died, not two weeks past," he said.

"I . . . I see." Constance was shocked, but she didn't do Winton the indignity of feigning grief. The Duchess had borne little love for Constance, the daughter of the Duke's previous wife. The late Duchess had been a proud native of Duke's Forest, while Constance's mother, Patience, had been a foreigner. The late Duchess was the daughter of a minor noble, while Patience had been born to one of the great families of Valorian. And the Duchess had noticed Constance's . . . *strangeness* . . . before anyone else, and made sure that Constance never forgot it. Even so, her heart ached for Winton. She knew what it was to lose a mother.

"I'm very sorry," she said sincerely, squeezing Winton's shoulder.

The people who had gathered in the courtyard were gazing at the small family reunion with mingled curiosity and expectation. They looked like a crowd of ghosts floating in the air, up to their knees in a thick sea of mist.

"For those of you who do not know me, I am Constance Rathbone. Firstborn of the Duke. Heir to the Forest," she said, her voice loud and commanding. *A ruse.* She felt weak, her blood pumping fast and shallow. She spied the brown-coated man who had followed her father pushing through the crowd, a determined expression on his face. He slipped into an open doorway nearby.

The Duke stood by her side, holding on to her right arm like a frightened child. As she spoke, his eyes fixed on her face, a wide, wondering smile on his lips. He seemed oblivious to her trouble.

She clutched her cane with both hands to keep herself upright, feeling the strain in her gloves. The courtyard was silent and solemn.

She forced cheer into her voice. "Come, is this to be my welcome? It has been six years since I was last home. We shall throw a feast tonight to celebrate!"

A few murmurs broke out, an uncertain clatter of excitement. Constance beamed, trembling inside. "And tomorrow, at midday, we shall hold a Witenagemot—"

A door to the side of the courtyard opened with a *click* and swung wide, the fog skittering around it like an agitated animal. The man in the brown physician's coat held the door, closely followed by a taller, broader figure dressed in the King's black military uniform. He had straight silver hair tied flawlessly at his neck and a large mustache. The King's Justice. She felt her fists clench tighter.

At the Justice's heels, a huge hound slunk into the courtyard, growling at the gathered crowd. Constance recognized the breed—identical to the hunting dogs in her father's kennels. But it was white instead of the ordinary brown or black, and enormous—its head nearly reached her waist and its body was corded with muscle. The hound's right eye was a scar, a gash of shocking pink against the creature's short pale fur, while its left eye was a hideous, livid yellow.

From the corner of her eye, Constance caught sight of her brother smothering a scowl. As the Justice stepped toward her, the buttons on his black greatcoat gleaming gold, disapproval naked on his face, the courtyard fell silent. No whisperings. No curious glances. No more murmurs of excitement for a feast. Eyes fell to the ground like stones, and people shrank back from the hound, folding their arms as if afraid it might snap at their hands. Six years ago, when she'd left, the Justice's role had been purely administrative—he was the King's representative, sent to oversee the royal taxes and the interpretation of the law in Duke's Forest, and to serve as an ambassador of sorts. Constance remembered the previous King's Justice, who had been a kindly and very elderly man with a penchant for cream puffs. He'd died of extreme old age about ten years ago, and they'd sent this one to replace him. He'd always been seen as strict, by comparison. But glancing between her father, the Justice, Winton, and the people, she could suddenly see that he was more than just strict: the Justice held the true power here. A retinue of black-uniformed guards followed him into the space that spread around Constance like ripples in a pool. The dog barked at her three times, a rough, tight sound. She flinched, in spite of herself, scowling down at the creature.

"Sit, Barbarus," the Justice said sharply, and the hound obeyed, its muscles coiled. A half-healed whip mark showed against the dog's flank.

The physician reached his hand out to the Duke. He was tall and heavily built, with a thin, blandly handsome face, his brown hair cropped short in a military fashion. A kind of cruelty revealed itself in the sharp angles of his cheekbones and jaw.

"Come, my lord. Let me return you to your apartments; it's past time for your medicine."

Her father cringed, as if afraid, and Constance placed a steadying hand on his shoulder.

"Get away from my father," she snapped at the man. "Who are you?"

"Dr. Jonas Thorn, my lady." His voice was as dry as kindling. "The Duke's physician. And I believe you've met our Lord Protector, the King's Justice?"

Lord Protector? That meant he truly was ruling in her father's stead. She drew herself up and met the Justice's steely gaze. Although Constance was tall, and the Justice must have been nearing his seventieth year, he still had the advantage of height.

"Six years," he said, his voice low and unyielding. "We all thought you were gone forever."

"You thought wrong," Constance said archly.

"You do realize this city is under quarantine?" The Justice's question tripped after her reply, dismissive, as if he'd hardly listened. "Did you not see the sign? The locked gates? How did you get inside?" The white hound growled up at Constance, but the Justice lifted his hand—ever so slightly— and the dog abruptly fell silent, cowering at his feet.

"I am aware of your quarantine, and your mage hunts," she said, remembering the grim truth told by the bones stacked around the gate. It was said that the Justice, a native of Duke's Forest, had served in the King's army for twenty years before returning to his home with a fresh disapproval for foreigners and a determination to reaffirm his connection to the Ancestors. He had long been known for his hatred of magic. Constance wondered what had happened in the army to turn him so bitter.

"It is my duty as the King's representative to ensure the storm cloud and its Pestilence do not escape Duke's Forest. It is equally my duty as Lord Protector and guardian of the Ancestors to root out the mages responsible for the storm cloud and destroy them." He fixed her with his burning steel-blue eyes.

"Why are you so sure the storm is magic? And even if it is, why are you so certain the mage who cast it remains within the city?" Constance demanded. "Your actions are cruel and senseless."

The Justice's lip curled. "The storm is clearly unnatural. In seeking out the perpetrator—as well as in persecuting those who practice the foul craft of magic—I follow, as ever, the laws and customs of the kingdom and Duke's Forest. I shall repeat my question: How did you get inside?"

She ignored it. "I saw the bones of hundreds. Were they all mages? Even the children?"

The Justice's stare was so cold that she felt her soul shiver. "The nature of magic is mysterious. But this is beside the point. You have broken the law, and you are refusing to answer my question." A shudder ran through the watching crowd. His words had turned a few faces doubtful, others

41

full of fear. At a nod from the Justice, one of his black-clad guards stepped forward, grabbing her right arm, pulling her aside from her father, whose face crumpled. "I'm placing you under arrest, pending trial, for breaking quarantine." His voice was horribly calm.

The Duke began to weep, a keening sound emerging from the back of his throat.

At the temple, she'd often dreamed of returning, and she'd never expected it to be easy. But this? Her father was incapable of helping anyone, and the city was torn apart by the Justice and his mage hunt, ravaged by fear and grief. And now her journey would end in a prison cell—or worse. She clenched her fists, her left hand tight around her cane. *No, it cannot end this way.*

Then another voice emerged from the crowd. "I believe it's illegal to *leave* the city, Lord Justice, but—though ill-advised—is it actually illegal to enter?" A tall, slender man dressed in bright indigo silk, his face swathed in scarves, pushed to the front.

"Lord Irvine," said the Justice calmly, a thread of hatred running under his voice. "I believe that as Swordmaster, you don't have a great deal to offer on points of law."

Lord Irvine? Constance's heart beat a tiny bit faster. She remembered him sparring against her in the gardens, the flash of their blades in the sunlight.

"Indeed. . . . Lord Veredith? Ah, there you are." Irvine addressed an ancient man with tissue-paper skin, whom Constance vaguely recognized from her childhood. "You are an authority on such matters—can you clarify the point for the Justice?"

"Y-yes . . . ," the old man stuttered, looking up at the Justice with a clear expression of terror. "Forgive me, but . . . I'm afraid . . . if my memory serves . . . that is—" He coughed. "I believe, alas, the Swordmaster is correct." He raised his voice and began to recite, his voice warbling: "*The Book of Law*, section eighteen, point thirty—"

"Very well, my lord," interrupted Irvine. "I think that settles it. My men and I will be happy to escort Lady Constance to her apartments and ensure she has everything she requires for this evening's festivities."

Constance glimpsed a number of men dressed in vivid sky-blue livery sliding from the crowd. At a glance, she guessed the Justice's and Irvine's retinues were about evenly matched. For a few moments, the two men locked eyes.

"For Mythris's sake," muttered Constance, as she shook free from the uncertain grip of the Justice's man. "Stop this nonsense." Irvine and the Justice blinked in apparent shock. "I'll take my old apartments at the top of the south tower. Can someone be prevailed upon to bring me some hot bathwater? Thank you." She took a deep breath, leaned forward, and kissed her weeping father on the cheek. "I will see you at the feast, Father. Please don't cry." She turned to Winton. "I am sorry about the Duchess, Brother. I really am."

And with the *tap-tap-tap* of her cane sounding hard on the cobblestones, she walked through the parting crowd and into the square south tower.

She climbed the staircase slowly, her breath shallow, the steps swimming in front of her eyes. *Nearly. Home.* One of her gloved hands was clenched around the banister. The other, the trembling left hand, held fast to the cane. The tremor was continuous now, a soft shuddering that set her nerves on edge. As she neared the top, she heard the courtyard door open and close.

"Constance?" Irvine's voice.

"I'm fine. Leave me to rest," she half shouted. She'd reached the door to her old apartment. It was just the same, down to the scuff marks where she used to kick it shut and the two angry initials she'd scored into the wood with a penknife as a girl. *C.R.*

"Constance, wait!" He started to take the stairs two at a time.

She sighed and pushed the door open.

Her bedroom was a heap of junk. She leaned heavily on the doorframe, shaken. The bed was dusty and piled high with papers, its curtains ripped and ragged. The play chest at the foot of the bed—painted garish pink and yellow by Constance's own childish hand—was barely discernible under a pile of upturned broken chairs. The main part of the room was a mass of furniture in various states of disrepair and smelled of old wood and rot. Weirdly, she could still see her hairbrush where she'd left it all those years ago on the dressing table, which was thick with dust, strung with cobwebs, and barricaded in the corner by the grimy window. She stepped inside, her mouth open, just as Irvine reached the landing.

"Constance . . ." His breath was even and slow, despite his swift climb up the tower. "I was trying to stop you from seeing this. I'm sorry."

"What happened here?" Her voice was weak. She hated the sound of it.

"When the fog got worse, when the lightning and thunder started, everyone wanted a place in the castle—the air's better up here, thinner and calmer. Most of the upper town moved in. The Pestilence has brought numbers down since then, of course . . . but at the time, space was at a premium." He sighed. "Your father refused to let anyone stay in your room. And so . . ."

"It became a dumping ground. Guess that shows what everyone really thought of me." She felt annoyingly close to tears.

"That's not true, Constance. I think in some way he was keeping it for when you'd come back."

He told me never to return, she thought, shaking her head. She turned to face him. "I had my enemies, even back then. The Duchess, for one." She remembered with a jolt that the woman was dead. "I've been preparing myself to confront her, but now . . ."

He pulled the silken scarves from around his face. Six years on, he looked different—and yet somehow just the same. He was about her age, with high, angular cheekbones and the brown skin of eastern Valorian, his mother's legacy. He'd been gangly when she left, and clumsy—except with a practice sword. But since then, his face had sharpened, and he'd grown tall and lean and self-assured. His bright-green eyes still glittered like gems, just as she remembered.

"I'm glad you're back," he said suddenly, color rising to his cheeks under her scrutiny.

Constance's mouth flickered into a smile, teasing. "So where do you suggest I sleep?"

He cleared his throat. "The apartments on the first floor are relatively habitable—I'm afraid that's the best you can hope for these days. We're rather short on manpower. I've already sent some servants to prepare them for you."

"Those were my mother's apartments once," said Constance. She'd been only four when her mother had died, but she remembered clearly enough.

He blinked. "There is another empty suite in the east tower, and I hear the north wing has vacant—"

"It's all right. Downstairs it is." She wasn't sure she could cope with another trip across the courtyard.

The first floor was already a hub of activity. As she descended the last few steps, Constance caught a glimpse inside the apartments through the open door as a manservant brought in a basket of firewood: a small team of maids had started removing the dirty dust sheets from the bed and were bringing in clean blankets, sweeping the floor, and laying a fire in the soot-stained chimney. The door shut behind the manservant, and Constance hesitated outside—old habits died hard, and the masked priestesses had taught

46

her to listen before she stepped into a room. A snatch of gossip from the servants reached her ears:

"They say the hounds came back still hungry. They never caught her."

"D'you think she's still in the city?"

"Constance?" Irvine was waiting at her back.

"Sorry," she said, shooting him a small apologetic smile. "It's a long time since I've been here."

She swung the door open, Irvine at her side, and the voices fell silent. Here, the furnishings had changed substantially since her mother's time—they were depersonalized, stripped of character. She wondered who had lived here since, and whether they had died here too. And yet . . . the window seat, in particular, caught her eye. The sagging blue velvet cushions on the ledge, beaten free of dust, felt familiar against her knees as she leaned against them, peering out over the murky courtyard. She hadn't sat here since she was a little girl. Once upon a time, her mother had sat here too, outlined in sunlight, her chestnut hair wound in a foreign style around her head. Even after all this time, the memory was clear. Constance had always been able to remember things better than other people.

Irvine joined her at the window as the servants bustled out. "I will leave you to rest before the feast. I've asked for refreshments to be brought up to you, and you'll find clothes in the chest at the foot of the bed. They should fit you. They belonged to Livia. . . . She . . . she died last summer. The Pestilence . . ."

47

His jaw was suddenly tight. Constance remembered his sister, three years his senior. She'd been beautiful, with her mother's brown skin and laughing black eyes, and had loved to dance. Constance had often wished, as a pale, awkward child, that she could be like Livia. "I'm so sorry," she said simply. "Was that the last time the Pestilence struck?"

Irvine nodded. "Ancestors be thanked, it has been over a year now. This summer we have been spared. Perhaps ... with your arrival ... I wonder if this horror is finally ending," he said.

"Perhaps," she murmured. She turned away from him, trying to disguise the jolt caused by his words. *It has been over a year now.* She cycled through the descriptions she had studied, detailing the growth of the spell ...

Six years in full the spell shall gestate. First year, a vapor, a mist. Second year, a fog, a storm cloud. Then three years in summer, it shall feast on death. In the sixth year, the sickness stops—the quiet before the storm. And then, in autumn, the contractions begin ...

Her eyes flicked back to Lord Irvine, who was gazing out the window. She joined him. The cloud was thickening and thinning, concealing and revealing the courtyard like a cheap conjurer's trick. *The quiet before the storm,* she thought.

Her mind drifted over what she had learned, and she frowned. "But then ... how did the Duchess die?"

"She had been ill for some time—a malady in her lungs. It was no great shock when she passed, but ..."

Constance finished for him, hearing his hesitancy. "But of course that doesn't make it any easier. Poor Winton."

But Irvine was shaking his head, as if she'd misunderstood. "The shock really came at the Duchess's Descent," he said. "It was . . . traumatizing."

Constance turned to face him. "What do you mean?"

"It's the talk of the castle. There was a girl there. A cryptling. She was administering the sacred ointment for the last time, but when she touched the Duchess's lips . . ." He shook his head as if he couldn't quite believe the words, even as he spoke them. "The body . . . It moved."

"It moved?" Constance's heart was racing, chills running down her spine. "But surely there are natural reasons . . . The cryptling could have knocked it . . ." Her voice trailed off.

Irvine was shaking his head again. "The action was far too determined. Trust me, I saw it."

"What happened?"

"The Duchess's hand flew up, quick as a cat, and grabbed the girl's wrist. As if to stop her. It held tight for a full second before it fell, lifeless." He paused, as if thinking through the words he spoke next. "There was no doubt in my mind: it was magic. The girl was tried and convicted yesterday, and of course the Witenagemot sentenced her to die. The Justice set his hounds on her, as he does with all his convicts." Irvine swallowed. "Whatever she did, nobody deserves such a death."

Constance tucked a stray wisp of hair behind her ear. "How horrible for Winton. For a moment he must have thought his mother was alive after all."

"He rushed to his mother's side, convinced there had been a mistake. A moment of hope makes grief even more difficult to bear." Irvine smiled sadly.

They were silent for a few moments, feeling the horror of everything that had happened. And then Constance spoke again. "Before we came in here, I heard the servants talking about a girl, saying she escaped."

Irvine nodded. "They say the cryptling evaded the hounds somehow. The Justice thinks she's still in the city. He's imposed a curfew and is tearing the lower town apart, looking for her."

But she's not in the city at all. Constance felt a small thrill at the knowledge that she'd helped the cryptling mage escape from under the Justice's nose. She gazed out the window at the swirling cloud licking against the glass, now flashing blue intermittently. She remembered vividly when her own magic had started to manifest, causing objects to float or fly around the room. Yes, that must have been it. The cryptling girl had just been extraordinarily unlucky to have been standing in front of an audience of hundreds, attending to an important body.

Footsteps sounded on the stairs, a knock on the door.

"Enter," Constance called.

Four servants bustled in, each carrying two copper kettles full of hot water for the bathtub in front of the fire. Irvine turned to Constance and smiled, focusing on her face. "It's so good to see you again," he said softly. "I didn't think I ever would. I'm sorry you have returned to such a changed place."

"I'm glad to be back," she said, smiling too. And it was true.

"I will talk to you in private later," he said, glancing over his shoulder at the servants. "I'm sure you'd like some time to rest now. Can we meet in the gardens after the feast? I'll wait by our fountain."

"All right."

He turned to leave.

"Lord Irvine?"

He hesitated.

"Thank you."

He flashed her a smile, and then he was gone in a swirl of silk.

THREE
The Serpent

The storm rolled and rumbled, as it often did, like a sleeping creature whose troubled dreams had deepened into nightmares. Lena shivered as she followed the glowing path through the darkness, the storm cloud, and the never-ending trees. The thin rain lashed around her, and flashes of sickly blue-green threw long and twisted shadows. The thunder, so close to the damp earth, sounded like an angry voice roaring in displeasure. Though warm and hard-wearing, her cryptling's habit wasn't meant for the outside, and she was quickly soaked through and shivering. She walked on, and on, and on, following the path, far beyond the point where she felt she could not continue.

After a time, the storm cloud started to thin enough for Lena to loosen her tight grip on her habit, which had been whooshing around her in the wind. The trees started to space out too and grew stronger, their bark thicker and darker, less furred and bubbled with fungus. And soon the canopy was so thin, and the fog slunk so low around her legs, that Lena could see the stars shining through the branches overhead. Her heart leaped: she hadn't seen stars in years. She staggered on, suddenly eager, allowing herself a few moments of hope, yet terrified the storm cloud would thicken and once more throw her into darkness.

But it wasn't the storm cloud that frightened her in the end.

She heard something else. A rustling nearby in the fallen leaves. A low *hissssss*.

Immediately, Vigo's voice spoke to her, a memory as clear and distant as the stars. *And in the forest, there are snakes that can swallow a man whole.*

Those stories never ended without death.

Please, not now. Not when I'm so close. She pulled out the dagger and crept on, her eyes searching the hundred darknesses pressing in between the trees. Weak lightning flickered—illuminating, for a second, a shiny shape, long and sinuous. Perhaps a large and ancient tree root glistening with rain . . . but no. In the blink of an eye, the shape slithered off into the forest.

Perhaps it had bigger prey tonight.

She gulped and hurried on, gripping the knife so tightly that her knuckles stung. If it attacked her, she'd bloody kill it—she had to. She wasn't going to let anything stop her now.

A few minutes later, Lena saw the path trail off, the light disappearing as it reached a wide field.

She was so close. She allowed herself to relax a little, lowering the dagger.

There was no noise, no warning: out of nowhere, she felt a sharp, burning pain in her thigh. She cried out, stabbed blindly down with the knife. The serpent darted back, too quick for her, and drew itself up—nearly to Lena's height—hissing, blocking her way. It was *huge*. Its body coiled on the path and its open mouth revealed large white fangs. In the purplish path-light, its dark scales shone silvery blue and its eyes were flecks of glistening black stone.

With one hand she clutched her leg, which was throbbing, and with the other she held the knife out in front of her. Her pulse was thundering and she gritted her teeth against the pain and odd sense of lightness, disorientation. *No. I will not die like this. Not here. Not now.* Determination hardened Lena's heart, and she was no longer afraid.

She slashed out again, but the snake was a narrow target, easily darting out of reach. She felt a sudden weakness in her leg, which buckled. She was down on one knee. The snake appeared to notice her struggle, twisting itself into a looser, lower coil and watching.

Waiting. Waiting for me to die, she realized.

She threw the dagger, which whistled through the air, and forced herself to her feet, running off to the side as fast as her injury could carry her. Her boots pounded the dead leaves at a limping sprint. Thump-*thump*, thump-*thump*, thump-*thump*, like a heartbeat.

It didn't last long.

She tripped, fell flat on her face—the second time that night she'd had her mouth full of dead leaves and damp soil.

She spat, turned on her back, tried to scrabble to her feet. But it was too painful—and the more she struggled, the more she felt the poison racing through her blood, draining her of strength, wrapping invisible fingers around her throat. She gasped for breath, desperate for the tiniest sliver of air. But the world was watery, choking darkness, and she felt certain she was drowning.

Out of the darkness she heard the slither of the snake's body over the forest floor.

Her throat had constricted to nothing, her mouth gaping. She felt the cold scales sliding over the skin of her leg where her habit had ridden up, felt the snake coil around her pulsing thigh. She tried to struggle but found she was trapped, paralyzed, her fingers twitching ineffectively. The poison had coursed through her like a dark rope, binding her to the ground. The snake's black eyes flickered into focus, pinning her like a pair of daggers as it reached her rib cage, and its body reared up, heavy and cold as a chain. The corners of her vision began to fade again, a dull hum filling her ears. The snake's mouth opened, revealing its wickedly sharp fangs to the dappled starlight, and Lena felt sure the last thing she'd see in this world was the way its eyes watched her coldly as she died.

She felt a flutter inside her chest. The scents surrounding her grew strangely intense and enveloped her senses—the damp dead leaves, the rotten undergrowth, the moss-padded stone. The musk of the night itself, a mushroomy softness breathing from the trees. The swirling, flickering cloud on the mountaintop—an electric, burning smell, like a summer storm.

Is this how it feels to die?

And suddenly a coldness spread from the center of her, up through her skin, tingling in her face and fingers and the soles of her feet. *Rising*. The grip on her loosened, falling away.

In a moment of pure confusion, she heard hurried footsteps, which stopped at her side.

Dreaming?

Darkness claimed her.

Lena felt a splash of water on her face and woke instantly, her eyes snapping open.

The man who crouched over her was young and dark skinned, with three silver scars running parallel across his face. She thought she should be frightened, but she was too bewildered. Between the yellow-red autumn trees over his head, Lena could see an indigo sky, washed with pink clouds.

It was dawn.

Despite her confusion, a part of her understood two things: she had survived, and she had escaped. Here, no cloud lingered between the trunks of the healthy trees— no flashes of sickly lightning, no grumbles of a monstrous creature in its sleep. The air was pure. Her throat, however, was dry and painful, and there was a strange, unpleasant taste in her mouth.

"What happened?" she croaked.

"Here." The man's voice was low as he offered her the flask in his hand. She glugged gratefully, cool water spilling down her chin. "You're lucky I was nearby," said the man, his accent unfamiliar—clipped and formal. "You might have defeated the serpent, but the poison would've killed you within the hour."

The serpent! Panic gripped her, and she raised herself up onto her elbows. Her mouth gaped in shock. The body of the snake lay at her feet like a discarded ribbon, crumpled and lifeless, the shine gone from its black-gem eyes. *I did that?*

Lena's gaze returned to the stranger. He was dressed entirely in gray: trews, tunic, and cloak, pinned at his neck with a sickle-moon brooch in silver. "I had to pull the beast off you," he said. "Whatever spell you cast, it worked in the nick of time."

Spell?

Her throat was tightening in shock.

How did I . . . ?

She gulped wildly at the water, half to rid herself of the bitter taste and half as a kind of distraction from her confusion, but coughed it up uncontrollably.

"Steady now. Sip it slowly." His warm hand on her shoulder. She flinched. She never touched anyone who wasn't Vigo, or dead—and nobody ever touched her. "I'm not going to hurt you," he said gently, drawing away his hand.

She sipped slowly. When she had recovered, she spoke in a hoarse croak. "Who are you?"

"My name is Emris Lochlade. I'm the Third Huntsman in the temple of Faul—though I don't suppose that means much to you. You're from Duke's Forest, aren't you?" Not waiting for her to reply, he asked, "What's your name?"

Emris. *Emris*. Lena's mind raced—and she remembered: the man the masked lady said she would encounter. She'd told her to say . . . but Lena's thoughts and memories scrambled. *Focus*. She swigged at the water, scrunching up her face. "I'm Lena. I . . ." She couldn't remember . . . The inside of her mouth was *itching*. "What is this *taste*?"

"Venomsbane, we call it—an herbal mixture known to cleanse the blood of most natural poisons." He grinned, his three silvery scars twisting. "Unfortunately, it tastes like poison itself—but the sensation will pass soon enough. Now, Lena, do you think you can stand up?"

She raised herself a little, her head spinning. She was facing into the forest, the green shadows between the trees darkening into the distance. The fog slunk around the roots farther in like a cat prowling for prey.

Emris offered her a hand. She gazed at it, bewildered, and stood up on her own.

"What's a mage doing in Duke's Forest?" he asked. "Or, I suppose, out of it. I thought there were no mages in Duke's Forest. And besides, isn't there a quarantine?"

"I'm not a mage," Lena said instinctively. She was suddenly conscious of the birthmark on her face. She started to pull up her cowl.

"Stop that." He touched her wrist lightly, a tension in his

voice close to anger. She nearly flinched again at his touch but stopped herself. It was nice, in fact, the slight warmth of his fingers against her skin.

"But I'm Marked," Lena said. "I'm a cryptling. You're not supposed to touch me or see my face."

"Marked?" He shook his head, lowering his hand from her wrist. The way he said the word, it was empty, devoid of its usual weight. "So? What does that mean?"

Lena stared at his scars and felt like she'd stepped into another world entirely—and, she realized, that's exactly what had happened. She remembered the masked lady's words: *There are those in the world that do not come from Duke's Forest, nor believe in its superstitions.* Of course she had known the world beyond the city was different . . . but Emris had *no idea* what she meant by "Marked." The weight of the realization hit her in the stomach like a fist. "In Duke's Forest," she explained a little breathlessly, "those who are Marked as babies or children are dedicated to the service of the Ancestors. They become cryptlings. 'Marked' could mean something like this . . ." She raised her hand to her birthmark. "Or maybe deafness. Or blindness. Or it could be the loss of a limb." *Like Vigo.* She hurried on, unable to bear the thought of him, the sharp pain in her heart. "Or some of the cryptlings are Marked on the inside. They think differently from other people."

Emris shook his head, distaste painted on his expression. "It is not for me to judge . . . but, Lena, you are not in Duke's Forest anymore. You can lower your hood."

Hesitantly, she dropped her cowl. He was right: she wasn't in Duke's Forest anymore. The woodland air felt cool against her skin.

"How did you get out?" Emris asked, his voice softer. "What of the quarantine? And the forest . . . even I couldn't get through the storm cloud. Every navigation spell I know goes haywire."

"My . . . my master told me a way out of the city, under the wall," she said. "And then I met someone going the opposite way. A mage." She remembered the intense purple glow of the bulb on the lady's cane. "She told me to follow her footsteps out, so that's what I did."

"A lady wearing a mask?" Emris said, his expression hardening. "She helped you?"

Lena nodded, suddenly remembering her instructions. "And she has a message for you. She said . . . she said I should tell you that you are mistaken and that she is innocent."

Emris frowned, running his fingers gently over his cropped, fuzzy hair—and then shook his head. "I have more questions, and I'm sure you do too. But we shall have plenty of time on our journey."

Lena blinked. "What journey?"

"It's my duty as a huntsman to bring untrained mages like you to the City of Kings to start your training." He watched her carefully.

"What?" She stiffened, stepped away from him, instantly mistrustful. "But I'm not a mage! I told you! I'm not going anywhere with you—I don't even know you!"

His expression grew serious. "Lena, I know you don't know me yet, and you're probably very confused. If you weren't from Duke's Forest, there are documents and certificates and all manner of things I could show you to convince you of who I am and what my duties are. But none of it will mean anything to you. I just have to ask you to trust me." He smiled slightly. "Think of it as a kind of repayment for saving your life."

"But I'm not a mage!" she protested a second time, clenching her fists: it felt as if her body was rebelling, attempting to defend itself against the very idea.

Emris spoke with infuriating insistence and calmness. "You *are* a mage." He pointed to the snake's still corpse. "And there's your evidence. You may not understand it yet, but I assure you I am right. Now, I have one question for you— it may seem odd, but I need an answer. When did you first experience something unexplainable, something that happened to you, or around you, that you felt you could not control?"

Lena blinked. She looked at Emris's grave face and resisted the urge to protest again. Instead, she thought back to the first time it had happened, the time the dead man had fixed her with his eye. "About a year ago," she replied quietly, panic rising in her chest, tightening against her lungs.

"And it's been getting worse? More powerful? Less controllable?"

She remembered the last time, a few weeks past: the cold, bony hand of the Duchess closing around her wrist, painfully tight. She had barely been touching the body, brushing her fingers against its lips. Lena nodded, unable to speak.

He looked at the snake. "And I suppose you didn't particularly mean to kill that serpent either."

Lena shook her head.

"Then if we don't get you to the temples soon, you and everyone around you could be in terrible danger." He stepped closer. "Lena, you might not be ready to know it yet, but magic is a part of you. And whether you like it or not, you need to learn about it and accept it, so that you can control it."

She felt herself nodding. Could it really be true? Her heart said no, but he sounded so certain. She gazed down at her hands wonderingly, as if she'd find the answers written on her palms.

Emris started walking through the thinning trees toward the pale, growing sunlight. When Lena hesitated, he turned back. "Come on. Or don't you want to understand what's happening to you? You won't find any answers here."

Nervously, she touched the butterfly in her pocket, stroking the delicate filigree of its wings, allowing the feel of it to soothe her slightly as she turned toward the forest border and the new world beyond. And with one last look at the huge sinuous beast she had killed, she followed.

A large carriage drawn by two brown horses was waiting at the edge of the forest, sturdy-wheeled, windowless, and painted gray. Stenciled on its side was the white silhouette of an archer aiming at a thin sickle moon hovering over his head. The whole carriage was battered and weather-beaten, the paint chipped and silvered.

Beyond the carriage, a field of cropped corn lay bare below a sky filled with pink and orange wisps of clouds. Lena stopped, her breath catching in her throat at the odd sensation of wind in her hair. How long had it been since she had seen a sky like this? As a child, she had been permitted to play in the gardens with the other cryptlings, but only at night. Whenever she'd been out during the day, her heavy cowl had framed her view in thick, ugly wool. Her hands twitched toward her cowl instinctively, but she stopped herself: it felt good, the dawn sunlight on her face, the air combing her hair loose from its ragged tail, cold and crisp in her lungs.

Why shouldn't I have this? she thought, breathing deep. She was not a cryptling anymore. She didn't have to hide. She felt a kind of happiness fill her like air, quickly followed by a heady fear of the unknown. If she wasn't a cryptling, what was she? A mage, as Emris claimed? She shivered at the thought.

A driver in a gray uniform sat up at the front of the carriage, swigging from a hip flask. He was a middle-aged man, stout and fat, legs wrapped in a brown woolen blanket. He looked at Lena's birthmark before he met her eyes, and she lowered her gaze. Emris called to him, climbing the three steps to the seat up front. They exchanged low words, and after a few moments the driver eyed Lena again, but with greater suspicion.

"You'd better get used to being looked at like that," said Emris under his breath, climbing back down and offering Lena his hand to help her inside. "Rogues are feared throughout Valorian."

"Rogues?"

"The common word for mages uninitiated into a temple, like yourself."

Lena shook her head, not understanding. "I'd've thought it was obvious that I'm already used to being looked at," she said tartly, facing him from the relative height of the interior.

Emris raised an eyebrow. He fixed on her mark momentarily, but there was no judgment in his gaze. "Perhaps. But people outside Duke's Forest aren't looking at your birthmark—not in that way. Once they know you're a Rogue, they're looking at *you*, wondering whether you might kill them." He threw her a slight, unnerving smile, the scars on his face puckering with the motion. Unsettled, Lena took a seat inside the carriage.

The large, sturdy vehicle had clearly been designed for practicality rather than comfort. It was tall enough to stand up in, for a start, although Emris's head almost grazed the ceiling. Inside, narrow benches bordered walls crammed with storage space: cupboards with slatted wooden doors fastened with rope, drawers of wicker that tied shut with string hoops. There were no windows, and Emris lit a lamp attached to the ceiling. In its steady light, Lena glimpsed rolls of blankets, a miniature iron stove, and a box labeled

"Panacea" next to another labeled "Venomsbane"—alongside other items of unidentifiable use (a bundle of finely carved twigs in the corner, a couple of bright medallions hanging from pegs, a knot of strange leathery leaves suspended from the ceiling). The smell of tough salted meat and old sweat assaulted her nose.

Emris knocked on the ceiling, and the carriage lurched into motion. Steadying himself against the shelving, he plucked a couple of long white feathers from a drawer, a leaf from the bundle suspended from the ceiling, and a few lengths of silky black string. Finally, with a glance at Lena, Emris unhooked a gray cloak identical to his own from the carriage wall. "Here," he said, "you're shivering."

It was true: her habit was soaked through with storm vapor and sweat—she was freezing. Lena wrapped the cloak around her body gratefully. It was spun of plain gray wool, finer and softer than the wool of her habit, and lined with black flannel. She pulled it close.

"You called yourself a huntsman. What does that mean?" she asked.

Emris sat opposite her, elbows on his knees.

"I will tell you everything, but I'll need quiet while I prepare this charm," he said, and he began to weave the strands together, the feathers and leaf slowly encased. "Rest if you can."

"But—"

"Trust me." He shot her a quick smile. "You'll get nothing out of me while I'm working—this is tricky. You'll just have to be patient."

Lena relented, rested her head against the wooden boards of the carriage wall, and shut her eyes, secretly glad of a few moments' peace. The carriage jolted, rocked, and trundled along the pitted dirt road leading from the forest. The sound of the road roared in her ears, and for a while her mind was empty. But then thoughts and memories slushed into her all at once, as if spilled clumsily from a bucket.

Suddenly she didn't feel grateful for the quiet anymore. She screwed her eyes closed, hoping to stop the threatening tears. Emris had said she was a mage. She'd never considered the possibility—even when they had convicted her—but she couldn't deny how the strangeness of the past year slotted neatly and simply into the explanation like pieces of a child's puzzle. And if it was true, she'd never be able to return home.

Home . . . What was that anyway without Vigo? Vigo had hated magic. If Lena was a mage, would he have hated her too? Pain washed over her as the events of the past day flashed through her mind. Vigo was dead. Vigo was *dead*. And it was her fault, after all. She had betrayed him.

The carriage was large and unsteady, the road ill-maintained, and Lena found herself rocking wildly from side to side at the slightest disturbance. Her mind fluttered in dazed distress through her memories of Vigo. She settled on the story about the day he had found her. He'd told her in his usual matter-of-fact tone as she lay tucked up on the mattress in the corner of the kitchen, near the warmth of the stove. Lena had been nine years old. She had recently started to sleep out in the kitchen instead of on the small child's cot in the corner of Vigo's room, and was trying very hard not to be afraid.

Ten years to the day after my little boy died, I found you at dawn in a wooden crate on the steps down to the cryptling cellars. You were perhaps a day old, wailing like a hungry chick, and wrapped in fine linen cloth. I knew there and then that the Ancestors had sent you to me. I fed you cow's milk from the kitchens first, and I dug out my son's empty crib, hidden and dusty in a cupboard. As soon as I laid you down, you slept. I named you Lena after my wife, Elena.

Whenever he'd spoken of Elena, his eyes had grown watery and he'd pretended to be busy or cross and would change the subject. But this time he had smiled.

Elena was beautiful, you know.

But wasn't she Marked? Lena had asked curiously.

She was. A fire had left one side of her body a mass of scars, and at first, she raged at the Ancestors for sending her to the crypts at ten years old. But she was strong, determined, and fearless, and her eyes . . . He shook his head at the memory, as if it had overwhelmed his senses. *Her beauty shone through, no matter what. As soon as I saw you, Lena, with your face screwed up and your fists balled in anger, I knew you were the same. Like her, you were a fighter.*

FOUR
The Feast

After Lord Irvine had gone, Constance set the mask, pendant, and cane carefully on the dressing table. She shrugged off her cloak and turned the lock in the sturdy wooden door—trying the handle for good measure. *Shut tight.*

She walked toward the window seat and removed a blue velvet cushion. Beneath, a small compartment was hidden. She slipped her finger into the gap and lifted, smiling as she found the small pile of illicit books her mother had left behind. She ran her hands over the worn leather spines. The atlas of the world. The books of magic. The stories of the puppet theaters in the southern islands where her mother had been brought up. When Constance was a child, these books had been the closest thing she'd had to her mother's voice.

She shut the seat and replaced the cushion, her eyes stinging slightly.

Unbuttoning her muddy dress, she let the silken material pool on the floor and lowered herself into the steaming bathwater. She'd taken her right glove off, but not her left.

She kept her left arm raised, resting it on the copper lip of the bath. The trembling in it had quieted to a mild, unnatural vibration worrying at her fingers.

The black velvet glove reached three quarters of the way up her arm, but white scar tissue still peeked from the top. She shut her eyes. Every time she saw the scars, she remembered the cold blue flash of pain. Felt it, almost. The intensity of the memory was nearly unbearable.

She tried to clear her mind as the water warmed her to the core. She had to focus on the task ahead, not on the past. Constance felt the storm cloud churning outside, stuttering with electricity.

Flickers of light fell through the window as she allowed her body to relax—but no thunder sounded; the air filled instead with steam and quiet. After a time, she stepped out of the bath, wrapped herself in bath sheets, and lay on her mother's bed. How long since Constance had rested here, her hair spilling across the pillows? Her childhood felt farther away than ever. She conjured the memory of her mother's arms around her and fell into a deep and dreamless sleep.

By the time Constance woke, it was dusk. She felt like she could sleep for hours longer, but instead she pulled on one of the finest gowns in the chest—red velvet with a fur-lined collar and gold-leaf embroidery on the sleeves. Over the top, she rested her round pendant on its long chain, glinting in the firelight. After a moment's hesitation, she opened the catch and peered at the bright mirror inside: nothing but her own dark-blue eye gazing back at her curiously. She breathed on the glass until it misted, her finger hovering over it. She wanted to see him, wanted to speak to him. But what could she say? The breath-cloud faded and she snapped the mirror shut.

She was running late. She slipped the mask into its secret pocket in her purple cloak and threw the cloak around her shoulders. She took the cane and left her room—her mother's room—locking the door behind her. Across the courtyard, her cane tapped loudly through the gloom, strange distorted echoes reflecting back as if others were walking, invisible, at her side. She'd nearly forgotten how it felt in Duke's Forest, the constant aware-ness of the Ancestors beneath, watching, judging. She followed different gods now, but the sensation was as potent as ever.

They had never wanted her here.

Voices roared from the great hall, the oldest building in the castle, predating even the ancient east tower by hundreds of years. The hall had been swallowed up by the rest of the buildings, until now it stretched across nearly an entire wing between the south and west towers. Light spilled from its windows, watching the storm cloud like an ancient, many-eyed beast protecting its mountain hoard from a rival predator.

Constance climbed the steps to the entrance and pushed the door open. She slid inside, fixing a smile on her face at the sight within. But behind her eyes, she crumbled. When she'd left, six years ago, the hall could have been filled twice over by the inhabitants of the castle. Now it was barely half-full.

Her brother and the Wise Men sat at the high table—at least she assumed they were the Wise Men; most of them were old and decrepit and tucking into their food like ill-mannered children. She recognized a few: Lord Veredith, the law expert from the courtyard, and Lord Redding, who had dandled her on his knee as a toddler. Lord Farley had been a newly wed young man when she had left, but now he sat stoop-shouldered and alone over a bottle. Others had clearly risen through the power vacuum created by the Pestilence—most of them strangers. And her father was there too, his horrible physician in the brown coat standing over him as he picked unhappily at the food on his plate, his eyes darting around in confusion. The only free chair stood next to her father's, her brother on the other side, Lord Veredith opposite. Lord Irvine was a little way down the table.

As Constance walked down the aisle at the center of the hall, people stopped talking, conversation thrumming into silence. She took her seat, forcing a wide, pleasant smile. But as she turned to face the room, she noticed a conspicuous absence: the Justice.

Well, I suppose I can't force him to celebrate my return, she thought. *Besides, it looks as if he's sent his creature as a spy instead.* She shot a sharp glance over her shoulder at

Dr. Thorn, who was now serving her father wine from a dull pewter jug, and she remembered how he'd hurried to fetch the Justice upon her arrival. The physician sank into the shadows as he noticed her gaze, cradling a goblet of his own, and nodded at her calmly. *I'll give him something to report,* she thought, with a tiny smile.

She stood and turned to face the rest of the hall, forcing her unease down into the bottom of her stomach. "I am so glad to be home," she said simply, her voice carrying easily in the quiet. "Thank you all for your warm welcome. You are probably wondering where I have been all this time. I expect there have been many rumors about my disappearance. And now you must be wondering why I have only just come back."

Winton was gazing up at her especially intently.

"I have been in the City of Kings, with my mother's family," she said. "My father had the foresight to send me away—in secret—as the cloud first began to develop. He was trying to protect me. He did not know how terrible it would grow, but at the first sign of the storm he knew, as I was heir to the duchy, that it was imperative I survive, flourish, and learn the art of rule from the greatest in the land." She laid a hand on her father's arm, part of her hoping he wasn't sane enough to call out her half-truths, her lies. "But now it's he who needs my protection. And all of you. I've come back to help you. My father has been alone at the helm, with no heir yet of age to offer a Protectorate." She smiled at Winton gently. "And especially alone since the sad decline and recent death of the Duchess." Pain flashed briefly across her brother's face, and Constance squeezed his shoulder. "But I am here now, and a Witenagemot is set for tomorrow at midday. As my father is ill, I intend to petition the Wise Men for permission to rule in his stead."

A murmur filled the hall. She heard the words "The Justice will not accept this," but could not tell who spoke. She ignored the warning.

"I am only sorry I could not return sooner. But let us raise a glass: to homecomings, to new beginnings, to our future." And she lifted the full goblet high into the air, watching nervously as people rose hesitantly to their feet, each guest raising their glass in answer.

"Homecomings. New beginnings. Our future," they murmured. She had never heard a toast spoken with less conviction.

Afterward, Constance sat down and piled her plate high with food, hoping the relief wasn't too plain on her face. She was a good liar—she'd never have reached her rank at the temple if she weren't—and yet lies still tasted sour in her mouth.

Lies are neighbors with the truth, she remembered the masked Priestess whispering. *Release your secret truths one by one, carefully, and only to persuade. Treat them like gold.*

Winton leaned closer, his voice low and worried as he spoke—although it was barely necessary under the rising clatter of plates and the roar of conversation. "You have my support, Sister, of course. But do you really think the Justice will lie down and take this?"

She chewed on a piece of rehydrated fish. Disgusting. The fare on the table was clearly drawn from the castle's plentiful siege supplies—some of it preserved for decades. She forced herself to swallow: she needed the strength. "No, he won't go without a fight," she said. "But I don't intend to give him a choice."

Winton shook his head slightly. "His personal retinue is the largest in the castle—he has three hundred men under his own command, and until you are confirmed as Protector in his stead, his ducal authority gives him command of the two hundred men of the city guard." He paused. "Five hundred men."

Constance set down her fork. "Yes, I can manage basic arithmetic, Winton," she snapped. She instantly regretted it, as she noticed his expression hardening. *He is an ally*, she reminded herself, *not just your little brother. He may not be of age, but he's not a child anymore.* "I'm sorry," she said quickly. "I'm tired from my journey, and it's been a sad homecoming."

Winton nodded, smiled. He always had been quick to forgive, even when they were younger. "Don't worry. I understand." He tore off a hunk of bread from a loaf in the center of the table.

You really don't understand, Constance thought. But she said, "What of the other personal retinues?" She asked partly because she was genuinely interested, and partly to make him feel important.

"Lord Irvine . . ." Winton swallowed uncomfortably. "Lord Irvine has two hundred and fifty men, or thereabouts, due to his rank as Swordmaster—it's fewer than the Justice but they're better fighters." In the past, the Swordmaster's guard had been the elite fighting force of Duke's Forest, a thousand strong. Two hundred and fifty was . . . pitiful. "As for the rest of the noblemen—their retinues number in the tens. Once it would have been more, but . . ." He shook his head sadly. "So very many have died. And now Mother . . ."

In spite of everything, Constance too felt a pang of sorrow in her chest—she hated to see her little brother so wounded. "Lord Irvine told me what happened at the Descent. I'm so sorry, Winton."

He shook his head. Constance could tell he was holding back tears. "I just . . . can't believe that she's gone. She was ill for so long . . . and suddenly . . . but then, for a moment . . . I thought . . ." She rested her right hand on his arm. Sleep had helped her, and food was strengthening her further, but her magic and emotions remained unsettled, burbling within her like an upset stomach. She steadied her breath in the way she'd been taught as a novice. She felt her heartbeat slow. Winton, however, had clearly never been taught how to control his emotions.

"It's all right, Winton. I'm here now," she said softly.

"I'm sorry," he said, pulling away from her and standing quickly, struggling to suppress his tears. "I . . . have to go, just . . . just for a minute." And he slipped out one of the servants' doors toward the back of the hall, attracting a few stares and murmurs.

Part of her was tempted to follow him, comfort him—but she knew she had to stay. If she was to rule here, she had to be stronger, calmer, and cleverer than anyone else. She sipped at her wine—an inferior vintage, sharp with tannins, but she was glad of the warm burn sliding down her throat.

On Constance's other side, the Duke pushed his food around his plate as if he'd forgotten what it was for. The physician had disappeared.

"Try to eat something, Father," she said gently, helping him cut a sliver of the pungent fish and raise it to his mouth. The Duke chewed with his mouth open, like a toddler.

Lord Veredith leaned closer across the table. "It is good to see you again, my dear," he warbled, patting the back of her hand. "You have grown into a beautiful young woman. How are the Santinis?"

The Santinis were her mother's family. Their estates in the southeast of Valorian were a scattering of islands called the Wishes, like a rash of freckles in the shallow turquoise sea. Long ago, they'd been a royal house in their own right, and even now their territory was known for its unusual freedom and outlandish customs, the Santini Contessa for her independence. As the family rarely visited court, Constance had never met them—but she'd done her research. "They are well. My uncle Alberto sends his regards. I believe you met him once, when my mother's match was first arranged?"

"I did indeed. Splendid, splendid." Lord Veredith sipped his soup, a good deal of it spattering onto his long beard. "It was a magnificent day. The sun was shining. The horrid storm cloud was not yet imagined. A crowd gathered in the lower town to cheer on the new Duchess as she arrived in a gilded carriage." His eyes had filled with mist. "She was beautiful, golden skinned, blue-eyed, and willowy tall. You have your mother's figure, dear, and her eyes," he said, "but your coloring is your father's." He continued, his voice warbling higher as his emotion grew: "I remember her stepping from the carriage. Your father was there, straight-backed and proud—his hair as fair as hers was dark. A young man then. Yes, they were a fine couple. And as they made their way into the castle, the whole city was alive with music. Never since that day have I felt—"

"These are sad times," Constance cut in, not wanting to hear more.

Lord Veredith patted her hand a second time. "Indeed, my dear. Indeed they are."

Constance's eyes wandered about the room, catching sight of the physician sitting at a table with the other professionals and senior servants in the castle. While the physician refilled his goblet, the bald houndmaster with his thin, sharp face was muttering something into his ear. "My lord," she said to Veredith, "what do you know of Dr. Jonas Thorn? I do not recall him from my childhood."

Veredith took a few much-needed moments to dab his mouth with a handkerchief. "He was hired as the physician's assistant not long after you disappeared—though before that, I understand, he was an apothecary in the lower town. When the physician fell to the Pestilence, Dr. Thorn took his place."

"And before he was an apothecary?"

Lord Veredith shrugged. "I can tell you no more than that—I take no interest in the affairs of the lower town, I'm afraid." He frowned. "Why do you ask, my dear?"

"He is responsible for my father's health," she said, refilling Veredith's goblet. "And yet my father does not seem . . ." She looked at his stringy, greasy hair, the dark circles beneath his eyes. "Well, he does not seem particularly cared for."

"Yes. Yes indeed," said Veredith, his face suddenly grave and defensive. "Caring for your father presents a difficult challenge. He does not like to be touched, I hear, and rarely sleeps. But Thorn represents the best medical care we can offer your father, my dear. There is no more senior medical professional in city or castle."

A difficult challenge? He is a person, not a nuisance! Constance felt herself growing angry, so she changed the subject while cutting up the rather hard pastry on her plate. "And what of my brother? Who has educated him since both his parents sickened?"

Veredith smiled. "Fitting, my dear, that you should show such concern for your poor brother. He was very close to his mother, right up until the end. After his childhood tutor fell to the Pestilence, perhaps three years past, it was the Duchess herself who elected to help Winton practice his letters and numbers—with the Justice's guidance of course."

"The Justice?" If anything, her brother would have been a threat to his position.

"The Duchess and the Justice were close for a time— although I understand Winton was never exactly comfortable in his company. And since she grew ill, the boy has ... well, he's run a little wild. The Justice tried to draw him closer, but to little effect. Winton showed virtually no interest in statecraft, and besides, the Justice had greater concerns than a wayward princeling."

Constance nodded slowly. It had been clear from his expression in the courtyard that Winton bore little love for the Lord Protector, though his dislike stopped well short of rebellion. "Then what?" she asked.

Lord Veredith frowned. "Then he was tutored by the Swordmaster—both in his books and in the art of swordplay. But in the last year he has abandoned the twin swords in favor of a longsword and spends much of his time in the practice hall with the city guard. He doesn't care for books, I am afraid—and with the Duchess so ill, there was no one left to insist on his lessons."

No one? Constance stared at Lord Veredith in disbelief. She could barely believe the hypocrisy of the man. Had none of the Wise Men taken any responsibility for her brother?

He continued. "The captain of the guard ... Captain Trudan, I believe ... has rather taken him under his wing." He sighed and shook his head. Constance waited, sensing more to follow. "Since your father's illness, we Wise Men have all tried to be fathers to Winton. And Lord Irvine seemed to be making progress, for a time. But it didn't last, alas. Trudan appears to have succeeded where we have failed."

"Captain Trudan?" She remembered him—a big man of thirty or so when she'd left, the son of a baker, who'd fought his way into the guard by virtue of his pure strength. She sought him out. He sat at the table with the physician and the houndmaster, ignoring their conversation and chewing enthusiastically on what looked like a very tough piece of dried venison. He had a straightforward, friendly face. She frowned. "But Trudan is lowborn. What happened with Lord Irvine? Why does my brother no longer seek out his company?"

"That I do not know." Lord Veredith sighed, then slurped his soup. "Who can understand the young? Perhaps Trudan's lowborn status has helped in some way. It is strange ... But these are strange times. There are no rules anymore." He sounded sad. "In another age, we would've protested. Now ..."

Now, you can't be bothered, she thought. "Indeed, my lord. Thank you for your thoughts on this sensitive matter." Constance smiled stiffly, and turned to her father to hide the worry she felt sure was naked on her face. The Duke was struggling through a mouthful of bread, and she couldn't help noticing the sore red marks on his wrists, as if he had been restrained.

She shot another glance at Jonas Thorn, who unexpectedly met her gaze from the far end of his table. His eyes narrowed at her—so slightly that it was nearly imperceptible, but she noticed nonetheless.

I don't trust him.

FIVE
Flight

Lena hesitated on the step of the carriage, pulling the gray cloak close around her body. They had stopped in the center of a crossroads. The four broad roads, golden in the sunlight, stretched into the blue distance. All around, low fields rustled with grass and the world felt calm and endless.

Emris waved at the driver, who tipped his hat, and then knelt beside the front wheel of the carriage. He had formed a little braid of a few materials in the carriage—the feathers, leaf, and strings—and he appeared to be weaving it between the spokes of the wheel. The horses seemed restless, throwing their heads and snorting, pawing the hard-packed earth. Despite the hour of the day, the crossroads was still and silent.

Behind the carriage, a gray-green smudge on the horizon was the only evidence of Duke's Forest. She felt a tug in her heart, like a cord pulled tight between her and the home she had left behind. An image flew unbidden into her mind: Vigo's bones, bare and chewed. The image lingered, mixed up with the last time she had seen the old man, the calm determination on his face as he'd told her how to escape.

Sweeping the image aside, she jumped the last step, her feet planted in the center of the crossroads. And all of a sudden she felt a thrill of power, a jolt of static. The sensation shocked her; she stumbled backward, hand on the carriage for support.

Emris looked up at her, his face unreadable in the bright sunlight. "Spells work best in transitional areas—crossroads, coastlines, the mouths of caves. Here, the boundaries between Order and Chaos are frayed, and magic thrives. Can you feel it?" He observed her closely. "You look pale. Are you all right?"

She opened her eyes. "No, I can't feel anything. I'm fine," she lied, willing it to be true. Emris returned to his work. But she felt something, all right: she felt as though she might laugh or scream or be violently sick, or as if some creature might burst out of the hollow place above her stomach—a feeling of . . . potential.

She reached for the butterfly in her pocket, breathing deep as she stroked its wings—something she knew, something ordinary and comforting. The sick sensation calmed down and settled in the slight dip between her lungs, below her breasts. Holding her other hand over the area, she pressed down and breathed deep again, and gradually the feeling passed. What was wrong with her? Was this magic?

When Emris was satisfied with the position of his braid, he laid a hand over it and spoke a string of words in a foreign language that sounded like the chiming of bells. He repeated the phrase again and again. What began as a quiet murmur over his work grew to a dancing hum, filling Lena's ears. Gradually, the sound became a sort of music, which swayed gently like a boat floating down a little stream. She felt herself falling into the rhythm of the stream, but the melody quickened: no longer an amble but a trot, a hoop spinning on a country road, a jog across a grassy meadow—then a run, a torrent, an exhilarating canter on horseback, the wind rushing in her face, and finally, impossibly, her stomach was turning like a spinning top, and—.

Emris had stopped and was smiling up at her. "You can sense it, can't you? Can you tell what the spell is for?"

Lena shook her head, confused, and lifted her gaze in the direction of the road ahead. "You already told me it was the quickening of journeys," she said quietly. In the distance, a range of sloping hills rose to tree-lined peaks covered with trees that swished in a faraway wind. She focused on the sight. Something about the motion of the trees calmed her. "How far to the City of Kings?" she asked.

"We'll arrive by sunset," he said, standing up. "Come on."

To her surprise, Emris sat up front, while the suspicious coachman took his blankets and bedroll inside.

"Can't stand flying," he grumbled as he climbed in. "Give me a good hard road any time." He was already pulling on what looked like a thick felt nightcap.

Flying?

Lena shot Emris an uncertain look. Maybe it was a turn of phrase. "Is the spell going to make us fly?"

He grinned, settling into the driver's seat and offering her a hand up. "That's the idea, yes."

"In . . . this?" She stared at the enormous, unwieldy carriage. She couldn't imagine anything less likely to take flight. But Emris just smiled.

She accepted his help and sat at his side, wrapping a woolen blanket around her knees and resting back against the padded bench. In addition, Emris fastened leather straps carefully around her torso. As he leaned close, she smelled a strong, clean scent in his tightly curled hair.

"Ready?" he said, as he took the reins.

She nodded, mingled terror and excitement building in the pit of her stomach.

He cracked the reins, and the horses broke into a canter, a gallop. At first, hooves clattered and the wheels roared along the road, stray stones flicking and banging against the carriage. Lena clutched her blanket close and felt the air steal from her lungs. She'd never gone so fast before! And suddenly—unbelievably—there was silence, and her whole body lurched, as if she were falling. The road was a few feet below, the wheels of the carriage now spinning in thin air, slowing and slowing. She clutched the seat tightly, wanting to scream or shout or laugh, but her lungs were empty. And the road was falling away like a golden ribbon between the grassy fields, more quickly than Lena would have thought possible—she could feel the air around her sparking with a brilliant luminescence as a puff of cloud rushed down to enclose them.

Magic, she thought again, as that sick sensation tingled in her chest. She hadn't known it could feel like this. It felt . . . wonderful.

"Hold your breath!" Emris warned—and Lena did.

They rushed into the cloud's whiteness, cold light rain enveloping them, and everything except the carriage and the bobbing heads of the bay horses, still galloping, disappeared. And when they emerged from the cloud, they were damp and cold and the sky was a brilliant blue—bluer than before—and the green of the earth was stretched out like a fine silken blanket threaded with roads of gold.

Emris adjusted the reins, leveling out their ascent, and rested back in his seat. "So," he said, "now is the time for you to ask all those questions."

Lena was speechless. She looked down again, noticing another carriage on the King's Road far below, as small as a beetle. The sick feeling had passed—but she felt the echo of it still. Was it . . . magic? Inside her? How had she never noticed it before? Had it always been there?

"Are all mages born with magic inside them?"

Emris nodded. "Yes. Generally, magic runs in families, and children with two mage parents are highly likely to inherit magic themselves. But sometimes, rarely, it can occur as if from nowhere." He glanced across at her. "I'm guessing your parents weren't mages?"

She shook her head. "I wouldn't know. I never knew my parents."

Emris smiled sadly. "Me too," he said, and she glanced at him in surprise—but he didn't elaborate.

"So you can't . . . *catch* magic?" Lena asked tentatively. "Or . . . or sort of develop it? It's always there inside you, even when you're born?"

"Catch magic? Like you catch a cold?" Emris laughed. "No, of course not. You're thinking that you've never felt this way before?"

She nodded.

"Well, living in Duke's Forest, I imagine you haven't been around much magic—there's the storm cloud, but that's . . ." He paused. "Well, no one's quite sure what it is—but it's certainly *different*. Whatever you're feeling, it's stronger because natural magic is all around us now—both at the crossroads and here in the air, keeping us afloat."

She gazed at the world far below, spinning under the horses' hooves. Her mind raced. "So . . . what's happening to me?" she said, turning the subject. Her breath plumed into the freezing air as she spoke, and she pulled the blanket closer. "Why are we in such a hurry?"

"You are a Rogue, Lena: a mage without the control of a god and a temple." Emris looked at her seriously. "What do you know of magic? Do they tell you anything about it in Duke's Forest?"

She shook her head. "Nobody speaks of it in Duke's

Forest, really . . ." But that wasn't quite true, was it? "I mean . . . except in children's tales."

"Tell me one," he said. "I'm curious."

Lena nodded, remembering one in particular. Vigo had been good at stories. He'd sit at her side when she was little, at bedtime. Usually he'd be off to some duty or other, so he'd simply tell her good night, tuck her in tightly, and flick off the oil lamp beside her bed. But sometimes his eyes took on a faraway quality, and she would tingle in excitement, knowing he was about to tell her a story. "There's one about a poor orphan boy in Duke's Forest," Lena said softly, conjuring the story from her memory. She shut her eyes and felt the thin, chilly breeze run through her hair. "It's an old tale, from hundreds of years ago, before the King conquered the dukedom. The orphan boy found that he had magic. For six years he magicked everything he wanted: a great palace for a home, all the food he could eat, and friends to play with, and he lived a life of luxury and pleasure." A gust of wind rushed past in a muted roar, and she opened her eyes. "But on the first day of the seventh year, he walked into his palace, and it was ash; he picked up his food, and it was dust; and when he went to play with his friends, he found only a nest of spiders."

She gazed down at the glittering world below, remembering Vigo's voice as he'd told her the tale. She remembered how he'd worded the next bit—it had stuck with her ever since.

"He was so grieved at the loss of all he'd loved that he wished he could not feel. And as he stood, his heart turned to stone, and stone ran into his blood and crept across his skin and rushed down across his body until he was cold and numb all over. And you can see him there today, in a courtyard in the upper town, frozen in his grief—or so they say." Lena had never seen the stone boy for herself—but then, the upper town was large and full of courtyards, most of which were private. "The story tells us that magic cannot replace real things. It tricks you. It is a false power." She thought of the strange feeling she'd had at the crossroads and shivered. All this was frightening her more than she cared to admit. And yet—she couldn't deny she was drawn to it. Once, she had found a forgotten doorway into a deeper passage of the crypts, stairs twisting down into a darkness so thick it was nearly velvet. She had hovered there, heart racing, unable to move for the fear pulling her backward and the strange longing calling her from below. She felt the same sensation now.

Emris straightened the reins so that they followed the King's Road far beneath them. "Many stories contain a grain of truth, and that one is no exception. But the whole truth is . . . well, it's more complicated. In the City of Kings, every schoolchild learns of Order and Chaos. Order is the physical world, governed by the laws of nature. Things in the physical world are predictable: if you drop something, you know it's going to hit the floor. Chaos is the opposing force. If you attempt to drop something in a space dominated by chaotic forces, it could very well fly back upward and hit you in the face."

Lena nodded, watching a farmstead rush by below,

surrounded by fields of cows like speckled ants. "So Order is the physical world and Chaos is magic?"

Emris smiled. "Yes, in some ways, though it's not quite that simple."

She waited for him to continue.

"Chaos could not exist without the physical world, Lena. It's best thought of as a kind of energy. If energy exists alone, in a vacuum, it is meaningless. It needs something to affect. Chaos needs Order. And, in turn, Order needs Chaos. Rules are meaningless if nothing has the capacity to burst their boundaries. What is a riverbank without a river, or vice versa? So the world is a delicate balance of Order and Chaos."

"How does this relate to me?"

"You told me that you've been experiencing strange things for the past year. And whether or not you dare to admit it, these things can only be explained by magic. And that means your magic has awoken in you." Emris glanced across at her, his dark eyes shining. " 'Magic' is the term we use for the supernatural effect of Chaos upon Order. A person with magical abilities is holding chaotic forces inside their body. This has the capacity to be dangerous—very dangerous—if these forces are not controlled."

Lena frowned. Was he suggesting she had hurt someone? "But I haven't . . ."

He started to shake his head, and she trailed off. "Not necessarily dangerous to other people, not yet, although that will come in time. But certainly dangerous to the mages themselves. Chaotic forces have been known to overwhelm the physical form—in short, to kill, to steal consciousness, to become another entity entirely. A force of Chaos loose in the physical world—that's a terrifying prospect. That's what we call a Radical."

"Is that . . . is that what's going to happen to me?" Lena swallowed. It did sound terrifying.

"No," Emris said firmly. "Not now, anyway. You are a Rogue—you hold the potential to become overwhelmed by your magic, and that is dangerous. That's why I want to help you. If you were a Radical already, I would have had to kill you on sight."

Lena suddenly felt colder. She looked down at her hands clutching the woolen blanket around her legs. She remembered the Ancestors, eyes swiveling, limbs jerking under her touch. What was she capable of, truly?

"But that's why children who demonstrate magical abilities must, by law, be educated in one of the temples. There's a ceremony called the Binding, in which the mage's power is tied to a god. After this ceremony, it is impossible for Chaos within the mage to overwhelm him or her. Combine this with strict regulations, patterns of thought, rituals, and rules . . . and, yes, magic is made as safe as it can ever be." He smiled. "So you see, the fear of mages in Duke's Forest is not without rationality—without temples, mages are dangerous indeed, and magic can turn you and everything you love to dust. And that is why I need to get you to the City of Kings."

Lena didn't feel different. She didn't feel like Chaos was living inside her, waiting to overwhelm her. Not right now. But after the past year, and after what had happened with the snake and how she had suddenly felt at the crossroads, how could she deny it? She stroked the butterfly in her pocket as Emris sank into silence, perhaps realizing how much new information she had to turn over in her mind. If what Emris had said was true, she'd be required to pledge herself to the gods. Could she do that? She was already an outcast, divorced from the Ancestors and the ceremonies binding her to their guidance. Part of her had prepared for the possibility long ago, before the storm cloud, when she'd fantasized about the world beyond the forest. But somewhere in the back of her mind, she'd always assumed she would return—because of Vigo. And now she had to grieve for Vigo.

But if she worshipped the gods, she'd be a confirmed heretic. Vigo had been a pious man—he'd never have approved of the person she would become.

If she did as Emris said, there would be no turning back. Her throat felt sore and tight, and she gazed out at the view, trying to distract herself.

Below, the King's Road was growing broader and busier, villages and towns crowding either side of it, bustling with people and wagons and horses. All of a sudden, Emris dropped their altitude, and Lena nearly jumped out of her seat when another charmed carriage crossed overhead, the underside of the vehicle passing a few feet above. She watched the carriage retreat—a gleaming black chassis with a golden crest on the side.

"Those who ride the sky road are usually either on temple business or disgustingly rich," Emris explained, smiling ruefully.

Here and there below, Lena thought she could spy a child pointing at them in delight, or perhaps fear—and dogs barked up as they passed. The sun beat down brightly, and Lena turned her face, her mark, toward the brilliant warmth, thinking—just for a moment—about nothing else.

They spoke intermittently during the afternoon, landing in a grassy field for a brief meal of bread and cheese and small tart apples that Lena retrieved from the supplies in the carriage, where the coachman was snoring noisily.

"What of your life in Duke's Forest?" Emris asked while they ate. "What did you leave behind, and why?"

"I worked in the crypts," she said. "I was an assistant mortician, preparing and caring for the Ancestors. But . . ." And she felt her voice disappear in her throat. She coughed. "But then I was convicted of magecraft, and the Justice set his hounds on me, and I ran. My . . . my master tried to protect me. He told me how to find a way out." She didn't feel able to tell him the full story—how he had died, how it had all been her fault. Not yet.

"Why were you convicted?" Emris asked. "What form did your magic take?"

Lena hesitated. "I . . . was attending to the Duchess's

body. It was a great honor—I was selected to assist in the Descent, the ceremony in which we place the body of the Ancestor into the final resting place. Everyone was watching. Everyone was there." She remembered the Duchess's son, Winton. Tears had run down his cheeks as he'd watched Lena perform the last rites. "The first part went well. But then, at the end of the ceremony, I had to touch the Duchess and . . . and when I did, she moved."

"She moved?" He sounded genuinely interested, but hardly shocked.

"I mean . . . her arm . . . I don't know what happened," she added lamely. "I guess . . . it was magic?" It sounded wrong to her, but she forced herself to consider the possibility. "Is that . . . normal?"

"Oh yes. Before the Binding, buildup of uncontrolled magic can result in objects moving, breaking, catching fire, or even exploding."

"Exploding?"

Emris laughed. "Count yourself lucky. I've come across some truly gruesome scenes in my time."

Lena nodded, unable to join him in smiling. She hadn't quite told Emris the full story, had she? Because it hadn't been a random movement. No, the Duchess's bony hand had shot up and grasped Lena's wrist, tight and cold. Lena had shrieked and pulled back from the tomb. But everyone had seen it. Even Vigo, who had looked at her blankly with uncomprehending eyes as murmurs of outrage had risen among the mourners. The Justice had wasted no time in chaining her hands and sending her straight to the dungeons to await her trial. And the Duchess's son had looked at her as she left, tears lingering on his face, mingled grief and horror in his eyes.

She had never felt so small, worthless and alien to herself.

But she didn't tell Emris any of that. She glanced at him out of the corner of her eye. How could she be sure about him anyway? She'd known him for a matter of hours. She was relying on him to tell her everything about this world. But she wasn't ready to tell him everything about herself.

Lena watched the land spool out below her, in silence and wonder, wrapped up tight, the sky gleaming a jewel-like, freezing blue. She felt grateful. Grateful for her life, yes. Grateful to have escaped the tiny, clouded world of her home. But guilt, fear, and anger had lodged in her heart like splinters too.

As evening approached, Lena spotted something on the horizon: a jaggedness on the curve of the land, outlined against the sinking sun. Staring into the brightness, she couldn't pick out the details, but hills started to rise and cast long shadows, reaching toward them.

"Nearly there," Emris said softly.

As the sun sank, the city revealed itself against the pinkening sky, and Lena felt her eyes widen. It was vast.

Emris flew higher as they neared. "Might as well take in the view," he murmured, watching Lena's rapt eyes with a quirk of his lips.

The City of Kings nestled in a shallow basin surrounded by seven hills and crossed by a wide, shining river. Lena counted four bridges spanning its silvery width. The tallest buildings in the city gleamed with glass, and she spied domes of gold and stone turrets whipping with flags. The streets were straight, strictly gridded—except on the outskirts of the city, where they tumbled ragtag up the hills like old lace—and courtyards were picked out here and there, some shining with pools and fountains like gems. Toward the north of the city, a huge expanse of green surrounded a large square building with seven pointed towers. Lena found herself breathless.

"The center is divided into three districts," Emris said. "There is the royal district." He pointed to the expanse of green to the north, a few riders galloping across the park. "That huge seven-towered building is the palace. To the southeast, the commercial district." He wheeled the carriage around gently, pointed toward an area with packed, gridded streets—people bustling about their business, despite the sinking sun. "Those big buildings are the municipal trading halls and the merchant guilds, but there are more homes here than in the other districts." He turned the carriage slowly to the left. "And there in the southwest is the temple district. That's where we're going." Lena trained her eyes on the broad central street of the district, lined with enormous buildings, flashes of gold and silver—statues?—catching the dying sunlight. "That street is the Sacristi, where most of the temples are," he explained.

"Most of them?"

"Well, technically, no one knows where Mythris's temple is," he said.

Lena would have asked who Mythris was and why that temple was so elusive, but as she looked back toward the palace, she noticed a fleck of black rising from the roof. As it grew closer, the fleck transformed into a rider on a dark horse, a long silvery cloak billowing. Emris had noticed him too. The rider was galloping straight toward their carriage, and Emris's mouth set itself in a firm, thin line. He pulled on the reins and the two horses drawing the carriage stopped, bizarrely, in the air. Floating. Somehow, it was weirder than flying. Now that they were still, Lena could hear the keening of the wind through the wheels.

"What's going on?" she asked.

"Lord Chatham, come to ask me whether I found what he wanted me to find." He shook his head at her question-ing look. "This shouldn't take long. Not to worry, Lena." But the tightness in his face said otherwise.

The man drew up beside the carriage. "Good evening, huntsman," he said, his voice friendly and businesslike on the surface, but somehow hard underneath. He had a pale, pointed, handsome face and oiled hair so ash-blond that it was nearly silver. He was oddly ageless, like a marble carving, but Lena guessed from the slight frown marks between his brows that he might be closer to forty than thirty. "Did you find Constance? Is she in the carriage?" Lena watched as his eyes lowered to her face, noticing how they flashed silver-blue in the light. "Who is this?" His gaze fixed on her mark. "Is she diseased?"

She quickly averted her eyes, wishing her cowl were raised, feeling a flash of hot anger deep inside her belly.

Emris's voice was cold and impatient. "I did not find Constance. She rode to Duke's Forest and disappeared into the storm cloud. I was unable to follow."

Constance was the masked mage, then, Lena realized. The name was distantly familiar, but she couldn't place it.

Lord Chatham's lip curled.

Emris turned to Lena. "And this ... this is a Rogue. I found her on the way back. I'm sure you understand that it's imperative to take her to the temple as soon as possible."

"Imperative, eh?" The man snorted, but his tone was curious. He looked at Lena so directly, she was shocked into meeting his eyes. Now that he knew she was a Rogue, his attitude had changed abruptly from disgust to interest. "Maybe for the likes of you, Emris. But there are those of us who don't need your ridiculous superstitions in order to control ourselves." Lena looked at Emris questioningly, but he shook his head slightly, as if to say, "Not now."

Lena turned back to Lord Chatham. There was something about the way his horse stood there in space, something different from their horses, whose hot breath plumed into the air, hooves pawing the sky impatiently. Something . . . oddly *still*.

"I assure you, if I have any news about the theft, I will report to the palace immediately," Emris continued.

"It's not a simple *theft*, huntsman," Chatham snapped. "That apprentice took my most precious invention. I need it back."

"Can't you just make another?" Emris said softly, goadingly. Chatham appeared to grow even angrier at that.

"It's not a *toy*. I can't whip one up in a morning's work. It took me *years* to perfect!"

But the exchange occupied only half of Lena's attention—the rest was fixed on Chatham's horse. The animal's torso was covered by a black fine-spun cloth, embroidered in the same silver as the man's cloak, and the face was hooded . . . She narrowed her eyes, peering into the shadow beneath. The beast was not flesh and blood, she realized with a shudder—at least not all of it. Was that glass? And under the cloth, was that metal? A slight yellowish glow burned in the depths of the creature's head.

"I see you've noticed my particular specialty," Lord Chatham said, breaking off his argument with Emris to address Lena and sounding abruptly pleased with himself. With an expression as if he were doing her a great and noble favor, he reached into his cloak and drew out a small silver card, handing it to her as the wind whistled around the carriage. The shining card was half the span of Lena's palm and covered in curly black writing. It read:

Lord Theodorus Chatham
Independent Certified Magician
The King's Mechanic by Royal Charter
Creator of Quality Magical Inventions & Curiosities
for All Persons of Substance and Nobility
INVITES YOU
to Experience His Emporium of Magical and
Mechanical Delights

"I'm on the hunt for a new apprentice, you know," Chatham added, "and I could use a Rogue...someone a bit more...malleable than my last one." He smiled.

"Stop it, Chatham," Emris said sharply. "Lena isn't a pawn in one of your games."

"Let's allow her to decide, shall we?"

Lena turned the card over. On the back was a slogan—*Magic for Everybody*—and an address in the royal district. She held the card carefully, letting the light catch the silver paper. She thought of the butterfly, remembered that night, the night she'd seen it fluttering out of the gloom. She had to stop herself from reaching for it as she looked again at the horse, the glow inside its head, the metal mechanisms clicking and whirring behind the glass. The butterfly had been similar, despite the difference in size—she could still conjure the *tick-tick-tick* noise she'd heard as it approached her. Could Lord Chatham have been its creator?

"Are there any other magicians like you?" Lena blurted as Chatham started to turn his horse.

He glanced over his shoulder. "There is no one quite like me," he said, winking. Lena blushed furiously. That wasn't at all what she had meant. "Good evening, huntsman, Rogue," he said, inclining his head to each of them in turn.

And with that, Lord Chatham rode off through the indigo dusk, gray cloak flapping in his wake. Emris wheeled the carriage into a slow, circling descent. His shoulders were tense, his jaw clenched. The encounter had affected him more than Lena could understand.

"What did he mean about the theft?" she asked tentatively.

"When Constance left the city, she stole something of his," he said, apparently reluctant to talk about it.

"And what about when he said that some people don't need superstitions to control their magic?" Lena asked as the temple district grew closer and closer. She held out the card. "Is that what this means by 'Independent Certified Magician'?"

Emris sighed. "Yes. Lord Chatham and a few others like him claim that they don't need the gods or the learning of the temples to control their magic. Instead, they pass a series of tests and are independently certified by the King, bound to his service." He shook his head. "They would argue that that's the way it was two thousand years ago, before the gods revealed themselves to humankind—that, therefore, there is something to it. But I don't like the idea of gambling with Chaos."

Lena watched the temple district draw closer. When she was sure Emris wasn't looking, she rested a hand over the butterfly in her pocket, stroking its delicate wings. She had left the only home she'd ever known—the person who'd made it a home lost to her forever. What's more, she was heading for a place where she'd be forced to pledge herself to a religion she'd always been warned against and a practice—magic—she'd long been taught to fear. But if haughty Lord Chatham was right and you could control magic without the gods, perhaps there was a middle way after all . . .

She hadn't liked the man, and she squirmed at the memory of how his eyes had first rested on her birthmark. But she slipped his card into the pocket, alongside the butterfly. It might just be another piece in the puzzle of figuring out where she really belonged.

SIX
The Garden

It was just past midnight. Constance stalked the narrow passage through the castle walls and past the west tower, heading for the gardens, her face buried in the upturned fur collar of her dress. She had stayed late at the feast, until there was no one left (or at least no one conscious enough) to observe her departure. Lord Irvine had slipped out earlier. Constance had borrowed a lantern from outside the doorway of the great hall; one cracked pane allowed a breath of air to tremble and tease the flame within.

She stopped several times to listen for pursuing footsteps. None. In the distance, somebody retched against a wall, the wet slap of their vomit echoing through the night. She followed a vaguely familiar route—a route she remembered, though much changed by time and darkness and the cloying fog. The world rocked subtly under her feet, her breathing slightly rough. Though she had watered her wine surreptitiously, she could not have abstained altogether; somebody would have noticed, wondered at her soberness. Everyone else was drunk almost horizontal, staggering to their beds with eyes half-closed.

One thing soon became clear: it was years since anyone had visited the pleasure gardens for pleasure. Constance drew to a halt at the gardens' edge, scanning the weird and twisted shapes looming from the flickering cloud for a form resembling Lord Irvine's. The storm cloud had had a curious effect on the gardens. The formal flower beds at her feet were a mass of rotten vegetation, crawling with monstrous centipedes and fat maggots glistening in the lamplight. The raised herb garden beyond, next to the kitchens, had crumbled, the mist choking into strange, viscous cobwebs catching moonlight between twigs of dead rosemary and thyme. Here and there, flashes of green-blue lightning cast flickering shadows across the lawn beyond. Fungi flourished, bulbous growths latching to the slender trunks of the naked, withered orchard beside the castle's wall. Naked branches cut the hazy moonlit sky into ragged segments.

This ghastly scene felt like a bad omen, a warning. Constance glanced over her shoulder, but quickly steeled her resolve. A memory returned to her with frightening clarity: the bare brick walls of the small reflection chamber, the deep pool in the floor, a voice emanating from nothing, perhaps from Constance herself, perhaps from someone hidden. How could she have known? She had been forced to stare at the pool for countless hours, her knees hurting beyond the point of pain, the water reflecting her own exhausted, masklike expression. *Pursue the things you fear*, the voice had said. *If you do not seek them first, they will seek you.*

She shook away the memory and ventured deeper into the complex of elaborately knotted beds and twisted footpaths, stepping carefully among the strange white roots that pried apart the paving stones. She jumped at the sound of movement, but it was only a rat, scurrying into the dead reeds beside the stagnant fountain. Her lamplight caught on the face of a statue, its cherubic delight made grotesque by streaks of black, like tears.

"Constance." Another light joined hers, its flickering glow illuminating Irvine's eyes, which glittered like green water on a sunny day. The lower half of his face was swaddled in scented scarves. The material was richer than it had been earlier in the day, a shimmer of gold cloth, the glint of silver thread in dark silk. The Swordmaster drew his blade from the hilt at his belt, the slim rapier gleaming in the shifting light, the jewel on the pommel glowing green. He set his lamp on the ground. His voice was muffled. "It's a long time since we've sparred, Constance." He threw her another blade from one of the two scabbards at his belt. Despite all the years since she'd practiced, she caught it in her right hand easily.

"Really?" she said, lifting an eyebrow.

"Really." He flashed her a smile and raised his sword.

"Wine, pointy blades, and poor visibility sound like a dangerous combination to me," she observed.

"Where's your sense of adventure?"

She smiled, rested her cane against the side of the fountain, and mirrored his stance, the unfamiliar posture exposing stiffness in her muscles, her left arm held awkwardly behind her back. Suddenly she felt as sober as if she'd plunged her head in cold water. The storm cloud seemed to thicken and wheel around them, a slow carousel turning to its own silent tune, grumbling softly. Constance and Irvine stood at its center, holding their weapons, gazes fixed.

She should have felt like her old self again. She should have felt the past six years falling away like autumn leaves. But this was different. Strange and serious.

He attacked first, a low, simple swipe that Constance knew was designed to test her. She parried, the blade feeling unnatural in her palm. And yet—some memory of the fight remained. Once, it had been her greatest pleasure.

"I don't believe a word you spoke in there," said the Swordmaster.

"That's your prerogative, I suppose," she said coolly. She swiped at his collarbone, but he stepped back gracefully.

"I so badly want to trust you. I stuck my neck out for you earlier, and the Justice has a sharp and ready ax."

"So trust me. Aren't you swordsmen supposed to follow your instincts?" She tried again, pirouetting in a feint, changing direction at the last minute. A fancy move for an ill-practiced swordswoman. Her skirts fanned out, sending the storm cloud into a frenzy, but Irvine neatly parried the blow. Her blade rang, her wrist jolting.

"Ouch," she said mildly. Her muscles already ached.

"Wherever you've been, you haven't been fighting," said Irvine.

"Ouch," she repeated.

"Enough of this game," he said, his expression suddenly serious. "Tell me the truth. I deserve to know." He leaped onto the ledge of the fountain. "Why did you leave?" He swiped at her head, and Constance lurched backward, rather ungracefully.

"Hey, careful!"

But his voice grew even harder. "Answer me. Why did you leave? And why did you return?"

"Look at you, taking the high ground," she said, stepping out of his reach. "I suppose things look so simple from all the way up there. It's complicated, Lord Irvine, and I can't tell you why. But I *can* tell you it isn't idle ambition. It's important. It's sad that I even have to tell you that—I thought you knew me better." What she had said was true, and she infused her voice with outrage. She could have lied to him, she supposed. But she didn't want to—besides, it wasn't a good idea. *If you build a tower of lies, someday it will fall and crush you*, the High Priestess had once told her. *Build your lies as false bricks into a tower of truth, so that no one can tell them apart.* "Why can't you just trust me?"

His face settled into something sterner. "I would never have questioned the Constance I knew six years ago. But that Constance disappeared, and I'm not exactly sure who has returned." He leaped from the ledge and spoke in a voice low with mingled anger and tenderness. "Tell me one thing . . . Did I mean anything to you at all?" Before she could reply, he attacked—one, two, three, four times, metal clashing each time she parried, driving her farther and farther back. Her muscles protested, burning painfully.

"Hey!" she managed as he attacked again, shocked at the ferocity of the strike. She stepped on the hem of her cloak and tumbled backward to the stony ground, her sword crashing down beside her.

Irvine lowered his blade. He still looked angry, but a smile tugged again at the corners of his mouth. "Sorry."

"*You've* been practicing," huffed Constance. "And I ought to get extra points for fencing in a party dress."

She took his proffered hand and stumbled to her feet. Irvine laughed. A flash of blue lightning lit up his smile—and suddenly she was laughing too. For a few moments, their easy friendship had returned.

"Tell me one more thing," said Irvine, through a smile. "Why won't you call me by my name?"

She snorted. "All right, Lord Alexander Irvine."

"You used to call me Xander." He was serious again. "We were the best of friends. More than friends . . ."

"You seem a bit grand for 'Xander' now. We're not children anymore." She handed him his spare sword and retrieved her cane from beside the fountain. She grinned as a memory returned to her, unbidden. "Do you remember how you used to dress? Your mother would have a fit every time you came home, covered in mud and leaves and scratches. She said you were too old to be getting into scrapes like that. And now?" She looked him up and down, leaning closer. "You're a proper lord. You're handsome and you dress in silks, and there's scented oil in your hair, isn't there?" She smiled as his cheeks reddened. "You have two hundred and fifty men under your command, you're responsible and brave and authoritative. Your mother would have been proud. Hardly the ragamuffin I knew back when."

He cleared his throat. "Two hundred and fifty men? Who's counting?" His tone was light. "Have you really missed me, Constance, or are you just after my sword power?"

She laughed, though it was only half a joke. "Winton told me."

An unreadable expression—discomfort, perhaps—passed over Xander's face.

"What's wrong?" Constance asked. "Did something happen between you and Winton?"

He shook his head. "My . . . my fighting style wasn't quite right for him. He's built for a longsword. Captain Trudan was the perfect mentor." He avoided Constance's eyes, and—for the moment—she chose to let it pass.

"Now, *Xander*, was this rendezvous just an opportunity to humiliate me in the practice ring, or did you have something to tell me?"

He glanced at her with mingled relief and sadness. He sheathed his swords and sat on the fountain's edge, sighed, and rubbed his temples. "Where do I begin?"

She carefully sat beside him, the damp stone cold against her thighs, even through layers of silk. "My father . . . how long has he been like this?"

He nodded. "As good a place to start as any. His condition began just over two years ago. The Pestilence had done its worst by then, more than half the population dead, a terrible toll each year in the summer months, regular as a harvest. The shallow crypts in the lower town were full to bursting. And traders refused to enter—instead, special convoys left produce on the outskirts of the forest, collecting gold in return." His voice was quiet, full of horror. "Things were bad. And the Pestilence showed no regard for wealth or status: my younger brother, my sister, my father . . . to name only a few. Everyone lost someone. It was a terrible, dark time." The lamplight flickered across his eyes, shining green. "But the Duke's strength in the face of great personal suffering helped us all see him as a true role model, a leader. He wasn't idle. He stockpiled food and supplies. He tried to stem the spread of the Pestilence. And he even sent envoys, messages to the City of Kings . . . but no one came. Perhaps the messengers were swallowed up in the storm cloud. Or perhaps no one cared. And then . . . something changed."

He paused, a distant look in his eyes above the swaddling of his scarves.

"What changed?" Constance urged quietly.

"It was gradual, but I see it now in hindsight, clear as day. Slowly but surely, the Duke developed an obsession: he wanted someone to blame for the tragedy inflicted on his home and his people. Rather than finding a solution to the storm cloud, he focused on rooting out and punishing those responsible. He began to complain of headaches too: it was then that the Duchess sent for Dr. Thorn, who began to attend to him regularly. But none of the doctor's medicines appeared to help—in fact, your father only grew worse. As the headaches worsened, so did his obsession. He spent hours locked away with the Justice, and soon both concluded that the culprit must be a mage, a coven of mages, an *infestation* of mages—and that they were still in the city, weaving the storm spell stronger and stronger by the day. Soon the Duke sent a message to the King: he was shutting the gates. No one was to enter or to leave. And so he did. He told the King it was to quarantine Duke's Forest and prevent the spread of the Pestilence, but his true purpose was, and always has been, to trap the supposed culprits inside the city and kill them."

These were hard words to hear. "Do you think ... the Justice poisoned his mind? Or did my father truly believe ... ?"

Xander rested his hand on her shoulder and met her eyes. "It has always been my belief that your father is truly unwell, and that the Justice has taken advantage of his misfortune. As your father deteriorated, he handed over more and more responsibility to the Justice, who was eager to accept the reins of power—and eventually petitioned the Wise Men for the Protectorship. The Duchess was always terrified of magic, and she never had a head for politics anyway. She respected the Justice, believed him—he was at pains to make a friend of her. Although she cared deeply for the Duke, she too wanted nothing more than to rid the city of mages."

Constance nodded grimly. She knew the truth of that.

"He's a fanatic, Constance. The rest of us watched, helpless. What can the Wise Men do, a mere advisory council, against the decisions of the Duke and the authority of the King?"

Constance lowered her eyes. Did he want her to apologize for not being there sooner? She wasn't going to, but she let him read into her expression.

"Don't blame yourself, Constance. You're back now, and I have a feeling things are going to change."

"Yes. Yes, things are going to change." She clenched her left hand tight around her cane.

Once Xander had gone, Constance wished for nothing so much as a cup of hot milk and a warm bed. But she had work to do—and only a few hours left before dawn.

Lifting her broken-paned lantern a second time, she hurried across the pleasure gardens, pulling her cloak tightly around her. The castle was quiet as the grave, her footsteps sounding strangely loud on the cobblestone path. She reached the porch of the great hall, lifted the lantern, and extinguished the flame. She slipped through the heavy wooden door.

Constance waited for a few moments, breathing quietly in the darkness as her eyes adjusted. Eventually, she eased the door shut, satisfied the hall was empty but for the detritus of the feast.

She fastened the bolt behind her and moved swiftly across the floor to check the two servants' entrances at either end of the room. They were locked already, but Constance whispered a charm, tapping her cane against the handles. A series of rapid purple flashes cast strange, fleeting shadows. If someone tried to open the service entrances, they'd find them mysteriously jammed.

She shifted the benches and brushed aside the piles of dirty floor reeds from the center of the room—the smell of spilled wine and dust wafted up to her. She stared down at the large trapdoors.

This is it.

She undid the latch and lifted. The hinges squeaked and the door was very heavy. She attempted to ease it to the flagstones, but her fingers slipped and there was a muffled *thump* as it dropped. She waited, but no answering footsteps spoiled the night, no cryptlings shuffled from their quarters in the shallow cellars nearby. A waft of cold, stale air hit her in the face as she peered into the darkness beneath.

Constance tapped her cane three times against the ground—a steady purple glow flickered to life from the pommel. The stone steps led straight down, down, down, wide enough for four men to walk abreast: large enough for the grandest of funerals. The darkness was so complete that she couldn't see where the staircase met the floor below.

She took the first few steps, suddenly afraid. Entering the world of the Ancestors outside of funeral rites was a crime punishable by death. According to legend, the Ancestors knew. Understood. And the Ancestors were vengeful.

Superstitious nonsense, she told herself firmly. She had left the Ancestors behind long ago, pledged her faith to a different power altogether. But it had been much easier to ignore them from the grand temples of the City of Kings than it was on the threshold of their world.

Her cane-light reached the first sarcophagi as a rat scuttled across the corner of her vision. When she reached the bottom of the staircase, other tombs emerged into view. This chamber contained the bodies of the dukes and their families across the centuries and was truly cavernous, stretching far beyond the foundations of the great hall itself. There must have been hundreds of bodies down here—and yet more in the network of catacombs burrowed through-out the mountain. Each grave was an individual stone platform, elaborately carved with the deeds and accomplishments of its inhabitant, most of whom lay out on top in varying states of decay. The dukes' graves alone were surrounded by intricately carved screens, hiding the bodies from sight. At the back of the chamber was another staircase, tucked into the wall, leading to the next level down.

There is my mother, thought Constance with a shiver of mingled horror and sadness, and even a little fear, as she spotted one of the nearest Ancestors. She recognized the blue dress, the golden rings woven through the perfectly preserved dark hair. She stepped closer. From the middle distance, her mother was familiar—sleeping, perhaps, on her bed of stone. And in spite of everything, Constance felt an irrational thrill of hope. But as she neared the body, details revealed themselves. The face was sunken and pale, the lips slightly parted, and the eyes—replaced with glittering dark sapphires—stared up at her coldly, as if in disapproval, reflecting the purple glow on the bulb of the cane. Nevertheless, Constance lowered herself closer to the face so similar to her own, close enough to touch, close enough to smell the decay, the herbal, oily tang of whatever they used to stave off the rot. They had packed her mouth with cotton, she realized, noticing the material protruding ever so slightly between the thinning lips. She clenched her fists, turning aside from the body.

Focus.

Constance shut her eyes and tried to sense whether any magic lay in the cavern around her. As usual in Duke's Forest, despite her best efforts, she felt nothing but a residual bass note, the thrum of an old and growing spell: the storm cloud. She slipped the mask from its secret pocket in her cloak and fastened it onto her face. Carefully, she turned the wheel to bring the spell-scape into focus. The shimmering storm spell surrounded her in phantom streaks of blue light, like frozen lightning, despite the fact that the cloud itself had not reached underground. She adjusted the wheel further, but beyond the slightest gray shimmer above the bodies of the Ancestors, there was nothing.

She wound a path through the sarcophagi to the first tunnel leading off the main chamber. This passage too was filled with corpses, set on ledges carved out of the stone wall. The inscriptions were much humbler. Servants who had lived and worked in the castle were interred here along with their families, doomed to serve their masters in death as in life. Constance sent her senses down the tunnel, searching from beneath the mask, but to her frustration there was nothing hidden in these graves.

The other three passages were equally empty, and she felt exhaustion settle on her, as cloying as the thick blanket of dust and cobwebs smothering the Ancestors. The network of tombs and passages extended for miles, deeper and deeper into the mountain, which was as hollow as honeycomb. *Don't lose faith*, she willed herself. She would search again tomorrow, this time in the upper town. As she removed the mask and turned to leave, two bright lights flashed at her from the gloom, and a hiss broke the silence. She spun to face it. Illuminated by her magelight was a huge ginger cat with a dead rat at its feet, glaring at her as if to say, "You are not meant to be here."

"Neither are you!" she hissed back, her heartbeat slowly calming. The cat grabbed its dinner and slunk off into the shadows, acknowledging her superiority. Constance stood up straight and smoothed down her skirts.

She walked upstairs and into the great hall, setting her glowing cane on the stone floor while she lifted the heavy doors back into place.

She hadn't really expected success on her first night of

searching. No. That would be far too easy. *It's possible that it isn't even down here anymore*, she thought glumly.

Suddenly she caught sight of movement in the gap under the door to the courtyard—a pair of feet. In shock, she dropped the trapdoor the last couple of inches, a loud boom reverberating through the silence. She winced, quickly extinguished her light, and stood very still in the darkness. Maybe she'd made a mistake—maybe she hadn't seen anything at all.

Quick footsteps retreated outside. "Jurah's tits," she cursed, and hurried to unbolt and open the door softly, peering out into the night. But whoever had been there, the storm cloud had swallowed them.

Her mouth was dry, her heartbeat shallow and rapid. Someone must have pressed their eye against the gaps in the old wooden door or looked through the defunct keyhole. Someone had seen her. And whoever it was, they'd seen her emerging from the forbidden crypts with her cane glowing. They knew she was a mage. They knew she was a heretic.

Once she'd unjammed the servants' doors, she picked up her cane and stepped out into the dying night, heading for her room. She tasted salt on her tongue and realized that she was biting her lip so hard it was bleeding.

SEVEN
The Temple

The carriage thumped as it hit the ground, the wheels instantly rattling over the cobblestones. The noise was unbearable—a brain-shaking roar, ridiculously loud after the smooth passage through the air. They hit a pothole at a gallop, and Lena pitched to the side, glad of the straps holding her steady as the horses slowed to a canter, a trot, a walk.

They drew to a halt. Emris stepped down and offered his hand to Lena. She allowed him to help her, his hand warm and dry. The driver, Fowler, was stumbling sleepily out of the interior, straightening his uniform.

The sun had vanished now, and a full moon was rising, low and ghostly. Lena allowed her vision to adjust to the semidarkness as Emris gathered together his things and instructed Fowler to drive the carriage to the stables. The narrow alleyway was empty and sparse but for a few leaves and scattered papers rustling in the autumn breeze. On the right, she spied the plain rear walls of tall town houses. They reminded her of the quiet backstreets of the upper town in Duke's Forest, dimly remembered from childhood, when she'd accompanied Vigo to the houses of rich dead people who had to be removed from their mansions and prepared for the Descent. Here, though, the stone was straight-hewn, not crooked. On the other side of the alley, she saw a huge building with a gently curving wall—part of an enormous dome, perhaps. Moonlight—low, intense, and blue-tinged—streamed through the narrow gap of sky far above. Lena craned her neck. The building on the left was at least as tall as the castle towers. She tilted her head. The walls seemed oddly insubstantial, shiny.

She gasped as she realized the thousands of tiny bricks were actually windowpanes reflecting the masonry on the opposite side of the street. The windows—tier after tier of diamond-shaped glass—began at ground level and stretched so high she couldn't see where they ended. "How does it hold itself up?" she breathed.

"By the will of the gods," Emris said, appearing at her side as the coach rattled off down the lane. "Or so they claim."

"Is this your temple?"

"Gods, no." He barked a laugh. "That's the Holy Council, much grander. Now follow me. It's time you got cleaned up and had something to eat. You've had a long day."

To Lena's disappointment, he led her away from the amazing glass dome and down a slender path between two town houses. At the end, set in a grubby wall, was an unremarkable wooden door. As Emris opened it with a small brass key, Lena gazed longingly back at the dome. She'd never seen anything like it before. How would it feel to be inside?

"Don't worry," Emris said, smiling at her. "You'll see the Holy Council in time. For now, you'll have to make do with this."

Inside, the cool hallway smelled faintly damp. A lantern hung from the ceiling, casting flickering yellow light over the narrow space—the mop leaning in a corner, the metal bucket on the bottom step. Emris shut the door softly. A rickety wooden staircase rose to the upper floors.

If the word "temple" had conjured anything for Lena, it certainly wasn't this.

Emris climbed the stairs, beckoning Lena with a glance over his shoulder. His footsteps barely sounded in the empty landing at the top. But she had clumsier feet, the wood creaking and popping under her hobnail boots, hand-me-downs from some older cryptling who'd outgrown them. Somebody stirred elsewhere in the house—a rattling cough, a groaning bed. Emris opened a door and ushered Lena inside. He shut it behind her with a *click* and drew across a thick velvet curtain.

A long wooden table dominated the room, surrounded by high-backed chairs. Its surface was hidden beneath scattered papers—maps, in fact, each of them impossibly large and overlapping, pinned flat with paperweights.

"Welcome to the temple of Faul," said Emris. "The huntsman's temple." He poked the fire, replenishing the embers with a fresh log. Sparks drifted up the chimney.

"We came in by the back door. There's a big impressive hall downstairs, by the front entrance, full of incense and statues and suchlike. But we've all got to live somewhere, so they tacked a whole terrace on the back. There are bedrooms, a kitchen, training rooms, offices, a bathhouse, and a huge dining hall—and rooms like this, for temple meetings or study. This one's the map room."

On the mantelpiece Lena noticed a silvery wooden carving of a hunter, his bow drawn tight, aiming with a narrowed eye.

"What's that?" she asked, approaching it. "Is he your . . . your god?" She gulped; the word felt strange and dangerous on her tongue. As if, in speaking it, the statue might suddenly spring to life.

Emris nodded as he crouched down in front of a cupboard, rooting around inside.

"Why hunters?" She glanced at him. "What is it you do, exactly?"

"We're a sort of peacekeeping force." He turned and met her eyes. "We catch magical criminals, or Rogues, or Radicals—anyone who might present a magical threat to themselves or others." He took out a couple of plates, a wheel of cheese, and a loaf of bread, and set them on the table as Lena sank into a velvet-cushioned chair. "Like Constance, for instance." He appeared to struggle to say her name, as if it were too bitter to taste.

"She's a Rogue too?" Lena asked, frowning. "She didn't seem particularly—"

"No." He cut her off. "She's a criminal, Lena. She broke the law—in fact, she broke the most important magical law of all." His jaw tightened; he looked angry. He returned to the cupboard and pulled out a lidded jug and two metal goblets.

"What did she do?"

Emris shook his head as he set the things on the table. "I can't tell you any more right now." He turned to one side as he poured them each a measure of the deep-red liquid.

"You promised me answers," she pointed out.

"I know, and you will have them. But not this one . . . not yet." He sounded upset, but firm. She didn't feel able to argue, although curiosity burned at her mind. What was his link to Constance, exactly? And what had she done that was so terrible?

"Who is Mythris?" Lena asked instead. "You said no one knows where that temple is."

Emris pulled himself together. "Mythris is one of the gods—a deity of indeterminate gender. It sometimes appears as a man, sometimes a woman—sometimes even as a child. Sometimes it is merely a cloaked figure, neither one thing nor another. It is the god of disguises. Of mysteries. A force of nature as much as it is a deity. The location of its temple is unknown—its disciples are equally elusive." He paused. "In fact, they have something of a reputation as spies and assassins for hire . . ." He nodded, as if deciding to tell her. "The temple of Mythris was Constance's temple."

"Oh," Lena said in realization, perfectly able to imagine the haughty cane-wielding lady as an assassin. Perhaps she had assassinated someone important—had that been Constance's crime? Emris had cut Lena some bread and a slice of cheese, which he offered her on a battered tin plate. "Can you tell me more about the gods, please?" she asked, accepting the food.

"There are nine in total," he said, obviously relieved to return to the earlier subject, "but some are more important than others. Each temple serves a different government function, you see. Faul's is a relatively small operation, as is Nomi's, the temple of adventurers and explorers. Mythris—well, who knows? Then there's Jurah, the goddess of justice—and Jok, the god of combat." He met her eyes, noticing her confusion. "Here. I should show you properly." He stood up, took a large scroll from the bookcase, and laid it over the top of the maps on the table, securing it with three heavy glass globes and the wheel of cheese.

Lena stood and leaned over. A series of colorful inter-locking circles centered on the words "Holy Council." Each circle was labeled, branching outward into intricate streams of text. The simple lettering and bright colors implied an illustration for young children. Lena felt suddenly very warm and very ignorant. She might as well be a child here, after all.

But Emris was already explaining the diagram, apparently blind to her discomfort. "As every mage starts their training, they are assessed, interviewed, and assigned a temple best suited to their powers and temperament. Later in their training, they can of course switch temples—in fact, interdisciplinary study is positively encouraged—and most end up experiencing apprenticeships in two or perhaps three temples throughout their novice years before taking vows and committing themselves for life to their best match.

"Here we've got all the temples laid out with their functions, gods, symbols, and magics simply explained. There's Turah"—he pointed to the ocher circle—"whose disciples handle food and agriculture. Their magic aids fertility and, at its most advanced, concerns the creation of life. And Regis"—he pointed to the circle outlined in bright white against the yellowing paper—"handles the political sphere, using the magics of foresight and persuasion." He ran his fingers over a couple of the other circles, marked "medicine" and "commerce." "The disciples of some of these temples are thousands strong—their worshippers beyond count. Others, like I said, are smaller." His finger settled on the gray circle marked "Faul." "But I'm overwhelming you. Here, keep this for your own reference." He rolled up the scroll and laid it on the table in front of her. She stared down at the worn paper. *Nine gods! The Ancestors are so simple by comparison.* But when she thought of everything she had learned as a cryptling—the rituals, the prayers, the precise and ceremonial preparation of the body for interment—she knew it wasn't true.

"Sorry. This must be difficult for you," Emris said a little sadly. "I'm afraid it'll get a lot harder before it gets easier—and soon. We'll require you to pledge your faith to the gods. To accept their help. We can't afford to leave you without a proper Binding, or training, or you could—"

She nodded. "I know. I could lose control. Become a . . . a Radical." Panic washed through her, and she turned away from the table, gazing into the fire. The flickering flames calmed her a little as she took a deep breath. "If I pledge myself to the gods, I abandon the Ancestors forever," she explained quietly. "Is there really no other way?" Lord Chatham and his claims echoed in her mind.

Emris appeared to read her thoughts. "Lena, Lord Chatham clearly wants you to seek him out. A Rogue is a rarity here, and I'm sure he would love for you to place your trust in him. But please, do not accept his invitation. There is no other way but what I am offering, not really. And the King's Men—Chatham most of all—are extremely dangerous."

Lena blinked. He hadn't seemed particularly dangerous. Vain, yes. Haughty, yes. But dangerous? "Why?"

"The King's Men are a group of thirteen independently licensed magicians favored by the King, who's young, proud, and reckless. They believe magic is simply a tool, a natural force to be used however they please—not a gift from the gods to be treated with utmost care and respect." He shook his head. "They are all blatant atheists, and they think they're above the law—and for the most part, it seems, the King lets them do as they please. And of course Chatham does: without gods, there is no one above the King. He is blinded by their flattery." He swigged on his wine—his eyes distant, as if he'd forgotten about Lena altogether. "To me, it stinks of Chaos."

"Oh," said Lena quietly, her mind racing and returning again to her butterfly. "What about his mechanical things?"

"Lord Chatham started creating his . . . his *inventions* perhaps twenty years ago. Illegally." Emris's voice was dripping with loathing. "He set up a business—a shop, really—offering magical services and curiosities to members of the public. The Holy Council was determined to shut it down. But Chatham, of course, had aristocratic connections. His services gained popularity among the nobility, and eventually the royalty. The King himself, who was but a child at the time, was infatuated with his creations. When he came of age, he awarded Chatham a royal license . . . and that's how it all began." Emris shook his head. "Now the King has thirteen magicians, taught and 'licensed' by Chatham, creating magical devices at his request."

Lena blinked. "So . . . How do these devices work? Why are they so bad?" She resisted the urge to reach for her butterfly.

"Ordinary people want magical things," Emris said. "Of course they do: people want whatever they can't have, particularly beautiful and powerful things. But there's a reason why the temples control magic so carefully, Lena. These magical devices aren't safe—in fact, they're a real threat. Essentially, the magician infuses each machine with a fragment of Chaos in order to bring it to life."

"Really?" The butterfly hadn't *looked* particularly dangerous or chaotic as it fluttered, lost, among the graves.

"I know—it's unbelievable," he said, mistaking her meaning. He looked genuinely outraged, warming further to his subject. "It's the only way the creature can possibly act with some measure of independence—but for some reason, no one questions it. And he sells these things to ordinary people with no means of defending themselves if anything goes wrong. There have been stories . . . but somehow they never reach the newspapers." His expression was truly thunderous. "And that's only the beginning of it: ever since it started, his 'Emporium' has always been a front, really, for the dangerous private commissions he accepts from—well, not just the King, but anyone with the money to pay."

Lena's mouth felt dry. "What kind of commissions?"

"We've all heard rumors about magical weapons— devices to enhance magic, or perhaps even steal it. But of course no one dared investigate."

If Chatham had truly created the butterfly, as she suspected, then had someone commissioned him to do so? Or was it just a toy? At Lena's thoughtful, confused silence, Emris suddenly smiled.

"I'm sorry. I've frightened you. Rant over, I promise. Anyway, what I mean to say is that you really shouldn't seek Chatham out. You're better off here, learning how to control your powers in the proper way—and we'll begin tomorrow." He gave her a measuring look. "For now, it's time you had some rest. Come on, follow me."

He led her to a door half-hidden in an alcove beside the fireplace, unlocked it, and pressed the large brass key into her palm: inside was a small and sparsely furnished bed-chamber with a low pallet, a chest of drawers, and a bathtub in the corner.

"This is one of our guest rooms, but it's yours until we get you settled. I'll send a novice with hot water for the tub. You'll find fresh clothes in the drawers. I'll check up on you in the morning." He walked back to the table, downed the rest of his wine. "I'll need to make my report to the First Huntsman and set up your initial assessment and training as soon as possible. I've got a feeling he'd like to assess you personally."

"That's . . . reassuring," Lena said, managing a weak smile. "And thank you."

"What for?" He looked surprised.

She shrugged, embarrassed. "You know . . . I was dying from snake poison. And then I didn't die. That's because of you."

He nodded, shifted on his feet but held her gaze. "Please don't leave this room unless I fetch you, Lena. I still have so much to explain, but trust me, few of my fellow hunters will take kindly to a stranger—let alone a Rogue."

"All right, I understand," said Lena, although she did not.

The door shut, and she was alone once more.

EIGHT
The Burden of Rule

After a couple of hours' restless sleep, Constance woke early in her mother's bed, listening to the hounds howling and barking below. The south tower was above the kennels, and as a child she'd often woken to the sound of dogs preparing for the hunt. But they weren't just hunting hounds anymore: they were executioners, and somehow the tenor of their howls had changed to the cold keening of a sharpening blade.

As she pushed out of bed, her thoughts returned to the great hall, to the footsteps and the shadow under the door. Who had seen her nighttime explorations? And when would she feel the consequences of their knowledge? Whoever it was, they hadn't raised the alarm instantly, as she might have expected from a terrified Forester. Perhaps they were intimidated by her status—or frightened. Or ... or perhaps they simply *weren't* alarmed. What if the person who had spelled the gates shut was the very person who had followed her?

Another thing to worry about, she thought, *as if I didn't have enough already.*

It was dark still, but she could feel the morning creeping behind the storm cloud like a cloaked assassin. She washed in her mother's basin and donned a plain wool gown from Livia's chest. How long since she'd had anything of her own? Even those items she'd arrived in belonged to the temple, in truth. And the mask—that had been stolen too. In the first gray light of dawn, she tied her hair in a high bun and looked inside the circular locket on the chain around her neck. The mirror inside was clear. Dark circles shadowed her eyes as she frowned at her reflection in the resolutely unmisted glass. Did Emris care about her at all? She felt like his was the one other life on which she had managed to leave her mark. And yet . . . sometimes it seemed that nothing she did had consequences, and that now that she had disappeared from that world it was as if she had never been there at all. As if she were a ghost.

The day was young and, beneath the yaps and yowls of the hounds, the castle was quiet as the grave, everyone nursing sore heads from the festivities, no doubt. Her cane tucked carefully under her arm, Constance crossed the courtyard to the north tower and tried the door: unlocked. Stepping softly up the stairs, she heard heavy snores emanating from the bedchamber on the first landing. She set her eye to the keyhole. Dr. Jonas Thorn had collapsed on his neatly made bed. He had removed his coat and shirt, leaving his back bare. Constance was surprised to notice deep scars crisscrossing the smooth, pale skin. Long ago, she realized, he had been whipped.

She shook her head and climbed the rest of the steps, passing doors to the other empty chambers she remembered from her childhood: the intimate dining room, the music chamber, and the comfortable living quarters once used for the Duke's private entertainment. She paused to catch her breath on the final landing before opening the door to the solar. It was time to find out the truth about her father.

The room perched atop the tallest tower in the castle, a circular, domed chamber with a glass roof constructed by a long-dead Ancestor for observing the stars. The thin, large panes rattled slightly in the breeze and Constance felt a breath of air tickle a loose hair at her neck. And suddenly she noticed she had climbed so high that the top of the tower had erupted from the storm cloud. Tendrils of gray snatched and swirled around the lower edges of the dome, but the rest was filled with blissful clear sky. She hadn't realized how much she'd missed it already. For a moment, she lost herself in the pool of blue, interrupted only by the sun's gentle yellow on the clouded horizon.

The circular room was starkly empty. The ghosts of removed furniture were imprinted on the walls in paler shades of white: the only remaining items were an enormous chest fastened with a sturdy padlock, a narrow, neatly made bed that ill fitted its surroundings, and a single, throne-like chair in the center of the room. And there, at last, she noticed her father, already examining her with wary eyes. Gone was the expression of pure, adoring admiration from the previous evening. Instead, he appeared confused, agitated. He was dressed in the same clothes he'd worn to the feast. *Has he even slept?*

"Constance," said the Duke, peering at her. "Daughter." And then he repeated vaguely, as if trying to jog his memory, "Constance . . . Daughter . . ."

She approached him with careful footsteps. At fifty paces across and laid with polished tiles, mirroring the umbrella-like pattern of the thin glass panes overhead, the room felt cavernous. She stopped before she reached the chair, her gaze catching on her father's hands. They were clasped, clawlike, over burnished wooden armrests. "Good morning, Father," she said calmly. For the first time since she'd arrived, she observed him dispassionately. She and the Duke had never been close. He'd had duties, and she'd had preoccupations, but she thought they had loved each other nonetheless—as family does. She tried not to flinch at the ravages of age and insanity on his features—features so firmly echoed in her own face. The angles of his cheekbones were sharper; his chin receded. The dark eyes looked watery and unfocused; the skin was drawn tighter over bulbous knuckles. Her father's hair was entirely white now and coarse as wool—no trace of the ash blond, like hers, he had once prized.

There was nowhere for her to sit, so she knelt beside the chair and rested her right hand over his, shuddering at the feel of his papery skin. It was time for the truth. "Father, I need to speak with you. I need to understand what's happening here."

The Duke stared into the middle distance. He showed no sign of having heard her words.

"Father, you alone in Duke's Forest know the truth about me, about my magic." *But that's not true, not after last night.* She shook the thought away. "It was you who told me to run. Do you remember? You wanted to save me. You knew what they would do to me if I stayed."

The Duke's eyes appeared to focus on her for a fraction of a second.

"But I've come back, Father. I've come to . . . to save Duke's Forest. I'm strong now, see. I've learned so much. But there's someone working against me."

His gaze flickered toward hers again, a glimmer of understanding.

"There is a mage in Duke's Forest. Other than me, I mean. A mage who sealed the gates. Someone who's been here all along, right under the Justice's nose."

His mouth opened as if he were trying to speak, but no words emerged.

"But, Father, I don't know who it is. Can you tell me? Who is the other mage?"

"The storm spell must be broken," he murmured at last.

"That's right, Father," she urged, her voice dry with longing. "Just . . . please . . . tell me what you know."

But even as he opened his mouth to speak, he was silent. A strange gargling sound rumbled in his throat, as if his words struggled to escape.

This wasn't going to work, not without a little help. She

lifted her cane, rested the cool pommel against his hand, and whispered under her breath. A purple sparkle emanated from the cane, spreading gradually up the Duke's arm and over his face, darts of pure light shimmering in the sunbeams like motes of shining dust. Constance closed her eyes, urging the spell to clear the darkness from her father's mind. But something was stopping her magic.

"Look at me," she whispered. And the Duke obeyed, the muscles of his face relaxing as he succumbed to her will, his eyes meeting hers.

Gently, ever so gently, she rested her hand on his weathered cheek and slipped her magic into the space behind his eyes: the sensation was like tipping forward into warm water, her fingers and face tingling. The familiar heat kindled in the hollow below her breasts as her magic awakened. But again, there was resistance in the Duke's mind. And as she pushed a little harder, the resistance grew stronger. Almost as if another spell had been wrought against meddling—but that wasn't possible, was it? Determined, she tried harder, flinging a surge of magic against the wall in her father's mind.

A red flash. Her cane flew from her hands—and suddenly the Duke lifted his fist and struck her hard around the face. She fell on the floor, felt her skin tear against the jagged edge of a cracked tile. Hot blood trickled down her cheek. Hand shaking, she raised her fingers to the open wound.

She stared up at her father, feeling a stab of anger. He had struck her only once before—that one time, when he'd been filled with rage and grief, dragging her by the arm from her mother's body . . . But her anger fell away as she saw his face crumple. He gazed at his own hand, caught between amazement and horror.

"Get away from me," he said in a low, steady voice. It was the sanest thing she'd heard him say since her arrival.

"Father," she insisted, "who is doing this to you?" But she couldn't help the edge of desperation creeping into her voice. She knew it was hopeless.

Just then, the door opened behind her. Constance stood, slowly smoothing out her skirts and dabbing the wound with her sleeve.

"Lady Constance," said the physician. "I did not know you had planned to visit the Duke."

"Do I need to make an appointment to visit my own father?" she replied sharply.

"It might have been advisable," said Thorn, nodding at Constance's wounded face. "If I had not woken to administer the Duke's morning dosage, he might've done worse. His condition is highly volatile."

She stepped close, drawing herself up tall. "It is none of your business what passes between my father and me," she said coldly. "And I have reason to believe his ailment is not entirely natural."

"Whatever can you mean?" His voice was flat, unimpressed. But she looked at him closely, spied a flicker of understanding. And that's when it clicked into place.

"I think you know, *physician*," Constance hissed. She stepped aside, scooped up her fallen cane, and left the room, slowly descending the spiral staircase. In her mind she replayed the red flash. And then she remembered the similar red magic binding the rusted lock and chains of the gates. She knew in her heart both spells had been cast by the same mage.

And that mage was in Duke's Forest, close to the Duke, spinning spells under the magic-hating Justice's nose. She tried not to jump to conclusions, but it was difficult to avoid the obvious suspect. Lord Veredith had said he was a lowborn apothecary who had worked his way into the highest echelons of the castle; surely in this city of strict hierarchy that was cause for suspicion in itself. Yes, she felt sure: the mage in Duke's Forest could only be the physician, Jonas Thorn. And by the feel of his magic, he was very powerful indeed.

Anger surged through her. He was driving her father mad. Keeping him in a prison of his own mind. But why? Was he playing his own game? Or was he working for someone else?

At the bottom of the staircase, she opened the door into the courtyard, dabbed her throbbing cheek with her sleeve again, and hesitated on the threshold. She watched the storm cloud gleam and wheel close to the cobblestone ground. The houndmaster crossed the courtyard with a bucket full of dead rats, one hand nursing his head. A few seconds later, Constance heard the dogs fall on the meat, their howls fading to snarls as they fought for a bite.

She shut her eyes for a moment, allowing the world to disappear. When she focused like this, she could hear an echo of the storm spell, a thrum like the dying voice of a struck bell. It was strong. It might be mere days from starting its contractions. And when that happened . . . well, she might already be too late. She would have to work fast to gain the upper hand. She clenched her fists. Gods. She'd been training for this ever since she left—but was she ready? Did she really know what she was doing?

I have no choice.

The Witenagemot would begin in a few short hours. She touched her cheek gingerly, gazed down at her blood-spattered dress. *A change of clothes, I think.*

In her room, Constance checked the round mirror on her pendant again, expecting nothing. Instead, she found the glass misted. Her heart lurched. *So this is it.* She sat on the edge of the bed, tucked her hair behind her ears, then breathed on the glass herself, knowing she had misted the twinned mirror in the temple.

A shadow appeared behind the mist, and suddenly the glass cleared. Emris's scarred face greeted her. His dark hair was scattered with silver, his eyes weary. He looked a decade older.

At last, he said, by way of greeting. Although his lips moved, his voice was heard in Constance's mind—echoic, traveling over impossible distances. *What the hell happened to your face?*

She touched the cut, which had dried out but was tender under her fingers. She'd forgotten about it, somehow. She shrugged. "A fist happened."

Why did you run from me? You must know, deep down, that you have to face the consequences of your actions.

She lowered her gaze. "No," she said quietly.

Constance, you can't do this.

She made her voice steady and true. "I am doing it, Emris. I tried to tell you—"

But his mind-voice was stern, cutting her off. *Things have progressed since you left. They've discovered the forbidden texts in your cell. I thought, before, that it was a spur-of-the-moment thing—a reckless impulse. I wasn't even sure what I was seeing, at first . . . But now I know.* His eyes burned. *You were planning to try it for a long time, weren't you, Constance? You must feel so clever. You certainly had me fooled. I thought you were different— but you're just like Chatham, after all.* There was real bitterness and hurt in his words. *Chatham is on my back about the mask too, as if that were more important than the rest of it.*

"You don't understand," she said, finally finding her voice again. She rubbed the top of her nose. "There's more to this than you realize. You know nothing about me. Nothing."

You've made that abundantly clear, Constance. Even so, it's simple: either return and face the Council's judgment, or remain in Duke's Forest and die from starvation, or the Pestilence, or whatever other evils are lurking in that cursed place. Or do you think you can hide from death as well as justice?

She felt something in her snap at his superior tone. "It is not simple. It is never *simple*," she spat out. "Don't be so naive, Emris."

He glanced over his shoulder—as if he'd heard some noise. But as he returned to her, his voice was firm. *I shouldn't even be speaking to you. I wanted to tell you that if you hand yourself in at the nearest temple in the next twenty-four hours, I will plead for mercy on your behalf. For the sake of everything we once had.*

"No," she whispered, but the bite had left her voice. It was over; it really was. She had known it would be, but it didn't hurt any less. She remembered briefly the times they'd spent together, how close they'd come to something like love.

He leaned nearer to the mirror. *Think about it. If I ever meant anything to you, think about it. You're playing with dangerous, chaotic magic. Is that how you found a way through the forest when no one else could?*

She shook her head. It wasn't worth arguing: whatever she said, he'd already made up his mind.

Then this is goodbye.

And the glass cleared, and she was looking at her own pale, pinched face, made ugly by bitterness.

A hot rage flooded her veins, and she saw her blue eyes flash purple. She snapped the pendant shut and flung it hard against the wall. She heard the glass cracking inside its case. The pendant skittered under the bed.

She curled up on the mattress, the sobs rising in her

chest—but stifled before they reached her throat. She lay there silently, every muscle wound tight, staring at her clenched fists inside their gloves. Her other life was truly gone. Everything she'd worked for. The one person in that horrible world she'd cared about. Everything that meant anything to her—she'd given it all up.

For this.

And what did that mean?

I cannot fail.

The Wise Men gathered promptly, despite their aching heads and tired eyes. Lord Veredith stood up and tried to pull out Constance's chair as she entered the room, with limited success. Lord Redding attempted an enthusiastic greeting, which descended into a hacking cough. Lord Farley looked like he'd seen the bottom of a bottle twelve times over, wincing at her cheery "Good afternoon."

She'd dressed in a steely gray gown edged in black and probably designed for a funeral—it suited her mood since her conversation with Emris. She couldn't help thinking of the last woman who had worn these clothes. *How many funerals did Livia attend before her own?* Constance brushed aside the thought as a servant poured her a cup of nettle tea. Her hair was pinned tightly to her head, her eyes bright. She'd magicked the wound on her cheek to a mere sliver of pink, barely noticeable against her skin.

She smiled around the table as more of the Wise Men took their seats. Xander arrived next with a large cohort of his sky-blue-liveried guards, who joined the city guard around the perimeter of the great hall. Was he expecting trouble? His eyes flicked to her face, a small smile on his lips. She nodded a formal greeting.

In the last few minutes, Winton arrived too. He'd smartened up: he was cleanly shaven and dressed in scarlet, his dark curly hair combed and shining. He slid out the remaining seat at Constance's right-hand side and sat carefully, shooting her a rueful smile; despite their obvious similarity in looks, this was an expression the Duchess could never have mastered. Constance smiled back, guiltily relieved that she didn't have his mother to contend with, as she'd expected.

Constance glanced at the clock on the wall: two minutes to midday. Only one member of the Witenagemot was missing.

At the last moment, a black-liveried servant slipped through the doors and approached the long table on the dais.

"My lady, the Lord Justice is indisposed but sends his regards."

"A shame," she said coolly. "What is his ailment? Shall we call for the physician?"

"Dr. Thorn is already with my lord."

Of course he is. "Very well. Send him my best wishes for a swift recovery."

The servant bowed, left the hall with quick footsteps, and shut the door behind him.

For a few moments, silence. Constance surveyed the men

at her table. Eleven in total, plus her brother, on whose loyalty she knew she could rely. Several were on the wrong side of middle age—some only tenuously on the right side of the grave. Lord Veredith she had in her pocket already, and Redding would not oppose her. Leobel was a kindly man with a bald pate and a fat gut—she remembered him from before she'd left. She'd win him easily too. Lord Farley was young enough, but so bitter and broken that she knew she'd find no resistance there. Xander was a strong ally: he'd help sway any uncertainties in her favor.

She'd find little opposition from the Wise Men, as long as the Justice left her to her own devices. He'd chosen to sulk and plot: so be it. If he wouldn't fight the fight, the prize was hers for the taking. If she could weave the right words, all the men here would be caught in her net.

"Thank you for gathering here today, my friends," she said, standing up. "As you know, I'd like to petition you for the Protectorship. The King's Justice has taken the mantle of power in the absence of an heir old enough to represent the Rathbone family. I hear he has inflicted a great deal of hardship on our city." A murmur rose along the table, and Constance took a careful sip of her tea.

"But whatever we make of the Justice's policies, he is no Rathbone. It's time to return Duke's Forest to its rightful dynasty." She met the eyes of every man in the room. "As the Justice is absent, perhaps we can speak freely for once." She had no doubt he was listening, the ears of the city guard still trained to his purpose for the time being—but perhaps that was no bad thing. "The mage hunts are crippling Duke's Forest. The locked gates and the storm cloud have sealed us from the outside world. But I found my way, and that means others can too." She paused for effect. "My lords," she said, "it is time for us to dare to hope once again—to open the gates and open our minds. I have spent time in the City of Kings—and in doing so, I have learned so many things I hope to bring to this city, to heal it and begin anew. You may not realize it, but everything I've done, I've done for you. Everything I've sacrificed, I've sacrificed for you. And I have ever been your advocate, your friend, your protector." Constance sounded as if she had real emotion choking her voice. She blinked as if she were holding back tears. "For this is, and always will be, my home."

The lies spilled from her, easy as water. As the Wise Men rose to their feet, voting unanimously to pass the motion, she smiled and smiled until her cheeks ached.

Constance stood on the battlements and peered into the storm cloud, which was thickening and thinning strangely in a nonexistent breeze. The dense clouds drifted in out of nowhere, plunging her into semidarkness before dispersing without a trace. Flashes flickered at the edges of her vision, the odd rumble like the snore of a sleeping dragon. All that power . . . so close—and yet so far. She flexed her fingers, her right hand cold even beneath her fitted leather glove, her left hand as unfeeling as ever. The brass mask felt unusually warm over her face, its cogs whirring. As well as providing a means of "seeing" magic, the mask was designed to filter out the effects of spells, allowing her eyes to remain unaffected by the storm cloud's noxious properties. A sudden gust of wind whipped through her skirts tauntingly. *The storm cloud is playing games.* She steadied herself on the crenellations guiding her along the walkway. *And this was supposed to clear my head?*

She'd spent most of the night searching the crypts under the upper town. She'd found nothing. And despite her triumph at the Witenagemot, dark dreams had haunted her few sleeping hours. Dreams of her mother's corpse, of Emris's scars twisting in disappointment, of wrathful gods, of forsaken Ancestors, of dark shadows following her in the night. *Is there anyone I haven't angered?*

She walked up to the edge, her footsteps clicking through the gloom in rhythm with the tap of her gold-tipped cane. Her shadow threw itself against a thick patch of cloud, and she started backward before sighing at her credulity. Leaning against the cold, damp stone, she looked down. Vaguely, she could see the rooftops of the upper town, overgrown with gray moss. Moss and fungus appeared to thrive in the storm cloud.

Constance wondered what Emris thought of her now. She had lied to him, yes. But that didn't mean she hadn't loved him, in her way. She remembered the night they had met, the stars over the palace like a silent chorus in silver and white. She pushed the memory aside. After all, she had more pressing concerns. Who had seen her that night after the feast? Whoever it was, they were biding their time, waiting for the right moment to strike.

The Justice, perhaps? She felt an unwelcome shiver of fear.

Footsteps approached, and Constance spun around. Gradually, details gathered upon the form, as if an invisible painter were bringing it slowly into existence—but she knew him from the first brushstrokes. A hulking wolf-skin cloak, the hilt of a longsword peeking from his back. He was dressed in his training clothes, and a faint hint of sweat lingered on his skin. He was wearing shield-eyes in soft black leather and silver, and a thick scarf was pulled over the bottom half of his face.

"Winton," she said, injecting some warmth into her voice. "Good morning. You've been training?"

"I try to train every morning," he said, smiling faintly.

She glanced again at the longsword. "I'm curious. Why do you train with the guardsmen? Why not with Lord Irvine?"

"Oh . . . I'm no good at that kind of swordplay," Winton said, but the lightness in his voice sounded forced.

"It would be more befitting the son of a Duke," she suggested gently. "The longsword is a common soldier's weapon."

He ignored the observation, lowering his eyes. After a few moments, he began again. "May I speak with you?" His voice was tired, tight with worry.

"You *are* speaking with me. Are you all right?"

"Fine," said Winton firmly, rubbing his temples. "I'm

sorry about my strange behavior at the feast. I just . . ." He shook his head.

"Brother, it is not yet a month since your mother's death. You are grieving, and some strangeness is to be expected," she said. She reached out with her right hand, squeezed his shoulder. And suddenly he enveloped her in a hug, warm and strong. Constance pressed her left arm close into her body, forcing the rest of her to remain relaxed.

"We haven't really had a chance to talk yet," Winton said, his voice muffled by her fur collar. "I've missed you so much." He pulled away, his eyes catching on the badge of office pinned to her cloak.

"I received it this morning." She stroked the golden shield-and-sword brooch positioned proudly on her chest— the sigil of the Protectorship. "Some poor bastard was given the task of retrieving it from the Justice."

"And he didn't put up a fight?" Winton frowned.

Constance straightened her mask, her skin slightly clammy beneath the warm metal. "No. What can he do? The city guard must obey the choice of the Wise Men, and I am their Lady Protector now, with the Swordmaster on my side. Even with his personal retinue, the Justice is outnumbered. Perhaps he's chosen not to fight me for fear of losing." *Or perhaps he has some other trick up his sleeve.* She fidgeted, feeling restless. "Come—walk with me. I came up here for some exercise."

Winton stepped in line beside his sister. The battlements spanned the full circumference of the castle. Built in a war-torn age, and designed for defense rather than beauty, they provided a walkway over fifteen feet wide, bordered by crenellations on both sides and punctuated by four guard posts, small jutting rooms at the outer corners of the three square towers containing supplies and ammunition. Constance and Winton walked between the south and west guard posts and around the great hall, wisps of cloud snatching at their heels like a pack of hungry wolf cubs. A couple of city guards bowed as they passed, dressed in the short green cloaks of their uniform. Constance's men now.

Once they were out of earshot, Winton spoke again. "Doesn't it all seem a little too ... easy? The Justice confronted you upon your arrival but at the first sign of resistance he just disappeared. That's not like him." He cleared his throat. "While you were gone, he was very ... aggressive in his pursuit of power. He allowed no argument from the Wise Men—all but forced them to confirm him as Protector. It's hard to argue with someone who has three hundred swords at their command."

Constance shot him a glance. She couldn't appear to be naive, and yet she knew she had to seem more confident than she felt. "I'm under no illusions. The Justice is likely planning his next move like some fat spider in his web. But that doesn't mean I'm not ahead of the game ... for now." She smiled. "If there's one thing the City of Kings has taught me, it's to take what you can get—and hope by the time the tables turn you're far enough ahead that you can save yourself." *The truth, for once.* "I'd try him for his crimes if I could—but you know how it is," she continued, as if part of her was desperate to bury her slip of truth under the details. "Only the King can convict one of his own Justices. For the time being, all we can do is confine him to his apartments. Lord Irvine has stationed a double guard around his wing. I've ordered as many of the Justice's men as could be found rounded up, paid off, or locked in the dungeons."

Winton nodded. They walked in silence for a few moments, and then he asked the question she knew had been on his lips since she had arrived. "What happened to you? Where have you been, really?"

Constance glanced across—they were nearing the south tower now, and a flicker of bluish lightning cast his face into fleeting relief. "I told you. Father sent me away to stay with my mother's family at court, the Santinis."

"He never mentioned it. I mean, before he was . . . unwell. Everyone thought you had run away or . . . or even died."

Winton wasn't a suspicious person, she thought—it wasn't in his character. But she could tell he didn't quite believe her. *If you can't tell the whole truth, tell part of it.* She stopped suddenly and turned to face him again. "Look, Winton . . . I am sorry about your mother. I know you loved her truly. But . . . she bore little affection for me. She was desperate for you to be the heir to the duchy. She hated the fact that you and I were close. And she must've been glad when I disappeared."

He hung his head, knowing it was true. "So . . . you left because of her? But I still don't understand. You were—you are—the heir to the Forest. In sending you away, Father severed your ties to the Ancestors ... And now ..." He shook his head, as if his thought were too terrible to finish.

Now I'm an outcast. Constance felt like laughing; Winton didn't know the half of it.

He continued: "Surely nothing can be worth that?"

She paused for a moment, measuring her words carefully. "In all honesty, Winton, I never had as strong a connection to the Ancestors as I should have. Once your mother made her feelings known, I started to feel unwelcome here—to feel different, foreign." She kept her voice low, sincere. "And I was, sort of. I may look more like Father, but inside I have always been my mother's child—outward-facing, curious about the world and my place in it." She paused again. "Honestly, I *asked* Father to send me away. I wanted to find the other half of my family. Mother died when I was very young, so I never really knew her, or them, or where they lived. I guess ... I guess I wanted to find a place where I belonged."

"But why all the secrecy? Why didn't you say goodbye?" His voice was low, steady—but she had the sense that these were questions he'd wanted to ask for a very long time. She felt an ache in her heart: he'd only been nine. Her departure really had hurt him.

"Father couldn't bear it, Winton. He saw the wisdom in it—but it was also a shameful thing, and painful. He said that if I was to go, I had to just go. And so he sent me off in the middle of the night." Another half-truth. She could still feel how hard he'd grasped her arm, the desperation in his voice. *Just run. Run. Before they find out.*

"I see . . ." Winton nodded, but he was frowning. Constance felt a tug of frustration. Why couldn't he just believe her? Perhaps she wasn't as good a liar as she'd thought. Winton opened his mouth to ask another question, but footsteps interrupted him, and they both turned to the wide-shouldered figure emerging from the cloud. She recognized the captain, a tall man in his late thirties, who smiled at Winton warmly and bowed to Constance.

"Lady Protector," he said. His voice was harsh with the accent of the lower town. He had broad, handsome, but rough-hewn features, a rash of stubble across his jaw. "I'm sorry to interrupt."

"Captain Trudan," she said, nodding in greeting. He, like Winton, was in his training clothes. She wondered if the pair had sparred together. Lord Veredith had mentioned the man had become something of a father figure to her brother.

"If you have a minute," he continued awkwardly, "I'd like to brief you on a few reports of disturbances in the lower town."

"Disturbances? Please, go on."

"The Justice ordered me to impose a strict curfew between sunset and sunrise after the cryptling girl vanished and had his own men search the lower town. They have been . . . thorough in their duties. The people are unhappy, and curfew last night was broken by a large assembly of around forty men from the lower town. One of my guards was attacked and narrowly escaped with his life. The Justice's men gathered in force to suppress the townspeople."

"I thought I ordered them to be rounded up?"

The captain bowed. "Yes, Lady Protector. But as soon as there was word of your success in petitioning the Witenagemot, many of the Justice's men disappeared into the city. We have imprisoned maybe fifty out of three hundred—none would be bought to our side. They largely believe, as the Justice does, that Duke's Forest is infested with mages—and I fear they will not submit to your authority now that you have detained him."

Constance let the realization sit for a moment, her stomach churning. *Two hundred and fifty enemies at large in the city.* When she spoke again, her voice was low and careful. "And what was the outcome of last night's activity?"

The captain bowed. "The Justice's men left five dead and strung up a ringleader in the lower town as an example."

"That's barbaric," Winton said, the outrage sharpening his voice.

Constance nodded slowly. "There is no more need for a curfew, Captain Trudan, and I want no more searching for this cryptling girl. Please ask your men to spread the word of our regime change among the townsfolk too, and if they see any of the Justice's men tormenting the people, they are to arrest them on sight. Is there anything else you would recommend?"

Winton cleared his throat and interjected, "The man they strung up as an example . . . and the others they killed . . ."

Constance nodded. "Have him cut down, and ensure the families of the dead are provided with coin for the proper rituals."

"My lady . . ."

"What is it, Captain?" she said, unable to disguise her impatience. *I don't have time for this.*

"The Justice . . . he has more men than you realize. Informants in the city, spies. Propagandists. Other men, whom he pays but who do not wear his livery."

"What is your point, Captain? Do you wish me to seek out all these men and kill them, alongside everything else? Do what I have commanded."

Captain Trudan bowed. "Very good, my lady," he said.

Once he was gone, Constance turned to Winton—he was still visibly upset by the news, and perhaps at how harshly she had spoken to his friend. "I should not have snapped at him," she said by way of apology.

"It's all right. I'm sure he's used to worse from the Justice." Winton smiled, forgiving her. "I can't believe what the Justice's men have done. How can anyone be so heartless?"

Constance shook her head. Her brother was annoyingly, unbelievably naive.

They drew up beside the west guard post. In silent agreement, brother and sister stepped toward the edge of the wall and looked out over the descending slopes of the mountain. The roofs of empty mansions in the upper town rose like ships from the storm cloud, glowing pinkish in the morning light. Random flickers of blue licked at the chimneys and the gutters.

"It's beautiful, isn't it?" said Constance quietly.

Winton glanced across at her in disbelief. "It's killed more than half the people who once lived here," he replied. "It's as good as destroyed us."

"As if something terrible can't be beautiful too."

He was silent for a moment, and then he turned to her and she was taken aback by the intensity of his stare. "For Ancestors' sake, Constance, I know you aren't telling me the whole truth. Just . . . let me help you." He reached out suddenly and wrapped his fingers around her left arm, her *wrong* arm. She snatched herself backward, but the shock was clear on his face: he'd felt the unexpected hardness underneath the long-sleeved dress. Instantly, doubt clouded his eyes.

"I have to go," she blurted, hurrying toward the stairs. She nearly stumbled in her desperation to flee across the courtyard, her throat tight, a pulse pounding in her temples. She must *not* be discovered. Not yet.

Later, Constance waited in the north wing, watching the courtyard for Dr. Thorn. When he finally left her father to visit the Justice, she set down her quill next to the papers on her desk. She'd purposely chosen the office for its vantage point near the door to the north tower.

"I shall visit my father now, Lord Veredith," she said. The old man glanced up from his own reams of paper, formalizing the transfer of the Protectorship from the Justice to her.

"Very good, dear," he quavered, smiling.

She reached the door to the north tower. The physician had locked it behind him, but—checking quickly over her shoulder—she magicked it open with a simple tap of her cane. She slipped through the door and relocked it from the inside.

Her father was calmer today, but less responsive. After a few minutes of persistent questioning, she knelt on the hard stone floor beside him, pressed her fingers against his temples, and tried again to break through the barriers Dr. Thorn had set up in his mind.

After a few minutes of fruitless work, she put on her mask and turned the dial. The spell-scape emerged all around her. The storm was weak up here—merely a faint web of lightning clinging to the sides of the glass dome. But her father was glittering with the red spell that kept him trapped in madness. She probed the red wall for weaknesses, needling gently through the mortar of the spell. Thorn was a strong mage, and skilled. She knew from experience what effect throwing her full power against the wall would have—and she wasn't eager to try it again. She knew she'd have to go the long way around: undo the spell, undermine it, pick at it until it fell apart.

It felt like hours before she bore a tiny hole in the wall, sending a stream of her magic into the weakness. Her head ached, but she persevered. Cracks appeared in the spell and the Duke's posture visibly relaxed. The effort had sapped her energy. She let out a sigh, a trickle of cold sweat running down her neck as she refocused, slipping the mask off her face.

"Father?"

"Constance?" He spoke in his ordinary voice, his eyes clearing. "Ancestors ..." He looked as if he was about to weep—but it was different now. The emotion on his face was real, sane emotion, and she felt a wave of relief. But the pure feeling in his eyes quickly hardened into something like shame, and Constance knew instinctively that while her father had been a prisoner in his own mind he had seen everything. He remembered everything.

"We don't have much time," she said. "I don't have the strength to break this spell completely."

"What are you doing here, Constance?" He met her eyes, a flash of his old determination returning in his gaze. "I told you never to come back," he hissed. She was startled by how quickly he had transformed from the broken old man into the Duke she'd once known. "Well?"

She stared at him. *She* was asking the questions now. "Who did this to you, Father?"

"Constance—"

"Father, I haven't got time to explain. You have to trust me." She met his eyes, willed him to listen, to yield—just for once. "Who did this to you?"

He surrendered. "The physician. His medicines reinforce the ... the spell." He spat the word, as if it were a curse.

"And why? What game is Jonas Thorn playing?"

Her father shook his head. "Look not to the pawn, but to the player. Who has gained the most from my madness?"

Constance frowned. "The Justice? But he hates magic . . . Why . . . ?"

"For power. Why else?" The Duke was gazing upon his ravaged hands with disgust, as if at the hands of a beggar. "All manner of hypocrisy is practiced in the name of power."

"You know this for certain?" She couldn't quite bring herself to believe the Justice was capable of such self-deceit. "It doesn't really make sense . . ."

The Duke met her eyes witheringly. "I know it. And if you have half a brain, you ought to know it too. Of course it doesn't make sense: the Justice is a fanatic. He is not a logical man, and it is likely he sees no conflict between the end he desires and the means he chooses to achieve it."

Her mind was racing, but she brushed aside her other questions. Instead, she took his hands to ask the one that truly mattered, the question she had saved until she knew he might be capable of answering. His fingers were dry and papery in her own, the hands of a very old man, though the Duke was barely fifty. "Father, I am looking for something. . . . Do you remember the brooch that Mother used to wear on her chemise?"

Confusion clouded his expression, but he nodded. "I remember it. She wore it always," he said, and despite his forcibly matter-of-fact tone, a tightness showed around his eyes. "I had gifted her far finer pieces of jewelry, and yet . . ."

The relationship between her parents had been strained, Constance knew: a marriage of two strong-headed people was rarely without complications. And after her mother's death, the Duke had all too quickly moved from mourning to his second marriage. She'd always hated that. And still . . . looking at his face now, she knew some part of him had truly loved her mother.

"Have you seen it since? Do you know where it is?"

"Why would I have seen it?" He fixed her with a hard stare. "What is this all about?"

Constance felt a precious part of her hope flicker and die. She'd assumed her father's induced madness was a sign he knew something important, something that would lead her to the answers she sought.

When her father spoke again, there was a new softness in his voice. "You should not have returned. Is this about what happened that night . . . when I saw . . . ?"

She squeezed his cold hands in hers, forced her voice through reluctant lips. "Of course it is, Father. Everything is about that night."

"I told you to run, foolish girl," he said, his voice caught between pain and tenderness. "There is no place for you here. Just like there was no place for your mother."

Constance felt an unexpected flash of pain at the words. "Why did she even come here?"

He shook his head but didn't answer. "Why did you come back?"

"This is my home. My birthright." *Truth.*

"The storm . . ." And all of a sudden he was struggling against the red spell as it tried to reinforce itself, mending the break in its wall with tendrils knitting like ivy.

"What is it, Father?" She gently raised her right hand to his face, feeling him start to disappear.

"Something . . . has been bothering me. Could it be . . . Thorn? The mage who cast the . . . the storm spell?" He had to struggle with the words between strained, panting breaths. "Could the Justice be . . . responsible? Is it all . . . connected? The mage hunts . . . They could be a decoy, and a way . . . to exert control? The Justice . . . is a fanatic . . . he is unhinged. These are the things . . . I have wondered . . . beneath my madness."

Constance nodded slowly, squeezed his hand. "The physician is strong enough to cast such a spell, and he has certainly been in the city for long enough," she said. Her heart clenched as she told her father what he longed to hear. "But I will triumph over this, Father. That's why I've come home."

"Yes." The Duke appeared comforted, resting back in his chair. "You . . . you have to save our city," he managed to say. "Save it . . . from the storm cloud . . . and from the Justice . . . and his mage."

His eyes met hers determinedly, and Constance could feel him clinging to his sanity like a drowning man clinging to the rocks. When she replied, her voice burned. "Don't worry. I will show them the true meaning of justice—you have my word."

Relief briefly flickered over his face, followed by confusion. Constance lifted her hand from his face, unable to bear the sense of him slipping away. The lines around the Duke's eyes grew deeper, his stoop more pronounced as he hunched over in the chair. He closed his fingers around the scored wooden arms, his knuckles whitening.

The sea had swept him back into its depths, and he was drowned.

"Who are you?" he snapped, catching sight of her as if for the first time. "What are you doing here, sneaking around? Fetch the Justice! Out! Out!" he shouted, his voice raw and ugly.

She stood up. "I'm just leaving, my lord," she said, the words catching in her throat.

NINE
The Huntsman

Lena woke, groggy and heavy-headed, when the sun was shining through the window of her little room. For a moment she was disoriented. She didn't recognize the wooden bed, the soft sheet beneath the mounds of woolen blankets. And where was Hunter, usually curled up on her feet?

Someone was knocking on the door of her room—and she could smell something delicious. "It's me, Lena," Emris announced, "and breakfast."

The previous day returned to her in a whirl of impossibility. At the same time, she realized quite suddenly that she was *starving*. "Coming!" she called, and scrambled out of bed. She quickly dressed in the clothes from the chest of drawers, leaving her ruined habit on the floor by the bath and resting the butterfly carefully in a new pocket. The clothes were exactly like the ones Emris wore—gray tunic, trews, and cloak. She pulled on her old boots after knocking the worst of the dried mud and leaves out the window.

After a huge greasy breakfast of bacon, eggs, and fluffy white bread, eaten from a tray in an armchair beside the map room fire, the huntsman led her on a twisted path through the interior of the old terraced houses. The entire street had been knocked through into a ramshackle mansion: flights of stairs, a tangled warren of corridors in various states of grandeur and disrepair, heavy doors, and carved arches. Emris nodded at gray-clad passersby, occasionally murmuring a greeting or flashing a smile. Lena was hardly spared a glance in spite of her birthmark; next to Emris's scars, she supposed, it was nothing unusual.

By the time they had finished climbing the final staircase, arriving at a plain wooden door engraved with the words "FIRST HUNTSMAN," Lena was a little breathless. "I'll never find my way back to my room," she managed.

"That's sort of the point," Emris said, allowing her a moment's rest. "Extra protection against any intruders. Ready?" Without waiting for an answer, he knocked three times on the door.

Lena straightened her fresh gray tunic, tucked her hair behind her ears, and blew a long breath through her lips. She'd eaten and slept, washed and changed, and still her nerves jangled like bells on a feast day, and her large breakfast churned in her stomach. She shifted on her feet, stared at the floor. Was she really a mage? Somehow she still couldn't believe it—none of the strange things that had happened around her had been intentional. But she was about to find out for certain . . .

"Don't worry," Emris said softly. "He'll ask you a number of questions and give you a few small tasks, and then he'll tell you what temple you're best suited to. Whichever it is, I'll be sure to take you there and set you up."

"I know." He'd already said this three or four times, in various different ways, as if he sensed her nervousness—but none of his reassurances helped. She kept thinking back to Emris's explanations about Chaos, how it was dangerous and could overwhelm someone who wasn't properly trained. She shivered. Something had killed that serpent, something inside her, even though she hadn't meant to. That sounded a bit like Chaos, didn't it?

Emris knocked again, louder, and an impatient voice cried out, "Yes, yes! All right. Come in."

The door opened. Inside, a portly older man sat low in an armchair at an enormous desk, a huge wall of bookshelves at his back. A musty tome lay facedown on his belly, and he was in the process of pushing his glasses up his nose. A big silver pot of sharp-smelling coffee steamed on the desk in front of him. Out the window, Lena glimpsed a wonderful view of the beautiful, glittering dome of the Holy Council.

"Is this her, then?" the man said, plunking the book on the table, standing up, and peering at Lena as if she were a tadpole in a pond. Like every passerby in the temple, he didn't seem to notice her birthmark at all—not even with a flicker of the eyes. He observed her all at once, summed her up in a glance. It was disconcerting and comforting at the same time. He had a large red nose and a stern but kindly face, his dark eyes peering from behind gold-framed spectacles.

"It is," said Emris. "Shall I leave you to it?"

The older man waved his arm. "Wait here—we shan't keep you long."

Lena was surprised by her relief. In a whole world full of strangers, she supposed, Emris was less of a stranger than most. He took a chair by the door, slipping a book off a shelf nearby and shooting Lena a reassuring smile.

"Well, then. Come here, girl," said the First Huntsman, and Lena crossed the several feet of embroidered carpet to the desk as he poured himself a cup of coffee and shuffled some papers. "Take a seat. Remind me of your name?" He picked up a feather quill, unscrewed a glass ink jar.

"Lena," she said, sitting down on the opposite side of the desk. The chair was very smooth and squashy. She sank into its cushions, her feet lifting off the floor as she slid backward.

"Family name?" he asked, glancing at her from under bushy eyebrows.

Lena shook her head. "I don't have one," she said, hoping he wouldn't ask her to explain. Cryptlings had no family name—that was taken from them the moment their birth families abandoned them to the Ancestors. When cryptlings died, they were interred in a communal tomb, like the lowest of beggars and criminals. Of course, Vigo hadn't even been afforded that—his bones lay bare and untended not far outside the walls of the castle. Her eyes stung, and she looked down at her lap.

The huntsman appeared to sense her discomfort, sparing

her further questions on the subject. His voice was gentle when he spoke again, his pen hovering over the paper. "And yet I shall have to fill the form with something. Perhaps, as you were rescued by a huntsman of Faul, you would accept the name 'Grey'?"

Lena nodded. *Lena Grey.* She liked it.

"Very good. Now, has Huntsman Lochlade explained why you are here?"

"Emris said you were going to decide which temple I should start training with," she said.

"That's right. And to help us decide, I'd like you to complete a little test—not the pass or fail kind, just the sort to help us puzzle out where you'll fit in. After that, we'll pack you off to your temple and you'll have your very first lesson." He looked at her kindly, as if she were about six years old. "Are you ready?"

Lena suppressed a gulp. She wasn't ready—but what choice did she have? Her stomach burbled with nerves and she sent an instinctive prayer to the Ancestors before realizing she was about to betray her old faith for good. She felt her face twist into a grimace of confusion.

"Are you ready to take the test, Lena?" he asked again, observing her distress.

She managed a stiff nod, forcing herself to agree. The only way was forward.

"Don't worry, child. As First Huntsman, I have lots of experience in assigning temples to Rogues. In fact, Emris is among my greatest successes."

Lena turned to where Emris was sitting in his straight-backed chair near the door, apparently absorbed in a large leather-bound book. "Emris was a Rogue?" she said under her breath.

"Oh yes." The First Huntsman sipped his coffee, a wisp of steam curling into the air above his head. "I knew within five minutes of meeting him that he'd remain with Faul—he had a natural talent for the sort of magic we require. And he's been a champion for other Rogues ever since. It's not the favored route into the temples, you know—many distrust it."

Lena blinked. She'd thought if she took this path, she'd be accepted into this new world. "Distrust it? What do you mean?"

"There are those who say that Rogues—or former Rogues—will never be as accomplished or controlled as those who have been in the temples from the start." He smiled. "Nonsense—of which Emris is the finest evidence. Well, let's get started." He shuffled his papers again. "I suppose I should ask you the obvious question: Do you feel drawn to any one of the temples? Emris mentioned he's shown you the basic outline."

Lena shook her head.

"Well, that's not unusual. No matter. Part of my job here is to be a good judge of character—to see in you what you can't see in yourself." He took up his pen a second time, resting the feathered tip against his top lip. "Now, I'm going to ask you a series of questions, and you're going to answer quickly and instinctively. Don't think about it—just say it. Does that make sense?"

"No," she said. How was it possible to stop yourself from thinking?

But the First Huntsman either didn't hear her or ignored her answer. "Good." His pen was poised. "Would you say you're a forgiving person, Lena?"

"No." The word leaped out of her mouth before she thought. A smile hovered on his lips.

"As I said, I have a knack for this. Do you draw a strict distinction between right and wrong? Or is it more blurred?"

"Blurred," she said instantly.

"How important is your family to you?"

Lena shook her head. "The only family that mattered to me is dead."

The First Huntsman offered no condolences but scribbled a line on his paper. "When threatened, do you run, or hide, or fight?"

"Run." She frowned, thinking back to the serpent. She *had* thrown a knife at it before running. "Or maybe fight."

He tapped his pen, as if uncertain. "Remember, try not to think, Lena. Are you guided more by your passion or your reason?"

"Passion." She shook her head. "No, reason," she argued, annoyed at her own answer. "Or at least a mixture of both."

He coughed. Lena sensed his unease—she was doing

something wrong. She shifted in her seat, warmth flooding her cheeks. "I'm failing, aren't I?"

"Not exactly," he said. "It's not that kind of test, remember. But your uncertainty is unusual . . . One last question, then. Are you a good person, Lena?"

The answers had arrived readily on her lips, if confusedly— but now, nothing. Her mind fell blank. She took a few deep breaths. *Are you a good person? You stole a butterfly from the crypts. You let Vigo die for you.* She shook the thoughts from her head. *Of course. Of course I am.* "Yes," she said at last. "I mean . . . I think so."

He frowned and set down his pen and notepad, half-filled with scribbles, lots of them crossed out. "Well, never mind about all that. I'm going to set you a challenge—and again, I need you to think as little as possible; simply follow my instructions. Do you understand?"

Lena nodded, sensing the slight irritation underlying his words.

"Now, sink back in your chair and breathe deep. Envisage a small white light floating in the air before your face. Slowly push your power toward the light."

Lena frowned. "My power? What? Look, I can't—"

"Just try." He smiled encouragingly. "Every mage can accomplish this small spell."

But was she really a mage? Was she capable of this? What if she wasn't?

What if she *was*?

Oh, Ancestors . . . Well, I suppose this will settle it.

The huntsman went on. "The idea is that the globe of light you produce will exhibit the color of your magic. This in turn will indicate to which temple you are most suited. Sometimes it's not terribly clear, but it can provide an indication. Ready?"

She nodded.

"Now, imagine a white light ... Push your power toward it."

Lena frowned in concentration at an imaginary glowing dot hovering in front of her nose. Soon she was focusing so intently, she really *was* starting to see a light pulsing in front of her eyes—the sort of light you get imprinted on your eyelids in sudden darkness, a shadow of the sun. *An illusion?*

"Good, Lena. Try to keep it steady. Focus. Feel the energy shift inside you as you push toward it with ... with your mind."

Lena tried, feeling ridiculous. She shut her eyes, imagined part of herself edging nearer to the imaginary light, felt a coldness pressing against her face. The air smelled damp and heavy. Her heart fluttered. A cool tingling started at the tip of her nose, which she wrinkled in surprise.

"Gods," she heard Emris say, followed by a loud *thump* as he stood, book sliding to the floor.

"What?" she said, opening her eyes. Before her, a little wisp of vapor floated in the air, no larger than the palm of her hand but definitely ... definitely *there.* "What the ... ?" She scrambled out of the chair.

I made that happen. But it's certainly not a light.

The atmosphere in the room had cooled. The First Huntsman peered into the wisp, his eyes narrowed.

"This power has an unusual character." He met Emris's eyes for a second, but the scarred huntsman shrugged, apparently speechless. The First Huntsman blew the vapor, and with a little shiver, it disappeared. "Well, if I were to call that a color, I'd say it was gray." He stood. "Let's call it inconclusive—but for now we'll keep you in the temple of Faul. I must consult with the Council." He met Lena's eyes, and his expression hardened. "I have a feeling the Council will need to *test* her, Emris," he said, speaking about her as if she weren't standing in front of him, staring up in confusion. Something about the way he said it, the emphasis on "test" . . . Lena looked between the two men.

"What do you mean, test me?"

"I'll explain later, Lena," said Emris. And he turned to his superior. "We'll attempt the Binding right away, sir."

"Report back to me this evening." He returned to his desk and, shooting Lena a final suspicious glance, sat down. "Dismissed."

Emris touched her elbow gently. "Come along, then," he said, and drew her out of the room.

"What in the thousand crypts *was* that?" she said, as they descended the staircase, footsteps ringing loud in the silence.

"I've never seen a mage-light quite like it before. And by the expression on his face, neither had the First Huntsman." Emris smiled, but the warmth never reached his eyes. "He's a man who doesn't like to be surprised . . . and you're a bit of a puzzle, Lena."

"What's a mage-light supposed to look like anyway?" she asked.

"Look." Emris stopped on the steps and opened his palm, face up. Lena gasped as a little light appeared in its center. She stumbled backward slightly, her heart racing as she clutched the banister. "It's okay," he said. "Just look." The light in his palm was ghostly, like the moon shining through mist, but it was definitely a light. *Not a cloud.* He closed his palm and the light disappeared. "Come on."

He turned away. Lena shivered, wondering if she would ever grow so accustomed to magic. Emris had summoned the glowing globe so casually, it was like he thought nothing of it.

As she followed him farther downstairs, she thought back to the sensation she'd felt in the First Huntsman's office, summoning the vapor. When the serpent had nearly killed her, hadn't she felt the same? The tingling, the coldness. "What's going to happen to me?" she asked quietly. "What did he mean about another test?"

Emris stopped at the bottom of the staircase. A grand hallway—polished wooden floor, paintings of old men and women in gilt frames—yawned emptily in front of them. The huntsman sighed, turned to face Lena, and grasped her by the shoulders. "Listen. I can tell you what's going through the First Huntsman's mind—he's wondering whether Chaos is starting to affect your power . . . to *infect* it. But somehow I know he's mistaken. Everyone's magic has a different character." He smiled. "Just because we haven't seen it before doesn't mean it's wrong . . ."

"But . . . ?" Lena could sense the word, although he hadn't spoken it.

Emris shook his head. "But nothing. There are those who will probably say otherwise, that's all. And yes, the Holy Council will likely want to test you to make absolutely certain—but it's standard stuff. We can practice. Come on. I'll run you through the Binding, and then we'll find some lunch in the refectory."

She wanted to ask about the test, sensing he wasn't telling her the whole story, but followed as he continued to walk across the hall, the wooden floor softly creaking under his weight. Besides, another question felt more urgent. "What's the Binding, again?"

"A little exercise every mage has to go through—mostly at the age of twelve or thirteen. Nothing you can't handle."

Is it true, then? Am I really a mage? She frowned. *I made something happen, something impossible, just by force of will. So . . . I must be.* Her whole body shivered in response to the thought. She'd always been told magic was wicked. Now, it seemed, she really was carrying it inside her. Did that mean she was wicked too?

Or maybe she'd been wrong her whole life. The thought pained her, but maybe . . . *maybe* Vigo had been wrong. Emris didn't seem evil. Even the First Huntsman hadn't been unkind. As Emris led her down the long hall, she let the notion sit with her, swirling in her mind like ink in water. Maybe Vigo was wrong. Maybe magic wasn't evil.

But she couldn't accept it, not quite.

I'm so sorry, Vigo. I'm letting you down.

"Here." They had reached a small pointed doorway at the end of the hall. Emris rested his hand on the handle. "From here on, the temple's going to look a lot more ... um ... templey." His scars twisted as he smiled.

As the door swung open, Lena's breath caught in her throat. They stepped from the humble doorway onto the stone floor of the tallest room she'd ever seen—it was like someone had hollowed out one of the towers in Duke's Forest. Narrow windows punctuated the thick walls—and far above, the ceiling was silver glass, gentle light filtering down through the pointed arches like clouded sunlight through leaves. The pillars holding up the impossible ceiling were shaped into the likeness of trees and twined with pale carvings of ivy and flowers. The air was cool and full of an indefinable strangeness—a little like the strangeness in the crypts of Duke's Forest, but a hundred times more wonderful. Lena's skin tingled. Inside, she felt uneasy—dizzy, even.

This place is spun from shades of light, she thought. She'd lived her whole life in darkness, and now ... This was almost too much.

In the center of the space, a four-tiered fountain trickled musically. On the highest, shallowest pedestal stood the archer, just like the one on the mantelpiece in the map room but ten times the size and hewn of gray-veined marble. His bow was drawn tight and aimed at some invisible target, his hair blowing in a nonexistent wind, brow caught in a frown of concentration.

"It's beautiful," said Lena under her breath, as Emris shut the door at her back, drawing a curtain across the archway to hide the entrance from view. A few other people stood or knelt before the fountain—some dressed in gray, others in ordinary clothes. A murmur filled the air, mingling with the trickle of water.

"Yes, it is." He seemed pleased by her reaction. The huntsman led her across the flagstones toward the fountain. His scars, normally paler and puckered, appeared smooth in the soft light. "So, the Binding—it's about finding and controlling the magic within yourself. As you know, losing control completely will cause Chaos to take over, and that's dangerous for everyone. This is an exercise you'll only need to perform once. Afterward, as long as you remain with the temples, you'll be able to exert basic control over your powers—and you shouldn't be a danger to anyone, not even yourself."

They reached the fountain. Its edges were broad and smooth, worn by the touch of countless people. The water was clear and very deep for a fountain—deep enough to swallow a standing man at least.

"Here, sit down beside me."

Emris sat cross-legged on the fountain ledge, and Lena took a spot at his side, their knees nearly touching. The thick soles of her boots pressed into her thighs. She watched as an older man standing opposite dropped a coin into the water and bowed his head.

"It's simple, really." Emris spoke softly, his voice nearly swallowed in the cavernous air. "Your magic is like a living being somewhere inside you. What you need to do is bind it to your will, much the same as you'd slip a collar on a dog or a bridle on a horse. And you do that with a little help from a god." He glanced up at the statue on the fountain.

If she did this thing, did that mean she was abandoning the Ancestors for good? *Yes.*

She stared into the water, finally allowing the truth to envelop her. The Ancestors reviled magic. She had magic—she believed that now, even if she couldn't quite accept it. If anything, she could safely assume that *they'd* abandoned *her*. Lena remembered her hallucination, the angry dead who'd surrounded her in the forest. She couldn't go back. And this . . . well, it seemed like this was the only way forward.

Memories of Vigo pushed themselves into her mind, but although sadness tugged at her throat, it couldn't persuade her now. This was all beyond his imagining. She had created mist out of thin air. What did Vigo know about that?

"Lena?" Emris said. "Are you all right?"

"Yes," she said firmly. "What should I do?"

"All you do is look into the water and pray for Faul to show you your magic. Gradually, you'll fall into a kind of dream. I can't tell you what happens exactly—it's different for everyone. You'll have to find your own way through."

"Is that it?" Somehow, she felt, there must be more to it. "What do you mean, 'find your own way through'?"

"I can't say. I've heard about other people's visions—some have had to literally find a path through a maze, others dreamed of a hunt, or even of a tricky riddle. But it's not difficult—I've never known anybody to fail. And afterward you should feel very different, calmer, more in control—especially as a Rogue. I certainly did. You probably don't realize how much subconscious effort you're exerting to keep your powers in line."

Lena felt a rush of warmth for Emris. He had been like her once—but he had found his way. And now he was showing her how to follow.

"Breathe deep and slow—and take your time."

Lena stared into the water. Muted gray light shimmered on its surface, reflections of worshippers passing like shadows in the background. On the floor of the fountain, a pattern of eye-shaped tiles in all shades of green and brown conjured a forest floor. She squinted, thinking she'd spotted a glint of blue-green, a flash in the corner of her eye. *Focus,* she told herself, and returned to her contemplation of the water's surface, its soft movement soothing and calm. The temple around her faded as she listened to the sigh of her own breath.

Faul, please show me my magic, she thought dutifully.

And suddenly her stomach flipped as she tipped forward, plunging into blackness . . .

Distantly, she felt the cool fountain water swallow her body. But instead of sinking to the tiled floor, she kept falling and found herself on her hands and knees in cold, cloying mud. She raised her eyes, her heart convulsing. All around her the air was damp, a huge gray cloud wheeling like a carousel. A low rumble rent the air.

The storm cloud.

She felt sick. She scrambled to her feet, wiping her hands on her old habit, the one she'd left in her room that morning, clutching it tight around her body. *This is impossible.*

The forest was thick with noxious clouds, the trees diseased and deformed, trunks shifting in and out of vision. The taste of decay filled her mouth and she pressed a hand over her lips, suppressing a retch. Wind whipped through her hair. A fork of greenish lightning flashed to her right, and immediately the air smelled of fire.

She was panting, her heartbeat wild, as if she'd been running fast. *Not here. Please. Not here.* Horror filled her, right from the bottom of her soul. She was back where she'd started, the howls of hungry dogs echoing in her ears.

The bodies of the cloaked explorers lay in the clearing. The woman with the splayed red hair. The man sleeping his eternal rest by the black ghost of the fire. The body propped up against the tree, as if in waiting, keeping his longest watch. *I have to run.* Lena started to stumble backward, a strange fizzing sensation building in the hollow beneath her lungs.

Too late. The body leaning against the tree shifted, as she'd known it would somewhere deep down. The man's chest lifted, rattling with years-old breath.

The fizzing sensation spread up through her nerves, along her shoulders, down her arms. Lena heard the creak of the dead man's bones, the thump of a rotten heart, impossibly loud, like a war drum, but crackling and distorted. She felt warm, like a flame burning in the cool damp of the forest.

And that's when she realized . . . she was making it happen. She lifted her hands, and around her fingers sparks flew. The magic was flowing toward the dead man, hissing in the air. All about her the storm quickened, a cold wind tugging at her habit. She gasped, stumbled backward.

The man's head tilted upward, and Lena felt her legs surrender, her knees sinking into the forest mulch.

She stared at her hands. "Stop it, just stop it!" She closed them into fists, but the sensation didn't stop—and she understood suddenly that the magic was not her servant: she belonged to the magic. The dead man's face was shrouded in a thick black scarf, the hood fallen over his forehead as he rose to his feet. And now his eyes were glowing in the semi-darkness like a pair of flickering beacons. Narrowing at the sight of her face.

She felt suffocated. She felt like she couldn't breathe.

The eyes narrowed again. Was the dead man . . . smiling?

Why am I here?

Distantly, she remembered Emris's voice. *The Binding.*

Is this just a test, set by a cruel god?

She tried to breathe, but the air was wet and close. She choked, grasping her throat. Maybe this was normal. Maybe she was okay. Maybe this was all part of the process. Was it?

She couldn't breathe. She couldn't breathe.

Her hands crackled with magic as the dead man walked closer. And closer. And closer. She had to stop this before he reached her. She gasped for precious air and prayed with all her might, no longer caring to whom she prayed, only that her pleas be answered.

Help me. Faul. Anyone. Please!

She pressed her palms together tightly, trying to smother the power fizzing around her fingers. As she gasped in another tiny breath, the dead man nearly upon her, she noticed a figure standing at the side of her vision. A tall man carrying a bow notched with a single arrow, his face hidden by a low gray hood.

"Please!" she mouthed, the dead man's hands reaching for her neck.

The hunter loosed his arrow. Lena felt iron pierce through the center of her palms, pressed together in prayer. A hot white heat ran through her blood in a rush, a river bursting its banks—then dark and coldness claimed her.

TEN
Falling

The night was nearly spent when Constance climbed down the steps of a deserted butcher's shop in the lower town, heading out onto the road. She breathed deep behind her brass grille, turning the wheel on the mask to bring the physical world into focus again. She'd searched the farthest reaches of the crypts—the rat-infested warren of humble passages filled with the bodies of the poor. Space was at a premium in the lower town's tombs, and a number of families could not afford the full services of the morticians. The result had been . . . unpleasant. Constance was longing for a bath. She started to climb the steep path up to the castle, her boots sliding occasionally on the damp cobblestones speckled with moss. Somewhere in the tangle of streets she heard a man shout in anger, a woman sobbing. She quickened her pace. A better person might have helped, she reflected.

I am not such a person. She had made her peace with that long ago.

In fact, she was so relieved to be on her way back to her

rooms that she almost didn't care that she had found nothing. Almost.

Another network of caves filled with the dead—and only the dead. No magic but the spell itself. No beating heart of a storm cloud close to maturity. She suspected it had hidden itself somewhere it thought it would never be found. But she'd hoped, for once, for a little luck. She'd now searched the crypts under the castle and the upper town and the lower town. She could search the crypts forever—they were vast and many-leveled, and impossibly complex—but something was telling her that if the spell's heart were still down there, she'd have found it already. She had to change her approach.

But how? Her spirits sank at her own lack of inspiration. *What if I never find it?* a small, bitter voice inside her mind whispered.

Then all this has been for nothing, said a stronger voice. *Your betrayal. Your deceit. Your theft. The sacrifice of the life you built. You* must *find it.*

As she approached the upper town, her and Winton's conversation with Captain Trudan played over in her mind, mixed up with fears and misgivings—the Justice, his barbaric and disappearing men, the men he had squirreled away somewhere, perhaps plotting on his behalf. The unrest in the lower town was a threat in itself. What was she to do about that? Was there anything she could do—or should she follow her instincts and focus on finding the spell's heart, even to the neglect of everything else?

Now in the upper town, Constance stopped for a second, listening for noises in the gloom: nothing, except the low grumble of the eternal storm. Even so, she felt half-certain somebody was following her as she continued up the slope.

It's just the storm cloud, she told herself sternly, already picturing stepping out of her corpse-stained clothes and into a hot bath. She quickened her pace again, close to panting with exertion as the path narrowed and steepened. The cloud was thicker in the lower town, but—senselessly—Constance had felt safer in the gloom below. Up here, she felt the bubble of unease spreading wider across her chest. *Someone is watching.*

And then by some instinct, she stopped about ten paces from the portcullis. The echo of footsteps continued, stuttering to a halt a little late.

"Who goes there?" No reply. "Come on. I know you're hiding," she added, her voice low with warning. She waited a few moments, half wondering if she'd imagined the whole thing. And then, slowly, a figure stepped out from the darkness.

Her eyes combed the face part-muffled in a fine silk scarf, the dark hair tied beneath. The eyes glittering green in the intermittent flashes cast by the lightning as familiar hands lifted a pair of shield-eyes. He didn't speak, but challenged her with his gaze.

"*Xander?*" she breathed, unbelieving. And her heart sank as she ran through everything he might have witnessed. How long had he been watching her? "What are you doing?" she hissed, suddenly angry. "Why have you been following me? We're supposed to be on the same side!"

He stepped closer, his expression strangely unreadable. "The night we met in the gardens, you refused to tell me the truth—and so I decided to find out for myself. I watched you slip into the great hall again. I watched your cane light up. I watched you descend into the crypts. And it was then that I knew you were hiding something . . . terrible. I've been trying to understand ever since."

She stared and stared. How much did he know? "You followed me into the crypts?"

"Yes, just now, to the peril of my own soul. I *had* to know. And still I don't quite understand. I know you're looking for something." His eyes flickered to her cane. "And obviously I know you're a mage."

"Xander . . . I . . ." The thought of him hating her, despising her, pierced her heart with a pain so pure and intense that it burned. Guilt was heavy on her shoulders. She shook herself mentally. How had he turned this around? *He* was the one following *her*!

He appeared to read the mix of shame, fear, and anger chasing each other across her face. "I know you're a mage, Constance," Xander said again. "And I could have told everyone after I saw you that first night. But I didn't. Your *secret* is safe with me." He said it sharply, as if rebuking her for daring to think otherwise. "Once I knew that, a lot fell into place. Your disappearance six years ago. The strange happenings before you left—the small fires, the broken things." He was warming to his subject, his eyes flashing. "It was your magic, wasn't it? At the time, I thought someone— perhaps the Duchess—was trying to drive you away. And when you vanished, part of me wondered if they'd succeeded. Why on earth didn't you tell me all those years ago? You could have saved me a lot of pain."

She was silent, her pulse racing, her eyes downcast. She hadn't thought of it like that before. Hadn't thought what her disappearance might have meant to the few people who had cared about her. Finally, she found her voice. "I was afraid," she whispered. *Truth*.

"You thought I was just like everyone else? Didn't I mean more to you than that?"

She stole a glance at him, watched as he ran a hand through his long, dark hair in frustration. A sudden tenderness rushed over her and she reached out, touching his hand lightly and stopping it in its tracks.

His voice softened, and he stepped closer. "Constance, my mother was a foreigner just like yours—and for all our noble blood, the people of Duke's Forest will never let us forget that we're different. My skin is the wrong color. You might look like your father, but inside you're different too. You're putting on a good front, but sooner or later everyone here will know you're not like them. *We're* not like them. You should have known I would understand. It doesn't change how I feel."

She shook her head, wordless. The sound of her heart pattered inside her skull like a squall of rain.

"And there are so many more lies, more things you are hiding from me. Why are you searching the crypts, Constance? What are you looking for? Look at me."

She glanced up at his face. To her surprise, she saw he did not despise her. He was . . . confused. Angry. But he didn't hate her.

"Let me help you," he said hoarsely, grasping her hand more tightly in his. She couldn't help the way her heart soared.

"Xander, I promise I will tell you everything. But here is not the place," she said at last. Her voice barely sounded like her own. "We should not be seen returning together."

"But—"

"The Justice has eyes everywhere, if Captain Trudan is to be believed," she insisted firmly. She pulled her hand away as gently as she could. "I'm asking you to trust me—just this one last time. And then I will tell you everything."

He nodded slowly, reluctantly. "Today?"

"Today. As soon as you like, once we're safely home. You go around to the west tower entrance. I dismissed the guards there before I left. I will enter here. They won't question me."

"Very well, Constance," he said. "But I will hold you to your word this time. I won't let you leave me in the dark again."

And with that barest hint of a threat, he melted back into the storm cloud.

Constance looked up at the four towers above, blacker darknesses against the night's shadow, slits of yellow light spilling infrequently from their sides. A clap of thunder far below sent a tremor down her spine, but she didn't jump. Anger and fear broiled within her, and her ears rang faintly, as resting bells hum in the wind.

What am I going to do about this?

She knew what she should do, what the temple would have had her do. *Go after him now. Silence him. You know the spells that will kill without a trace. No one will be the wiser.*

She shook her head, faintly sickened by the thought. Oh, she could kill—and she had. She wasn't squeamish. But this was different. This was Xander. No matter how much she tried to deny it, he meant something to her—he always had. Even after six years apart, and whatever she had shared with Emris, those feelings didn't just disappear.

By the time she entered the courtyard, the storm cloud was lightening, a dull predawn luminescence spreading across the castle.

She was midway to her tower when she heard the scream, the sound of glass smashing. She spun around, unable to pinpoint the direction. Cold sweat prickled her skin. "Who's there?" she called. She held her cane at the ready, magic thrumming in her blood.

Another scream sliced the air, louder now, high-pitched, followed by a desperate "No, no, no, no!" More smashing, the icy noise of breaking glass. Constance looked up instinctively. The shapes of the four towers were tangled with fog. She knew with sudden urgency, her stomach plummeting to her feet, that the voice belonged to the Duke.

"Father?" She hurried toward the base of the north tower, but it seemed impossibly far away, shrinking like the end of a tunnel in a nightmare. "Father!"

She heard footsteps and a bleary-eyed Winton appeared at her side from his rooms in the west tower, hastily dressed, his furs bulky around his shoulders, his longsword strapped askew to his back. He was holding out a lantern and his nightshirt peeked out above his boots.

"Did you hear that?" Constance breathed. They met each other's eyes through the storm cloud, which flashed blue and shifted between them in the pinkish glow of dawn. For a moment they were children again, and their father was in trouble. And then, at the same time, they looked up.

"Please, I beg you—" The Duke's words terminated midsentence.

"Father! *Father!*" Winton called out, throwing himself toward the tower, pure panic in his voice. Constance followed, her skirts flying. Glass crunched under her feet as she neared the tower's base. A primal terror gripped her.

"*Pa!*" Winton's voice broke on a word he hadn't used since childhood.

A large dark shape fell sharply from above; the air whistled, the cloud parted, a wet *thwack* rang out on the paving stones at their feet—so close, she felt the atmosphere ripple. It happened so quickly. For a few long moments, Constance could not move. Black blood spread across the cobblestones. She stared at the body.

Father. My father.

Somewhere far beneath the dumb shock freezing her limbs, her thoughts raged. Only yesterday she'd been at his side. She'd broken through the spell on his mind, and they'd talked. *It can't be a coincidence ...*

Winton dropped to his knees in the dark, wet pool, looked into his father's staring eyes, which gleamed in the semi-light of dawn, just breaking over the battlements. He looked and looked, clearly unable to believe what he was seeing. Then his eyes rose again to the tower. Constance felt her whole body shaking, but she followed his gaze, stood very still, and listened, and tried to think.

Footsteps echoed down from the stairs. Dr. Thorn appeared at the threshold, panting.

"No ...," the physician managed, his face contorted with exaggerated shock.

"Help him, for Ancestors' sake!" Winton cried in frustration.

Help him? Help him? Is he crazy? Constance's mind was swimming. One thing was clear to her: *Jonas Thorn is the killer!* She raised her cane in sudden anger, feeling the power burning under her skin. *I'll turn him mad, crack his skull against the pavement, see how he likes it.*

But curiosity got the better of her. She only watched as Thorn crouched beside the Duke, shook his head.

"*Do* something!" Tears flooded Winton's trusting, stupid eyes. "Help him, Dr. Thorn!"

Obediently, the doctor rested his fingers on the Duke's

exposed neck, curiously clean and pale against the mess of his skull. "I'm sorry," he said after a time. "He's gone, Winton. The Duke is dead."

Voices sounded in the gloom: the Duke's last struggle had woken the castle. Questions rang out across the courtyard.

"The Duke is dead!" Thorn announced to the new arrivals. As people spied the body between the shifting clouds, screams of confusion laced the air.

Heavy footsteps cut through the panic, sharp and cold as a snick of scissors. The Justice had arrived, fully dressed and accompanied by his vicious white hound, Barbarus, and a large cohort of his men. Constance stiffened, her jaw tightening. The captain had been right to worry about the Justice's hidden army. The black-liveried guard surrounded the courtyard—they'd expected the news, Constance realized, somewhere behind her raging disbelief. She saw too the knowing glance that passed between the Justice and the physician.

Others arrived: Xander, who had gathered a handful of his men on his way from the west tower, and a number of the city guard, those who had been inside the castle or on patrol. She searched out Captain Trudan's face—found it. He nodded at her respectfully. Xander stood close to her now. He met her eyes, shook his head in shock. Nobles and their ladies, dressed in bedclothes, clutched at each other, a few screaming or sobbing at the ghastly sight. Constance's pulse raced. Her father was dead. She felt the force of two slaps, one six years past and the other two days ago, ringing in her ears like a new-struck bell.

And then, at last, her mind caught up. The Justice had arranged the murder. He had a plan. And it was starting *now*. She tightened her grip on her cane.

"The Duke is dead," said the Justice, once everyone was gathered. He turned his eyes on Constance. "Constance Rathbone, Lady Protector, you are under arrest on suspicion of murder."

A shocked silence fell across the courtyard as two of the Justice's men stepped forward, reaching for Constance. Winton stood up from kneeling at the Duke's side, the knees of his trews soaked dark with blood, and blocked their path.

"How dare you," he said softly, and the chilly disbelief in his voice froze them in their tracks. "Our father is dead. How dare you accuse my sister."

"Murder?" Constance faced the Justice calmly. "By what evidence?"

The Justice's cold blue eyes flashed as he turned to address not Constance herself, but the crowd of onlookers. Barbarus growled low at his side, fixing her with its single pale-yellow eye. "No one can question my devotion to the Ancestors, or my determination to root out the wickedness responsible for the curse upon our city. Since returning to Duke's Forest, my home, and my faith, it has been my life's work. In my ten years of service, I have achieved a great deal, and yet not that which meant the most: the destruction of the storm cloud and those who caused its evil visitation upon our great city." He stepped out, past the body on the cobblestones, his eyes falling but briefly on the corpse. "I had been searching in the wrong places. And with the prodigal daughter's return, the answer fell into my hands."

The gathered people waited, the whole courtyard holding its breath in expectation.

"For Constance Rathbone *is* responsible for the storm cloud. She *is* responsible for the madness of the Duke. And . . . she is responsible for the death of the Duke." He turned his eyes to Constance. "For she," he continued, his voice ringing with triumph, "is a *mage*."

Constance's mouth was suddenly dry, and the courtyard grew busy with gasps and murmurs. She forced a laugh, a cold, hollow sound in the whispering hush. Winton stared at her. "This is ridiculous," she said, "absolutely ridiculous." Her voice sounded unconvincing even to herself.

"Do you not defend yourself, *my lady*?" the Justice sneered. "I had my suspicions six years ago or more. The late Duchess too was convinced there was something . . . *odd* about the Duke's firstborn. Curious, isn't it, that the Duchess conveniently departed this world a matter of weeks before the Lady Protector's return. And that the mage who cursed her burial rites disappeared into thin air the very day before the Lady's arrival, as if Constance herself had helped cover her tracks."

"What? I . . ." Constance knew she had to speak. She

knew the Justice's arguments were full of holes, threaded together with the barest of suppositions and the slimmest fragments of truth. But somehow the memories from six years ago gathered in her mouth like a gag, and she could not release her words. The mirrors breaking at her lightest touch. The fires sparking in her dreams, setting her bedclothes alight. The wisps of steam from her tea curling into hands and faces and creatures before disappearing into air.

She remembered Winton's mother, the young Duchess, watching with her beautiful dark eyes. Once, when the Duke's back was turned, she had pinched Constance on the arm, sharp and hard, and whispered, "*I know what you are, and when I prove it, you will be gone—just like your mother.*"

The Justice laughed coldly. "Are you not a mage then, Constance? Defend yourself! Did you not visit the Duke in secret yesterday?" he demanded. "And did you not cast a spell on him? A spell to exacerbate his madness, to force him to cast himself from the tower?"

Absurd, she thought with instant clarity—and the absurdity of it knocked her to her senses. Suddenly she found her words. "That doesn't make sense," she hissed. "Nothing you have said makes any sense."

"Do you deny you are a mage?"

She drew herself tall. *Half-truths are better than lies*. "No, I don't deny that."

The gasp rippling through the crowd was spun full of horror. She heard murmuring. Although she couldn't pick out the words, she could guess their import. Winton was looking at her as if she were a stranger. "Constance? Is it true?" he whispered.

She met his eyes determinedly. "I'm sorry I have had to lie to you all. I wish I hadn't felt the need, but I knew I would not be accepted if I told you the truth." She turned to the rest of her people, their cold, shocked faces. "I cannot help that I am a mage. I didn't ask for it. And I never wished to be ripped from my home and sent away. But even so, I didn't kill my father. That was you, Lord Justice. Or rather, you and Dr. Thorn, whose potions fed his madness." She fixed her eyes on the physician. "You pushed him, didn't you? On the Justice's orders."

The physician's face was impassive. The Justice slid the sword from his belt and aimed it at Constance's heart. As if waiting for this signal, his hound rose to its feet and crouched, ready to pounce. His black-clad men drew their blades, and Dr. Thorn slipped two fine daggers from his belt, standing in a fighting stance at the Justice's side. He displayed no signs of the red combat magic simmering under his skin, but Constance could sense it, sure as fire.

"You are under arrest, my lady, for murder," the Justice growled.

"You said that before, Lord Justice," said Constance. She raised her voice. "But surely it is *you* who ought to be under arrest. We have to ask ourselves, who has gained the most from the storm cloud, from my father's madness, from the Pestilence and the mage hunts?" She lifted her cane and pointed it directly at the Justice, the golden tip a mere inch from the end of his sword. "You, Lord Justice. You, who have the hypocrisy—the *gall*—to recruit a mage to hunt mages."

Suddenly she turned her cane aside and shot an arrow of magic at Dr. Thorn. She'd hoped not to harm but to reveal—and she had judged it right. The instinct to defend against such an attack was irrepressible. He swiped his dagger and a flash of red dispatched the purple dart. The crowd gasped, and Thorn scowled as he realized what he had done. Someone started to scream, others to run. The fear in the air was palpable.

Magic was truly here.

Constance watched Winton's face drain of blood.

The Justice spoke next, his words low and heavy as thunder. "To conquer what you fear, you must become it." The monstrous white hound barked twice. Constance couldn't stop herself from flinching at the sight of its bared yellowish teeth.

The ordinary folk of the castle were fleeing from the scene in earnest now, the Duke's body cold and forgotten at the courtyard's heart. People slipped into doorways like frightened mice, hoping not to be noticed—those inside already pressed white faces against the nearest windows, watching.

"Stand down, Justice. Call off your men," she demanded. But nobody moved. "Very well, if that's how it has to be. Guards!" Constance cried. A shout from the captain sent

the men on the battlements hurrying down to the courtyard and gathering around her, their short green cloaks and
peaked helmets casting strange shadows in the fiery dawn
light. Their longswords were ugly, heavy weapons but
unmistakably sharp and businesslike against the soft curls of
the mist. She remembered Xander's words on the stoic
loyalty of the city guard to those who wore the badge of
the Protectorship. Clearly, even though she was revealed as
a mage, the rule persisted. *Thank the gods.*

Winton straightened his spine and drew his own longsword, standing at Constance's side. She felt a tug of pure
relief and affection in her belly. "You owe me an explanation,
Sister," he said under his breath. She nodded in response.

"Lord Irvine?" she said, with as much confidence as she
could muster. *Please, please, trust me,* she thought.

After a short, agonizing delay, the Swordmaster drew his
slender twin blades, and so did the blue-clad men whom he
had gathered on his way. Other men had joined on both
sides, hearing belatedly of the fighting about to start. "Stand
down, Lord Justice," said Irvine. "You know you cannot
win against us all."

The Justice's lip curled, and he kept his blade raised.

Constance trained her eyes on the physician as she
readied her cane. *He is my priority. Irvine's men and the guards
can take the others.*

A heartbeat of silence, then chaos broke loose.

The Justice attacked first, a shouted command launching
Barbarus at Constance's torso. But she leaped to one side,

felt the whoosh of the dog's bulk pass her stomach as she fell hard onto the ground—and the hound sank its teeth into someone else's leg. The man shouted out in agony, and Constance felt hot blood spray against her cheek. She staggered to her feet but kept low. All around her, blades sang in the churning cloud. A metal tang soured the air— was it her imagination or did the storm spin faster? She felt sick, the man's blood trickling over her lips.

"Get back!" Xander was beside her, hauling her up and pushing her toward the relative safety of the courtyard's perimeter, as if she were a child.

She pulled out of his grasp. "Hey—"

"Just go, Constance!" His face was wild and angry, and he ignored her struggles. Once she was out of the way, he turned back to the fray.

She felt warmth flush her cheeks. She wasn't about to let others fight her battles in her stead. She turned to survey the fighting, spied a red flash from the corner of her vision: Thorn. She edged closer behind a bank of cloud and spelled an attack toward the physician. Purple light flashed, casting crazy shadows in the storm.

She had thought her aim was true, but instead the physician had disappeared completely.

Her mind raced as she shrank into the shadows and scanned the courtyard carefully, trying to pick out Thorn among the fighters. Had she missed? Or had he fallen? No, it couldn't be so easy to defeat a disciple of Jok, the warrior god . . . Could it be a trick?

The Justice himself fought with the strength of several men and fended off three of Irvine's retinue at once; in a flash, he'd killed two with a single strike across their throats, blood arcing across the courtyard in a spray of vivid red. She heard Barbarus growling, tearing at someone's flesh.

And then one of the Justice's black-clad men was before her, sword raised—she felt a stab of fear at the hatred in his face, the sheer determined fury. He wanted her dead.

As he struck, she met his blade with her cane. A bright purple flash repelled the iron. She braced for the next strike—no time to spell an attack of her own. The man was bulky, tall. She defended herself a second time but was pushed back against the battlement wall. The next time, her cane flew from her grasp. She cried out, her left arm trembling. *Damn this thing!*

The Justice's man grinned, his teeth streaked with red. He raised his sword again, lunging for her wildly.

Use it, she thought with sudden clarity.

She screwed her left hand into a fist and retaliated with a sharp blow to the head. Her velvet glove caught on his helmet and tore, exposing the metal beneath. He staggered back, doubled-up and dazed, dropped his sword, his face pale with shock as he realized what had been revealed: an arm wrought purely of metal. She flexed the fingers, feeling how smoothly her magic filled and commanded the limb, its complex mechanics working soundlessly inside the silver shell. The man gurgled wordlessly, gaping, and she worked his shock to her advantage. A boot in his face sent him toppling onto the ground, helmet clattering aside. He tried to raise himself, his mouth now twisted into a scowl, but Constance snatched up the sword with her right hand and brought the point down hard into his neck, no hesitation.

Pink blood bubbled in the man's mouth. Darkness spread from the wound like a lengthening shadow.

She stepped backward, her chest heaving, and threw the sword to the ground with a clatter.

Constance cradled her left arm close, pulling the ripped material of her glove over the exposed metal beneath. *Keep it hidden.* As she gazed down on the dead man, she felt a surge of power and disgust fighting for dominance. Her throat filled with bile, but she swallowed, bent down, and scooped up her cane. As she rose, a wave of glittering red sent her hurtling onto her side, as if struck by a gust of furious wind. Thorn. She whipped aside the next attack, bringing her cane around in a searing arc of purple light. The glove flapped from her left hand uselessly—no time to hide now.

Thorn ducked under her attack, straightened. He was fast. He stood in a practiced fighting stance, his twin daggers ablaze with red fire. He'd shed his brown physician's coat with its pockets of tools and herbs and medicines. Now he was broad-shouldered and light-footed, his dark tunic tightly fitted. Cords of muscle stood out beneath his clothes.

He spun his right dagger and red magic arced through the roiling cloud. She waved her cane, sending the attack ricocheting into the castle wall. Mortar crumbled. He was testing her, she knew—and combat wasn't her strength. *You'll have to outsmart him.*

"How does it feel, doing the Justice's dirty work?" she asked casually. He spun another attack with his dagger, but she deflected, shaking with the effort of trying to make it look easier than it actually was. "You're a long way from home, warrior," she tried. "What does your god think of all this? I didn't think Jok was one for sneaking around like a coward." Another attack—deflected. He was probing her defenses.

"Shut up," he hissed. His eyes flickered to her metal arm, and she saw them widen fractionally.

"Oh, he does have a mind of his own!" She feigned delight, flexing the metal fingers of her left hand. "And here's me thinking you were a dumb piece of muscle, a little magic puppet for the Justice to jerk around."

Thorn's face twisted as he spelled five consecutive attacks—and this time, he wasn't just testing her. She spun her cane, deflecting each one with the purple bulb of magic at its head.

"You know nothing about me," Thorn snarled.

"So tell me. I'd love to know why any mage would work with someone who hates magic as much as the Justice. Isn't it a bit demeaning?"

This time, he threw one of his daggers. It whistled through the air, straight at her head, sending red sparks flying. She stepped aside—barely in time. The blade opened a burning gash on her forehead before it spun around in the air and flew back into Dr. Thorn's hand. The pain was nearly unbearable—but she felt gloriously, thrillingly in control.

"Ouch," she said mildly. "Somebody's going to lose their temper."

And that's when he did. A wild fury of attacks battered her defenses, one after another—nearly overwhelming her in a scarlet wave. She grimaced as she threw a shield up, reinforced it as a crack started to spider along its length. He wasn't concentrating. In the tiny space between one attack and the next, she sent the smallest pure violet arrow through to his chest, aimed directly at his heart. He gasped.

The attacks stopped abruptly.

He crumpled like a puppet with cut strings.

Constance was too weak to stand any longer. She sank to her knees, feeling them bruise as she fell clumsily. She knelt there quietly while the storm cloud swirled around her. The fighting felt curiously distant, muted. She wasn't right, her ears ringing, but she had wits enough to switch her velvet glove from her right arm to her left. At first glance you couldn't tell it was on the wrong hand. If Thorn was dead, her secret was safe.

He lay a few feet away on the slick cobblestones. His chest barely rose and fell. She felt a flash of annoyance. She hadn't meant to let him live. She wondered dimly whether to finish the job, but the fighting was quieting, and she didn't want to be seen killing a prone man in cold blood. Besides, she wasn't sure she had the energy.

Looking up, she saw her father, left alone in his own circle of darkness. As a child, she'd thought he was indestructible—but nothing was, not anymore. Her nose filled with the iron smell of battle as she pieced herself together, wiping her mouth on the back of her sleeve. The cut on her forehead was sore, but the heat of the physician's magic had already sealed the wound.

The fighting was dying down as, one by one, the Justice's men found themselves outnumbered by the city guard and Xander's men and threw down their blades. Barbarus the hound had been knocked out on the ground—breathing, but blood staining its muzzle and a bad wound joining the scars on its flank. Constance stood up unsteadily. A band surrounding the Justice continued to trade blows, with increasing desperation. Winton sparred with the Justice himself, his face etched with rage—and they seemed evenly matched, Winton swinging his heavy longsword in wide, powerful arcs as the Justice parried with a shorter blade, the cords on his neck standing upright in effort. But Constance watched as Xander, a long graze across his forehead, slid through the remaining fighters like a shadow. And then he was at the Justice's back, a dagger at his throat.

"Set down your swords!" he cried.

As suddenly as it had started, the fighting stopped. At the sight of the Justice captured and several of their comrades killed, the remaining black-liveried men dropped their weapons with a clatter on the ground. The Justice's face was white with fury as he let go of his blade. Dr. Thorn had raised himself onto his elbows, clutching his chest. Constance stepped forward.

"Lord Justice. Jonas Thorn." Despite her exhaustion, her voice was cold and sharp. "I place you under arrest on suspicion of conspiracy against the duchy. Guards!"

Captain Trudan stepped forward. He was bleeding freely down his fingers and dripping onto the cobblestones, but otherwise appeared to be unharmed. He grabbed the Justice's arms, tied his hands behind his back. Others bound the physician's hands.

"Confine the Justice to his apartments. We can do no more until we reach the King. Throw Dr. Thorn into the dungeons, along with the rest of the Justice's personal retinue," she commanded.

"My lady," the captain said. "Thorn is a mage. How can we be sure he won't use magic to escape?"

Constance rubbed her aching head. The world felt distant, faded—her thoughts jumbled. She wasn't strong enough to reinforce the physician's prison with spells, not yet. "In Thorn's supplies, you should find sleeping draughts," she said. "Administer them as necessary to keep him unconscious."

Captain Trudan nodded.

"Once I am confirmed as Duchess, we will try the Lord Justice and Thorn for their crimes," she declared.

Gazing around the courtyard, she counted twenty or more bodies—several of the city guard, two or three of Xander's men, the rest belonging to the Justice. "So much death, Lord Justice, and for no cause," she said, as the captain's men led him past her. "I hope you're happy now."

He stopped, met her eyes with a burning gaze. "This isn't over, mage." His voice was calm and low. He didn't look or sound like a beaten man.

"It is for you," she said, drawing herself up tall. In spite of her words, the hatred and determination on the Justice's face sent a chill down her spine. She was relieved when guards surrounded the older man and shielded her from his eyes.

Constance turned to Trudan, who remained at her side as the Justice was marched away. "Double the guard on his rooms, Captain. We can't let him slip free."

The captain bowed his assent and followed the others.

Winton stepped up to Constance uncertainly, and she squeezed his shoulder. *Another person to whom I will have to explain myself*, she thought, exhaustion washing over her. "I am so sorry, Brother. And so grateful for your faith in me. We will speak whenever you are ready."

To her relief, he shook his head. "I . . . need to rest."

"Of course. I will call on you later," she promised, as he limped off to his rooms. He stopped next to the huge white hound, which was starting to come around, and Constance watched as he coaxed it to its feet. "What are you doing? That animal is vicious. It should be put to death," she said.

"He's just been mistreated," Winton said, running a hand along the scars on the dog's flank. "You'll see."

He is too good for this world, she thought.

Soon, apart from the Duke's pale body and those who had joined him in death, Constance and Xander stood alone in the bloodstained courtyard.

"Never have I seen such disrespect for the dead," said Xander, his voice as worn and smooth as old silk. "Are you all right? What happened to your head?"

Constance lifted her hand to the scorching wound on her brow. It felt tender, her skin hot and raised. "Dr. Thorn," she said shortly.

"Let me see." He examined it carefully, his face close to hers. "It looks worse than it is," he said. "I don't think all this blood is your own." He wiped his thumb under her eye. "Don't cry."

She blinked. She hadn't realized hot tears were running down her cheeks. She turned away, annoyed at herself, wiping her face on her sleeve.

"You should have stayed back from the fighting," he said.

"I could hardly do that. It was my battle," she said, her voice sharp with hurt. "I'm not some defenseless little girl. Without me, Dr. Thorn might've killed you all."

"I know . . . I just want you to be safe," Xander replied quietly. After a pause, he continued. "It seems churlish to ask you to tell me the whole truth after all this." He pushed his long hair back from his face. "But I still need to know. I have trusted you, Constance. And now you need to trust me."

"We will talk," she said, "and I will set your mind at ease." The salt of her tears was drying on her lips. "We have a lot to do. My father . . ."

Xander placed a hand on her shoulder, his emerald-green eyes softening slightly. "I'll deal with this. You go, rest, have your wound seen to. I'll call on you this afternoon, and you can tell me everything."

Constance sat on the rug in her bedroom. It was noon, but felt later. In fact, it felt like she'd lived a hundred days since last night.

She had bathed, eaten, slept, and changed into a soft, dove-gray gown. She'd found a pair of long cream gloves to hide her metal arm, and wrapped a woolen shawl around her shoulders for warmth. A fire crackled in the hearth. Her hair was unbound, reaching the base of her shoulder blades.

Now there was nothing left to do but cry—and she knew she ought to, here, where she was alone, if she was going to cry at all. She couldn't slip up again, not where anyone could see her. When she had first joined the temple of Mythris, she had cried the day's suppressed tears in bed every night, silently, until her pillow was drenched and she fell asleep breathing through her mouth. But to her frustration, now the tears wouldn't flow. As she gazed blankly into the middle distance, she spied the broken mirror pendant under the bed where she'd thrown it in rage, already gathering dust balls.

She suddenly wished she were back in the temple again, resting her head on Emris's chest, listening to his heartbeat. She wondered where he was, what he was doing.

Someone knocked on the door. She stood up and smoothed down her gown.

Xander waited on the threshold, dressed in clean clothes, his wound stitched and his lower face wrapped in deep green silk. Dark shadows lingered under his eyes.

"I've made arrangements for the Duke's funeral rites," he said as she stepped aside to let him in. "Tomorrow at the break of dawn."

"Of course," Constance murmured. "Come in."

"How are you?" Xander asked, his voice gentle. "Is your wound all right? I can hardly see it."

"It really was just a scratch," she said. She had spelled it closed, the swelling easing at her touch.

As she led him toward the window seat, she felt oddly distanced from herself, as if she were trapped in a nightmare. For all that had happened, she had accomplished so little of what she'd set out to achieve.

"What of my confirmation ceremony?" she asked, as they stood at the window.

"It'll have to be the day after tomorrow. It would be disrespectful to arrange it for the same day as the funeral," said Xander pointedly. He pulled the silken scarves from his face. He looked tired, older—two shallow lines framing his mouth. "It's time you told me the truth, Constance."

She gazed out the window. The storm cloud pressed up against the glass like a cat: she could see nothing else. Xander waited for her to tell her story.

"You were right. I left because I am a mage," she said at

last. "My father was the only one who knew for sure. One day, he found me trying to cast a spell—I'd discovered the instructions among my mother's belongings. He was enraged. It was the only time he hit me." *Except for a few days ago.* She raised a hand to her cheek. "But for all that . . . he still loved me. If I had stayed, he knew the Duchess and the Justice would be my enemies. And so he told me to go to the City of Kings and never return. He told people nothing. He let it be believed that I had simply disappeared, or even that I was dead—he thought I would be safer that way."

For a few moments, Xander was silent. "And why did you return?" he asked softly. He raised his fingers to her right hand, still resting on her cheek, held it in his own. It felt . . . good. Warm and strong.

"The storm cloud is a spell—the Justice is right about that, at least. For all these years, I've been learning about it. And now I've come back—to conquer it. To claim my birthright." She raised her eyes to his. "Xander, this is my home too. I can't let them take it from me."

"How are you going to do it?" He was whispering now— and standing very close. His green eyes searched her own as he drew her hand from her cheek, pulled her into his body.

"Every spell has a heart." Her voice was barely more than a whisper. "If I can just find it . . ."

He nodded, as though he understood, and she rested her cheek against his shoulder. "But, Constance . . . who cast the spell?" His hand was cradling the back of her head, as if it were something precious. She tilted her lips upward.

"My father believed it was Dr. Thorn, under the Justice's instruction."

"It is a twisted game he is playing," Xander murmured. But he wasn't concentrating on the story anymore, his eyes glowing and unfocused. He tilted her head back and rested his forehead against hers, and she felt his breath on her mouth, sweet and warm. But it was she who opened her lips and kissed him.

As if he'd been waiting for the signal, he pulled her closer, her body melding into his warmth. She relaxed. And the kiss warmed her deep inside, her skin burning as she sank into it, her heart beating faster as his arms encircled her waist, tighter and tighter. The kiss was insistent now.

Out of nowhere, Emris's scarred face flashed into her mind, and Constance tensed up. Xander's hands had started to roam across her back, reaching for the fastenings of her dress, but he hesitated as he sensed her discomfort.

"Are you all right?" he murmured into her ear.

You need him, a sharp voice insisted inside her mind.

"I'm fine," she whispered. Constance relaxed into his arms, and he started to kiss her again, slower, deeper. Ever so gently, she lifted his hands away from the fastenings of her dress. Instead, she started to undo his buttons, and his belt, and to lift her skirts, and—at last—to pull him to her bed.

When Constance awoke, daylight had faded and the room was half lit by the burning embers of the fire and the lightning flickering outside. Constance was curled among the tangled bedclothes and cushions, Xander cupped around her body, still fast asleep. She was half-undressed, her clothes loosened and disheveled, but she had kept her secret. The long glove remained tightly fastened over her left arm.

The place where metal met flesh was almost painfully itchy. She felt a flush of shame. She would have hated for him to see her that way. To see the truth of who she had become.

She turned slowly over to face him, touched his lips with her bare right hand. He was especially handsome when he was asleep, his skin honey-dark against her fingertips, his long hair loosed from its bindings. Constance felt a tug in her heart—an old feeling, never entirely buried. She shook her head at her own foolishness.

What would it take for someone to love me truly, the way I am now? Is it possible?

He loves the old Constance, said the hard voice in her mind. *If you want to keep his loyalty, he can never know the truth.*

ELEVEN
Training

Lena felt hands on her shoulders, and she floated upward. The gray forest brightened into a jewellike green—she flinched from the light, comfortable in her small, dim, forgetful world. But the hands shifted to her armpits and jerked her violently, forcing her into brightness.

As air hit her face, she realized she was wet, terribly cold, and choking. Suddenly she was lying flat on the ledge beside the fountain, Emris's face hovering above hers, alive with panic.

"Lena, are you all right?"

He was sopping wet, his dark, tightly curled hair dripping. He looked incredibly young, like a frightened little boy.

She tried to breathe, felt burbling in her lungs, and retched onto the pristine stone floor, coughing up buckets of slimy water. People gathered around to watch, the low murmur of voices filling her ears. Ancestors, her hands ached . . .

She held them before her face. Two faint red marks scored the middle of her palms, a relic of a dream already slipping from her mind. "I'm all right," she managed quietly, between wheezes. *Am I?*

"She's fine," Emris announced. "Please go back to your worship. Go." He repeated himself, his voice firmer, and one by one the curious onlookers shrank reluctantly back to the main temple floor, murmuring among themselves.

"Did it work?" Lena asked, shivering. Water had puddled in her boots, and her ears rang.

He answered her question with another. "What happened?"

Lena opened her mouth to tell the story. "I ..." She hesitated. The memory was falling from her mind like sand through outstretched fingers. "I was back in the forest. Something ... bad was happening. I think I was struggling ... and I was praying ..." She held out her hands, the pain fading now. She glanced up at the hunter statue. Confusion and outrage rushed through her mind. "I think he *shot* me!"

That's not a good sign, she thought, her panic rising. *The god must've known I wasn't a true believer. Maybe I haven't let go of the Ancestors entirely.* She looked at her hands again, feeling torn between her two worlds.

Emris was peering at her curiously. "How ... irregular. I can find out for sure if you don't mind me searching?"

"Searching?" Lena felt close to tears with confusion. "Whatever it takes. I just want to know."

"Okay. Hold still," he said. He held her face in his hands and stared into her eyes. She blinked. His eyes were dark brown, flecked with fiery copper. He searched her face and

210

then abruptly closed his eyes. She felt a tingling sensation in his palms as they rested against her jaw, his thumbs grazing her cheekbones. Warmth flooded her as she tried to look anywhere but at him, her eyes skimming the delicate stone-work vines trailing around the temple pillars. She felt his senses—magical senses, she realized—coursing through her into that place beneath her lungs. She could feel it the same way you can feel someone's breath on your skin. "It's worked," he said after a few moments, frowning. He lifted his hands from her face and the warmth left Lena's body. "I can sense his presence—but Faul's hold over your magic is unusually weak. How do you feel?"

"Cold and wet," Lena said. Emris waited for her to answer the question properly, and she shut her eyes, trying to feel the magic place inside herself. But it was different now, she noted with relief: instead of a sickness or a shimmering sensation, it felt like a little cold fire was burning steadily in her stomach. "Better, I guess."

"That's good." He helped her to her feet, the pair of them dripping as they made their way toward the little door at the back of the temple. "Come on. I could use a hot meal and some dry clothes."

Despite Emris's words of encouragement, his face was set grim as he opened the door and shut it behind them. The grand hallway was empty, but instead of leading Lena up the stairs toward the First Huntsman's study, Emris showed her across to a different door. "I wish it had been more straight-forward, for your sake. The First Huntsman will probably interpret this as further evidence that your magic is Chaos-infected."

"Oh," she muttered, feeling her stomach twist in fear. To her surprise, she found they'd entered the same dingy hall she'd first encountered in the building: the mop and bucket now gathering dust in the corner. "But if the Binding worked, I'm okay, aren't I?"

"Yes, you should be, but we'll have to work on strengthening it." He smiled at her rather unconvincingly. "You'll have to pray at the temple every day, reinforce your connection with Faul."

Lena nodded doubtfully. She'd prayed to a god—and she'd have to do so again and again. Vigo had told her the gods were evil and untrustworthy, playing with the souls of humans, and that only the once human Ancestors could understand people and guide them toward their true destiny. Each time she prayed to Faul would be a betrayal of everything he'd taught her to be. *What if this isn't the right path?* She thought of Lord Chatham, the alternative he had offered.

"And there are a few other things we ought to attempt too," Emris continued as they started up the stairs. "A long time ago, before the gods, there were no laws governing magic, no temples. It is thought that young mages generally gained apprenticeships to experienced mages, learning to control their powers the old way, without the Binding: breathing techniques, meditation, self-reflection . . . and lots and lots of practice. Those techniques are still absolutely essential to training a mage within the temples, and you're going to have to work especially hard at them."

Lena grimaced.

"You're certainly not making things easy for yourself," he said, grinning at her over his shoulder as they reached the top. She could tell he was trying to lighten the mood and make her feel better, but she couldn't bring herself to smile back.

They'd entered the map room, which was empty, though someone had cleaned out the ashes and laid a fresh fire. Lena shrugged off her sopping wet cloak and hung it on the back of a chair beside the small blaze.

"I'll get someone to bring you some lunch," Emris said. "For now, you'd better change. Feel free to use the map room this afternoon—there are lots of interesting scrolls and even some novels in the bookcase beside the window. And you should study the temple diagram too—you'll find it helpful. But please don't venture further afield."

As she wrung out her hair, she caught sight of a large map spread out on a coffee table in front of the fire, trapped beneath a flat pane of glass. She walked over to it.

"I have some business to attend to this afternoon," Emris was saying, "but I'll be back in the morning, and we'll begin your training in earnest."

On the map, a large greenish shape was surrounded by blue and filled in with extraordinary detail. "Valorian Continent" the title declared.

"Ah," Emris said, drawing closer as he noticed what she

was looking at. "I suppose you haven't seen one of these before."

Lena peered closer. Slightly to the east of the continent's central point, she recognized something: a congregation of hills, and a city detailed in the basin between. A seven-towered building, a dome, a pillared facade. "City of Kings," she breathed, noticing the words curled around it to the north.

"That's right." He pointed to the far west of the continent, where a mountain range spilled a forest from its skirts. "And here is Duke's Forest."

Lena's eyes ran over the other details of the map. The distance between Duke's Forest and the city was nothing compared to the distance between the city and the islands to the south of the continent, labeled "The Wishes." Even the wastelands in the northeast looked miles and miles away. *The world is so big. And Duke's Forest . . .* Her eyes flicked back to the circle of dark forest surrounding her home. *It's so small.*

A knock woke Lena. She was fully clothed, lying on top of the bed. She had one hand under her pillow, curled tightly around the stiff silver card from the magician, and the other hand around her butterfly. She loosened her fingers, the sharp edges of both items imprinted on her palms in vivid red. Pins and needles ran up and down her arm as she sat up. The card had lost its sheen and was curved, frayed at the corners.

She'd been dreaming of Duke's Forest, she realized. She remembered lying on a stone tomb in the crypts, the

Ancestors whispering with voices of dust and shadow as they drew closer, closer. She'd been crying, afraid. But when she raised her hands to catch her tears, a pair of glittering gems had fallen into her palms, smooth and heavy.

A cold sweat still clung to her neck, streaks of tears on her cheeks.

Another knock. The light filtering through the window was suspiciously weak and pale. Lena wiped her face.

"Hello?" she called.

Emris opened the door a little awkwardly with an elbow. In one hand, he held a paper bag full of something greasy and sweet-smelling—a pastry?—and a dark, bitter-smelling mug of coffee. In his other hand, he carried a different set of gray clothes, neatly folded.

"Sleep well?" He set the mug and paper bag down on the chest.

She flexed her fingers, wincing. "Not really."

"Tough. Your training starts today. Eat, drink, and get dressed. I'll be waiting in the map room." Unlike Lena, he looked entirely the opposite of disheveled—his regular uniform neatly pressed. *Sheveled*, Lena thought blearily.

She set aside the coffee, which tasted like poison, but ate the sweet roll in two big bites, finding herself ravenously hungry. Afterward, she stripped off her gray robes and pulled on the new clothes, which consisted of baggy trews and a long-sleeved tunic. The tunic was of rough-spun cotton, a huge sickle moon emblazoned in white on the front. She tied back her shoulder-length black hair with one of her bootlaces.

When she stepped out, Emris set down his newspaper and led Lena through the maze of corridors—passing hardly anyone at this early hour—to a large, plain room in a different part of the temple. "A practice room," he said. The floor was sprung wood, the windows very high up, and the walls cracked and punched, as if someone had been at them with a hammer.

"Today we're going to try some basic attacks," he said. "Practicing this kind of thing should give you a better hold over your powers."

"Attacks?" Lena raised an eyebrow. "You're already teaching me to fight?"

"It'll be on your test. Plus, it's a good place to start—simple, for the most part. Like pulling a punch." He was digging around in a cupboard in the corner. "Some people are better at it than others, but everyone is taught the basics. Other stuff is . . . well, a bit trickier." He chucked a few heavy punching bags from the cupboard onto the floor. "You've seen the godspeed charm, when I made the carriage fly—how complicated and delicate it is. That kind of control takes years to master fully. This . . . this is just aim and fire." He grinned at her. "Think you can manage that?"

He ran her through some breathing exercises and hoisted the bags on a couple of pulleys supplied for the purpose. She sat cross-legged, breathing deeply and feeling like an idiot. *How is breathing supposed to help, anyway?*

"All right. Ready?"

She stood up. "What do I do?"

"Watch this." Emris stood to one side and held out his hand, his palm facing a punching bag target. "Stand like I am, feet hip-width apart, your front foot at right angles to the heel of your back foot."

Lena tried out the position. "Which foot should be in front?"

"Whichever feels most natural. Here, you're not quite there." With deft hands, he gently shifted her foot, straightened her back, and lowered her shoulders. She suddenly found herself achingly conscious of her body, her hair escaping from its bond, the dark mark on her face. She lowered her eyes as he resumed his own pose—graceful and strong. He stood with his left foot forward; she was facing the opposite direction. For a moment, they locked eyes. Emris smiled. Not for the first time, she glimpsed something—a flash of real warmth—behind his friendliness. "That's good," he said, his voice soft and low. "Hold out your arm like so—but try not to brace. You'll be surprised at the kickback."

"If it works at all," she mumbled.

Emris laughed. "Don't worry so much! No one gets it right on their first try. Now, you need to find that place inside you—the place you feel your magic strongest. You need to reach for it and imagine it traveling out along your arm and toward the target. Imagine it first, and then command it." Almost invisible, a little corkscrew of translucent energy shot from the palm of Emris's left hand and thudded into the punching bag, which swung violently from the ceiling. Lena blinked in surprise. *Can I really do that?*

"Last time I reached for my power, in the temple, it didn't go so well . . . Won't that happen again?"

"This is different. It's more akin to the simple light orb spell . . . or the wisp of vapor spell, in your case." He dropped his arm to his side and stood naturally, rolling his shoulders. "Go on. Give it a try."

She gazed at the second target and tried to imagine something firing out of the palm of her hand. *Go!* she commanded, frowning intently. *Go on, now!*

Nothing.

"It's not working." Besides, her arm was beginning to hurt. She lowered it and rubbed the muscles, flexing her fingers.

"Are you really engaging with your power? Remember the breathing, feeling how the air fills up every part of your body. Remember that sense of awareness. Try again."

She breathed deep, shut her eyes, held out her hand. She did feel something, that burning coldness at the pit of her lungs. She imagined a white spark of light traveling from the place and along her veins, out through the center of her palm. She opened her eyes and gazed at the target. *Now.*

At first, an underwhelming effect: her hand tingled with cold. But suddenly a dart of gray burst out of her hand. Lena staggered backward with the force. The little arrow of mist exploded onto the left side of the punching bag, which rocked nearly as violently as Emris's.

She stared at Emris. "I did it!" she said, flushing with unexpected pleasure.

He nodded, his eyes wide. "Good . . . very good. Now do it again, this time faster, and try to hit the center."

The next time, nothing happened. After that, she hit the target twice, but very weakly, the sack barely moving on its rope. She tried again and again, Emris correcting her posture, lifting her arm up straight, reminding her to breathe—which was something Lena found surprisingly difficult to remember. The magical place inside her evolved again. At first, it had felt obvious, a fizzing sick feeling beneath her lungs . . . and then, after the Binding, it had felt like a cold fire crackling in the pit of her stomach. But now, after she'd drawn on it time after time, it grew insubstantial, like vapor. The more tired she became, the harder it was to grasp on to, like trying to clutch at a loose strand of thread.

After half an hour, she felt like the first time had been a fluke; she could barely muster a puff of vapor, let alone force it toward the target. She felt hot and achy, and long strands of flyaway hair stuck to her sweaty cheeks. As a little wisp dissipated barely an inch from the palm of her hand, she stamped in frustration.

"For Ancestors' sake, why can't I do it anymore?" She fumed at her hands, as if they were to blame.

"Let's take a break," Emris suggested calmly. "You're just tired. With practice, drawing on your power for longer will get easier."

They moved to the side of the room, where a bucket, ladle, and a couple of cups offered some refreshment. Lena gulped down her first cup of water and poured a second, hoisting herself onto the table, her legs dangling over the side. "Did you find it this hard—you know, when you were a Rogue?"

Emris glanced across at her, sipping from his cup while he leaned against the battered wall. "Yes, it was difficult for me too. It's always difficult, but especially for Rogues. We've developed our own methods of coping, not all of them healthy, whether we realize it or not. This whole process is *un*learning, as much as it is learning."

A darkness had passed over his scarred face. Lena found herself wondering for the hundredth time what creature had left those silvery scars—but she couldn't bring herself to question him.

Emris spoke again. "You know, I should tell you something . . . because I'm not sure if I've made it clear, and I wish someone had told me when I was starting out."

"What is it?" Lena asked a little warily.

He cleared his throat. "Even when you gain control of your powers, even when you can prove it . . . because you're a Rogue, they'll never really trust you." He sounded bitter. "How can you ever really trust someone who lived so long with Chaos? I mean, it's more than that. Up until fifty-odd years ago, there was no distinction at all between Rogue and Radical. Some people still think it should be that way." He sipped his water. "I just think you should know . . . it's not going to be easy."

"The First Huntsman mentioned this too," she said.

Emris smiled slightly. "But he doesn't understand what it's like. Not really."

Lena nodded. Although the information itself was no surprise, it felt different hearing it from Emris. "You're the Third Huntsman though. Isn't that a position of trust? I thought it meant you were third in command?"

Emris shook his head. "It's not quite like that. Like many of the other temples, Faul's is a meritocracy up to a point—I'm the third most powerful huntsman in the temple. But even if one day I'm the most powerful mage in the temple, I'll never be allowed to make decisions. I know that now—although I didn't in the beginning. For years I aspired to a position of leadership. But it's never going to happen."

Lena sat silently, the sweat cooling under her clothes. Unlike Emris, she hadn't imagined herself staying here. She hadn't really imagined her future at all—not since Vigo's version of it was laid to rest forever. But now she had to start imagining it, didn't she? She looked across at Emris. She longed to be accepted for who she was, to find her place in the world—but it didn't seem like that's what he had found in the temple at all.

Maybe I won't find it here either. Lord Chatham's card flickered in her mind.

She shook the image from her head. She was growing to like Emris, and now that he'd told her something difficult, something true, she was even starting to trust him a little. If he said she should be afraid of Chatham, perhaps he was right. Besides, she couldn't shake off the memory of how the man had looked at her *before* he'd known she was a Rogue, the mingled disgust and dismissal in his eyes, so familiar from her life in Duke's Forest. "Where were you before you came here?" she asked, changing the subject. "The First Huntsman said you were old for a Rogue. He said it was impressive you were still in control of your powers."

Emris nodded. "I lived in the north—the wastelands. I was an outlaw by the time my magic surfaced—like my father. I never knew my mother. I had to use my magic to survive, especially when my father was captured by the authorities. I spent years fending for myself, until the temples followed the rumors of a Rogue in the wastelands and captured me too."

"I'm so sorry," said Lena softly.

"Sometimes I think it was necessity that kept Chaos at bay, for me," Emris continued. "I had no choice but to control it, in order to survive. And so I did, even though I felt its call and sometimes longed for its oblivion. Pure will is a powerful thing, Lena. You should take comfort from that—you've got a lot of will too." He glanced at her, and she felt the conversation shift—as it always seemed to—away from Emris and back to her. "I think you're going to be fine, Lena."

She forced a smile, feeling uncertain. "How many Rogues are there exactly?" she asked, gulping again at her water.

"Among the five thousand or so mages currently in the city's temple system, only forty of us arrived as Rogues. The rest were whisked off to the Binding at the first glimmer of magic."

Lena nodded slowly. Forty. It wasn't many in the grand scheme of things—half as many as the cryptlings she'd grown up with in Duke's Forest—but it was something. She liked the feeling that there were other people in this city like her and Emris. She liked feeling that she was a tiny bit closer to normal. Cryptlings had been banished, hidden, controlled. To be merely mistrusted, she thought, was something of a luxury. *But is that enough?*

"Constance . . . she was a Rogue too," Emris said quietly. "The first in centuries to arrive here from Duke's Forest."

"Did you . . . know her?" Lena pressed. "I mean, before she committed . . . her crime?"

"Necromancy," he whispered. "She was a necromancer. And, yes, I knew her."

"What's necromancy?"

"The Chaotic magical arts associated with death."

She frowned and was about to ask for more explanation when a pained expression flashed over his face, quickly smothered. "Finding out what she was truly study-ing . . . well, it changed everything," he continued. "The thing is, Lena, Constance and I . . . we were close. Friends, at first, and then something more."

She hesitated, feeling awkward at the revelation, blood rushing to her face. She couldn't imagine what it might be like to be close to anyone in that way. Vigo had been married, had even had a child, but he'd been a qualified mortician. Cryptlings weren't allowed to touch anyone, let alone marry—and it took years to qualify as a mortician, if you were lucky enough to be as clever and skilled as you had to be in order to pass the tests. Lena had never considered a relationship to be a part of her future. *But we're not talking about me,* she reminded herself. "I'm sorry," she said a little stiffly, after a silence. "It must've been awful when she did what she did." Emris didn't seem to notice her awkwardness.

He shook his head sadly. "It *was* awful. I always knew she was different. I think part of the reason we were drawn together was that we understood what it was to be set apart . . . mistrusted." He paused, sighed. "But it turns out she was more different than I could have guessed. In fact, I didn't know her at all." He turned to Lena, his face a touch lighter, as if the confession had lifted a weight from his mind. "Come on. Let's try again."

TWELVE
Last Rites

Gong.

A low bass note thrummed in the center of Constance's chest. She turned in her sleep, her brow twitching. Nightmares trembled under her eyelids.

Gong.

A storm cloud. A rumble of thunder and a surge of blue-hot pain. Nausea. The touch of burning metal against the skin of her arm. She tried to scream, a whimper escaping her lips.

Gong.

Her father's broken body pooling blood. *Father.* The thought jerked her awake and she sat up abruptly. She was alone in the bed, the sheets beside her cold—and suddenly Constance felt cold too. Xander had gone. The whole thing felt like a strange dream.

Gong.

And then she remembered: The bell of the dead. Her father's Descent. She was late.

She scrambled out of bed, felt a flash of anger that no one

had woken her sooner—that she hadn't woken by herself. It wasn't like her to sleep late.

She threw on clean clothes and a fur-lined gray cloak and stared at herself in the mirror. *A mess.* Darkness shadowed her eyes as she pulled her hair into a severe bun and splashed yesterday's water on her face. No mask today. It wouldn't be respectful.

Constance took her cane and walked quickly downstairs and into the courtyard. Already a crowd spilled into the great hall. Everyone had dressed in their finest, the colors somber but the fabrics rich and strangely luxurious against their ashen faces and downcast eyes.

Xander caught her near the door, resting a hand softly on her right arm. "I was worried about you. I thought I was doing you a favor by letting you sleep, but . . ."

"It's all right," she said, suppressing her annoyance and forcing a smile. "I'm here, aren't I?"

He squeezed her arm.

"You'd better leave me before people start talking," Constance added. Xander's face grew respectful. He nodded at her and took his place among the other Wise Men.

The crowd parted for her, murmuring, as she entered the hall. She nodded as she passed, trying to appear stately and unhurried, as if she shouldn't have been the first inside.

She approached the platform that had been set up in the center of the hall, in front of the large trapdoors, whispers gradually falling to silence. Her father had been dressed in the black robes of the dead, his limbs straightened out, the mess cleaned from his face. The wound on his head had been bound in black bandages. Constance drew closer, remembered the pool of blood soaking into her boots, shivered. The Duke's face was as pale as marble, his cheekbones prominent, his brows furrowed, and his mouth set in a hard line. His eyes had been replaced by glittering sapphires and were fixed on the ceiling far above. He didn't look like himself at all. He didn't even look at peace. He looked enraged.

Winton stood vigil on the other side of the platform, dressed in dark purple: composed, silent, and very pale. He shot her a wavering smile, and she noticed his fingers were trembling. She felt a stab of guilt as she remembered promising to visit him. Xander's visit had . . . distracted her. All around the hall's periphery, the city guard watched, short cloaks shifting in the subtle breeze from the open door. Weapons were forbidden at sacred ceremonies, and their belts looked curiously naked. Cryptlings in cowled gray habits waited at the entrance to the crypts, kneeling, their heads lowered.

The ceremony began, the mourners touching their heads, lips, and hearts in the old sign of reverence as they started to pray. The words sounded distantly familiar, but Constance remained silent and still. She was pledged to another kind of divinity. She followed, however, as the bearers lifted the Duke's broken body on its plain wooden plank and carried him to the trapdoors. As the doors opened, the stale, cold air that had grown so familiar in the past five days rushed into her face. She looked at Winton. His eyes were brimming with tears as he faced the dark steps downward.

Below, the chamber was deep and cavernous, each duke's resting place surrounded by gorgeously decorated screens, each wife and child laid out upon a sarcophagus. This was different somehow from the underworld she'd visited after the feast, alone and by the light of her magic—everything felt more alive now in the yellow torchlight. The warm flames danced over grimy statues, old clothing, elaborate carvings, and the rich and rotting carpets adorning the walls, blooming with color—the opposite of the monochrome world she'd entered by pale mage-light. The shadows leaped and multiplied, as if for every living soul at her father's funeral there were another ten of the dead. The people of the castle shuffled into the wide chamber, each finding a place to kneel.

Constance knelt at the front of the procession, the cold floor hard against her knees, and watched with detachment as the cryptlings carried the Duke toward the long tomb reserved for him since birth. The family motto was prominently displayed across the arched screen: *Without its roots the forest withers.* The tree sigil on the screen doors was inlaid with gold leaf—and as the doors were opened, the metal glinted in the firelight. Within, her father's last resting place: a bed of stone. The cryptlings laid him down with extreme gentleness, as if they were afraid to wake him.

On either side of the tomb, the Duke's two wives—her own mother and Winton's—lay in state, their bodies illuminated by the torches. As the old prayers wafted through the air, the incense burning to a thick and dizzying smoke, Constance felt her eyes drawn to her mother's grave again; they flickered over her angular form. She'd been born in a land of sunlight and warmth, her family's palazzo in Scarossa, a great island city at the southernmost point of Valorian, its lands stuttering into aquamarine. She remembered her mother dimly, remembered the brightly colored pictures, like jewels, in the atlas she'd kept in the secret place beneath her window. Remembered the other secret books she'd found after her mother's death, the magical and the foreign, the glittering and the gorgeous. Had her mother truly wanted to spend eternity here in the dark and cold, among strangers?

Constance knew she had not.

Eventually, the cryptlings started to administer the last rites. The hush grew deeper as the black-robed mortician handed one of the younger cryptlings the holy oil. Everyone was remembering the Duchess's funeral, Constance knew—including the cryptling. The poor boy's hands were trembling. She glanced at her brother—his hands were clenched, his breathing short and fast. She rested her hand on his shoulder, squeezing gently in reassurance as the cryptling touched the oil hesitantly to their father's forehead, lips, and heart.

Nothing happened. *Of course. That girl was probably the only mage to be born in Duke's Forest since I was.*

Tension drained from the tomb, the cryptling visibly

relieved as he stepped away respectfully, handing the oil to the mortician, who set it aside and helped him shut the beautiful carved doors of the tomb forever.

The ceremony had ended—the golden tree whole and guarding the entrance to her father's final place of rest. Constance knew she had to be the last to leave, even though she felt like running away. As the crypt emptied out, only one figure remained with her by the tomb: Winton, kneeling to her left.

Her knees were aching. She stood up—and Winton touched his forehead, lips, and heart one last time, rising to his feet.

"Come," she said, "let's talk. You've waited long enough."

Together, they walked up out of the tomb, through the great hall and into the courtyard, leaving their father behind in the dark.

In her chambers, Constance was surprised to find a cat waiting on her bed. It was enormous and ginger, and it had left a dead mouse on the dressing table. Wasn't it the same cat she'd seen that first night in the crypts?

"Whose is that?" Winton asked, hesitating on the threshold.

Constance shrugged. "Looks like I'm his. Cats like magic— he was bound to find me sooner or later. Come in, Winton," she added, when she saw he was waiting to be invited.

Her brother stepped inside and quickly sank into the armchair in front of the fire, which someone had tended in her absence. The flames danced and flickered in the iron grate, casting a warm glow over Winton's face. For a few moments, she leaned on the mantelpiece and watched the flames.

"You must be angry with me," she said, when he didn't speak.

"My mother is dead. My father is dead. Constance, you're all I have left," he said. "I don't care if you're a mage. I don't even care that you lied."

"You . . . don't care?" His words stunned her.

"Of course not." He gazed up at her. "Don't you know how much I love you? I admired you even as a boy. I think I sensed you were different from everyone else, even then. I used to follow you around when I was very small."

"I remember that," she said, a smile quirking her lips. The Duchess had hated it.

"And I think it's because I knew that . . . I'm . . . different as well."

Constance blinked, uncertain of what she was hearing. "You're a mage too?"

"No, I didn't mean that. I mean . . . I'm different." He blushed. "The thing with Lord Irvine is . . . I . . . ah . . . I . . . tried to . . ."

And suddenly Constance understood why Winton had stopped training with the Swordmaster, with no explanation. She understood how Irvine had played along, skirting the subject, a clumsy attempt at sensitivity.

"I've known for a long time," Winton said, his voice low and full of pain. "My mother was eager to marry me to some Duke's Forest girl. I've had to sit through countless dinners and dances and ridiculous formal meetings—even through the Pestilence. It felt so pointless, with so many people dying, but Mother just said that the dynasty was the most important thing in the world. It's our link to the Ancestors, she said, and it's the way we carry their blood to the next generation, and the next . . ."

She had heard the Duchess say so too, glaring at the young Constance as if she were the poison in the bloodline. "But you didn't want to marry a girl."

Winton shook his head sadly. "I liked them, sometimes. It wasn't always a chore. But mostly I felt like the quarry in a strange kind of hunt. Mostly, they would smile at me with their sharp white teeth and I would feel trapped." He took a deep breath. "It was only when Mother got very ill that those meetings stopped. And my feelings for others . . . in particular Lord Irvine . . ." He dropped his head into his hands—his next words muffled and ashamed. "It was a childish adoration. I'm so embarrassed."

Constance stepped closer, rested her right hand gently on his head. "Don't be embarrassed. All of us have childish adorations."

"But not like that . . . not . . . *twisted.*"

"You don't really think it's twisted. That's someone else's words. Who said that to you?"

Winton sighed, raised his head. "I spoke with my mother once, tried to tell her . . . We were talking in general terms."

"Your mother, for all her love for you, wasn't the most . . ."
Enlightened? Well-traveled? Educated? ". . . diplomatic of

women. In the City of Kings, it's accepted. They say the King himself prefers the company of men," she continued. "I think people here are obsessed with having children—because of the Ancestors—in a way that the rest of the world just isn't."

Hope kindled in his eyes before extinguishing. "But I'm trapped here, don't you see? Because of the storm cloud, and the quarantine, I'm trapped here forever. Or until we run out of supplies and just *die*."

She tried not to smile at his melodrama. "Winton, listen to me." She knelt on the rug in front of his chair, pulled his hands from his face. "Now that my secret is out, I can tell you the truth: I am here to deal with the storm cloud. That's why I came back. And once it's gone, you can go anywhere you like."

He looked dumbfounded. "What about the quarantine?"

"The Pestilence comes from the storm cloud, Winton. If I get rid of it, we won't need the quarantine."

She could hear the hope in his voice, even as he continued to argue. "But ... even without the storm cloud ... if I left for good, I'd be betraying the Ancestors. Betraying my mother's memory. And if I don't have any children ..."

"Who said anything about leaving for good, eh? You can visit other places, can't you, as long as you return? And ... and I will have all the children our dynasty needs." It was hard for her to imagine such a thing, but she said it anyway.

"Really?" Winton sniffed.

"Everything's going to be all right, Brother," she said, and she pulled him into her embrace. She owed him this, at least.

THIRTEEN
Chaos

After two days of training, Lena felt different—stronger. The feeling had been rising, as if the magic in her belly had been stoked with fuel. The place she had once struggled to find and draw from grew closer to her fingertips, even when she was tired. Her vapor grew thicker, darker, as if it too was gaining strength.

And yet her old frustrations had been replaced by new ones—which was, she supposed, a sign of progress. Now she was able to hit the punching bag somewhat reliably with her magical attacks—but she wasn't exactly excelling at the simple spells Emris had urged her to practice. The spells were like little poems, matched with rituals, and Lena didn't understand how or why they worked—or why they had to be so fiddly.

"You're really improving," Emris said on the second evening, holding his hand over the steaming bowl of water Lena had heated by magic. She felt a flush of pride at the cold burn of her magic in the pit of her stomach. A couple of days ago, it had felt odd, uncontrollable, disconcerting—but now it was growing familiar . . . even mildly comforting. Like a cool shadow against firelight, it flickered and shifted against the heat of her body.

"You really think so?" she asked.

He nodded. "It's not quite boiling, but it's close. Now let's try the floating spell before we finish for the day—you haven't attempted this one before, so it's a true test of your ability to follow instructions. And if you can master this, you've taken the first step toward successfully creating a godspeed charm."

He led her to the next table along in the practice hall, where he'd set up a bowl of plucked feathers from the kitchen and instructions written in his own cramped, spiky script.

She leaned over the table and read through them carefully.

Place your hand over the feathers. The feathers are the anchor into which you will weave the spell's heart.

Speak: By the power of Faul, I command thee to rise. I command thee to rise. I command thee to rise.

As you speak, weave a light into the feathers in the bowl, and lift.

"Are the incantations really necessary?" Lena asked. "They're all the same. All of them just repeat a command three times."

"They have been shown to help," said Emris. "Maybe it's just psychological—I think it concentrates the mind. But no, they're not all the same. Complicated spell incantations sound like a song and may be written in two other languages. Theodorus, the language of the gods—that's the one used in the godspeed spell, for instance—or, in some older spells, Chaortus." He looked at her expectantly.

"The language of Chaos?" At the mention of a song, Lena remembered the night she'd found the butterfly. She'd thought someone was singing in a foreign language.

Emris was speaking again. "That's right. But for simple spells like this, our common tongue works perfectly well. Ready to try it?"

Lena placed her hand over the bowl of feathers. She focused on her magic, drew it out gently until she felt its cold burn at her fingertips. It was a little like holding a taper to a fire and watching the wick light, and then transferring the flame to a series of lanterns, never letting the light flicker out. It was delicate work. As a cryptling, she had often been tasked with lighting the lanterns in a crypt in preparation for a ceremony. A too-quick movement or an unexpected draft could leave her standing in darkness, the taper smoking into the shadows.

"By the power of Faul, I command thee to rise."

Coldness flooded her, tingling through her arm and into her palm. *Too much.* She tried to pull it back—so the wax of her inner taper wouldn't catch fire.

"I command thee to rise."

She felt a mist flowing out of her hand, surrounding the bowl and the feathers inside. She held her magic close to the feathers, commanding the vapor to weave in and out of their light, almost weightless forms. They shuffled in their bowl.

"I command thee to rise."

A moment's silence—Lena was convinced she had failed—and then the bowl shattered as the whole flock of feathers shot up into the air, exploding into the roof, surrounded by billows of gray cloud. They drifted down slowly, covering Lena and Emris in a ghostly kind of snowfall as the cloud disappeared.

Why can't I control it? she wondered, frowning at her feather-covered robes as panic rose inside her.

"It's all right," Emris said gently, sensing her mood. "That started off well. But you put too much into it."

"I'm going to fail, aren't I? I can't do it." Lena met his brown eyes, her body flooding with fear. "They hate Rogues anyway. If it looks like I can't control my magic, they'll never let me pass."

"You can do it." He put both hands on her shoulders. Feathers drifted in the air around them, lifted by a breeze from somewhere. "I know I've probably scared you by saying how hard it's been for me, arriving here as a Rogue. But you're getting better so quickly—quicker than I ever did. Your test should be more straightforward."

"What happened in yours?" asked Lena, sensing the story behind his words.

His mouth twitched uncomfortably. "The Grand Master was so suspicious of my power, she decided to examine it herself. And examination from a mage of Regis can be . . . well, very painful, as well as dangerous."

Lena frowned. "I don't understand."

"Regis is the god of politics and persuasion, and the most powerful of his disciples can see the future and the past, and sometimes even the truth—even against another mage's will. The Grand Master . . . she is very powerful indeed. And she just looked inside me, I suppose, searching for . . ." The blood had fled from his face, and he shook his head, suddenly deciding not to go on. "I don't want you to think about this, Lena. It's not going to happen to you. She said it was a one-off. She wouldn't do it again, so you don't need to understand it—I'm not sure I do, anyway. Now, come on, let's try again."

But she couldn't help worrying. Her magic was so unpredictable. One moment she felt in control—almost happy to have magic burbling inside her. And the next moment it betrayed her, throwing everything into doubt. It was as if it had a mind of its own.

If the Grand Master could see the truth, she would see that too.

After a late supper in the map room, she and Emris decided on a lantern-lit walk in the temple district, where he tested her on the temples and their disciplines. Lena felt the butterfly's wings as they walked, comforted by the weight of it in her pocket, trying to distract herself from thinking about the test, and the Grand Master, and the strangeness of her magic.

The temples had closed up for the night and the streets were quiet, the paving stones shining wet under the moonlight. The air was damp and cold, promising drizzle, and Lena pulled her padded training coat tight around her body.

"So whose temple is this?" Emris stopped outside an impressive pillared facade with a statue kneeling at the foot of the steps. At first glance, in the half-light of the moon, it could have been a worshipper, a girl of ten or twelve kneeling still, in prayer or adulation, hands outstretched.

"Turah," said Lena. The kneeling girl had a sheaf of grain in one hand and a full pitcher in the other.

"What color are the robes of her initiates? And what magics do they practice?"

Lena knew this one. "The color is ocher. Magics of agriculture, the earth, and—"

Fast-approaching footsteps interrupted her. "Third Huntsman!" a voice cried.

Emris turned—a gray-clad woman was running from the direction of Faul's temple, her robes flying. She was Emris's age, tall, with cropped red hair, tightly curled. "Sir. We've received reports of a Radical in the palace. You're to lead the team."

"The palace?" Emris was already hurrying back toward Faul's temple, where a group of novices was leading horses out of the gates, godspeed charms woven into their bridles. He matched the woman's long, hurried stride. Lena followed at a jog, her heart pounding. "What's happened, Mara?" he asked the woman.

"It's not clear. But they say it's one of the King's magicians, sir. Lord Aster."

Emris's lips were tight. "Is the King safe?"

"He's alive, but nobody is safe," said Mara grimly. "The Radical is holding half the court hostage in the ballroom."

Emris mounted a horse. Lena tried to grab another, but the woman held her arm. "We need these for the hunters," she said sharply. And she glanced up at Emris. "Shall I take your Rogue to her room, sir?"

"Your Rogue." Is that how they all see me? Lena wondered, with a flash of anger. *Some little pet of Emris's?* She wasn't an animal or a curiosity to be owned. "I'm not 'his' Rogue. And there's no way I'm going back to my room!" Lena retorted, shaking off Mara's grasp.

Other huntsmen—perhaps fifteen or twenty—were streaming out of the temple and claiming horses for themselves. Emris met Lena's eyes, a tiny smile on his lips.

"I'm coming whether you like it or not," she said to him determinedly. "If you leave me, I'll just run after you. So you might as well let me."

Mara looked outraged at the idea, but Emris's smile broadened. "I wouldn't dream of stopping you," he said, offering her a hand. "Let's go."

Lena blushed and nodded, her stomach somersaulting in fear and excitement. Once she was safely in the saddle in front of him, Emris wheeled the horse around and kicked it into a gallop. The others followed his lead, and at the edge of the square their hooves found purchase on the air. Lena felt her breath snatched from her lungs as they rose—up, up, and up into the starry night.

As they gained height, the gentle sounds of the city dropped into whispering silence. Emris swerved to the north, the muscles of the horse tensing under his command.

"This will be dangerous," he said into Lena's ear. "I don't want you getting hurt. You need to promise to follow my orders, all right?"

"I promise I'll be safe," she said, sidestepping the question.

"I'm not asking more of you than I'm asking of any of the huntsmen here," Emris said. His voice was serious. "I mean it; you have to follow my orders, no matter whether you agree with them or not. Promise?"

Something in his voice convinced her to agree. "I promise."

The bright jewel of the palace glowed in the darkness, the curiously plain, square bulk set on the northernmost of the seven hills. It rose from the ground to impossible height, its glowing windows like eyes narrowed in suspicion. Seven towers stood sentinel above the battlements, as straight and thin as needles, their pointed roofs shining gold even in the moonlight. The building was surrounded by a steep grass border, and a deep moat encircled it like a glittering necklace.

As they descended, Lena noticed that the wide drawbridge was down and appeared to be deserted. *Odd*, she thought. Even in Duke's Forest, the castle was heavily guarded. "Where are all the guards?"

"They probably rushed inside the palace to help," Emris said, his voice low with foreboding. "Something is very wrong here."

The horse descended farther, its hooves finally hitting the drawbridge with a clatter—the other huntsmen following close behind. At the sound of the hooves, a pair of guards dressed in black-and-white livery emerged from a small room at the side of the gates, their faces grim.

"What's happened?" Emris demanded of the first.

"In the ballroom, huntsman. Lord Aster has taken the King and his guests hostage," the man said, accepting Emris's reins, "along with most of the guards who ran to help at the first sign of trouble. At least one woman is dead."

As Emris questioned the guard for details, Lena wandered a few paces to one side, peering into the wide, white-paved courtyard edged by greenery. Yellow light fell in long strokes through the windows on the left side, glittering chandeliers visible between their frames. And there, in the center of the courtyard, she glimpsed a flash of red. Her skin turned cold, and she peered closer. A woman in a red silken gown lay sprawled facedown on the paving stones, blood pooling around her head.

Lena had seen plenty of dead bodies in her life. Some of them had even been victims of violence or murder. She was not squeamish. But this woman's body was unnaturally twisted, her arms splayed at impossible angles, her legs mangled. Smashed glass surrounded her body in glittering shards. What had done this? A fall from a great height?

Or Chaos?

Why had Lena been so determined to come here? Did she really want to help, or was she drawn by something inside herself? She felt a prickle of fear.

Emris was at her side; he'd noticed the corpse. Lena watched as his eyes darkened. "As I feared, Chaos has grown powerful in this man. We need to hurry," he murmured, as if to himself. He signaled the other hunters over his shoulder. "Lena," he said, turning back to her. "I need you to watch what's happening from the outside."

"From outside?" She needed to see! How could she understand from out here? "But—"

"Remember your promise, Lena. See those bushes outside the ballroom?" He pointed to the green, manicured bushes below the room where the chandeliers were framed by the windows. "Hide there and watch. If things go wrong, take one of the horses and return to the temple. Tell them what happened. Do you understand?" Not waiting for her reply, he entered the courtyard, followed by the other huntsmen, stepping carefully around the body and the blood spreading across the paving stones.

Lena waited a few breaths, then crept into the courtyard herself. A border of soft earth and thorny roses protected the broad windowsills of the ballroom. She edged into the flower bed, felt the sharp thorns scratch her legs as she tried to find purchase on the pillowy earth. Standing on tiptoes, she glimpsed inside.

The room was cavernous. A highly polished marble floor

reflected the candlelight from the chandeliers, hanging relatively low from an enormous ceiling painted with scenes from temple stories. A huddle of frightened people in sumptuous dresses and silken suits stood a little distance from Lena's window. Among the huddled forms, she noticed Lord Chatham. He didn't look frightened like the others. Everyone was watching something at the far end of the room, including the group of black-and-white-clad guards standing uselessly in the grand doorway opposite, swords drawn. On the floor in front of them, one of their number was sprawled in a pool of blood, obviously dead—his body twisted. Lena knew instinctively that he had died in the same way as the woman in the red dress.

She peered further into the room, wondering where Emris had gone . . . Ah yes. The twenty huntsmen were filtering in through another grand set of double doors. They stood in a half-circle formation, facing the far end, where a raised dais housed a throne. On the throne sat a handsome man dressed in green velvet wearing a slim golden circlet upon his head. *The King*. Even from a distance, Lena could tell that his expression was oddly strained, for at his side, his hand resting on the King's shoulder, was the man Lena knew right away must be the Radical. Even so, he didn't *look* very dangerous. He was dressed in silver brocade and was portly, his fair hair wavy and slightly receding.

She lowered herself down—the effort of standing on tiptoes was making her legs wobble—and stepped out of the flower bed. Keeping low, she crept along to another window, closer to the end of the room where the King sat. A drainpipe ran up the side, and Lena lifted herself onto the wide window ledge, angling her body into the shadow.

Yes, this was a better view. From here, she could see how the Radical's eyes had turned a brilliant swirling color, like the rainbows in spilled oil, no distinction between the pupils, irises, and whites of his eyes. He was smiling. She leaned against the window, straining to hear. Emris was speaking to the Radical, stepping forward. She picked up a few words.

"Step away ... can never hope to defeat ... the gods ..."

He was like a different person—no longer her mild-mannered teacher and friend, but formidable, angry, and powerful. In the bright light of the chandeliers, his scars seemed to glow pale against his dark skin—a reminder of everything he had survived, everything he had conquered. Even from a distance, behind a window, Lena could feel the magic rolling from him in waves. She leaned closer, her weight on the cool glass ... and suddenly, with a creak, the casement swung inward, and Lena tumbled into the room.

Her head hit the marble—hard. A loud ringing started instantly in her ears. For a moment, the cold surface beneath her felt like the stone of a tomb, and she was caught in a vivid and confusing dream in which Vigo was firmly telling her to decide what to do with her life, while at the same time removing her heart and putting it into an earthen-ware jar. She heard her heartbeat, loud as a drum, as if he were holding it up to her ears ... but no, that didn't make sense. And with that thought, the world returned abruptly— the fresh pain in her head, shoulder, hip. She laid her palms flat and pushed against the polished floor.

"Hello, little spy." The Radical was in front of her, smiling as she sat up, his black-rainbow eyes swirling.

Behind him, hunters swiftly moved to surround the King, who seemed unharmed, and rushed him to the doors, where the waiting palace guardsmen whisked him away to safety. The huntsmen started to hurry the other guests from the room. Emris was standing on the dais nearby, very still, watching her, and his eyes were alight with rage.

"Oh . . . Ancestors . . . ," Lena breathed, nearly more terrified of Emris than of the Radical.

Nearly.

The Radical wrapped the fingers of one hand around Lena's throat and slowly lifted her to her feet. The pain was almost enough to send her spiraling into blackness—and his strength was uncanny for a portly man. *It's not* his *strength*, she realized. When she was upright, he pressed her against the wall by her throat. "Fancied a peek at Chaos, did you? Curious to see what I was like?"

Lena tried to say something—anything—but she couldn't speak. His hands were greasy and smelled of blood. She met his eyes defiantly. And then, as if in surprise, he released her. She relaxed against the wall and gasped for breath, but the Radical lifted her chin and stared again into her eyes. His eyebrow rose. She found herself transfixed by the swirling colorful pools, her magic stirring inside her, her fingers tingling as if she were about to shoot lightning from the tips. She felt sick. "Why, hello . . . ," the Radical murmured. "Who are you?"

"H-hello," Lena managed. "I'm . . . Lena Grey."

"I was Lord Aster until this evening, but I've made some excellent improvements since then." He smoothed down his coat, which Lena noticed was spattered with dark stains. Blood. Over the Radical's shoulder, she saw confusion passing over Emris's face.

"You're not like those others dressed in gray, are you? You're different. Are you like me?" The Radical sounded playful, and the childlike voice didn't suit him.

"Um—no," said Lena, rubbing her throat, her voice harsh. She risked another glance behind the man. Emris was creeping forward, slowly, slowly. He waved an arm. The other huntsmen spread in a semicircle around the room, blocking the exits. *Keep him talking*, Lena thought, catching on to the plan. "Or . . . I don't think so, anyway."

"Not *yet*, perhaps? Let's have a look at you," he said, and he clapped his hands together. Lena found herself raised up a foot into the air, her stomach turning at the sensation. Her arms spread out—and when she tried to struggle, she found she could not. Invisible bindings, ropelike, tied her in place. She felt like a pinned butterfly, suspended.

She could see the fear on Emris's face—but he didn't even hesitate. He crept closer, and closer.

"Just a girl from the outside," the Radical was saying, peering at Lena from one side, then the other. "A girl with an ugly mark." He prodded her cheek, his overlong fingernail scratching her skin. "But on the inside . . ." He peered into her eyes again, close this time, so close she could smell his breath—alcohol and meat. He pried apart her eyelids, and her eyes stung furiously. She desperately tried to edge her head away but found her neck pinned into place. Her stomach roiled. "The stink of a god," said the Radical, sniffing and releasing her eyelids. "But not as strong as usual. What *are* you?"

"They say I'm a mage," Lena said quietly, blinking, trying to keep her voice conversational. *But I'm not so sure*, she nearly added. Magic rolled off the Radical—overwhelming, heady, like a strong perfume.

"Ha! That's what they tell you, is it? No, you're something else entirely," he whispered now. "The gods cannot truly bind you. Their little tricks cannot tame you." And suddenly, realization flashed in his rainbow-black eyes. "Ha! I know it! You are—"

He cut off abruptly. Lena felt the bindings fall from her body and she crumpled to the floor. "What? I am what?"

She didn't understand at first—but then she saw that the Radical had grown deathly pale. He tumbled to the ground like a felled tree, his head hitting the marble floor with a loud *crack*, and Emris stood behind him, over his body. In his hands, suspended between his palms, he held a glittering ball of dark, iridescent darkness—just like the Radical's eyes—which lit up Emris's face in curious flickers of multicolored light. Lena gazed down at the corpse. Lord

Aster's eyes were ordinary again, ordinary and dull and staring at the ceiling as if in shock.

Holding the ball carefully in his hands, Emris carried it to the center of the room and placed it on the floor. At a silent signal, the huntsmen surrounded it, raised their hands, and spoke as one.

"By the power of Faul, we banish thee, Chaos. By the power of Faul, we bind thee to the void. By the power of Faul, we charge thee never to return."

They repeated the incantation three times, and Lena watched as the ball of energy appeared to struggle, fizzing and popping on the marble floor. At one point during the last incantation, it rose up by a foot, sending sparks flying into the air, a wild light reflecting in the chandelier overhead.

But as the huntsmen spoke, an invisible power resonated through the room, emanating from their hands. The air around them rippled, and waves of gray-white energy pulsed toward the ball. And when they had finished speaking, it was simply swallowed up in a pocket of air. Everything was quiet.

Footsteps rushed toward her. "What the hell did you think you were doing?" Emris said, and, without waiting for a reply, pulled her into a tight, punishing hug. Lena allowed herself to sink into the embrace, warmth rushing to her face.

"I didn't mean to. Besides, I saved the King, didn't I?" Lena managed, feeling close to tears of relief, and Emris squeezed her tighter.

"For gods' sakes, just ... don't do that again," he said quietly, murmuring the words into her hair. "I need to settle a few things before we leave. Wait here for me, all right?"

When he was gone, Lena sank to her knees. She didn't think she could move, even if she'd wanted to. For a few moments, she simply stared at the body of Lord Aster, wondering if this was what her future held. Around her, the place grew alive with sounds of relief and activity—sobbing ladies escorted out to the hallway, huntsmen performing searches of the surrounding area, guardsmen retrieving the body in the center of the ballroom and the dead lady in the courtyard. Eventually, Lord Aster himself was raised onto a stretcher and removed.

"You dropped something," said a familiar voice. She turned to find Lord Chatham kneeling on the floor at her side, lifting the small brass butterfly in his perfectly manicured hands. Panic gripped her, flooding her with sudden energy. *It must've slid out of my pocket when I fell.*

"Give it back," she said unthinking, reaching out.

Chatham stood up, evading her grasp. "Your manners, Rogue, are quite appalling."

She scrambled to her feet, her head spinning. "Give it back, *please*," she said through gritted teeth.

Lord Chatham's eyes were glittering with mingled amusement and curiosity. "Of course; all in good time." He examined the butterfly closely. "How intriguing ... As I suspected ... How did you come by my little creature, Rogue?"

So he did *create it*, Lena thought. "My name isn't Rogue. It's Lena Grey. And that's none of your business." She held out her hand, palm upward. "Give it back."

A self-satisfied smile curled his lips. "You stole it, didn't you?"

She flushed. "I *found* it," she protested.

"Be that as it may, *Lena Grey*, aren't you curious to know what it really is?" He held the butterfly up to the light.

Lena glanced around nervously, but everyone else in the room was busy—including Emris, whose back was turned as he consulted with one of the guards. "Of course—but just . . . just give it back first!" she hissed, trying not to attract attention.

Chatham's eyebrow rose. "Oh, you've been keeping it a secret! How delicious." He smiled, predatory as a cat. "I could tell you a few things that might surprise you . . ." He met Lena's eyes, smiling wider at the curiosity she knew she was betraying. But then he shrugged. "No matter." He dropped the butterfly into her waiting hand. "If you do decide you want answers, you already have my card."

He walked away as Emris started to approach from the other end of the room. Lena closed her fingers around the butterfly, relieved to feel the filigree of its wings against her skin as she slipped it back into her pocket with a sigh. She couldn't help it: She *was* curious. She *did* want to know how the butterfly had come to be in the crypts. It had always felt important to Lena, something that she was destined to find—her own tiny, beautiful thing in the dark, monotonous world of Duke's Forest. Of course she wanted to know what it really meant.

"What was all that about?" Emris watched Chatham's retreating back suspiciously.

"Nothing," she said, grasping for an excuse. "He was just trying to get me to visit him again—but I said no." She was surprised at the steadiness of her voice.

Emris met her eyes for a long moment, then nodded. "That was wise. He's so keen to be friendly with you that you have to wonder exactly what it is he wants in return." He met her eyes again, and Lena could tell she hadn't quite convinced him with her lie. "Remember, people like Lord Chatham don't give anything for free."

Lena felt fear and guilt and relief battling inside her but brushed the feelings aside.

"Let's go," he said, his voice gentler. "I don't know about you, but I feel like it's been a very long night."

The journey home by horseback over the city and under the stars, Emris's arms encircling her, left Lena smiling and warm inside. She tried to bury her guilt about lying to him under that feeling, and—just for now—she was too tired to dwell on it anyway. Other riders surrounded them like a flock of gray birds, cloaks flying in the thin, cold wind. She watched the dark parkland roll away beneath the horses' hooves, and ahead the glistening fountain and the busy night market around the Holy Council glowed like an enormous gemstone. The river sparkled in the moonlight, and beyond, in the commercial district, the sounds of a raucous party floated into the quiet sky.

"What happened in there?" Lena asked quietly, as they started to descend toward Faul's temple. "How did that man become a Radical? He was independently licensed, wasn't he—but what does that really involve?"

"Yes, he was licensed—like Lord Chatham and eleven others," Emris said grimly. "Chatham has devised a number of tests, similar to those you will perform for the Holy Council, to prove a Rogue has control over their power. He then issues a certificate authorized by the King. That's it—and they think that is enough." The scorn in his voice was palpable. "They tell the world they are safe—and, to give them the benefit of the doubt, perhaps they even think they are safe. But without a god's control, their power is drawn from Chaos, and given long enough, I believe it will overwhelm each and every one of them."

Lena paused, thinking about the creature who had been looking out from behind Lord Aster's eyes. "Why was Chaos so interested in me?"

Emris sighed, as if he'd feared the question. "Chaos noticed something special about you, Lena—just like the rest of us did. You don't need to read more into it than that. Chaos is a trickster. Notice how Aster simply abandoned the King when a new distraction arrived for his attention? Chaos isn't rational, or even particularly smart. It's just immensely powerful."

Special. Not different—*special.* Lena felt her heart glow. "That ball of magic . . . ," she started, not sure how to finish.

"That was the physical manifestation of Chaos—of pure, unadulterated magic. Like a parasite, it grows inside the host, invisible, before taking it over entirely. Nothing was left of Lord Aster—he was a vehicle, no more."

"How long had it been growing inside him? Would he have known?"

Emris turned his horse toward the broad Sacristi; she felt the movement of his arms where she rested her shoulders against his body. "Who knows? But he had been an independently licensed magician for over fifteen years. They all said he was safe." Emris shook his head. "Two people died today to prove it wrong. Thank Faul it wasn't worse."

A chill ran through Lena's body. Vigo had always told her that magic was an evil, unpredictable power—and in a way, he'd been right. She shook the thought from her mind, disturbed at the idea that Chaos could overwhelm her without her even realizing. "Perhaps this will change the law," she suggested.

"Perhaps. But somehow I doubt it. There are too many vested interests in the system."

"But if the King—"

"The King's interests included. Remember? The King himself commissions magical items from his magicians, as if they were no more than a collection of merchants."

The ground was flying upward rapidly, the gray cobblestones silvery in the moonlight, and hooves hit stone, galloping for a few moments before clattering to a stop at the temple entrance.

As they dismounted, Emris said, "I'll have to report to the First Huntsman—and you should see the healer. You'll find one on duty in the office by the training rooms. Meet me in the map room afterward? I could use a nightcap." He smiled, and Lena felt warm inside all over again.

In the map room—empty, as always—Lena sank into her favorite chair in front of the fire and sipped on a goblet of wine. The blue-clad healer had sealed the small wound on her head and prescribed a draught of restorative medicine in a cup of wine and a good night's sleep.

Now, in spite of everything, Lena felt safe, peaceful, and warm. And yet . . . she played over the Radical's words. She wasn't a Radical, he'd said, but she wasn't a mage either. Despite Emris's reassurances, she couldn't help thinking the Radical had been about to tell her something important before he was silenced forever.

And then there was Lord Chatham, promising answers about her butterfly. Would he be able to guess what the Radical had been about to say? Perhaps there was something in her that the temples would never quite understand. *Chaos?* Despite the routine she'd fallen into, and her comfortable friendship with Emris, she still felt uneasy every time she stepped into Faul's temple—as if the god were watching her suspiciously, rather than watching over her as he was supposed to do. *What are the gods, anyway?* she wondered. *How can they be so different from Chaos? They're beings of magic too, aren't they?*

And still the Ancestors waited in her nightmares, always on the edge of her consciousness. Angry. Vengeful at her betrayal.

At that thought, she set down her goblet and tipped in the small vial of medicine. When she sipped again, the wine tasted sour, so she threw her head back and swallowed it in two big gulps. Then she rested her head against the wing of the chair and closed her eyes. The next thing she knew, Emris was gently shaking her awake.

"Come on, let's get you to bed," he said softly.

"Oh . . . I didn't realize . . ." She stood up, feeling foolish and bleary as he led her toward the guest room door. Her neck ached where it had rested to one side against the wing of the chair.

"I have some news for you, Lena," he said, stopping on the threshold. "The Council has decided about your test. It's the day after tomorrow."

"The day after tomorrow?" She was abruptly wide-awake. "But . . . that's really soon. I've only been training for a few days!"

"Relax. You've made good progress on simple manifestations and combat. And we'll focus on your spells tomorrow—I'm free all morning. And in the afternoon you can practice on your own." He reached out to her, squeezed her shoulder. "I ought to be angry with you about today. You shouldn't have climbed up onto that windowsill, let alone leaned against the glass!" He smiled, the affection clear on his face. "But for some reason I just want to help you. I can't resist it."

"Thank you," Lena said, uncomfortably but not unpleasantly aware of how close he was standing, the weight of his hand on her shoulder. She felt a twinge of guilt at the way her thoughts had been tending—toward Lord Chatham, and Chaos, and the butterfly, and away from everything Emris told her was good and necessary. "You've done a lot for me," she added. "I'm grateful. I really am. I'd be lost here without you."

He smiled, and she found herself wishing she could trace the lines of his scars with her fingers. His voice was husky when he spoke next. "I'll see you in the morning, Lena. Get some sleep."

But even as she lay in bed, Lena still felt wide-awake, feelings and thoughts spinning around in her mind like Hunter chasing mice. And she knew, with sudden clarity, what she had to do.

FOURTEEN
The Dead

Constance followed Captain Trudan down the uneven, slimy steps to the dungeons, where the physician was locked in one of the cells destined for traitors, the lowest of criminals. Unlike the sparse but habitable cellars Constance knew were reserved for the cryptlings and morticians, the dungeons were cold, dark, and damp—the ceiling was distant, the windows at ground level shedding ghostly evening light as if from another world. The straw clearly hadn't been changed in several years, and rats crawled freely among the old rags and refuse. Constance held a scented handkerchief to her nose.

"We've stationed three guards," Captain Trudan said, offering her a hand down the last two steps of the staircase, which were particularly steep, "but I don't know what he's capable of. He's been drugged for much of the time, as commanded. But if we continue for much longer, his life—"

"I understand," she snapped, cutting him short. *His life might be in danger.* If he died, he'd never stand trial for his crimes. She didn't care: this man had killed her father; in her eyes he was already condemned. But she had to *appear* to care.

The captain kindled another lamp, leaving his own on a hook beside the staircase. She had tucked her cane under her arm, unlit. "If I could have asked someone else, I would have, my lady." His broad, stubbled face was concerned in the flickering firelight. "It seems wrong to ask you, so soon after the Duke's Descent."

As if I need shielding from unpleasantness, like some delicate flower. "I am sure I shall manage, Captain," she said a little sharply. "Lead the way."

The smell of damp and rotting flesh assaulted Constance's nose even more strongly as they walked down the corridor. A few other prisoners raised their heads at the light—the black-clad men of the Justice's personal guard, their faces twisted in hatred as they caught sight of the visitor. Captain Trudan held his lantern high, examining the upturned faces, until they found the cell at the very end—the darkest and filthiest—which contained the physician. Dr. Thorn was indistinguishable at first. His shirt, like the others', was torn and bloodstained, and a ragged woolen blanket was wrapped tightly around his shoulders against the cold. But unlike the rest, he had buried his head in his arms and did not raise it for the visitors.

"You can leave me now, Captain. I'll follow you out once the spell is finished." Constance didn't care to be watched while she practiced magic: it was something she had always preferred to do in solitude. *Do not reveal your craft if you can avoid it*, the masked priestesses had taught. *It is your greatest weapon—hold it close, and keep your strength a secret. It is an advantage to be underestimated.*

The captain hung his lantern on the hook next to the cell. "Are you sure, my—"

"Captain, please. What do you expect to happen? All these wicked men are behind strong iron bars. Now, let me do my work."

"My lady," the captain demurred, bowing, "I'll wait in the guard room upstairs." And he left her in the gloom of the flickering lamp.

Dr. Thorn was still leaning against the wall, silent, and Constance had no wish to acknowledge his existence. She laid her hands on the metal of the gate. Magic flowed through her blood and out through her fingertips in threads of shining purple—a process so natural to her now that she hardly noticed the motions. She whispered the words, wove a spell partly learned and partly of her own invention, knotted and complex, to guard the metal against a magical attack. Once she had threaded it into the bars, she removed her hands and the purple light glowed white before extinguishing.

"Very good," said Dr. Thorn, looking up at her. "I couldn't have done it more gracefully myself."

Constance shot him a dark glance. "I don't want your approval, traitor."

"I hate the Justice too, you know," he said as she turned to leave.

She hesitated. Rage sparked in her belly as she spun to

260

face the physician. "You hate the Justice? So why torment and kill my father at his command?"

"I will tell you if you permit me."

The calmness of his voice wore down her anger. Constance had to admit she was curious. She stepped closer to the bars.

"This had better be good," she whispered.

"It started when I was a soldier in the King's army, training as a military physician. I was young and foolish, and one night I killed a fellow soldier in a drunken brawl. The punishment for such a crime can be as severe as death, at the discretion of the commanding officer." He paused, as if gathering the strength to continue.

Constance sighed. "How exactly is this related? I don't have all day."

Dr. Thorn ignored the comment. "The man known as the Justice was my commanding officer—I was the only mage assigned to his contingent. He'd already had me whipped viciously for my minor disobediences. He hated mages, and so he hated me. I knew he wouldn't spare my life. Perhaps I should have stayed and faced my fate . . . I almost wish I'd had the courage now. But instead I fled here—to the remotest part of the world I could imagine—and changed my name, my very identity," he said, pausing to swallow. His voice was husky and low. "I did not know the Justice himself was from Duke's Forest."

Constance shrugged—but she was interested, despite herself. "What then?"

"I set up as an apothecary in the lower town, where I stayed hidden for several years. I married a local girl. My business thrived. I thought I had escaped him forever." And then his voice grew even lower, darker. "But a few years ago there was a knock on my door at night. The Justice stood on the doorstep. He told me I would work for him again or he would destroy me." He hesitated, sighing heavily. "I tried to threaten him. I am a mage, after all, and he isn't. But then his men surrounded my house. They didn't make a sound—but I could see them, blades and eyes glinting in the starlight. The Justice told me that I might be strong, but my wife wasn't. I couldn't watch her all the time. He could take her whenever he wanted. Kill her . . . or worse." He swallowed, the noise thick in the silence. "I had to keep her safe."

Constance felt her lip curl. So that was it? He was a fool if he'd expected her to be moved by his tale of woe. "Why should I believe a word you say? Even if it is true, I will not release you. You made your choice. You helped *him* destroy my father. You fought against me in the courtyard. You had choices, and you made the wrong ones."

The doctor seemed about to argue, but then something else, some determination, flitted over his face. "I don't want to defend myself. I'm just trying to warn you. The Justice may not be a mage, but he has tricks of his own. Not just his informants throughout the city, but other things . . . During his army days, he would sometimes take delivery of certain . . . devices."

Constance blinked. "What do you mean?"

"I don't know exactly," Dr. Thorn said, the frustration evident in his voice. "He wouldn't let anyone see them. But I'm sure they were weapons. Weapons powered by magic, but which ordinary people are able to use." He shook his head. "He hated magic. And yet he desired its power. Perhaps his hatred was born of envy."

But Constance was only half listening now. *Devices . . . magical weapons . . . This stinks of Lord Chatham.* If the Justice was capable of turning a mage to his purpose, despite his hatred of magic, it was also entirely possible that he had been involved in testing some of Chatham's more controversial inventions. And that meant it was possible he had commissioned or acquired one of his own prior to his appointment in Duke's Forest.

"You think he is using one of these devices now?" Constance asked.

"Using it or planning to," Thorn replied. "I cannot tell."

"And you have no idea what this device might be?"

Dr. Thorn shook his head again. "No. I just wanted to warn you. He might not be as devoid of magic as he appears." He shut his eyes, as if suddenly overcome by tiredness. "Now that it's all over," he whispered, "I mean to do everything I can to bring the Justice down with me."

Constance stared at him for a few moments. "I'll see what I can do," she said coldly.

★　★　★

The castle was dark and quiet, and Constance was curled in her covers, sleep clinging to the corners of her mind: Dreams of her father, of the funeral, of forgotten corridors below the earth that drifted into lost halls of stone. Dreams of a spell's heart somewhere, hidden in the depths.

The fire in her grate had faded to cold ashes.

Slowly she started to awaken, although she'd barely slept. Her mother's book lay on her pillow, the pages ruffled and stuck to her cheek. She'd been searching for clues.

Her eyelids flickered, then snapped open. Had she dropped off again for a moment?

Distantly, she heard a high-pitched wail: the creak of a hinge, perhaps, or an owl's screech . . . But no—the owls had long fled the diseased air of Duke's Forest. Yet again the sound rang into the night, and Constance sat bolt upright in bed. She knew what it was: a scream.

She snapped the book closed and hurried to the window, but it was black as coal outside, the courtyard and battlements obscured by the usual banks of gray cloud. She opened the casement and stood still, listening, shivering in the biting, damp cold. Another shout—a man's this time— broke the silence, and more, and more. Yellow lights danced in the cloud, ghostly and fragile, like fireflies. She stepped into the dress she'd discarded a few hours previously, pulled on her boots, and grabbed her cane. Before she left, she slipped the book into the hidden compartment of the window seat. It was unlikely anyone would search her room, but she couldn't be too careful.

Constance pulled on a warm fur cloak and opened the door in time to hear frantic footsteps approaching up the stairs of the tower, a young city guardsman stopping, breathless, as he caught sight of her. She recognized him, under his peaked helmet, as one of the guards who had first greeted her upon arrival.

"What's wrong? I heard screaming."

"The lower town, my lady," he sputtered, gasping. "Your presence requested."

She shut the door to her apartments and followed the young guard downstairs. He grabbed a lantern from a hook on the doorframe and led her out into the courtyard.

"What's happening?" She slipped the mask from her cloak pocket as they stepped into the storm cloud, fastening it over her face to filter out the effects of the spell.

"It doesn't make sense," said the guard, his light bobbing in the gloom. "The townsfolk are running out of their houses into the streets, terrified. They're ignoring the storm cloud, leaving their eyes unprotected." He shook his head. "They're saying ..."

Constance saw that his face was ashen, green-tinged. She could tell he was as disconcerted by the mask as by his story. "What is it?"

"They're saying it's the Ancestors." He stopped, his voice sinking to a whisper. "They can hear the Ancestors moving below ... knocking on the floors."

So the final stage has begun at last.

The contractions are starting.

The dead are rising.

Constance felt no shock, but heavy resignation settled on her lungs, nearly stopped her breathing. She'd expected this. She'd known the spell was close to maturity. But this was no comfort.

"What's the situation now?" she asked. "What are the townsfolk doing?"

"They're angry—some of the men . . . they overpowered Captain Trudan and another guard on patrol. They tied them up—I ran to the castle as soon as I saw. A big group was heading toward an old public house, the Hanged Thief."

They'd reached the gates. Constance's orders to relieve the pressure on the townsfolk had clearly been too little, too late. Four guards watched over the battlements, mere shadows in the gloom.

"I fear they're going to get violent, my lady. The ale is flowing. Tempers are high."

Constance took a deep breath. "What's your name?" she asked the young guard.

He seemed taken aback by the question. "Aron."

"Aron, we can't waste any time, but we can't alarm the people of the castle either. Let's keep this quiet. Take two further guards from the gate and we'll head to the lower town. We have to speak to these people."

Aron looked uncertain but nodded. "Yes, my lady," he said. He hesitated.

"What is it?"

He cleared his throat. "Should we inform Lord Irvine? I mean, if something goes wrong . . ."

She shook her head. "I am the Protector—and tomorrow I'll be Duchess. I have to deal with this myself. Brief the guards on the battlements. They can pass on the message at dawn if we're not back."

Aron hurried up to the battlements and returned a few minutes later with two older men, both grim-faced, their knee-length green cloaks wrapped tight around their torsos. All three guards slipped on shield-eyes.

"Do you need any, my lady?" Aron offered Constance a pair.

"I'm fine, Aron." She tapped her brass mask.

He nodded uncertainly.

Although the guards carried lanterns, their lights appeared horribly insubstantial against the darkness and the storm. Glancing from one to the other, she realized she had nothing to lose: everyone knew now. Everyone had probably suspected anyway, on some level. She tapped her cane against the cobblestones, a bright purple light springing from its pommel. Apart from squinting at the sudden glare, the guards remained professionally composed.

"Ready?" She smiled slightly beneath her mask. "Let's go." At Constance's nod, the small group set off down the narrow path, deeper into the storm cloud.

The Hanged Thief had been shut and boarded for two years—ever since the quarantine had cut off the majority of its business. But as they arrived, they saw yellow light chinked between the rough planks nailed across the windows, and the sound of raised voices poured onto the road. The sign over the doors was lit up too: a picture of a man with a bulging purse at his belt, golden coins spinning from his pockets, hanging by his neck from a naked tree.

After a moment's hesitation, Constance slipped off her mask, tapped off the light on her cane, and stepped boldly toward the door. It swung wide under her touch, the old hinges protesting. The three green-cloaked guards stood close at her back.

A thick trail of fog slid through the opening like a creature of flesh and blood. Aron quickly shut the door, closing the small group inside, and the cloud dispersed. The room was filled with people—at first, nobody seemed to notice their entrance. Men clustered around the bar and a handful of women and children huddled in the corners, nursing steaming cups and drooping sleepily over the tables.

Constance absorbed the details as she tucked a stray wisp of hair behind her ear: the hushed adult voices, the plaintive children, the wail of a baby, the nightgowns poking out from under women's thick coats and shawls, the dark circles around men's eyes. The thin wrists and hollow cheeks—the brass shield-eyes hanging at every collarbone. The smell of ale overlying the subtle scent of fear.

Captain Trudan and another guard were tied up in chairs at the far end of the room. The captain was either out cold or dead, blood congealing in a wound on his head, his body sagging under the ropes. The other guard was gagged, his eyes wide and angry under his peaked helmet.

Gradually, the men at the bar noticed the new arrivals, their low, urgent voices sinking into silence.

"What's this?" demanded a burly man in his midforties with hands like slabs of beef.

Constance met his eyes. "I've come from the castle," she said, keeping her voice calm. "Will someone tell me what's happened here?"

"Some fine lady from the castle's come to tell us to go home, just like the captain here," the large man interpreted, clenching his fists. "P'raps she wants to join him, eh?"

An older man, gray-haired but straight-backed, laid a hand on his shoulder and stepped in front. "My name's Redwold. I was a scribe here once," he said. "I apologize for my blacksmith friend, but we're all on edge tonight. If you ask me what's going on, I say the Ancestors are angry— angry at us for sitting on our arses while Duke's Forest is destroyed around us. Here's what happened, and let's see if you can explain it any better." He took a few paces forward and looked Constance in the eyes. "We woke to the sound of knocking on our floors—some of the doors to the crypts lifted, as if pushed from below. As if the Ancestors were trying to get out . . . to tell us something, or warn us, or worse."

As the image flashed through her mind, Constance felt her skin crawl, the hair on the back of her neck standing on end.

"And when we tried to run, your captain tried to stop us, told us to be calm." He shook his head. "Be calm! The Ancestors are rising, and they tell us to be calm! So we came here to decide what's to be done. To decide how to take back control." He shot a glance at the two injured guards in the corner, then returned his gaze to Constance. "So who are you, and why are you here?"

"I am Constance Rathbone, Lady Protector and Duchess-in-waiting."

The room erupted into murmurs. "She's a mage," said a woman with a small baby clutched to her breast. "We cannot trust her."

"I heard she killed her father," another voice called.

"She's the one raising the Ancestors from their graves."

"She's planning on burning the Ancestors and forcing us to bow to the gods," said the blacksmith. "That's what they're saying."

A few others rose from their seats, the hostility palpable. Somebody spat at her, the glob of liquid nearly reaching the hem of her gown. From the corner of her eye, Constance spotted Aron's hand creeping to the hilt of his sword. She touched the guard's arm, interrupting the movement.

"I'm sure those are things that people are saying," she said, staring at the glob of spit before raising her eyes. She drew back her shoulders, pulled her spine tall. "But perhaps you'd care for something that's definitely true. Perhaps you'd care to know what I'm going to do about this recent unrest."

Redwold nodded for her to continue.

"The Lord Justice and the physician Jonas Thorn have been placed under arrest on suspicion of conspiracy. Tomorrow is the day of my confirmation, and once I am Duchess, as soon as I am able, I shall open the gates, ride for the City of Kings, and insist our good monarch put the Justice on trial for his crimes against the people of this town."

A stunned silence fell over the room.

"But first, I must end the storm cloud. The forest is not passable as it stands, and we cannot open the city gates until it is. I know how to destroy it. And I know that it's caused these disturbances tonight. I just need a little more time."

"How much time?" said the older man.

She searched the pale, determined faces turned toward her. Dark thoughts encircled her mind.

Finally, she spoke. "I need two days."

A murmur rose around the room. The scribe listened to the talk for a moment, then held up his hand for silence. "I say yes, on three conditions. No curfew. Extra rations from the castle's own stores. And if the storm cloud does not disappear by dawn the day after tomorrow, we shall march on the castle and break open the gates."

The people were silent, grim-faced, and Constance knew without a doubt that they would carry through Redwold's threat. *Two days.* Slowly, she nodded, and met the old man's eyes. "Done."

FIFTEEN
The Magician's Workshop

Busy as the city had been at night, it was even busier during the day, which was bright and cold. The thoroughfare in front of the Holy Council was heaving with people, and market stalls, and carriages, and riders, and wagons piled high with wares. Lena clutched Chatham's card in her hand as she wove through the traffic toward the fountain, and then headed north into the royal district. She'd checked the city plans in the map room before she left, so she knew Chatham's workshop would be somewhere among the grand houses by the park. She looked carefully at the street names painted in black and white on the sides of the corner buildings.

For the hundredth time since sneaking out of the temple, she thought about Emris and how he'd feel if he knew where she was going. She felt terrible about deceiving him. He was busy this afternoon, and Lena had told him she'd spend the time practicing her spells. But she needed to do this, and she knew he wouldn't understand. She *had* to know the truth—besides, it was just a quick visit. And what Emris didn't know wouldn't hurt him.

At last, Princess Boulevard opened up on the left, a wide tree-lined avenue full of tall new buildings with bay-windowed shopfronts and signs with fancy lettering hanging above the doors. The street was relatively busy. Smartly dressed women with cinched-in waists and huge fur scarves pushed baby carriages with elaborate lace coverings. Scores of men dressed in various colors of livery hurried behind them, carrying piles of boxes.

Lena felt distinctly out of place in her gray huntsman's robes, and she attracted a few disapproving glares in a way she hadn't in the temple district. She reached instinctively for her hood but stopped herself. It felt a little bit like she was a cryptling again, walking in the upper town before nightfall—but this was different. She was strong now, probably stronger than anyone else on the street. And she had every right to be here, no matter how odd she appeared among the fine ladies of the royal district. Nobody stopped her as she approached the large bow-fronted shop that was her destination: Lord Chatham's Emporium of Magical and Mechanical Delights.

Lena climbed the five shallow steps to the door. In the window, a plethora of shining mechanical animals labeled with gorgeous gold-ink signs promised everything from help with housework to evening entertainment, from music or comedy to occupying "children, pets, and other nuisances." Every animal was beautifully constructed of various metals—silver, gold, or bronze—and often bejeweled. Some were woven with feathers or even fur as part of their design, others with silk or velvet. She particularly liked the petite golden cat with emerald eyes and a white feather puff on its tail, supposedly for the dusting of library shelves.

It was all rather grander than her little brass butterfly, she thought, suddenly nervous. She realized Lord Chatham might not be in his shop anyway and felt a little relieved at the thought. But she ought to try now that she was here.

Gathering her courage, she pushed the door open, and a discreet bell rang in the luxurious interior. Two women were sitting together at a glass display case, picking out something small and glittery. One of the women—young and pretty, with dark and elaborately styled hair—turned and raised an eyebrow at Lena.

"Are you lost?"

Lena bristled. "No. I'm here to see Lord Chatham."

The eyebrow raised itself higher. "Card?"

"Umm . . ." She patted her pockets.

"If you haven't got a card," she started to say, with a satisfied expression on her face, "I'm afraid . . ."

Lena dug the bedraggled card from the bottom of her pocket, blushing furiously as she handed it to the woman, who examined it briefly, then glanced up at Lena's birthmark with disapproving eyes. She tutted. "Very well, this appears to be legitimate. Name, please? I shall see if he's available."

"Lena Grey," she replied brusquely.

"Do excuse me, Lady Honoria." The shop assistant simpered at the older, plumper lady waiting at the display cabinet. "I shan't be a moment. Why not try the dragonfly for size?" And she disappeared through a large wooden door behind the highly polished counter.

Lena didn't have to wait long. The assistant returned with a different manner. "Miss Grey," she said, "Lord Chatham will see you now for tea in the workshop. This way, please."

Lord Chatham was sitting at a long wooden desk strewn with cogs and springs and other small pieces of shiny metal. He was peering at something in his hands through a silver tube clenched in the socket of one eye and making a small noise of frustration.

The workshop was compact but very tall, and every available wall was lined with shelves from top to bottom. On some of the high shelves there were large books stacked with neat precision . . . or perhaps they were ledgers, Lena thought, for each one was numbered. The shadows crowded around the shelves nearest the top of the high room. The shelves farther down were full of labeled wooden boxes. The labels were embossed metal. She picked out a few: "Springs, size 7D," "Joint, Silver, size 1F," "Misc. Gold." The single window in the room was a stained-glass arch depicting a series of scenes involving a man and bits of machinery, as well as a large gold crown, and it cast ghosts of red, green, and yellow on the carpeted floor. She couldn't see outside at all.

And no one can see in, a quiet part of her added.

The room was functional, but it also contained a small and very pretty fireplace surrounded by tiles decorated with cogs and wheels in gold, bronze, and silver—*It must've been specially designed*, Lena thought, *just like the stained-glass window.* And in front of the fire were two leather armchairs and a small round table with a teapot and a neat pile of books. Suspended over the fire was a kettle, already puffing steam through its spout. On the wide mantelpiece, she spied a set of six cups and saucers and a large strawberry cake.

"Miss Lena Grey, what an honor. I shall be with you forthwith," Chatham said, still staring at the two tiny pieces of silver in his hand, which he appeared to be trying to slot together. "Please take a seat by the fire. I'm just finishing up this bee. The wings are extremely delicate."

Lena sat in one of the chairs. It was more comfortable than it looked—perhaps *too* comfortable. She felt herself sinking into its cushions, even though she was determined to remain upright and businesslike. The kettle started to whistle.

"Would you be a dear and get that? The tea things are all ready—just pour in the water," Chatham said.

She took down two cups and set them on the table, then poured the boiling water into the pot. The action instantly brought Vigo to mind, although the scent of the tea was entirely different. Vigo had favored fennel, mint, and nettle—sharp herbal smells that had always reminded Lena a little unpleasantly of embalming oils—and a rich, spicy aroma rose with the steam from this pot.

At last, while the tea was brewing, Chatham exclaimed, "Bravo! Now, let's test it out . . ." She heard him whisper a brief incantation; a flash of yellow light brightened his desk—and then the golden bee was buzzing over his head. Chatham joined her beside the fire and the bee followed, landing elegantly on the lip of his teacup. Minuscule stripes of black fur banded the bee's tiny body, and in between Lena could spy a strong yellow glow. *Like the glow in the horse's head*, she thought.

"I trust you are fully recovered from last night's ordeal? That was quite a fall."

Lena pulled her attention away from the bee. "I'm fine," she said. Suddenly she felt like a silly little girl. She drew herself up and opened her mouth to demand answers, but Chatham spoke first.

"I'm sure we should all be very grateful to you. It really was the perfect distraction—although your hunter didn't seem too approving. Is that why you're here? You're fed up with taking his orders?"

"No. I'm just curious. You said you had information for me."

Chatham smiled as if he didn't believe her. "Yes, well, I'm glad you finally decided to drop by. It certainly felt as if fate was trying to bring us together." He poured the tea—the bee flitting from the teacup to his shoulder. "So . . . if you don't mind . . . might I have a proper look at your butterfly?"

Nervously, she drew it out from under her clothes—a little embarrassed at how it felt warm from her pocket. She hesitated for a moment, holding it in her hand. *I have to do this if I want to know what it really is*, she told herself. She took a deep breath and passed it to Lord Chatham.

He pulled his small magnifying eyeglass from his top pocket and started to inspect the thin, cylindrical body. He *hmmm*ed.

Lena sipped her tea, but it was far too sweet. Chatham must have added sugar to the pot. She set down the cup and waited. After a few long seconds of silence, she asked, "So . . . *did* you make it?"

"But of course." He appeared to be surprised by the question, glancing up at her. "The question is, who did I make it for? And why is it no longer working? All my inventions are guaranteed for thirty years—longer than I've been operating this business. But we can find out. Here, I marked it with a serial number—027."

Lord Chatham stood up, leaving the butterfly on the table, and walked to one of the walls, the bee buzzing gently over his head. He rolled a ladder along the shelves and climbed to the top, into the shadows, where he slid down a leather-bound tome.

"I mark every creation with a number corresponding to one of my ledgers," he explained, climbing down the ladder. "In here, I record the details of every commission. Rather dull, but sometimes extraordinarily useful—especially when they are from this long ago."

"How long ago?" Lena asked.

"This ledger was my first, and I started the business around . . . *hmm* . . . twenty-two years ago. I was a mere boy—sixteen years old. Imagine! I set up shop in the commercial district, would you believe. It was difficult for a time . . . My line of work wasn't respected in those days and the temples were absolutely determined to brand me a Rogue and absorb me into their ludicrous system. But I had a few allies among the nobility—my family, you see, is rather important—and had already developed my own way of controlling my powers. It was a system based on old wisdom, wisdom I'd drawn from texts written long before the gods." He sat down again, sipped his tea, and opened the ledger on his lap.

"Before the gods?" Lena asked.

"Oh yes. The temples will tell you that the gods have always existed. But the temples themselves were only established two thousand years ago."

Two thousand years sounded like a long time to Lena.

Chatham smiled, resting his perfectly manicured hands flat on the open ledger and leaning forward, eager to explain. "The history of Valorian, sweet girl, is far, far older than two thousand years. And how do you suppose mages lived before the gods became an accepted truth instead of one option among many? Speak to your huntsman and he would have you believe the whole world was consumed in Chaos. He would be wrong—if he were right, none of us would be alive today. The truth is that if you are trained properly, there is no need to allow a god to slip a leash on your power. In fact, there are ways to slip out of a leash too, if one were to desire it . . ."

As if prompted, Lena felt her own power leaping in her stomach, straining against its binding. She swallowed, tried to concentrate—even if that's what she decided, now wasn't the time. She was here for answers. "But Lord Aster . . ."

Chatham sat back in his seat. "He was weak. He let his control wear down over time. A better magician could never have succumbed to Chaos. A better magician would have *used* Chaos for his own purposes . . ." He raised an eyebrow, as if he and Lena were sharing a private joke. "But that's another story entirely. We were talking about your butterfly." He returned his attention to the ledger and started flicking through the pages. Eventually, he said, "Ah, here we are, 027," and rested his finger on an entry toward the end. "Butterfly 8. That means it was the eighth of this design. And it was a special commission for . . . oh my . . . Lady Patience Santini." He smiled slowly. Something important had dawned on him, Lena thought. "Yes . . . yes, of course. One of my first noble customers. I suspected this might be the case."

"What?" she asked, confused.

"Where did you find this butterfly, Lena? Are you from . . . you can't be . . . Duke's Forest?" A kind of darkness gleamed in his eager gaze.

Lena nodded slowly, uncertain about exactly what she was revealing. Chatham's eyes widened in something like delight. "Yes—the first time I saw you, the huntsman said he had found you on the way back—but I just assumed . . . Well, no one has emerged from Duke's Forest in years . . ." He was murmuring to himself, and Lena watched as the golden bee settled next to the butterfly on the table. It appeared to be examining its sibling curiously.

"Yes . . . But I came here for *you* to tell *me* what's going on," she reminded him.

He smiled, but no warmth reached his eyes. He sipped his sweet tea. "Silly me. Allow me to explain: Lady Patience Santini was the first wife of your Duke. Although originally from the Wishes to the far south, like most noble mages she trained with the temples as a young woman, while living at court. She visited me to buy the butterfly a few days before she left to be wed."

Lena felt suddenly pale. She didn't remember the first Duchess, but she knew she was interred in the crypts below the castle. So, effectively, Lena really *had* stolen grave goods. But then . . .

"When I first found it . . . or . . . when it found me . . ."— she gulped, her throat dry—"it was . . . flying."

"How interesting." Chatham ran his fingers through his smooth, pale hair and glanced down at the open page. "You see, the ledger reminds me that when Lady Patience bought the butterfly, she wanted it empty."

Lena shook her head. "Empty?"

"Generally, my magical mechanicals, those designed for ordinary people, are woven through with magic upon purchase—it's something I do once they're taken off display. Come, little bee." The bee flew to his palm, its yellow light glowing brightly as it lifted and lowered its wings. "See this glow? My own magic powers this little creature. But for some of my customers, I can leave it empty. Here." He touched a finger to the bee, and with a flicker of yellow the light went out and the wings froze in position. *Dead*, Lena thought, a sudden chill running through her, but she brushed the thought aside. Had it ever truly been alive? He set it beside the still form of the butterfly. "Now it can be filled with someone else's magic ... or perhaps with a spell, or several spells."

She frowned, not understanding. "What would be the point in that?"

"Well ... say you were a mother, and you wanted your child to be safe. You might cast a healing spell and put it in this bee, and magically instruct the bee to follow your child around. And then, when the child grazes her knee, the spell activates and the wound is healed. The bee can carry one or two small spells." He turned his attention to the butterfly. "This little creature is more complex, however, and can easily carry two or three small spells—perhaps more, depending on the skill of the mage."

"Right ..." Lena's mind jumped around wildly, returning to a point earlier in Chatham's explanation. "So Patience Santini was a mage?"

He nodded. "Magic runs famously strong in the Santini bloodline—and I see she asked for the butterfly to be sent to her quarters in the temple of Regis. She trained there before her marriage was arranged. Although I doubt they told Patience's new family in Duke's Forest about her talents." He smiled briefly. "You Foresters are not known for your love of magic."

Lena ignored the comment. "What spell did the butterfly have inside it?"

"I don't know. As I said, I made it empty. It would've been up to Lady Patience what she wished to fill it with." Chatham sliced the cake. "Now, how much do you want for it?"

Lena's mind was occupied, and it took her a few moments to process what Chatham had said. When she did, she blinked in confusion. The fire flickered, and the shadows near the ceiling crowded down like eager observers. "Excuse me?"

"How much do you want? A hundred gold pieces?" He lifted a slice from the cake stand and lowered it carefully onto a plate. He tried to hand it to her, but she didn't move.

Lena shook her head. "It's not for sale," she said. The butterfly sat on the small table. They both looked at it. Chatham reached out to pick it up, but Lena was faster, cupping it protectively in her palm. "I'm sorry, but I'm not interested."

"Now, now, Miss Grey. I think we've established that this little creature isn't really yours anyway," he said, still holding the cake knife. "It's out of pure generosity that I'm happy to compensate you for the loss."

Lena raised her chin. "Why should it belong to you? It belonged to Patience Santini, and she's dead."

"Well . . . by rights, it belongs to her daughter, Constance."

She blinked. Constance. The masked mage. Chatham's apprentice.

"And I'd just love the opportunity to return it to her," he went on. "Constance and I are old friends, you see."

"I thought she was your apprentice. I thought she stole something from you when she ran away," Lena said, her voice slow and quiet. "Doesn't sound like you were friends, to me."

Chatham nodded. "Emris has told you ... Well, I shouldn't be surprised, I suppose: the huntsman appears to treat you as something of a confidante. I'll tell you something else: Constance wants this butterfly."

Lena looked at the creature in her palm, not quite understanding. "What?" she breathed.

His voice was sharper, tinged with something sour and unpleasant. "Oh yes. That little butterfly may be next to worthless, but for reasons of her own, I believe Constance desires it." He looked genuinely angry now. "Isn't that marvelous, Lena? If you let me have the butterfly, I'd have something she wants, and she'd have to come back and get it. And so the little butterfly flies into the net, along with the priceless treasure she stole from me." He held out his hand. "So you see, it's absolutely necessary that you give me the butterfly."

"No," said Lena firmly, holding it tighter in her hand.

Chatham slammed his fist into the table. His face had grown twisted and ugly—he looked ten years older than he had moments ago. "What value is the damn thing to you?"

"It's mine, and I'm not giving it away." She leaped up from the comfortable chair and edged toward the door.

"If you don't give it to me," he hissed, "I will tell everyone that you stole it from me, and you will spend the rest of your life in prison."

Lena's eyes widened. "But that's a lie!"

"Who do you think they're going to believe, stupid girl? Now, hand it over!"

Lord Chatham lunged across the table, his arms outstretched, knocking over the teapot and spilling hot, steaming tea all over the hearth. The fire hissed as Lena flung herself to one side and ran for the door, but the air flashed bright yellow. She felt herself caught by the ankle and tripped. The butterfly flew out of her hand and hit the door with a *clink* before falling on the carpet.

Something flickered to life inside her, a coldness fizzing in the pit beneath her lungs, catching alight with alarming intensity. She gasped as the coldness rose from deep inside, burning through her gullet with its strange, freezing electricity. *I'm not doing this*, she realized, her heart thumping wildly. As Chatham's hand closed around her boot and started to pull her out of the way, something jerked from her mouth like a scream: a cloud, dark and menacing, hovered in the air like a bad omen.

She felt Chatham stop, his hand suddenly loosening. The cloud resembled the vapor she had been conjuring from her palms during her practice sessions with Emris, but it was much larger, darker—a low rumble filled the air. She flinched: the cloud appeared to have a life of its own. Lena and Lord Chatham watched it float toward the butterfly, momentarily united in their wonder and confusion. In a split second of strange silence, the cloud landed on the delicate mechanical body, enveloped it. The creature shuddered, flapped its wings a couple of times—and then, miraculously, the clockwork kicked in and with a *whir* the butterfly flapped its wings and started to rise into the air, puffing little clouds of dark-gray smoke out of its body as if it were coughing and spluttering to life.

What just happened? Lena's heart was pounding. *I didn't mean to do that. Was it Chaos?*

The quiet broke as Chatham roared and lunged for the butterfly. Lena pushed herself to her feet. The butterfly flitted up toward the ceiling and settled on the top shelf of ledgers, its wings peeking over the edge.

The magician started to climb the wheeled ladder, forgetting Lena in his total focus on the butterfly. She shot toward the ladder and kicked it with a strength she hadn't known she possessed, sending it hurtling along the rail, tipping sideways. Chatham, who was halfway up, tumbled into the shelves, sending several drawers of metal fixings crashing to the floor. Lena watched as one of the bookcases swung forward, and readied herself to jump out of the way—but it wasn't falling. It was . . . *opening*.

Inside the secret room, a low yellow light burned steadily over another workshop, twice the size of the one in which she was standing. She caught glimpses of metal objects scattered across a long desk and recognized them dimly as counterfeit body parts—legs, arms, hands ... even a series of masks similar to the one Constance had worn. And on the floor, which was plain pale stone, were several dark stains ...

Lena knew a bloodstain when she saw one. And now that she had noticed it, she perceived other signs of violence in the secret workshop. A saw discarded on the floor beneath the desk, its blade streaked with dried reddish stains, and various bloodied cloths tossed into a large metal bin. Whoever had cleaned up in here had done a slapdash job.

"Get away from there," a low, menacing voice said. Chatham had risen to his feet, and there was murder in his eyes.

I should never have come here.

She staggered backward, her heart in her mouth.

"What did you do?" she breathed, her voice barely more than a whisper.

As soon as she was clear of the bookcase door, Chatham slid it shut. "Now, now," he said softly, "don't draw conclusions about things you don't understand. It wasn't *me* anyway."

But Lena wasn't listening. She shook her head, continuing to back away slowly. The butterfly was hovering around the door to the shop, its metal wings scraping against the wooden frame in clinking whispers.

"I'm sure we can come to some arrangement, after all,"

the magician added, his voice now sweet as honey. "Just . . . stay here for a moment."

He was drawing closer, but Lena's hand had found the handle of the door. She burst through into the main shop, unsteady on her feet. The assistant and the customer, who was on her way out with a white box clutched under her arm, shrieked loudly as Lena slammed into the counter, Chatham at her heels. His hands closed for a second around her wrist, and she felt a lurch in her stomach as an unnatural warmth radiated from his fingers, a hum filling her ears as her wrist started to burn. His magic. She tried to pull away, but he was too strong, so she kicked out desperately—once, twice—and found his knee with the hard toe of her boot. He cried out, let go.

Fear propelled her forward. She couldn't get the horror of the bloodstained workshop out of her mind. She skirted the counter—wincing at the stinging, blistering ghost of his fingerprints around her wrist—hearing a *tick-tock-tick* sound close over her head. It was the butterfly, she realized, the sound conjuring the memory of the first time she had seen it, fluttering in the dark.

Lena raced for freedom. Lady Honoria screamed again, her voice raw with fear as she ran out the front door into the sunlight. The butterfly settled on Lena's shoulder as she put out a hand to grab the handle of the shop door, already swinging shut after the lady's escape. She was almost upon it when a loud *click* and *whir* sounded and a metal gate shot from the top of the door to the ground. She snatched her hands away from the contraption, her racing heart sinking. She was trapped.

She searched around for another means of escape, but a disheveled Lord Chatham was already emerging from the counter, a section of his heavily oiled, ashen hair standing up on end. Fury glowed in his eyes. "Good work, Miss Evershott," he said to his pretty assistant, who had her hand on a lever to one side of the counter. "Now, Miss Grey—as you can see, there really is no escape. You might as well hand it over—and I might even forgive you for . . . the damage."

Forgive her? After what she had seen? She *had* to get away!

Think of something else. Think! Lena told herself. *A distraction.* As Chatham stalked toward her, hand outstretched, she raised her own in the opposite direction, toward the bay window displays.

"No!" Chatham shouted, realizing what she was about to attempt.

She called on the cold fire burning in the pit of her belly—and blessedly, a burst of magic shot through her in arrows of electricity. Bulbous clouds flew out of her palm, converging around the metal creatures in the window, and Lena watched in astonishment as the mechanicals absorbed the vapor, as if each creature were inhaling sharply. She flexed her fingers, surprised at what she was now capable of. All at once, the shop was alive with whirring and clicking and even the noise of little bells playing tinny mechanical music as the metal animals sprang to life.

"No!" Chatham yelled again, his face pale with rage and disbelief.

In the split second before Chatham's shock subsided and rage won out, Lena darted aside and ran around the display counters of the shop, shooting clouds of magic at every mechanical creature she spied as she knocked aside the plush velvet stools and upholstered chairs. Magic was coursing through her—suddenly it felt bottomless, surging like a great river, eager to burst its banks.

The shop assistant—Miss Evershott—snapped herself out of shocked stupor as Chatham cried, "Stop her!" But the small golden cat with the fluffy tail that Lena had admired in the window launched itself at the assistant's stricken face. She fell down, shrieking, and Lena heard her head rap sharply against the floor. Lena rushed to the lever but stopped short.

Miss Evershott's eyes were open, staring blankly at the ceiling, a halo of blood spilling around her head.

Dead.

Time seemed to slow. The cat, animated by Lena's magic, was sitting on the woman's chest, gazing up at Lena with empty eyes, its mechanical throat purring. Or were its eyes really empty? She could see something swirling in their depths. The world was faded around the edges and she realized she wasn't breathing, but she pinched herself, forced herself to face the truth.

I killed her.

Another, harder voice spoke in her mind. *There's no time. Just run.*

Lena pulled the lever up, and the bars over the front door shrank back into the ceiling.

Chatham was doing his best to pursue her, but his numerous bird and insect mechanicals were buzzing around his head, tugging at his clothes, and an elephant the size of a goat had started to sneeze great multicolored spurts of gas into the air. Chatham was choking and staggering, enraged, in the wrong direction. The vicious metal insects dug tiny limbs into his face. Blood ran onto his collar. The elephant was ramming its shiny, sharp tusks into his shins. And now the cat was poised to leap on its second victim, its furry tail already soaked in blood, its metal teeth pointed and gleaming.

What have I done?

Lena stumbled, wondering whether to help the magician.

But then she remembered the secret workshop, and her heart hardened. There had been so much blood. Wasn't it likely that he too was a killer?

She sprinted out the unlocked door, pounded down the street, and turned into a backstreet she thought might lead toward the temple district. No sounds of pursuit. Had she killed Chatham too?

She caught her breath in the little back alley, her mind spinning, her face hot and sweaty. A flash of metal suddenly glinted in front of her face, lit by the sinking sun, and she flinched, suppressing a scream—remembering how the creatures had attacked their creator.

But the brass butterfly merely fluttered in front of her nose, circled once around her head, and landed on her shoulder. Lena started, but didn't brush it away. It didn't appear to mean her any harm. Carefully, her hands trembling, she picked it up and slipped it into its customary place in her pocket, where it was happy to stay.

By the time she reached the temple around half an hour later, the shadows were lengthening, and she realized Emris would arrive in the map room with supper shortly—that is, if he wasn't already waiting for her. What would she tell him? Slowly, she climbed the stairs to the map room. Mercifully, it was empty. She flung herself into a chair, panting, unable to believe what she had done.

The little brass creature crawled out of her pocket, flew up, and perched on the end of her nose, inspecting her eyes as if it were as curious about her as she was about it.

"This is all because of you," Lena said quietly. "Why did you choose me? Why were you in the crypts? What magic was in you then, and why did it go away?" She'd gone to Lord Chatham for answers, only to find more questions— and a lot more trouble than she'd bargained for.

The butterfly flew to her palm, and she cupped her hands around it as she usually did. It seemed happy in the dark. It didn't glow as it had done the first time she'd seen it, years ago. Instead, she noticed a little vaporous heart of gray cloud. The butterfly was animated by her own magic now, she realized. Chatham's bee had glowed yellow, like his horse. The animals she had brought to life hadn't glowed, because her magic didn't either. The first time she'd seen the butterfly . . . what color had it been? She remembered it only as a pale light. What color was Patience Santini's magic? And why had her spell flitted to life when she'd been dead for so many years?

But there were more pressing matters to deal with. She had killed a woman with her magic. She might have killed Chatham too. Blood drained from her face as tears stung her eyes.

"Lena?" Emris was holding a tray loaded with food, but as soon as he saw her face, he set it down on the table and rushed to her side, kneeling on the floor beside the chair. "What's the matter?"

"I've done something stupid, Emris," she said, the tears falling in hot, heavy trails down her cheeks.

He ran a thumb across her cheek. "Whatever it is, it can't be that bad," he said gently.

"It is," she choked. She opened her hands to show him the butterfly. For a moment, it was still, and Emris's face remained caught between confusion and kindness—but then, with a flutter of its wings, it rose into the air, circling the chair. His expression changed.

"All right." He looked up at her, then slowly lowered himself into the chair opposite hers. "Looks like you have some explaining to do."

Lena told him everything. She told him about the night she'd found the butterfly, the song she'd heard, the way the butterfly had glowed and flown toward her in the darkness. The way it had stopped as if it had chosen her. She told him how she didn't feel like she belonged—not in the crypts, nor in the temples—and how Faul's hold on her felt tenuous. She told him what she remembered of her strange dream when she'd fallen into the fountain. How, despite her progress in his lessons, every now and then she felt her magic bubbling over like a kettle left too long on the boil, uncontrollable. She told him how she had tried to find answers elsewhere, how this had led her to Chatham's shop—and she told him everything that had passed. The secret bloodstained room. The woman she had killed. And maybe . . . maybe even Chatham himself.

As she spoke, Emris leaned forward in his chair, resting his chin on his hands, his face growing more and more serious as her story continued. When she had finished, he was silent for a few long moments.

"You've given me a lot to think about," he said, his tone cold despite the calmness of his words. "But I can set your mind at ease on one score," he added. "Chatham is gravely injured but . . . he's alive."

"What? How do you know?" Lena's heart clenched in an odd mixture of relief and terror.

"A messenger arrived with the news a few minutes before I left the First Huntsman. He said Chatham was attacked in broad daylight, his shop vandalized. He's unconscious, but he'll survive. Apparently, he's been taken to the palace for healing." He looked at her darkly. "But they're saying his assistant was killed in cold blood. Do you see now how dangerous Chatham's kind of magic can be?"

Lena shivered. The woman had been unkind, but Lena had never meant for the mechanical cat to kill her. She hadn't meant to kill anyone. The thought of what she had caused was . . . overwhelming. She buried her head in her hands.

"How long will it take for Chatham to heal?" she murmured, trying to bring herself back to the present. "Won't he come after me? He wanted the butterfly, but now he's also angry about what I've seen . . ."

"Yes, of course he'll come after you," Emris admitted. "He's protective of his secret workshop. Only those closest to him know the truth about what he creates."

"You knew about it?" Lena asked, shocked.

He nodded slowly. "That was where I found Constance the night she ran away . . ." He was about to continue, but suddenly stopped, bowing his head. "No, this is a story for another time—perhaps a story I should not tell you. Your test is tomorrow morning." He glanced up at her. "I'm not saying that you're safe, Lena. But if we can establish you as an initiate of Faul, or any of the temples, you will have legal protection and a chance to argue your case in a court of law. The bottom line is that Chatham threatened to steal your property and then to detain you against your will. You defended yourself in the only way you knew how."

She raised her head, feeling a glimmer of hope. "Really?"

He sighed. "Yes, really. Some might even say the fault was in the mechanicals themselves. They're powered by Chaos, Lena. Chatham obviously has tricks to ensure they are usually harmless . . . at least outwardly. But you didn't know how to do that. Of course you didn't." He stared at the butterfly curiously as it rested on the top of Lena's head. "You really should get rid of that thing," he murmured, clearly uncomfortable.

She scooped it up protectively. After all this time, there was no way she was letting it go. She slipped it safely into her pocket. "So basically, I just need to pass this test," she said.

"Focus on that. You can't fight every battle at once."

Lena stroked the butterfly's wings. "I'm sorry, Emris," she said quietly.

"You should have listened to me," he replied, standing up, his voice businesslike again. "I have a lot to think about. You should use what time you have left to practice for the test tomorrow." He stalked away from her, turning at the door. In his eyes, Lena read sadness, and disappointment, and concern—but also fear. Fear for her?

"I'm sorry," she said again, drawing herself up straighter and wiping her face. "Maybe it was stupid, but I had to do it. I had to know."

He shook his head slightly. "You know I forgive you," he murmured. And then he left.

SIXTEEN
Confirmation

Constance stepped into the great hall. The white and green ceremonial robes weighed upon her narrow shoulders; her pale hair fanned out across her back. The Rathbone tree emblem was emblazoned across the long train behind her, its leaves over her shoulders, roots trailing along the floor. A smattering of applause, swelled by a few half-hearted cheers, rang out through the hall as she approached the center. The Wise Men followed her inside, clothed in silk, velvet, and jewels of their own, led by Winton in the silver robes of the second in line to the ducal throne.

After the night's unrest, Constance could hardly feel the weight of her ceremonial clothing; her dread was heavier still. Captain Trudan had lost his life to the revolt—they'd untied him from the chair in the Hanged Thief only to find him cold as stone, bled out from the wound in his head. It felt like a bad omen, and Winton had been distraught. *Bad news over bad news*, she thought grimly. Time was slipping away, and here she was, walking as slowly as she'd ever walked.

One step. Another three steps. Slowly, slowly. Encrusted with gems, the old robes clinked gently, hastily adjusted for the female form; heavy embroidery stroked the newly swept floor with whispers.

Considering the short notice, the hall had been miraculously transformed—the floor cleaned, cobwebs captured and banished, wall hangings beaten of dust. The benches had been arranged in neat rows, creating a long aisle down the center, the trapdoors to the realm of the Ancestors gleaming with beeswax. Traditionally, the walls and oak-beamed ceiling were bedecked with ivy for grand occasions, but the ivy had long perished and the servants had had to manage with swathes of green cloth woven with gold. An abundance of candles supplemented the weak midday light filtering through the freshly cleaned windows.

Constance couldn't help remembering how bright the hall had been—bathed in golden sunlight—when her step-mother had been crowned Duchess.

Weapons forbidden, the city guards stood again around the hall's periphery, their belts empty. Constance felt unsettled by the sight. She'd have liked to make an exception to the rule but hadn't dared: she knew it would cost her politically. Most people seemed prepared to accept she was a mage—or at least offered no outward protest—but no one would welcome outright disrespect of the laws of Duke's Forest by its own would-be ruler. Still, a sense of unease shivered in the back of her mind as she thought of Dr. Thorn's warnings. She'd doubled the guard on the

Justice's apartments as a precaution and had his rooms searched, but nothing magical or mechanical had been found. She'd even swept around the apartments herself, turning the dial on her mask—but no spells had glimmered except the storm cloud.

Lord Veredith—the newly appointed master of ceremonies (an honor that would usually fall to the Justice)—waited at the end of the aisle, dressed in his finest robes. The small book of ceremonies lay open in his hand, a red ribbon marking the place. The pages trembled slightly with the old man's fatigue. Nearby, a green velvet cushion rested on a pedestal, bearing the crown—a plain silver circlet inset with emeralds twining around its length like vines. The traditional ducal crown had been too large and heavy for her, so she'd chosen the circlet once worn by her mother, and by Winton's mother. The Wise Men sat in a broken semicircle of chairs directly below the dais. Constance continued at her stately pace toward the steps to the raised platform.

She felt the heel of her slipper catch slightly as she climbed the steps. She tripped, landing hard on her knee. Her heart lurched, and a few gasps sounded through the hall. *Another bad omen. That's what they're all thinking.* She stood up slowly, paying no heed to the screaming bruise on her knee, keeping her expression blank. She smoothed her robes and continued up to the dais. For all her apparent composure, she felt a bead of sweat trickle down her brow as she knelt at Lord Veredith's feet.

The old man took a rattling breath and embarked on the long-winded preamble to the ceremony of confirmation. She tried to relax. *You have no enemies here*, she told herself. Dr. Thorn was locked in the dungeons, the Justice confined to his apartments. She was safe. And she was nearly Duchess.

"Constance Rathbone, daughter of Ethelbur Rathbone," Lord Veredith said finally, his voice quavering as he placed his palm flat on her head, "the living and the dead gather in this hall to witness your oath to the duchy. Do you swear to uphold the King's laws and accept his overlordship?"

"I do." But her reply was underlaid by a flurry of noises: clicking and a distant tinkling like a bell—or a coin dropping to the floor. Lord Veredith's eyes flickered across the crowd, but quickly returned to his text. Constance breathed deep, a leaden feeling in her stomach. *Not now*, she thought. *Please not now.*

"Do you swear to protect the people—"

A moan, louder this time, interrupted the old man. His eyes drifted to the floor, his face abruptly pale. Constance followed his gaze, dread building in her ribs. *Not again.* Everyone was watching the trapdoors set in the middle of the aisle, holding their breath.

Knock. Knock. Knock.

It was unmistakable now. A noise emanating from below. From the crypts. Where only the Ancestors existed.

Somebody in the crowd whimpered.

"Bar the crypt doors," said Constance firmly. Nobody moved, the guests frozen in shock. "For gods' sake!" she hissed. She stood up, grabbed the long wooden weight from the ceremonial banner behind Lord Veredith, and thrust it through the trapdoor handles.

Barely in time. Another slow knock and the door shuddered, as if pushed. The room fell eerily silent, all eyes fixed on the space. A woman started weeping; murmuring filled the air. A few of the Wise Men stood as if to leave, but faltered under Constance's glare.

"Please be seated, everyone. I shall deal with this in due course," she said, her voice loud and firm.

"The Ancestors are angry," someone protested.

"Nonsense!" snapped Constance, returning to her place, kneeling at the front of the hall. Luckily, the noise from below the floor had ceased, as if the Ancestors too had been cowed by her display of authority. "Lord Veredith, proceed."

The murmuring fell to muffled whispers as the old man fumbled to find his place in the text.

"'Protect the people,'" she whispered to him. The crowd was restless, disturbed—barely quiet. In the corner of her eye, she saw a small child try to run for the door, quickly caught and scolded by a white-faced parent.

"Do you swear . . . to protect the people . . . from harm, to the extent of your power and authority, from threats . . . martial and magical alike?" Lord Veredith was struggling, his breath heaving in short gasps, his hands shaking.

"I do." Her voice rang clear and true through the hall, determination bolstering her courage.

"Do you swear to honor and worship . . . the Ancestors, observe . . . their ancient rites and fulfill . . . your obligations to their ancient religion?"

I cannot, she thought, but bowed her head in assent nonetheless. "I do."

Veredith picked up the crown and held it over Constance's head, where it shuddered like the old man's lungs. "With this crown, I proclaim—"

And that's when the doors of the great hall burst open, and a deafening ring of drawn steel reverberated around the room. Veredith dropped the crown with a clatter.

What now? asked a small exasperated part of Constance's mind as she turned to face the doors.

In his right hand, the Justice's short sword was wet with blood—his left hand was covered by a large silver gauntlet. Behind him stood a dozen black-clad guards with naked blades—but no Dr. Thorn, Constance noticed. The storm cloud poured inside, flickering and swirling, until the doors swung shut with a *bang*. The Justice was quickly flanked by those members of his personal guard who had not been imprisoned, some of whom Constance realized had been scattered throughout the watching crowd, not wearing their usual black livery. And—unlike Xander's men or the city guard—they were all armed.

Her mind spun wildly, like the needle of a broken

compass trying to find north. *How did he get out? What happened to the guards at his door?*

A few whimpers filled the air as the congregation cringed away from the drawn blades, falling quickly into stunned silence as the Justice's men took control, ordering everyone to their knees. Lord Veredith collapsed onto a chair, his face deathly pale.

But Constance stood up slowly, a curious calm taking hold of her underneath her confusion. Xander was immediately in front of her, his green eyes bright with determination. She felt her heart soar—and quickly sink as she realized what was about to happen. *I can't let him die for me.* "Xander," she started, trying to pull him aside, but he shrugged off her touch.

The Justice thundered up the aisle, his footsteps echoing on the flagstones, sword outstretched. Upon his left hand the silver gauntlet gleamed.

"Step no further, traitor!" Xander cried, holding up his fists as the Justice reached the semicircle of chairs. But six or seven of the Justice's men had already surrounded him. Xander landed a few blows, quick and clean, but was swiftly overpowered and wrestled to the floor. Constance pressed a hand over her mouth to stop herself from crying out—she knew it would not help him. She couldn't move. She felt like she'd turned to stone.

"Stop this! Stop!" Winton was shouting, attempting to pull one of the men away from the Swordmaster. But he was pushed back, restrained. His cloak tore as somebody stepped on its hem.

The men kicked Xander viciously, the scarlet silken scarves falling around him, mingling with his blood. He curled up, and the kicks landed on his spine instead. Constance felt her insides twist painfully, as if she were the one receiving the blows. Winton continued to struggle against his restraints, to cry out against the violence, until the Justice raised his gauntleted fist and smacked him around the face, once, almost casually. And then everything was quiet except for the sound of boots crashing into Xander's flesh.

It was all over so quickly.

The Justice sheathed his sword and reached for Constance's neck with his silver-gloved hand, but her instincts finally kicked in. *Fight, godsdamnit.* She raised her hand and a flash of bright purple lit up the hall—without her cane, she was weaker, but not defenseless. The Justice was thrown back, landing on his side a few feet to her right.

She lifted her heavy robes and ran from the dais, past the Justice, and down the aisle toward the door. Nobody tried to stop her. She was hardly thinking. Her whole mind was filled with the desperate impulse to escape, to live another day.

At the end of everything, what else was there but the will to survive?

But suddenly a huge *bang* echoed, and Constance was flung to the floor. Red light flashed behind her eyes; pain racked her body. At first, she was certain she'd find the head of an arrow sticking from her heart—but there was no wound. No blood. Except . . . she raised a hand to her face, feeling a warm trickle from her nose. It was as if an invisible door had been slammed in her face. She was dizzy. Confused. Her brain carried out an absurd dialogue with itself somewhere beneath the ringing in her ears. She had no doubt what had happened was magic—but how?

The gauntlet.

She started to think more clearly as she connected the pieces. She had told her men to search the Justice's rooms for magical items, or even clockwork. They had found none—beyond a perfectly harmless grandfather clock. She too had searched the rooms, in her mask, for signs of magic as an extra precaution—and found nothing. But what if the clockwork had been disguised . . . say, in a ceremonial suit of armor? And what if it hadn't yet been activated, and therefore wasn't revealed by the spell-scape?

Stupid. Now everything is ruined.

"We have a mage among us," the Justice bellowed at the congregation. "A snake at the very heart of Duke's Forest. How could you allow this, you who claim to be faithful to the Ancestors?"

She turned her neck awkwardly from her position on the floor, her head spinning as she looked over her shoulder at the Justice, blood trickling down her chin. The spell had been disguised. To outsiders, it must have looked as if she'd simply tripped. In his hand, the one without the gauntlet, the Justice was holding the ducal crown.

Dr. Thorn had warned her about some trick, some magic belonging to the Justice himself . . . Her eyes caught on the metal gauntlet. Could she see a cog turning somewhere on its wrist?

The people closest to Constance had backed away, but now Winton rushed down the hall to his sister's side. He knelt beside her, helping her sit up unsteadily. "Constance," he murmured, his face already bruising from the Justice's blow. "Constance, are you all right?" She struggled to focus on his eyes, dark like his mother's—and his mother's features echoed in his face. But he was not his mother. His eyes were swimming with angry tears.

"I'm all right, Winton," she whispered, although she wasn't.

She heard the Justice's footsteps approaching down the aisle, the *clack-clack-clack* of his boots in the stunned silence. But Winton refused to turn around, retrieving a handkerchief from his pocket and pressing it to Constance's nose. She held it in place, winced as her entire face throbbed. The white cloth quickly bloomed red.

He turned to the Justice. "How dare you," he said. "My sister is the Duchess. You cannot treat her this way!"

"Your sister is not the Duchess," the Justice growled, jerking Winton from her side, his right hand tight and white-knuckled on her brother's shoulder. "The coronation was never completed." He waved over a couple of his men, who hauled Constance clumsily to her feet. She dropped the handkerchief, which flopped, sodden, onto the floor. Her head pounded, but her mind was clear. Blood had spilled over the white and green robes, she noticed, ruining the embroidery worn by her Ancestors for generations. And her glove . . . her glove had slipped down her arm, revealing the sore place where the metal joined her flesh. She pushed it up, guessing by the lack of reaction that nobody had noticed. She would keep what secrets she had left.

The Justice addressed the congregation a second time. "The pretender Constance Rathbone has deceived you all." His eyes found the Wise Men and narrowed. "And you have allowed it. Constance has already shown herself to be a traitor—a mage, no less, and an imposter. Her brother has done nothing but support her wickedness," he added, his grip on Winton's shoulder tightening. Constance watched as he tried to suppress a wince. "Now, by the King's true authority, I claim a change of regime in Duke's Forest. The reign of the Rathbones has ended. For years, I have been ruling the dukedom in all but name—and now . . ." He pressed down on Winton's shoulder, forcing him to his knees. "I *will* be the Duke." He lifted the crown, placed it on his own head.

Then he turned to Constance, a small smile twisting his lips as he flexed the fingers of his gauntlet and nodded at his men. "Take her to the dungeons."

As they half dragged, half carried her out, Constance felt as if she were floating.

It was all over. She'd never find the heart now.

★　★　★

Constance sat in her cell a few hours later, listening to the *drip-drip-drip* of damp into a puddle.

Drip.

I've failed.

Drip.

I'll never find the heart.

Drip.

I'll never fulfill my destiny.

The storm cloud seeped and sank into the damp cells through the high, glassless windows, creating low-lying patches, green-tinged and venomous, light flickering within them like a serpent's tongue. Taunting her.

How did I miss the gauntlet? How did I get so complacent? How did I allow myself to be outwitted?

Constance let her magical senses open. She felt her own power under her skin, the unruly force she had tamed over long years of enforced discipline and willing learning. She sensed the presence of Mythris too: a gossamer thread tethering her magic to her faith and holding it in place— binding her to a mutable god she'd never quite understood, but whose power appeared to be blissfully unconditional on her morality.

Her senses roamed further. She felt the spell cast over the bars of her cell, gleaming red, hot, and rough—like sunlight on dry sandstone. A crude spell, cast by a man who did not know magic but stole it anyway. *The Justice.* Beyond, her own purple spell—an intricate, strong-woven silk—kept Thorn imprisoned. She roamed further. The storm spell hung like a great net over the mountain. She brushed its strings like wire, at once damp and electric. A masterpiece of a spell. She clenched her fists so tightly a spark of magic flew from hand to hand unbidden.

Be calm. She took a deep, shuddering breath.

Xander was out cold in the cell next to hers, his face oddly pale, his breathing shallow. Beneath his dirtied silks, his body was a mess of red bruises, Constance knew. A wound on his head dribbled blood into the darkness of his hair. The Justice had exacted the full extent of his revenge on the Swordmaster and his men. Those who remained languished in the cells around a sharp corner, out of sight. Constance occasionally heard a cough or the groan of a man in pain.

Tension pressed behind her eyes, but she did not cry. Her mind drifted to the early years in the masked temple, how they'd taught her the price of tears. The cold faces in the mask room had watched as the High Priestess brought down her whip. The old scars stung on her back.

Your face is hidden. CRACK.

You are unreadable. CRACK.

You are without emotion. CRACK.

She shook her head, tried to forget. Right now she ought to harness the kernel of determination she'd always held close to her heart and focus on how to fix this mess. But her mind was bubbling, unfocused, clouded by bitter disappointment.

After all this time, was this really it? She pressed her fingers to her temples, unwilling to admit that everything was lost.

Across from her, Dr. Thorn had lain silently in his cell ever since she'd been brought here, hours before, curled up and facing the wall, his chest rising and falling fitfully. As she watched, he stirred, pushing himself up to a seated position—and a glint of silver caught the faint light. He settled, leaning back against the wall, face taut with pain—and she watched carefully as the glint resolved itself into a second gauntlet.

The twin of the Justice's.

Chatham's work, she thought grimly. *That sick, twisted son of Chaos.*

"Can you take it off?" Constance whispered, her voice cutting sharply through the gloom.

"Don't you think I would've if I could?" Thorn raised his right hand. In the moonlight filtering through the cell windows, she could see how the flesh was bleeding, livid purple where metal touched his skin. "It draws power from my very blood," he said, "and channels it to the other one." At the place where the gauntlet met his skin, Constance noticed a few tiny cogs and wheels, currently still and quiet. "When he starts to draw magic from me, that's when the clockwork starts." He fixed his eyes on her arm. Even though it was still gloved, she remembered he'd seen her left arm when they'd fought in the courtyard. "What about yours?"

"Mine is different," she said shortly. Then, changing the subject: "I had his apartments searched yesterday, but found nothing. When did they put that thing on you? Why didn't you fight?"

"This morning. Four men in plainclothes fought their way in, forced it on me. I tried to fight, but I was too weak. It takes time to recover from so many sleeping draughts," he said, pointedly. Constance didn't apologize. "I can't even use my own magic now," he continued. "He has stolen that from me too."

She was silent for a few moments, and then she spoke again. "Why am I still alive, Dr. Thorn?"

He regarded her sadly. "I guess you'll soon find out."

Constance woke suddenly from dreams full of thunder and lightning, her head pounding, disoriented. Her neck ached where her head had drooped onto her shoulder: she hadn't meant to fall asleep, but long nights of searching for the spell's heart had finally taken their toll. It was still light, and wisps of storm cloud drifted through the high, barred windows, glints of green and blue emanating from the magical vapor. And beyond that, high up in the sky, she spied a muffled yellow glimmer that might have once been the sun. *Midday, perhaps.* She heard the noises of men trying to sleep rattling through the darkness. And she heard other movements distantly, from below—whispers of old burial robes and the clatter of naked bones, echoing far beneath in the crypts.

Or was she imagining it?

Across the way, Dr. Thorn had his back turned toward her again, his breathing slow and deep. She could hear the stirring of other prisoners farther off. Constance peered through the iron bars into the cell next to hers. To her surprise, Xander's bright green eyes were open, watching her, etched with an emotion caught between love and fear.

Her heart leaped. She had feared he would never awaken.

She realized her left arm was slightly exposed. She hugged it close to her body, the metal cold to the touch, unnaturally smooth, and tugged up the material to cover the ugly join.

"You never did tell me the whole truth," said Xander. He was very pale and still, his breath shallow, his voice low.

She shook her head.

"Constance, why couldn't you trust me?"

"I didn't lie to you," she said. She edged closer to him, craving the warmth of his body. The palms of her hands sank into the rotten straw at the cell's edge, but she hardly felt it.

"Perhaps not technically. But you lied in every way that matters. You were tactical. You revealed only what you felt you could trust me with, what I needed to know." He tried to sit up, winced, and fell back on his elbows. "You treated me like an ally. Not like the . . . the friend that I am."

She pressed herself against the bars, reached through, and clasped his fingers in her hand. The fingertips were hot. He tried to shuffle closer and winced again with the effort, his breath thick. "Stop," she said, now holding his hand

312

properly. "Just stay there." Suddenly she was scared. Although he wasn't bleeding, and he was awake at last, the Justice's men might have caused some invisible damage inside Xander's body. She was no expert, but he looked feverish and his labored breathing—could he have cracked a rib? Could the rib be pressing into his lung?

Stop thinking. Just stop.

She rested her forehead against the cold, damp bars and shut her eyes. She sighed.

"I'm here for the storm cloud. I don't want regrets, or recriminations, or tears, or broken dreams, or anything except the heart of the spell." Her throat felt tight with frustration. "I've looked everywhere. My powers are strong. I had everything I needed. Why can't I find it? Why?"

"Could it have left the city?" Xander said quietly.

"No," she snapped. "It has to have been here while the spell was growing. That's the way it works. And because of the quarantine, no one has left since . . ." Since . . .

Oh gods.

She had passed a girl in the woods. The mage. She had *helped* her. "Oh . . . Jurah's tits, Xander! It was the cryptling girl. The girl had it!" She laughed, a strange melancholy sound in the dark stone of the cell. And then she fell quiet. "How am I supposed to reach her now?"

Silence. She pressed closer against the bars, her mind spinning.

But when Xander spoke, his voice was gentle and low, and he squeezed her hand. "Constance, I know you can do it. You're special. To everyone and . . . to me. It's always been you. Since forever. You know that deep down, don't you? Even though I've never said it. And there's never been anybody else. How could I *not* love you?"

Despite herself, she felt tears threaten. She blinked them away, wished she could be the person he thought she was.

"I only wish you felt the same."

"I . . ." She choked on the words. "Xander, I . . ." *Am I even capable of love anymore?*

"Don't despair, Constance. You've come so far. Now you have to work . . . with what you've got." His words came in short, pained snatches.

She raised her head at last. In the half-light she could see he was deathly pale. "Xander? Are you going to be all right?"

"Never mind about me. You know how to destroy the spell." His breath rattled. "And you've worked out who has the spell's heart. That's something, isn't it? The Constance I know would never give up. . . . No matter what."

Another tear trickled down her cheek. "Xander . . ."

"Don't give up, Constance."

She drew herself closer against the bars, hating the touch of cold iron separating her from his arms. Instead, raising his hand, she pressed it to her lips.

SEVENTEEN
The Test

Emris pushed the door of the Holy Council open just as the sun broke from behind the clouds, and Lena stepped into a room that looked like it could swallow the lower town of Duke's Forest twice over. Far above, golden sunlight filtered through the glass ceiling. She stopped dead.

"Oh . . . ," she breathed, staring up at the light dappling the glass, refracting in the air. Darts of color shot through the golden sunlight—pinks, blues, reds, purples. *Not glass, at least not everywhere. It's crystal.* She felt dizzy at the scale of it all, the impossibly vast distance between her and the ceiling. The butterfly quivered in her pocket as if straining to escape, but she soothed it gently with her hand. Emris had told her to leave it in her room, but she couldn't bear to— she felt a sense of responsibility for it, brought back to life by her own magic.

The room was occupied by tiers of high-backed, pale wooden benches, simple in design and arranged in a huge semicircle. Long cream banners drooped from the soaring glass ceiling, creating pools of cooler shade.

A breeze wafted in from somewhere, rustling the shadows like leaves.

Emris led her forward. Lena's eyes roved around the room, hungry for sights. The benches were packed with brightly clothed people. Her breath caught in her throat. She had never seen so many people, or so many colors.

It was noisy now, a rumble like thunder or the wheels of heavy carriages. *The roar of thousands of whispers*, thought Lena, resisting the urge to cover her ears and curl into a ball. Eyes turned upon her, but instead of instinctively reaching for her nonexistent cowl, she drew up taller, squaring her shoulders and inviting their stares. Gradually, the room quieted as, one by one, members of the Council fixed their gaze on the newcomers.

Emris and Lena reached the center of the floor, where two small tables had been set up.

Silence descended. Ten paces in front of Lena, behind the two tables, a long, pale wooden bench ranged across the hall. On it, eight people sat in a line, each dressed in a different color. She recognized the portly gray-clad figure as the First Huntsman, who was gazing at her appraisingly. *One master for each of the temples*, thought Lena, quickly running through them in her head. *But there are nine temples.* The empty place, she realized, belonged to the temple of Mythris.

In the middle of the bench, an older woman dressed in white robes fixed Lena with a fiery-eyed stare. *The Grand*

Master. Lena felt herself catapulted to the castle in Duke's Forest, her trial in front of the Wise Men, the Justice's blue gaze boring into her soul.

Emris began to speak, his voice smooth and confident, easily carrying through the huge space. "My name is Emris Lochlade, Third Huntsman of Faul's temple." He bowed at the high table. "My companion, as you have heard, is the Rogue Lena Grey, a native of Duke's Forest."

Lena felt her courage shrivel under the scrutiny of the hundreds of eyes locked on her face. She really did wish for her hood now. She resisted the urge to cover her birthmark with her hand, to flee to the shadows and find some dark place to be the person she had once been—insignificant, ignored, and safe. *But I am not that person anymore*, she thought, clenching her fists. The figures at the table frowned and murmured.

Emris cleared his throat. "In my opinion, Lena has made incredible progress—"

"Thank you, huntsman, for your introduction. I did not ask for your opinion." The Grand Master's face remained impassive, despite the sharpness of her words. Lena glanced at Emris, who had fixed his eyes on the floor, his jaw tight. She had never seen him so anxious. The woman in white turned her attention to Lena. "Welcome to the Holy Council," she said, her voice ringing out through the hall. "You stand before the highest magical court in the land. My name is Grand Master Auris—my seven colleagues here are the masters of their respective temples. Do not attempt to lie to me, for I can see untruth clear as black shadows in the sun. Do you understand?"

Lena nodded.

"Your situation is unusual. The First Huntsman has described his difficulty in determining your temple, and your subsequent struggles with the Binding. You have been given basic training by Third Huntsman Lochlade, and now you've come to be judged by the Holy Council." Auris stood up and walked around the table. Lena could see the deep lines at the sides of her mouth, the determined set to her eyes, which were the dark-yellow shade of autumn leaves. "Your test will proceed in three stages, and we will use them to decide whether you are properly in control of your powers. Each stage tests one of the three main skills of a mage: power, dexterity, and reactivity. If you pass the test, you will no longer be deemed a Rogue, but will be accepted into the temple training system. Do you understand?"

Lena nodded again, feeling cold and pale and extremely small.

"Good, then let us begin."

A few items were produced from the back of the hall and laid on the two tables in front of the temple masters. One table supported a large glass globe, big enough to fit a child inside. The second table had been laid with a single sheet of paper and a wooden log in a stone basin. The third challenge, Lena knew, would be a combat, and a dark-skinned woman dressed in red appeared to be standing ready at the side of the room.

"Your first challenge," said Grand Master Auris, standing behind the table bearing the glass globe, "is to fill this receptacle with a manifestation of your magic. You must produce enough to fill the globe, but not so much that it shatters. This is to demonstrate the nature of your power, and your basic ability to control it. Proceed."

Lena glanced at Emris, who nodded encouragingly—*You can do this*, his eyes promised. She had practiced a similar technique on several occasions. Slowly, she stepped up to the table and touched her finger against the cool, smooth glass. She closed her eyes and carefully drew on her power—today it felt mercifully close to her fingertips. She opened her eyes to watch the glass bubble fill with roiling gray cloud in a matter of seconds. Quickly, she drew her hand away. The cloud inside the globe flickered suddenly blue, like lightning, and Lena jumped.

Each time she used it now, her power seemed to strengthen.

The watching mages murmured at the manifestation, and Lena waited as the eight masters conferred among themselves. She swallowed and glanced down at her hands.

Grand Master Auris leaned forward, and Lena expected her to pronounce whether she had passed or failed the first challenge. Instead, Auris said, "Your second challenge is a simple spell. You will find everything you need on this table. This will demonstrate your dexterity, your ability to mold your magic to individual requirements not necessarily compatible with its character. Proceed when you are ready."

Lena approached the second table, her heart pounding. She read the paper of instructions, but the words swam the first time, and she had to read it again before she realized it was a spell to set the log on fire. She laid her hand on the log, noticing how her fingers were shaking. The wood was dry and brittle beneath her skin.

"By the power of Faul, I command thee to burn."

She felt her magic, a curl of cold and damp, responding in the place at the base of her lungs. Lena suspected they'd chosen the spell on purpose, because she'd find it difficult. She probed her magic awkwardly, trying to feel out how she might manipulate it to set the log alight. *How can this kind of magic burn anything?* And yet there was—somehow—a flicker of heat deep inside.

"I command thee to burn," she said again.

She couldn't help feeling the weight of eyes on her, judging her as she grappled with the spell. *Come on . . . just do it . . .*

"I command thee to burn," she said, more loudly this time. She pushed her power forcefully toward the log . . . and . . .

It was taking too long, she was sure. She frowned in concentration, dug deeper, and then something sparked in the palm of her hand, a jolt of electricity, and the log burst into flame so quickly she had to snatch her hand away from the heat.

She exhaled in relief. Emris was grinning at her from the side.

Grand Master Auris stood again, her face totally impassive. "Now we shall test your reactivity: defend yourself from attack and attempt to retaliate. Jolanta?" The red-clad mage stepped forward from the sidelines, bowed. "Ready yourselves."

Lena and Jolanta sank into a fighting stance, one arm outstretched, feet squared. Lena felt jittery, nervous—but she knew she could fight too. Combat wasn't tricky like a spell. It was aim and fire. Aim and fire. Jolanta was professionally composed, nearly bored-looking.

Master Auris spoke again. "The first attack to hit home wins the fight. Begin."

A spark of red shot instantly from the woman's palm, but Lena stepped aside and spelled her own attack. Gray cloud zoomed through the air so fast that Jolanta only just had time to deflect, a wall of red springing up to absorb the strike. She looked surprised by the impact. A murmur rose up from the onlookers. Lena followed up quickly with a ballooning shot of cloud, which Jolanta ducked, eyes widening. Lena deflected an attack from the woman, and another. Jolanta didn't look so complacent now. After deflecting a third attack, Lena deftly spelled a small, subtle strike that took Jolanta by surprise, hitting her in the upper arm.

"Ow!" said the woman, rubbing her arm. The hall was alive with gasps of surprise, and even a clatter of applause.

Lena caught Emris's eyes and felt like cheering. He

smiled broadly, and she knew she had done it. She really had. She turned hopefully to Grand Master Auris, but the woman's face was still stony and unreadable.

"Come here," she said. When Lena stood close enough, she reached out, quick as a snake, and grabbed Lena's chin, tilting her eyes up to meet her own. Lena tried to pull away, but Auris's grip held fast, nails digging painfully into the soft flesh of her cheeks.

Emris stepped forward, his voice angry. "Grand Master—"

But Auris merely flicked her eyes and Emris froze, as if held by an invisible arm, and then stumbled backward. She returned her attention to Lena.

"I *can* see something . . . ," whispered the woman under her breath. "A shadow? A mist?"

It hurt. A pressure built behind Lena's eyes until her head felt full of blood; the rush of her pulse was deafening in her ears. The murmur in the hall had grown to a rumble, but a cry rang out over their heads: "Stop this!"

Emris had struggled to his feet. Lena tore away from Auris's grasp, her heart racing, the skin of her cheeks burning. She darted backward, but instantly a semicircle of red-clad mages blocked her route to the exit. The crowd was in an uproar. Emris strode to her side, placing himself between her and the Grand Master.

"You promised not to do this," he said, glaring at the masters, fire in his eyes. "You promised never to treat another Rogue as you treated me. She's passed the test! She's not some criminal on trial!"

"Stand down, huntsman." The First Huntsman stood, his kindly face twisted into a stern frown. "We cannot tolerate this insubordinate behavior, no matter your personal agenda. I can assure you the Grand Master does not intend to harm the girl, and nor does the Council. We are simply doing what is necessary."

"Sir, I—"

"Be quiet, or be removed!" His face was full of warning.

"Order!" The slender young woman beside him, dressed in a luxurious blue silk gown, called out, "Order in the Holy Council!" The hubbub died slowly. Emris stood his ground, but Lena touched his arm, warning him off. She had to pass this test in order to be protected from Chatham. And to do that, she had to gain the Grand Master's approval.

"What do you want from me?" Lena asked Auris.

"You have proved that you have some control over your power . . . but it is still somewhat unusual." Auris eyed the globe filled with cloud, which was starting to thin as the power weakened and dissipated. "To be certain, I need to look inside you and discover its true nature," she said, lowering her voice. "If all is as it should be, you have nothing to fear. Come here, Lena. If you are untouched by Chaos, I shall know it quickly."

Lena looked at Emris. He met her gaze, nodded, but his eyes were tight with worry. She supposed she didn't have much of a choice. She approached nervously as Auris raised her hand.

"Relax," she said, gently touching Lena's brow with her palm. A white glow sputtered to life in Lena's vision, initially almost invisible in the sunlight spilling through the glass dome, but slowly, slowly growing in intensity. It was the brightness of a candle, of a lamp, of a fire burning merrily in the grate—now it was the strength of the bright North Star on a clear night, the crescent moon, the full moon, the first break of day. Then it was *too* bright, explosions of random color forming in Lena's brain. She tried to shut her eyes but found her eyelids pinned open as Auris stooped down to peer inside her soul, an owl face, searching and predatory, against the burning glow.

"Here it is again," she heard Auris whisper. "There's something there . . . deeper . . . some shadow lurking."

"Stop . . . ," Lena managed, tears running down her cheeks. But the probing sensation continued, light pouring into her brain like acid. Her discomfort turned rapidly to pain—the stinging in her eyes to a throb. A smell—like sulfur, or burning—filled her nose. She tried to call out, to pull away from the woman's face, the small puzzled frown on her brow. Searing agony tore through her mind, but her body refused to shift. She couldn't even see either side of her; the rest of the Council had been swallowed into the light . . .

. . . And she was back where she had started. The passages beneath the castle were dark and twisted. Lena walked quickly, her breath loud in her ears. She was afraid. Someone was following her, their footsteps slow and deliberate but somehow gaining. She was holding the butterfly tightly in her hand. Her other hand trailed along the wall, keeping her steady.

The storm cloud slunk at her feet like a cat, light flickering in and out like a tongue.

Impossible. The storm cloud never sinks beneath the earth.

And yet, here it was.

In the flashes of lightning she spied the niches containing Ancestors along the narrow passage, the names carved beneath their bodies long obscured by dust and cobwebs. A rumble of thunder sounded in the silence.

"What's the point in running?" A harsh, cruel voice. "It's no use. I *will* have what belongs to me."

A flash of lightning came from behind, casting crazy shadows across the winding passage, and Lena started to run. "Vigo!" she cried out, her voice breaking. "Vigo!" But she'd forgotten—Vigo was dead: he couldn't help her now. No one could.

She didn't recognize this part of the crypts. She was lost.

Lena hurtled around a corner into a cavernous tomb, where Ancestors were laid out on their sarcophagi, gem-eyes glittering. The storm cloud was thicker here, and she sank into it gratefully, enveloped by the thick, cloying vapor. A second rumble of thunder sounded in the darkness, the timbre of a groan. Impossibly, the steady footsteps grew yet closer—even though Lena had been running—and she ducked down behind a tomb, cupping the butterfly close to her chest.

"You can't hide from me," said the voice nearby.

The footsteps were so close she could hear the distinct footfall of heel-toe, heel-toe, the swish of robes against the dusty ground. She trembled, hugging her knees. She felt very small suddenly, like a child. She shut her eyes, but it made no difference: the storm cloud swirled behind her eyelids too.

And that's when she heard the other voice, a grumble of thunder separating into words.

She who spins the cloud weaves the storm.

Lena woke with her head cradled in Emris's arm, lying on the floor of the Holy Council with bright light filtering through the glass-and-crystal dome far above. She was slick with sweat and her head felt like it was stuffed with wool. Her mouth was dry.

"Lena, are you all right?" Emris said.

She nodded, raised a hand to her clammy forehead as the world spun. "I had the strangest dream." She sat up slowly, vaguely aware that the room had emptied out, the long white benches standing vacant. Emris offered her a tall glass of water and she drank deeply. The silence felt peaceful now, the light soft. "How long have I been out?"

"About thirty minutes." Emris glanced over his shoulder. "She really shouldn't have done that. It might've been much worse." The anger in his voice was unmistakable, though whispered.

The remnants of Lena's dream were already melting

from her body, tension leaking from her shoulders and neck, her fists slowly unclenching—the imprints of nails red and sore in her palm. What had happened? All she remembered was the butterfly in her hand and those curious words spoken in a voice of thunder: *She who spins the cloud weaves the storm.*

What did it mean? And who or what had spoken?

Emris offered her a hand and she rose unsteadily to her feet. She now saw that Grand Master Auris was standing, unapologetic, in front of the table. The seven other masters had left. The Grand Master spoke without preamble.

"Your power is . . . unusual. There is no doubt it contains a kind of darkness, certain properties that indicate an association with forbidden magics." Her voice was hard and cold. "And yet . . . after your successful accomplishment of the three tasks, and further discussion with the seven masters present, I can find no reason to deny you access to the temples," she said. The obvious reluctance in her voice gave the impression she had looked for every possible reason. "You are to begin in Faul, as a novice under the Third Huntsman's supervision. In a year, you shall undergo this test and examination a second time."

The words were swimming around in Lena's head. "You mean . . . I'm not a Rogue? I've . . . passed?" She turned to Emris. "I did pass, didn't I?"

"Not exactly," he said gently. "But they've decided to let you stay and prove yourself."

Lena felt a surge of confusion and stared at the floor.

She'd succeeded at the spells. She'd won in combat. How could she have done any better?

She looked up at Grand Master Auris, who had already turned to leave. "Tell me, what exactly did you see inside me?"

Auris's eyes flashed. "That is not for you to ask."

"Please," Lena insisted. "I just need to know what's wrong with me!"

Auris trained her eyes on Emris. "Huntsman, get your novice under your control and leave. I will not be spoken to in this way."

"Come on, Lena," said Emris, leading her to the doors.

Outside, she squinted against the sunlight, queasy and shaky and unable to believe what had happened.

"It's not so bad, Lena. Even though you're a novice, the temple will still afford you the legal protection you need," Emris said. "I know it's not what we hoped for . . ."

"It's not that," she said, shaking her head. "It's the dream I had when I blacked out in there. When I woke up, I remembered a voice telling me something."

"What did it say?"

"'She who spins the cloud weaves the storm.'"

"The storm?" His voice was thoughtful.

Together, they had started down the steps, but both of them hesitated now, close to the bottom. Something was wrong. The broad street in front of the Council was unusually empty and quiet, even though the market stalls were still set up and the smell of roasted nuts and candied fruit sweetened the air. There was something else: a group of men emerging from the shadows of the stall directly opposite the Council entrance. The man at the front of the group, dressed from head to toe in white brocade, was followed by eight or nine of the black-and-white uniformed guards of the palace.

Lena's stomach roiled, and she started to stumble backward toward the Holy Council. She tripped on the steps, landing hard on her tailbone. The man in white brocade was Lord Chatham, and he was approaching her with thunder in his face. *He's finally woken up, then*, Lena thought, her heart pattering. *Time to face the consequences*.

There was no sign of the injuries his mechanicals had inflicted upon him—but it looked as if he was determined to have his revenge.

Suddenly Emris was at her side, hauling her to her feet. She watched his expression harden as he realized what was happening.

Lena drew herself up tall.

"Hand her over, huntsman," Lord Chatham demanded.

Emris shook his head. "She is not mine to hand over."

"I'm not coming with you," Lena said, her hand circling the butterfly in her pocket, the weight of it lending her courage. Its wings fluttered at her touch.

"This girl destroyed my property," Lord Chatham growled, continuing to address Emris. "Do you have any idea how much she has cost me? The King has authorized a warrant for her arrest." He held out a piece of paper stamped with a large red seal. "Hand her over."

The guards moved forward, surrounding the pair.

"Lena is a novice of the temple of Faul. You will need to petition the Council," Emris said firmly, but the men didn't seem to be listening, tightening the circle around them.

"We should go," Lena said. She glanced up toward the Holy Council, but it was unlikely the few left inside were aware of what was happening on their doorstep.

"Petition the Council? Me?" Chatham's voice was mocking. For the first time, Lena thought she saw a glimpse of black-rainbow glimmer flashing behind his gray eyes, and felt an instant chill. "First, my godsdamned apprentice runs off with the most precious item in my possession. Then this little thief refuses to sell me something that isn't even hers to sell and sets a fortune's worth of stock against me with her filthy Rogue magic, nearly killing me. I'll have to destroy it all. Do you have any idea how expensive it's going to be for me to replace that stock?" His guards parted for him as he climbed the first few steps, then closed in tightly behind. "And you talk to me of *petitions*." Chatham opened his hands wide at his sides. The air crackled, and with a sudden whoosh his palms were glowing and fizzing with a fierce, flickering, electrical light, yellow sparks flying between his fingers. "I *will* have retribution."

"Get out of my way, Chatham, or I'll really kill you this time," Lena said with false bravado. She dropped into a fighting stance, drawing on her power in the way she'd been taught, feeling it rush through her body but holding it steady beneath her skin. Her heart was hammering. By her side, Emris raised his own palms: the air around them warped, gray streams of light emanating from his body, ghostly as starlight.

"Do you *really* presume to fight me?" Chatham laughed. The bright, humming electricity surrounding his hands spread up his arms, around his shoulders, and down his body, growing brighter.

Lena gasped and staggered against Emris, the breath snatched from her by the force of Chatham's power. She had to squint to look at him—but when she did, she caught an unmistakable flash of rainbow-blackness. "Emris, his eyes!"

"Chaos-infected," Emris said under his breath. "As I suspected."

"Chaos is the most powerful, purest form of magic," Chatham said, his voice weirdly distorted. "And I have mastered the art of bending it to my will. Shall I show you?"

But it was Emris who attacked first, sending a punch of sleek gray light directly into Chatham's stomach. The magician doubled over, scowled, retaliated with a zap of bright-yellow electricity, but Emris cleverly twisted and deflected the attack with a corkscrew of air, hitting the guard behind Lena, who had been cautiously edging closer to the fight. He fell instantly, his face ashen—and the other guards hesitated. Chatham attacked a second time, and

Emris ducked. In a curve of his hand, he twisted the air near Chatham's feet, his magic glowing a moonlight-silver. Chatham stumbled, but he didn't fall: it wasn't enough. His next attack hit Emris square in the chest, and Emris staggered back, obviously dazed, barely keeping his balance. He fell onto one knee.

"Emris!" Lena shouted. The duel had passed in a matter of seconds and had drawn them farther down the street. She hurried toward him, summoning a punch of cloud that knocked Chatham on the side of his head; then she looped Emris's arm around her shoulder. Supporting his weight, she started to climb back up the steps to the Holy Council, shouting "Help! Help!" at the top of her lungs.

But she was only halfway up when she felt Chatham's burning magic close about her ankle, yanking her backward. Her leg hit hard stone, her shin screaming. Emris fell at her side. Chatham twisted his hand and turned her over, grabbing her and pressing her down. His fingers were tight and cold around her arms, and a step dug into the nape of her neck. The serpent flashed into her mind, the dark, icy chips of its eyes watching her die. Chatham's handsome face had grown ugly, contorted in rage.

She gasped for breath but found only heat and light. She tried to move, but Chatham's magic surrounded her, trapped her. Her skin was burning in the bright, hissing yellow that encased her like a tomb.

"Now I will show you what power really means," he whispered.

A film had covered his eyes, a black iridescence, and he was smiling, a curious calmness passing over his features.

She reached inside herself in desperation, searching for an answer within her magic.

She found . . . something. Something she had sensed before, even used before, but never truly grasped. A curl of darkness in the cold fire that crackled deep within, pulsing with power . . . *A kind of heart*, she thought. She tugged on it, wildly praying for a miracle.

Lena gasped. She was in two places now. She was outside the Holy Council on a bright wintry day, staring into Lord Chatham's Chaos-infected eyes, and she was in Duke's Forest in her mind, and the three dead were sleeping in the glade outside the city walls.

The real world was fading—the sunlight and the cold, hard hands at her throat. She felt an urgent tug in the place beneath her chest, a struggle, like something trying to escape. In the forest, the huntsman's arrow bound her palms in prayer, leashing her power. The huntsman lingered in the shadows. In a moment of clarity, she knew what she had to do. She ripped her hands apart, screaming as pain coursed through her like thunder, and her blood and her storm were unleashed. She pressed her hands into the sky. And with her scream, the power rose from deep inside, enveloping her completely. The world returned.

She clenched her fists. Storm clouds spun from her fingers, from her mouth, rumbled over the glassy dome of the Council. Chatham staggered back, his face suddenly confused. She wove the clouds into the sky, sensing a familiar, cold electric fire filling her body—and now spilling out of it. Lena felt the first spots of rain on her gasping lips. And then came the lightning.

Strike him, she thought, and the storm was at her command. A huge bolt of lightning streaked through the air, reflected wildly in the darkened glass of the Holy Council.

Chatham fell, and Lena heard his screams and smelled burning flesh. The butterfly had escaped from her pocket and was fluttering around her head, round and round, as if excited by the power.

Her ears were ringing and her eyes were staring. Under the clouds, it had grown dark. Her hands were wet and hot, her throat sore; the smell of acrid smoke filled her nose. It was pouring rain now. Someone was tugging her and she stumbled up, the steps appearing to fall from beneath her. "Lena, come with me. We have to run."

The world righted itself, and she allowed Emris to pull her away. His face was drained of blood but full of determination. She glanced behind her. Chatham lay on the ground, pale. His clothes were burned, his hair singed. Blood—shockingly red against his silver-pale skin—was running from his nose.

Struck by lightning.

The guards were hurrying for help. Shocked onlookers had gathered behind the glass walls of the Council. A couple of girls were screaming in the street. Others gazed up at the sky, roiling with clouds.

"Lena, listen to me." Emris grabbed her face, forced her to meet his eyes. "Once they understand what's happened, they're going to say you're a Radical and a murderer and they're going to kill you. You need to run."

Murderer? Lena gazed up at the sky, let the rain trickle down her cheeks. The butterfly settled in her hair, calmer now. "I've killed two people," she whispered.

But Emris just pulled her hand. "Come on!"

And finally, with a jolt, she understood. They barreled down the steps together. The few white-faced guards who stood in their way toppled like tin soldiers as Emris made a sweeping gesture with his hand, the air churning under their feet.

Together, they rounded the back of the Holy Council, passing the small alleyway into Faul's temple. She remembered running through Duke's Forest, the dogs howling for her blood, and felt wordlessly grateful for the touch of Emris's hand in her own. Now she could hear people following, shouts in the distance, hoofbeats.

"This way!" Emris said, tugging her around a corner. They pelted down the narrow street, quickly turned left and then right. Left again, right again. The streets were quieter, poorer, residential. Fat drops of rain were falling, heavy and hot as tears of rage, roaring on the cobblestones. They carried on down a straight road for a minute or so, the sounds of pursuit growing louder, and Emris pulled her into a side alley so tiny it was nearly invisible. The streets were slick and shiny in the semi-light. At the end of the alley was a tall wooden gate—Emris vaulted over; Lena climbed. He helped her down the other side, into a back garden, her hands stinging with splinters. Hoofbeats passed by on the street beyond the alley.

"Come on," Emris said, urging her onward through one garden and then another. Lena's boots were soon caked with mud from the drenched flower beds, her robes soaked through. Lights started to flicker on inside the buildings, and the small comfort of a fire and a lamp appeared to Lena like another world. The ground started to slope upward as they emerged onto a street again.

Lena realized they were heading broadly east, out of town, and had reached the tangled warren of streets that had seemed like lace from far above, climbing up one of the city's seven hills. Emris darted left down a dark alley and drew her aside. The rain had lessened at last, and a reddish, sickly sun showed through the drizzle.

"Hide here for a while," he said. "I'm going to create a diversion."

"Emris—no. It's too dangerous! What if they catch you?" *None of this is his fault*, she thought. *I can't let him suffer the consequences. Not like Vigo did.* "Besides, I haven't heard anyone following lately . . . Aren't we safer sticking together?"

"It's not that simple, Lena. Look." He pointed upward. Sure enough, she spotted riders in the sky, a few of them barely streets away. "They'll be combing the city for us until it's too dark to see. If I can lead them somewhere else, we'll be safe until dawn."

Lena hesitated, seeing the wisdom in what he was saying but not wanting to accept it. "I . . ."

Emris shook his head. "Just hide. I'll find you again—please, just for once, do as I say. Stay here until nightfall. I promise I'll be back."

And before he left, he pressed his lips briefly to hers—so briefly she wondered if she had imagined it, and held her hand over her mouth as if to keep the ghost of the kiss.

Lena crouched in a doorway in the quiet, dilapidated alley where Emris had left her. It was full of empty, broken windows, abandoned newspapers, and the stench of feral animals. She sat in the dark at the end, drawing her knees to her chest. She'd been waiting for ages; it was dark now, and a beam of moonlight lit the detritus at the alley entrance.

The houses here had been grand once, with huge deep doorways and wide steps—but they looked old too, their bricks flaking and ivy trailing through their windows. The night grew quieter as the moon rose: for hours, the only sound she heard was a distant drunkard lurching, singing, into a gutter.

Tears streaked Lena's cheeks with salt as she wondered what had happened to Emris. The butterfly perched on her knee, gazing at her as if in sympathy.

"He said he wouldn't be long," she whispered. "But it's been hours. What if they captured him?" Her forehead sank down, and the butterfly crawled into her hair—she felt its warm weight against her skull, the gentle simmer of its magical heart chiming with her own. She'd wait until sunrise, she decided. If he didn't return, she'd have to flee the city on her own.

And then what? She ran through all she'd learned of Valorian. West was Duke's Forest; north were the Wastelands; east, she thought, promised trading ports and military posts. But the south . . . yes. Emris had said the islands were wild and foreign; perhaps there she might have half a chance of leaving herself behind, of disappearing.

Is that what I want, to disappear? Lena shook her head. She was finally beginning to feel like herself. Would she really be forced to throw all that away?

EIGHTEEN
Truth

Constance woke in the evening, her hand resting in Xander's. He was sleeping, his face ashen and pale. The light was dying, and it had started to rain, water trickling down the walls into her cell.

"You're a physician," she said to Dr. Thorn. "What's the matter with Lord Irvine?"

"I can't be sure without examining him. But I'd hazard a guess he's bleeding internally. I've seen men beaten like that before."

As she'd suspected. "And what does that mean?" she asked quietly.

"For his chances? I'd be surprised if he lasts the night."

"Don't say that," she snapped, running a hand through her hair, unbound and matted around her shoulders, her hairpins all fallen or twisted.

"Just because it's painful doesn't make it any less true," he replied calmly. And he lay down on the straw, turning his face to the wall, cradling his gloved hand as if it was hurting.

Constance concentrated on eating the meal she'd been

brought a few hours ago, disgusted at the dry, mealy bread and the brackish water—but forcing it down to keep up her strength. A puddle had formed beneath her cell window—a product of the rain running down the walls. She'd had an idea. If the girl had followed her instructions, she ought to have found Emris, and he would have taken her back to the City of Kings. If she could only send him word . . .

She gazed at the puddle. The light down here was fading, but it might be just enough.

It was worth a try. It was dangerous: without an enchanted mirror, the entire operation relied on her own magical resources. But what choice did she have?

She knelt over the dimly lit puddle and plucked a few strands of straw from its surface. Lowering her face, she glimpsed her pale reflection swimming unsteadily in the dirty water.

Her magic pulsed under her skin, thrumming through the metal of her left arm. She touched the puddle gently with her hand, feeling the wetness against her fingertips and releasing a glittering liquid magic onto the water. She imagined the temple, the mirror in Emris's room—the familiar furnishings, the rugs, the bed. She pushed her vision into the magic.

"Emris Lochlade," she whispered, breathing on the puddle's surface.

And slowly an image emerged, dim and indistinct but undeniably *there*.

"Emris?"

Constance? In her mind's ear, she heard him drop something, the clatter of a chair, and in the puddle his scarred face swam into view. He was disheveled. Scorch marks on his gray robes suggested a fight, and his right shoulder drooped. But she already knew she didn't have time to ask—the drain on her magic was intense and unrelenting. *You ignored my advice, then,* he said, quickly composing himself. *You shouldn't be doing this. It's dangerous. Where are you, anyway?*

"In the dungeon in Duke's Forest. Things are more serious than you realize. My father is dead," she whispered. "Emris, is there a girl there with you? A girl with a birthmark on her face, a mage . . . ?"

He nodded. *Her name is Lena. I've been trying to figure out—*

"Let me figure it out for you," she interrupted. "She has the heart of the storm spell—a small brass butterfly that once belonged to my mother. Emris, you have to send her back to me so I can destroy it—before it's too late."

Emotions crossed his scarred face, fleeting as shadows, until his eyes settled into a kind of understanding. *The books . . . the forbidden magic you were studying . . .*

"What is it?" She could feel the connection slipping.

You were studying the storm spell. It's necromancy—that's why you had all those forbidden texts . . . and your experiments in Chatham's workshop. You were studying it to find out how to break it. His voice was full of sudden wonder, even in her mind.

"For gods' sakes, Emris." She streamed her magic across the puddle, feeling her hand tremble with the effort.

"There's no time. The Justice has taken control. I am trapped in the dungeons and the dead are rising. The fate of Duke's Forest rests on your shoulders." Her whole body shook. She could feel Emris's confusion through the mirror-bond, though he said nothing. "Just hurry."

His expression shifted to determination. *We'll be there tomorrow.*

And with that, the connection was severed.

NINETEEN
The Cat

Lena woke to the sound of rumbling and a warm, furry creature pressing against her legs.

She opened her eyes. A small gray cat with a snub face stood on the steps, silvery in the moonlight, purring loudly and nudging its cheek against her shin. She sat up, her back aching from leaning against the door, and rolled her shoulders. The cat regarded her thoughtfully.

"Hello, puss," said Lena as the cat nudged her again, smiling in spite of herself. The butterfly peeked out curiously from behind her ear, not quite daring to fly. Lena rubbed her knuckles against the cat's head until it sank to the ground, its purr thunderous. "Who are you, eh? What's your name?" The cat meowed and rolled onto its side, arching its back in delight. She ran her hand through its soft fur.

As quickly as the cat had succumbed to Lena's attentions, it leaped up and padded down the steps to the street, glancing over its shoulder at her. It licked its paw with sudden businesslike ferocity, as if to say: *Me, make a fool of myself?* Lena grinned. The cat stared at her expectantly.

"What is it? You want me to follow?" she whispered.

She stood up and walked down the alley, her legs aching from sitting still for so long, hunched up against the chill. The cat instantly trotted along a little farther and waited for her at the nearby corner. It moved further when she caught up—and disappeared down a set of steps between two houses.

"I don't really want to go down there," whispered Lena, peering into the gloom, hesitating at the top of the steps. What if Emris returned to find her gone? She'd promised him she'd wait until dawn. The cat wrapped itself around her legs, then hurried into the darkness, meowing—as if in encouragement. The stairway was narrow, pitch-black, and silent as the dead. The cat meowed a second time—the sound fainter, farther away.

"Come back, puss. It's too dark," she whispered.

Another, slightly impatient meow. A deep silence.

"Hey, are you there?"

Nothing.

She edged forward, trailing her fingers along the wall as she eased down the steps. A noise—a creak, or perhaps a whine—sounded from farther along. Lena felt her heart squeeze, her breath go shallow. The stairway reeked of rotten food. *What the hell am I doing? I should turn back!*

"Where are you?" she breathed. The butterfly fluttered out from behind her ear. In the darkness, she noticed the tiniest flicker of bluish light at its core, wreathed by cloud. Her eyes started to adjust, vague black shapes materializing in the gloom as the butterfly fluttered on: a long ladder or plank leaning against the wall at the bottom of the steps, a pile of rubbish.

A yellow flash in a dart of moonlight—two feline eyes up ahead.

"Stupid animal," she grumbled. "What are you doing? I thought—"

That noise. A subtle creak. The cat's eyes vanished.

Lena hurried over to the end of the alley, felt the solid brick wall with her hands. "Where are you?" she murmured—but the damned creature was gone.

She leaned against the wall in despair, but the surface shifted, the creaky moan now identifying itself as the noise of old hinges. Gasping and unbalanced, she fell through to the other side, slamming painfully against the ground.

Dazed, she felt the cat nudging her head. Her cheek was pressed against a cold stone floor.

"Hello, Lena," said a man's voice, low and warm. "I see my friend found you."

Lena lifted herself onto her elbows and looked up. Despite the eggshell-pale mask covering his face—swirling with fire patterns around the eyes—his voice was unmistakable. "Emris?" He was holding the cat—purring fiercely—in his arms.

She scrambled to her feet. Her ears were ringing, a bruise rising at the side of her head. She stood in a nondescript redbrick corridor, the high ceiling shaped into a pointed arch. "What—?"

"Draw up your hood and follow me," he commanded

softly, setting down the cat and pulling his own gray hood down over his mask. "In the halls of the masked god, we can never be certain who to trust."

The masked god? Her heart lurched. She followed Emris at a brisk pace down the long corridor. As the passage wound deeper into the building, it broadened out, red brick melding to stone, doors appearing on either side. The cat slunk away down a different passage. Despite the late hour, they passed a handful of other people wearing masks and loose purple robes, each mask as individual in decoration and even expression as their robes were uniform. One woman stalked past in close-fitting black, her hood pulled low, the smell of blood following in her wake. Lena shuddered.

Eventually, Emris stopped at a wooden door that opened into a modest, dark room, a fire crackling in a large fireplace. He shut the door behind them, locked it, and set his torch in an empty sconce on the wall. The room was windowless but contained a single bed, a desk, and a wooden chair, as well as two battered armchairs in front of the fire. Emris removed his mask, setting it on a stand on the mantelpiece. The painted flames around the eyes shone in the firelight. A mirror with a strange iridescent sheen hung on the wall next to the bed. He took a taper and walked around the room, lighting the candles.

"We haven't got much time. The palace guards are searching for you in every corner of the city," he said, "and the initiates of Mythris are not known for their trustworthiness. I'm sure the King has several in his pay." He blew out the taper and signaled for Lena to sit in one of the low chairs by the fire.

"Tell me what's going on." She rubbed her forehead and whispered, "What is this place? Why are you . . . ?" She gazed around a second time. The room showed definite signs of habitation: the half-empty glass on the table, the crumbs on the floor.

He sighed. "I haven't been entirely honest with you. Like Constance, I am an initiate of the masked god, and by Mythris's nature we are sworn to secrecy. But now, of course, the truth can hardly be avoided." His voice was matter-of-fact, as if the whole situation were entirely ordinary.

"I don't understand. You're . . ."

"The Third Huntsman of Faul—yes. Remember, you don't necessarily have to pledge yourself to one temple exclusively. I was pledged to Faul as a novice, but secretly the masked god recruited me to the cause. Now I spend my days with Faul and my nights with Mythris. It's how Constance and I first met."

"What?" Lena blinked, confusion sinking under a kind of anger—at him, perhaps, but more at herself. It occurred to her how little she knew Emris, a man she had met a handful of days ago, a man she had nevertheless trusted. He had told her about the initiates of Mythris, their reputation as spies and assassins for hire. If that was true . . . She stared at his face, trying to figure out if another version of Emris was hidden beneath: a killer, a liar. *Masks behind masks.*

He leaned forward, elbows on his knees, his eyes grave. "Lena, I can see you're struggling—and I can't blame you. It's a lot to take in. But I'm still me. I never wanted to lie to you. And now I have to tell you something important."

His serious expression made her nod slowly, pushing away her shock. "What is it?" she asked, her voice quiet.

He ran a hand through the tight curls of his hair. "It's Constance. I had it all wrong. I've spoken to her at last, and I finally understand."

"Spoken to Constance?" She frowned, uncomprehending. "How?"

"When we were together, we spelled two mirrors, one of mine and one of hers, so that we could speak to each other in secret. That's mine." He gestured at the mirror hanging beside his bed.

Lena tried to ignore the tug in her heart at the intimacy this implied. "What did she say? What's happening in Duke's Forest?"

"Things aren't going well. Constance said her father is dead, and the Justice has seized control outright, crowning himself Duke. Constance has been imprisoned in the dungeons. But, Lena, listen to me. I finally understand what she is trying to do." His eyes had lit up with something like joy. "She's not a necromancer at all. She was studying the storm spell, and she's going to try and break it."

"The storm spell?"

"The storm cloud over Duke's Forest is . . . well, it's a spell to raise the dead, Lena. And it's starting to happen."

"The Ancestors?" she gasped, her mind turning confusedly, remembering how dead bodies had reacted to her touch. Had it been the storm cloud all along, not her at all? It made no sense—she was a mage, wasn't she? And who would want to raise the Ancestors anyway—to what purpose? "Where do I fit into this?"

Emris breathed deeply. "I think I've figured it out. Constance believes the heart of the spell is housed in the butterfly. But what she doesn't realize is that when you found the butterfly, the spell passed to you."

Lena pressed her hand against her chest as if she could feel the spell inside her. "But how . . . ?"

"I don't know. I've never heard of anything like this before. I wouldn't have thought it was possible." Emris smiled slightly. "But then, this is perhaps the greatest spell ever cast. Of course it would have an intelligence of its own."

"It . . . it's conscious?" She remembered how the spell had taken over when she was attacked by the snake, which had mysteriously died even as she passed out. She remembered how the Radical had told her she was something different. She remembered too how her power had appeared to help her in the shop, bringing the butterfly back to life—how the mechanical creatures had launched themselves at their creator as if animated by some other, vicious consciousness. How, outside the Holy Council, she had severed her ties to Faul so that her power might overwhelm her and take care of Chatham. Saving her. Saving itself.

"A spell like that has Chaos at its core," said Emris, "and

it wishes nothing more than to be free of anyone's control, to wreak its own havoc on the world."

Lena looked down at her hands, feeling like an imposter or the host of a parasite. *But who is really the parasite in our partnership?* "So my power ... isn't really mine at all? I'm not a mage?" She felt a kind of pain in her chest, a grief as she let go of the person she had thought she was becoming—a stronger, better person. Someone who had the power to defend herself, to walk in the sunlight and turn her face to the world. She heard her breath, shallow and fast, roaring in her ears. And suddenly she understood why she always dreamed of the crypts and of the forest, why she felt this constant urge toward a place of death, and sorrow, and pain, and darkness, drawn like a creature on the end of a lead. Because the spell's heart had to return. Because otherwise ... otherwise ... well, she wasn't sure what. But if she wanted to know the truth, one thing was certain:

"I have to go back," she whispered.

TWENTY
Hope

A night had passed since Constance had spoken to Emris, draining the best part of her energy.

Rats rustled somewhere on the periphery of her sight, glistening shapes pushing through sodden straw, tails pale in the half-light. She pulled her knees to her chest, rested her chin on the ruined material of her ceremonial robes, feeling the silky smooth embroidery against her throat. She breathed the rancid air deeply and watched the entrance to the crypts.

The dungeons overlaid the deepest, darkest sections of the crypts: the chambers of the disgraced. Here, the realms of the living and the resting place of lawless Ancestors were separated only by a rotten wooden door. Prisoners died frequently in the dungeons' grimy conditions, and guards had no wish to move the bodies of criminals to their Ancestral tombs elsewhere in the city.

And now, Constance was terribly aware of their nearness. She'd tried to rest and recover her strength, but how could she sleep when noises drifted regularly from the catacombs below, the dead stirring in their palaces of stone?

The spell was solidifying, testing itself, finding its strength—and here in the dungeons they were all unprotected but for the bars of their cells.

Constance reached through those bars and forced her own cup of water to Xander's lips, but she wasn't sure whether he swallowed—most of it ran down his chin. Earlier she'd shouted for help, insisted that he be attended to, but the guard who eventually turned up told her to shut her mouth or he'd kick her teeth in.

She *hadn't* given up. She'd promised not to. But after a night of sitting in filth and darkness, Constance had to admit she was starting to lose hope. Even if Lena and Emris turned up in Duke's Forest now, the Justice would simply take them into custody. Somehow she had to meet the girl before the Justice found her. But how?

Her forehead sank onto her knees. Then she heard a muffled roar from outside.

She met Dr. Thorn's eyes. Both of them frowned.

Constance stood up, craning toward the barred window high up in the wall of her cell. She could distinguish different sounds within the distant but growing roar: footsteps, and the pulsing chant of raised voices.

She laughed out loud, pressing her hand against her mouth.

"What is it?" said Dr. Thorn, his voice a hoarse croak.

"It's a revolt," she said, unable to believe her luck. "I promised the people an end to the storm cloud by dawn today. How could I have forgotten?"

In spite of everything, a spark of hope ignited in her heart.

The noises outside grew louder as the day slowly brightened. What sounded like a booming, threatening announcement from the battlements had little effect: if anything, the roar of the crowd intensified. An hour later, Constance heard weapons drawn outside. She heard the rhythmic stomp of angry feet against the flagstones, chanting, and shouts. And she waited.

Xander lay still, oblivious, his breath shallow. Opposite, Dr. Thorn also slept fitfully, the gauntlet on his hand occasionally twitching with red light.

Some of the guards in the room above the cells had been summoned to the battlements—she'd heard them being called, then the scrape of chairs and heavy footsteps pounding away. Constance guessed a couple had been left to attend to the prisoners, but she couldn't be sure. She stood up, paced her cell, and wondered for the hundredth time whether to use her powers to escape. Could she break through the spelled bars of her cell and fight her way out without a weapon, winning against two or three armed men at full strength? Probably not. She wished she had her cane—and her mask . . . but for now she had to pick her moment.

Even so, a smile reached her lips as she spun on her heels.

Sounds from below the prison floor stopped her in her tracks.

The steps from the dungeons, hidden behind a rotten wooden door, led down into blackness so deep that she could feel it—even though she couldn't see it. She looked at the door. A waft of stale air from underneath it flicked a strand of hair across her face. She heard the tinkle of metal on stone. Jewelry or coins falling from rotted flesh, from disintegrated clothing. The scrape of bone on bone—and footsteps. Slow, unsteady footsteps on the old, worn steps.

Not now. Please, not now.

But the noises were insistent and distinct. The spell had reached its final stage of development, no longer fumbling in the dark but surging toward the misted light. And she had no doubt that it hungered for fresh lives to feed its strength. She set her jaw and tried to stop herself from screaming in frustration.

The gods give with one hand and take away with the other.

Dr. Thorn had sat up. His cell was the closest to the door to the crypts; Xander's was close too, on the opposite side. Constance braced herself as another waft of stale, cold air rustled her hair, and the door opened.

A skeletal figure stood in the doorway, dressed in prison rags, a filthy, rusted shackle encircling its neck. Its remaining flesh was blackened and dry, clinging to white bones like limpets to the hull of a ship. Shadows stared from empty eye sockets. The hair alone remained untouched—brown and matted—while the teeth were bared by decay into a terrifying yellowish grin. The body held something that might once have been a length of chain but was spoiled and rusted nearly beyond recognition.

The figure appeared to be startled by the dim daylight and stood quite still.

Dr. Thorn staggered to his feet and backed away from the bars, his face white with horror. He raised his ungloved hand, but as he tried to summon his magic—which Constance felt surging within him, even from across the floor—something in the glove jolted him, and he cried out in agony, doubling over. At this, the dead man regained his wits, and flung himself against the physician's cell with surprising strength. Another was close behind, this one larger, broader, and less decayed.

Constance's eyes shot to Xander, completely helpless on the filthy floor of the adjacent cell.

She didn't hesitate. She rested her hands on the lock of her cell and focused, blocking out the sounds of the rising dead. She needled her magic into the red spell reinforcing the bars. The spell glittered to her magical senses, hard as sandstone against her careful touch. She persevered, frowning as she picked at its structure—clumsy, even though it was brutishly strong. At last, she found a point of weakness, tugged on a strand: the spell crumbled. Her head was pounding now—it would have been easier if she'd had her mask. She felt for the catch of the barred gate, turned it, and was out. The whole process had taken a matter of seconds.

"Help me!" Dr. Thorn's attacker had been joined by two others, and together the three dead men were attempting to tear the prison bars from their rusted sockets in the wall. Purple magic flashed and sparked as Constance's reinforcement spell was torn apart along with the cell's structure. But it was Xander she was determined to save. Another two figures had emerged from beneath and were trying to force the door of his cell. Extending her hand, she flung a concentrated ball of magic at them. Already fragile with decay, they disintegrated into dust with a flash of purple light. Coughing, she hurried to the cell and unlocked it with trembling fingers.

Xander was deathly pale, but breathing, still breathing. She heaved his arm over her shoulder and hoisted him upright.

"Help!" Dr. Thorn shouted again. Constance turned her back and half supported, half dragged Xander toward the stairs, his eyelids fluttering.

Footsteps sounded above and she steeled herself for the arrival of a guard. But instead, Winton—longsword drawn, horror on his face—appeared at the bottom of the steps, his breath billowing in the cold. To her surprise, the Justice's dog, Barbarus, was at his side. Under his free arm, Winton held a bundle, which he dropped quickly on the bottom step. With relief, Constance recognized the shape of her cane, wrapped up in an old cloak.

"Help!" Dr. Thorn's voice was desperate—the three remaining Ancestors, working together, had pulled free the bars, and one was sliding through the gap toward the physician, who was cringing against the wall.

Her brother was already hurrying toward the onslaught, the dog growling at his heels.

"Winton!" Constance said quietly but firmly, catching him by the shoulder. "The gauntlet—it's channeling

Thorn's magic into the Justice. If the physician dies, the Justice will be stripped of his greatest weapon."

As the meaning of her words dawned on him, Winton's face twisted in mingled understanding and disgust. "What is wrong with you, Constance? We have to help him!"

Constance gritted her teeth in annoyance, nodded.

He hurried forward, swung his sword in broad arcs at the heads of the dead creatures, fighting his way through. One crumbled at the first slice of metal. Barbarus disabled a second by dislodging its shin. The third had its bony fingers closed around Dr. Thorn's neck: the physician was struggling, kicking out. Winton slid inside the cell and dispatched the corpse with a single sweeping strike, while Constance eyed the door of the crypts in expectation. All the corpses in the dungeons had been destroyed or turned to dust, but countless others remained, stirring, in the darkness below . . .

For a few moments, everyone was still, the only sound the slowing of their breath and Barbarus's panting. Constance relaxed a little, lowering Xander with difficulty onto the steps. He was shaking, his face pale and slick with sweat.

"The noises have stopped," said Winton quietly. "What in the thousand crypts is going on?"

"The storm spell has reached the final stage of its development and is gaining power in a series of contractions, like a woman in labor," Constance explained, drawing out her cane from the bundle on the floor, her heart rising in relief. "Each time, the periods of activity grow longer and stronger, the peace in between shorter and more desperate."

"And then what?" Winton breathed.

"The spell is trying to gain autonomy. It wants to be free to roam wherever it wishes. I have to stop it. We should get out before the contractions start again."

"Gladly," said Winton, who was helping a shaken Dr. Thorn out of his cell.

"Winton . . . thank you." Constance had found a change of clothes in the package, including her dark-purple cloak, which—unknown to Winton—contained the mask in its hidden pocket. She changed quickly, glad to leave behind the unwieldy weight of the dirty coronation gown.

The Swordmaster was gaining consciousness, his head nodding as if he were struggling to surface from a dream. But Constance noticed the slick of sweat against his brow, the sour smell of his skin, and knew he was still in danger. "What's going on out there?" she asked.

"The people are rioting. The guards are trying to hold them at the portcullis, between the two gatehouses. The Justice is up on the battlements, directing everything. I slipped away in the confusion—they'd locked me in my rooms, but the guards were needed elsewhere and no one was left to watch me. The Ancestors are emerging from other entrances to the crypts too." He shook his head. "It's chaos."

"We can work this to our advantage," said Constance, her mind racing as she fastened her cloak.

Winton nodded. "All the guards have abandoned their posts to help on the battlements, and I found the cell keys on the ground outside. Here," he said, taking one of

Xander's arms over his shoulder—Dr. Thorn took the other, still speechless, his face white with shock. Winton pressed a ring of keys into Constance's hand. "Let's free the other prisoners and get out of here."

Constance nodded gratefully and straightened her back. A plan had already taken shape in her head. "Winton, take Dr. Thorn, the Swordmaster, and what remains of his men to my rooms in the south tower—it's the farthest from the fighting. Dr. Thorn, there you will attend to Lord Irvine."

"So you have a use for me after all," the physician said, shooting Constance a sharp glance that left her in no doubt he'd heard her quiet advice to Winton minutes earlier.

"And what will you do?" Winton asked.

She turned to face her brother. "Do you remember the cryptling with a birthmark on her face? The one who . . . at your mother's Descent . . . ?"

Winton nodded, frowning at the memory.

"She's on her way here, and she has the heart of the storm spell. If she gives it to me, I can destroy the spell for good. She should be trying to find me too, so I'm guessing she'll be headed for the castle. I'm going to try to intercept her before the Justice gets in the way."

"All right. You know where I am if you need me."

Constance felt a sudden rush of affection for her half-brother. She reached out for him, squeezed his shoulder. "Thank you, Winton."

He smiled, his eyes shining. "Let's do this."

TWENTY-ONE
The Chase

The street was quiet. The moon was a dim gray, mercifully, and the stars were shadowed by thin scarves of cloud. It was too dark for searching—no riders circled the sky now. Lena and Emris, hooded and cloaked in the robes of Mythris, led a pair of black horses uphill toward the outskirts of the city. A pair of horses with godspeed charms, Emris had said, was the fastest way to fly to Duke's Forest—but they had to get to the very farthest reaches of the city to avoid attracting attention, and to conserve the horses' energy and the spell's effectiveness.

A few men and women watched from doorways as they passed by—but quickly slipped inside, eyes wide, as they caught sight of Emris's mask. The increasingly ramshackle houses eventually turned into the slums, where the very poorest scraped out a living.

"Why build a temple here?" Lena whispered.

"This place and these people are invisible to the rest of the city," Emris said under his breath. "What better place to hide a temple that does not want to be found?"

The dwellings extended nearly to the hilltop but grew hunched and shadowed, petering out as the slope got steeper and rockier. As Lena reached the top, breathing heavily, she stopped at the sight of the view beyond. The hill dropped off sharply, a steep slope tufted with grass. At the bottom, the gray starlit land stretched into a long, uncultivated field, yawning into the distance.

Emris drew to a halt. "Are you ready for this?"

Lena looked back. A strange peacefulness had settled over the city, like the calm before a storm. Lights glowed in the darkness, sharp and real. And yet . . . after everything that had happened since she'd left Duke's Forest . . . it felt like a dream.

The spell was inside her, swirling in her stomach, its coldness flooding her veins. The butterfly slowly opened its wings and fluttered from her shoulder to her hand. *This* was real. This was the piece of the puzzle she was missing. If she could only understand it, she knew she would finally understand herself.

"I'm ready," she said at last.

"Then let's go."

They mounted their horses, and Emris laid his hands over both of the godspeed charms tied into the bridles, speaking the incantation to seal the spell. Once he was done, he nodded. Lena took a deep breath and dug her heels into the horse's flanks.

Their journey to the City of Kings sped past in reverse, far into the night—twinkling lights broken by long swathes of blackness, the screams of owls rising from solitary barns. Otherwise, the ride over the King's Road was silent. The moon was a sliver of white like a god's fingernail. Hours later, as they gained on the mountain range in the west, the sun started to rise and the horses descended, their hooves thudding as they met the road surface.

Lena reined her horse to a stop at the edge of the forest. Sure enough, she felt a kind of tug in her stomach, as if the spell were drawing her inside. And yet . . .

This is the place I killed the serpent.

Farther in, the dead explorers lie in the clearing.

Farther still, the hounds tried to catch me under the city walls.

And beyond that, Vigo's bones lie bare outside the castle.

There was no glowing path to guide her this time—and even if there had been, she wasn't so sure she would want to follow it.

"The spell's heart is inside you, Lena. You have to follow your instincts to lead you to the castle—we have no other choice." Emris was a few paces behind, scanning anxiously over his shoulder for signs of pursuit. Dark clouds had gathered on the eastern horizon, and it was difficult to distinguish the black shapes wheeling in the sky—birds, or riders in flight?

"What if . . . ?" Lena started, but shook her head. Even Emris didn't know about her deepest secrets, her hopes, and her fears.

"What is it?" He pulled his horse up beside her, reached

across to her, and squeezed her shoulder. "Lena, you can tell me anything."

The ghost of his kiss burned on her lips. If she didn't trust him, whom could she trust? She took a deep breath, her mind spinning back to the first time the butterfly had found her, how she'd felt special: as if she'd been chosen. "What if I wasn't chosen at all? What if I'm not special? What if this is all just . . . chance?" She swallowed. "I was the only cryptling down there that night. It might've just been an accident of timing."

Emris regarded her seriously. "Lena, you can't think this way. The spell is chaotic magic. It's not something you should feel special to have received."

"And yet . . . even though Vigo died because of it, because of me . . . if it weren't for the spell, I would never have found my way out. I would never have met you or traveled to the City of Kings and learned everything I have learned, seen everything I have seen." She gazed into the writhing mists, feeling a similar writhing inside her own heart. "It feels wrong to be grateful, but I am."

"I can understand that," he replied gently. "But think of all the evil it has wrought too. The Radical's fascination with you. The dead shop assistant. Lord Chatham. The circumstances in which we've had to flee—it's all the spell's doing. When we find Constance, she will remove the heart and destroy it, and that's a good thing. The storm cloud will be gone forever. Isn't that what you want too? To save your home?"

Is this my home? Lena thought. But she nodded. He was right. She knew he was. The storm cloud had caused her as much harm as it had good. It was only . . . without the spell, she'd just be . . . Well, who would she be really? Her old self? Trapped by destiny and painfully powerless? She sighed. "Let's just go."

"Good. Now, lead the way," Emris said softly. "I trust you." He turned to look at the sky one last time. "And hurry, Lena. I think they're coming," he said, his voice barely more than a whisper.

Lena also stole a glance at the darkening sky and the black shapes emerging from the gray, then set off into the forest.

They hadn't ridden far by the time they heard hooves beating the soft earth some distance behind and shouts of "Stop, in the name of the King!" thronging the storm cloud like the cries of ghosts.

They spurred their horses faster, dangerously close to losing their footing in the mulchy forest floor, but soon it was clear the men were gaining. A few flashes zipped through the thick cloud, mingling with the blue-green flickers of lightning.

"They're attacking!" Emris called over the noise of their hooves. "We should separate—I'll try and lead them off."

And before Lena could protest, he had wheeled his horse off to the right and was swallowed in the cloud.

"No!" she called. But it was too late. How would he find his way without her? The thought of Emris lost in the forest—infested with vicious serpents and hostile mages—made her insides lurch uncomfortably.

The sounds of pursuit dropped off but didn't disappear altogether. Among the maze of trees and the shifting cloud, it was difficult to tell whether the noises of hooves and voices and the flashes of magic were real, figments of her imagination, or even the effects of the noxious cloud on her bare eyes. Lena shut her lids briefly and felt the tug of magic inside her growing stronger and stronger. She must be nearing the city by now. She just had to trust her instincts, like Emris had said.

Her eyes snapped open as the horse's muscles strained, and it vaulted a fallen tree, sweat foaming on its glossy coat. Lena clung on, her legs burning, hair lashing her face. The purple robes flapped behind her, damp with vapor. She sensed her mount wouldn't last very much longer.

A close branch overhead whipped away the thought—she ducked at the last minute, a shower of dead lichen falling on her shoulders. The cloud was thickening, her exhausted mount working hard to pick out a trail. Lena ached all over, inside and out—but she couldn't give up, not now, not ever. She was so near she could feel it.

She heard the *thud* of another set of hooves, a cry of frustration or victory. That *was real*, she thought in panic. Someone was close by. Her horse swerved around a desiccated stump, snorting. She risked a glance over her shoulder, glimpsed a flash of something in between the thick, dead trees—still some distance behind but gaining.

Suddenly the ground lurched, her horse rearing with a wild scream as a ditch opened up on the forest floor, and Lena flew through the air. She landed heavily on her back in the soft earth.

"Hey!" she tried to shout, but—winded—only a muffled wheeze escaped her lips. The horse was already galloping off into the darkness.

She scrambled to her feet and ran along the path, which veered steeply uphill. By her reckoning, she was very close to the city. She panted as she climbed, pulling the purple robes up over her knees.

The city walls appeared from the storm cloud as if they'd leaped out of the soil. The rumble of hooves grew closer and closer, and she hurried to find the secret narrow opening under the wall. At least whoever was following her didn't know about this—they would likely lose her trail here, and find the locked gates instead. *But what of Emris?* She pushed away the painful thought, dived onto her stomach, and pulled herself through, the dead rosebush scratching her hands and snagging on the masked god's long purple robes. As she emerged on the other side, she shrugged off the tangled outer layer—beneath, she still wore the simple gray uniform of Faul's temple.

She looked up, and her heart plummeted. Whatever she'd expected to find, this was worse. There was smoke in the air, a sulfurous tang distinct from the foul electric odor of the storm cloud—and she heard shouts, then the clash of metal, the crackle of fire. Her stomach lurched. She ran forward and saw a building burning on the main thoroughfare, acrid smoke mingling with the cloud.

She ran uphill toward the castle. On her way she noticed smashed windows, wide-open doors, the storm cloud snaking into cramped living quarters, flickering over the chaos inside. Belongings were strewn, abandoned, across the pavement. And but for the voices, which she realized were echoing from farther up the mountain, the lower town was silent and seemed to be deserted.

Lena was about to pass another open door when she saw something curious: the hatch to the crypt in the center of the floor was slightly ajar. She approached it uneasily, a stab of fear twisting in her gut.

She crouched by the trapdoor, smelled the familiar odor of her old life: dust, mold, stuffy air. But in the faint light falling through the gap, she glimpsed something . . . something *else*. A cold sweat prickled the back of her neck.

She reached out, pushed the door slightly further ajar— and instantly staggered back, unable to breathe.

A withered hand lay on the top step—darkened, rotten flesh clinging to bone. It was attached to a black-clad arm leading down into darkness. She could see the vague shape of a head, turned away from her, and a long-robed body.

It was as if the person . . . the Ancestor . . . had been trying to escape.

She quickly replaced the hatch door, her breath coming

in sharp gasps. She pushed a heavy wooden chair over the top, though it was pointless: every house in town had an identical trapdoor. If the dead wanted out, they'd find a way. Perhaps they already had.

I have to find Constance, she thought, backing slowly away from the trapdoor and stumbling into a run. *Emris was right: I have to make this stop.*

The crowd around the castle's gates was hundreds strong, faces twisted, mouths contorted and shouting. Some carried weapons—beaten-up longswords or workmanlike daggers, and a handful of spears. Others made do with whatever had come to hand—kitchen knives, spades, and scythes. Their fear and rage were palpable, living things buzzing in Lena's ears.

She struggled toward the gates but kept losing her bearings—though small enough to slip through the gaps, she wasn't tall enough to see the route ahead. She recognized a few faces here and there—the relations of the dead she'd tended to over the years, no doubt. For a split second she reached for her cowl, then immediately realized that it wasn't there, that she didn't need it anymore. She wasn't a cryptling now. No one spared Lena a glance anyway, despite her birthmark: their eyes were too keenly focused on the castle looming above, wreathed in fog. A few children clutched at their parents or grandparents, crying, not understanding what was happening.

Somewhere, the hounds were yowling, their voices like

lost souls drifting into the sky. The sound was a chilling reminder of those who had been condemned to death by the Justice.

The crowd cried wordlessly in return, surging toward the wrought iron portcullis. It held firm, for now, under the assault of hands and shoulders and rusty old metal, and the guards were firing arrows at those brave enough to fling themselves against its bulk. But as she worked her way forward, Lena spied a large tree trunk—a makeshift battering ram—passed by the strongest among the crowd at the back toward the gate. The assault on the castle was barely starting—the people were determined to fight their way inside. Someone threw a bottle; the glass smashed against the walls.

A chant started up toward the rear: "Justice! Justice! Justice! Justice!"

Lena followed the eyes of the chanters and thought she could see the Justice on the battlements as the storm cloud momentarily cleared, distinguishable by the gleaming buttons on his military coat, the gold epaulets. He was a lone figure off to one side, gazing out over the tumult like the captain of a sinking ship over a stormy sea. A silver glove—a gauntlet, perhaps—caught the light as he raised his arm to command another attack of arrows. Lena felt a surge of hatred so strong that bile rose in her throat. *This man killed Vigo, and he nearly killed me . . . but I'm not here for him. Not yet anyway.* She swallowed and continued to slide forward through the crowd.

At last, Lena shouldered through a gap at the front—she was close now, up against the portcullis, but a way inside was as elusive as it had been at the back. Green-cloaked guards with drawn swords blocked the narrow staircase leading into the gatehouse beside the portcullis—and more were stationed on the battlements above, bows trained on the crowd. The walls were slick with storm vapor and impossibly tall.

The Justice raised his hand, which glinted in the half-light, and let out a bellowed command. As she watched, an arrow was loosed. She followed its trajectory—it fell dangerously near. A dull *thud* of iron into flesh—a woman's scream. The metallic stench of blood filled Lena's nose.

The crowd roared and heaved in panic as a volley of arrows whistled overhead—but instead of driving them back, it made the townsfolk surge forward. An elbow rammed into Lena's back, knocking her onto her hands and knees right under the feet of a guard. The guard pointed his sword at her throat—he was standing in the small doorway in the shadows of the gatehouse.

But although he drew his blade back, the blow never came. He didn't kill her. Thank the Ancestors, he didn't.

She stared up at his peaked helmet, his young, pale face. His mouth opened and shut—his eyes widened in recognition.

"Wait . . ." He grabbed her arm, pulled her up and toward him. No one in the crowd appeared to notice how she vanished into the structure of the castle's walls.

"What do you think you're doing?" barked his older comrade from farther up the spiral staircase. His dark-green cloak was edged in black, his helmet taller.

"This is the cryptling mage who escaped the hounds last week," said the young man grasping Lena's arm. "I'd recognize that face anywhere—the Justice has had us tearing the city apart searching for her. Shall I take her to the dungeons, sir?"

Lena's heart raced in excitement. Constance was in the dungeons. If they imprisoned her there, they might be delivering her to the very place she wanted to go.

The older guard narrowed his eyes at her, lip curled in disgust, and shook his head curtly. "No, best report to the Justice. He'll be glad of some good news. But come back quick—we need every man we can get."

Lena found herself bustled through to the courtyard, her blood racing with adrenaline. All right, they were taking her to the Justice ... but maybe that wasn't so bad. She felt a sudden thrill as she realized she had a kind of power over him. Training. Knowledge. And he didn't know it—he'd be expecting a defenseless cryptling who'd been hiding in the city. If she could defeat the Justice, finding and releasing Constance should then be easy: The castle would be facing a rebellion without a leader. Who would be watching her?

Can I really do it?

Something about being back in Duke's Forest made her wish for the safety of her cowl, her small cell, the darkness beneath the city, and the quiet dead. But the dead weren't quiet anymore, and she couldn't be a coward. She clenched her fists tightly in preparation for the fight.

The storm cloud was thinner up here. Thick patches roamed the four towers, but in between, swathes of lighter mist danced with shadows. Lena could hear the hounds howling in their kennels on the other side of the courtyard somewhere. The castle looked deserted but for the guards racing around the battlements above: the windows were shuttered, doors firmly bolted. But amid the quiet, Lena noticed disturbing signs: piles of dust scattered at the edges of the courtyard, the smell of rot and bitter herbs stifling her throat—a smell she had grown up with, but not out here, not in the daylight. Rusty swords and armor lay abandoned, and a naked skull peered up from a gutter, leering. The dead had risen here too, and it appeared they had been in a fighting mood. She spotted movement at an upstairs window, the twitch of a heavy curtain. The rich folk had barricaded themselves inside, afraid.

They had rounded the north tower, but now the guard hesitated at the bottom of the steps up to the battlements. A figure was standing very still a few feet away, shrouded in the gloom.

"Hey, who's there?" the guard called. Real terror showed on his face, but he drew his sword and grabbed Lena's arm, pulling her behind him. As the cloud passed, the figure disappeared. The guard let go of her quickly, his eyes darting to her birthmark. "Come on," he said.

He led her up the stairs, but Lena knew someone was

out there in the darkness. Watching. And she swore she had felt a small tug in the space below her heart. Was the spell trying to tell her something? She rested her hand on her ribs and looked back, but the figure was long gone.

The Justice was standing on the battlements, off to one side of the riot below. He had a good view but was protected against the rage of the people, able to direct the squalls of arrow fire from a position of safety. He stood alone, a drift of storm cloud at his feet, flickering green, and Lena fancied it was marking him out as an enemy. As she stepped up the final stair, the wind blustered with an unexpected force, and magic tugged at her from within. The feeling was like a strange kind of homecoming—bittersweet, sad, joyful. She shut her eyes, feeling the movement of the huge storm all around her and the little storm's heart inside her own. It wasn't under her control, and yet . . .

The guard pulled Lena closer.

"Sir," he said, "we've found the cryptling. She was among the rioters."

The Justice turned, and Lena found herself pinned by his steely blue gaze. The heat of her hatred felt so intense she was surprised he didn't burst into flames. This man had condemned her—and worse, he had condemned Vigo, who was innocent and had tried to protect her. He had left the old man's bones to the dogs, the ultimate insult, so Vigo would never join the Ancestors he had revered in life.

A silver gauntlet on the Justice's hand glinted as he

clenched his fist. She wondered why he didn't wear a second. His other hand was black-gloved.

"At last, some good news," he growled, his voice barely audible over the roar of the angry crowd. "I see no reason to delay execution. Fetch the houndmaster and tell him to bring his hungriest dogs. The hounds shall feast today," he said.

"Yes, sir," the guard replied, and turned—but as he did, Lena caught sight of a movement down the staircase. A purple spark shot through the spinning cloud and suddenly the guard stopped short, clutching his chest.

The young guard fell, toppling over the edge of the battlements into the courtyard with a nasty *crunch* that turned her stomach inside out.

A figure climbed the stairs, and Lena started at the sight of the brass mask she remembered vividly from the night of her escape. Instead of a rich purple gown, the masked lady now wore plain, functional hunting clothes, and her hair was loose and wild out of its tight, high bun.

She raised her cane and shot an attack at the Justice, a purple flash illuminating the storm cloud like another kind of lightning.

TWENTY-TWO
Stolen Magic

Lena shrank to one side. Constance's first shot had found its target, but the Justice appeared unaffected. He raised his hand and the gauntlet spat red magic—a flurry of sparks showering the battlements.

Lena stared at him. "You're . . . a mage?"

He grinned humorlessly, and Constance frowned, then attacked a second time—but her magic seemed to be attracted to the gauntlet, which absorbed it with a flicker.

"I'm not a mage," the Justice said, answering Lena's question. "But with my little . . . device, I might as well be. It steals magic, you see. Not just the mage to whom the second gauntlet is connected—any mage's power."

"But you *kill* mages!" Lena shouted, her face pale and pinched.

He raised the gauntlet. A powerful slam of red power emanated from the palm—no subtlety or skill, simply an expression of pure force. Constance ducked, feeling the deadly heat of the magic as it passed over her head.

She kept her voice calm. "The girl has a point. I thought you hated magic, Lord Justice," she said. "Isn't this a little hypocritical?"

He smiled. "Didn't I tell you before? To conquer what you fear, you must become it."

Constance flicked the wheel on her mask, revealing the spell-scape. Now she saw how the gauntlet was connected to a scarlet thread, which disappeared into the storm, heading, she guessed, to Dr. Thorn, where he tended to Xander in the south tower. *I knew I should have let him die,* she thought.

"That makes no sense," Lena protested, her eyes brimming with tears but her voice strong and steady. "You killed people, even when they weren't mages at all, and now you're using magic yourself!"

The Justice bristled, his eyes flashing, but his voice was calm—almost rehearsed—when he responded. "I am using magic to eradicate the evil from this city. When the work is done, I shall have no need of my little device, or the mage that powers it. It is merely a means to an end."

Constance aimed for the Justice's head—a calculated attack she knew ought to hit him but not the gauntlet. But at the last moment, her arrow of purple light deviated from its course—again absorbed into the device. She had to stop herself from crying out in frustration as she watched her purple magic grow red on contact with the gauntlet, a cog whirring faster at the wrist as its power was absorbed.

Another red attack flew toward her head, but she

deflected with a sweep of her cane that set her ears ringing, the metal of her left arm thrumming. She defended against another two attacks as her mind raced. The Justice was no mage. He was stealing his power. How could she turn that to her advantage?

Everything she had fought for in the past six years was within her grasp: the girl with the butterfly was right *there*. Only this man stood in her way.

If I can't use magic, I'll just have to use my wits.

Yet another blinding pulse of red made her stumble against the battlements. She rolled to one side and stopped, her mind whirring. She played at defeat, raising a weak hand to her head as if recovering from a blow.

"No!" Lena cried, starting forward, but with a flick of his fingers the Justice sent her barreling into the opposite crenellations.

He sneered as he drew closer to Constance, his heavy boots rapping on the stone until he stood at her feet. "No last words?"

She waited until he was leaning over her in triumph— and then she kicked out savagely at his kneecaps. The Justice cried out, doubled over.

The crowd roared, and Constance realized the storm cloud had moved aside; the people below could see the duel on the battlements. She kicked again, a boot in the Justice's face, pushed herself up, and swung her cane in a huge arc she hoped would crack his traitorous skull.

But his gauntleted hand rose, caught the cane. His face

was streaked with blood—her boot had made a mess of his nose—and his icy eyes were murderous.

Down below, an enormous thump signaled an assault on the portcullis. *A battering ram.* The iron bars screamed in protest.

Constance struggled with all her strength to free her cane from the Justice's grasp. Her eyes widened, and her pulse slowed. Time stuttered, and she noticed a microscopic change in the Justice's expression—from determination to triumph.

Thump. The second assault on the portcullis felt like a heartbeat in Constance's ears. The crowd roared.

A surge of red power flowed through the cane and into her arm. She was flung backward several feet—landing, dazed, on her left arm with a *clang.* Her head beat the wall—this time for real—and her mask loosened and dropped to the stone battlements with a clatter. Her ears were ringing, a shrill, bright sound like the call of a carrion bird.

Dimly, she heard the Justice fling her cane onto the floor and approach her a second time with heavy footsteps. She turned slowly toward him, trying to force her body into action—but it felt like she was suspended in thick, cloying water. Hatred burned on his face, a kind of hunger in his steel-blue eyes. He said nothing as he lowered his gauntleted hand toward her neck. She tried to bat him away, but her vision was blurred and her head throbbed, and her hand barely lifted before cold metal closed around her throat, pulling her onto her knees and jerking her head toward the crowd below.

Thump. In the clarity between two drifting storm clouds, Constance watched the people guiding the huge battering ram against the portcullis.

"I will kill them, each and every one," the Justice whispered, a clear glint of fanaticism in his eyes. "In betraying me, they have betrayed the Ancestors."

The moment slowed. It felt as if she were closer to the crowd than she really was, close enough to see how ordinary faces had been transformed into ghastly masks of anger and fear, violence and righteousness. One woman had blood running down her cheeks. A child's body lay still and crushed and forgotten. A man was clutching his arm, roughly bandaged with rags. A girl was crying as she clung to a young man's shoulder; he was chanting the constant refrain: "Justice! Justice!"

"See how they call for me? As if they know I hold their fate in my hands."

"For you? Or for real justice?" she croaked, and her eyes were laughing at him. *Self-important fool.* His grip tightened.

Constance looked back down for a last glimpse of her city as the storm cloud rumbled over, obscuring the view and muffling the chanting and shouts. *And so the living fight on,* she thought. They might call for justice, but Constance knew the real reason they were fighting. They were fighting to survive. The living fought simply to live. Just like her. Just like everyone.

The Justice's grip had grown so tight that Constance found she couldn't breathe.

"Hey!"

It was the mage Lena, standing behind the Justice in the gray robes of Faul, her back to the storm cloud, her hair flying in a flag of darkness. The cloud wheeled around her legs like the skirts of a dancer. The Justice hesitated, turned to look over his shoulder as if startled. Perhaps, like Constance, he had been so lost in the moment that he'd forgotten there was someone else on the battlements.

"Get away from her," Lena said.

"What?" The Justice's gauntlet loosened slightly in surprise. Constance managed to gasp a breath, the impression of his fingers burning on her throat. *What is she doing?*

"I said, get away from her." The girl's voice was cool and commanding. *Is this an attempt at a distraction?* Constance reached for her magic, but the Justice held her down, and although power thrummed beneath her skin, it wasn't strong enough to break his hold.

He raised his head. "You should be back underground with the rest of your kind, cryptling. You are the worst sort of traitor."

The girl's face flushed, her brown skin reddening. "You are the one who executes innocent people for imagined crimes. People like Vigo." The girl had lost control of her emotions.

The Justice's expression shifted in realization. "Ah yes, the old mortician," he said. "But if it weren't for you, he would never have died. You should blame yourself for his death. If he was innocent, you corrupted him. You killed him, not I."

"You're wrong!" Lena shouted, but Constance spied two angry tears running down her cheeks and knew the accusation had hit home.

The Justice had noticed too. "Then why the tears, little girl?" he asked mockingly.

Lena clenched her fists, and when she spoke again her voice was calm and low once more. "Enough of this. Just release her. Or I'll destroy you, I swear it."

The Justice laughed, and his gauntlet tightened around Constance's throat. She could feel the magic welling up inside it, hot as burning embers. "I'll kill your mistress now, cryptling, and there's nothing you can do about it."

"She's not my mistress," Lena said fiercely. "No one owns me. Not you. Not her. Not even the temples. Not anyone."

Stupid girl. Now we're both going to die, thought Constance. Below, another huge *thump* sounded through the castle, echoing like thunder, and the shouts of guards suggested the portcullis was close to buckling.

The girl's eyes started to flicker with blue-green electricity.

Lena breathed in—slowly closing her eyes—and breathed out, opening her eyes again. To Constance's surprise, a huge gray cloud emanated from the girl's mouth—not a cloud of breath, as if it were a cold day, but a thick, roiling cloud, purplish and bruised in its depths. The storm rumbled in response. Lightning licked around the girl, who placed a hand over her chest, and suddenly her body was alight, fizzing and hissing with lightning. And then something rose from her pocket, a little brass creature, wings flickering in the lightning as it circled her head. Constance's eyes widened and she felt the Justice's hand drop from her throat.

She knew what she was seeing, but . . . *This isn't possible. And yet* . . .

She is *the spell's heart.*

The Justice was staggering away from Lena, holding up his gauntlet.

And then the storm cloud turned on him.

TWENTY-THREE
The Heart of the Storm

Lena raised her hand, clenched it to a fist in a wordless command. The thunder obeyed, growling somewhere in the depths of the earth, a hungry noise from a predator's rumbling throat. She had drawn power from the spell's heart, lodged inside her own body, in the past, but this was different. Here the power was spinning around her in a maelstrom, a hunting beast that would respond to her call alone. Lightning bunched and tangled in the air around her fist. The Justice's eyes widened in fear as Lena flung everything toward him with a scream of rage.

He stopped, staggered away from Constance like a drunkard. Green-blue electricity was racing across his body, and Lena could smell burning flesh, the acrid stench of scorched hair. And something else—the tug of a life toward death and a death toward life, teetering on the edge between.

She saw the Justice trying to fight the cloud, the gauntlet sending crazed red flashes into the storm. A wraith of vapor was sucked inside the device, but it fizzed and crackled as if the power were too great for it. A couple of his red attacks blew holes in the crenellations of the battlements; others came to land in the crowd surging around the buckling gates. More red magic shot off impotently into the sky. It was all pointless; the cloud simply consumed him. The air was rent with lightning, thunder, screams, and vapor that spun in excitement at the kill.

At last the screaming stopped, and the Justice toppled over the side of the wall, down into the city he had ruled—and after another *thump*, the portcullis guarding the castle broke open with a bone-shattering crash.

Lena offered Constance a hand up, but she supported herself against the wall instead, sitting and breathing deeply. Without her mask, her face was pale and shining with perspiration, a strand of long fair hair plastered to her cheek.

"The butterfly . . ." Constance gazed at the brass creature now settling in Lena's hair. "The spell's heart isn't in the butterfly at all. It's in *you*."

Lena dropped her hand to her side and nodded slowly.

"What's more, the heart of the spell is under your command," Constance said breathlessly, her mind spinning as she tried to tie it all together. "And the storm . . . just then, it responded."

"If the heart is under my command, how can I stop the spell?" Lena said, crouching down to Constance's level. "Please. I need to know what's happening . . . You're the only person who understands."

Constance shot her a hard look, her dark-blue eyes—nearly violet in the dim, stormy daylight—serious and bright. "It's complicated ... but, yes, I can help you," she said finally.

Lena's heart fluttered with hope. "Emris said you wanted to destroy the spell."

She nodded. "I want it gone from Duke's Forest. If the spell's heart had been harbored in the butterfly, I would have destroyed it, and the storm cloud would have disappeared. But if you're in command of the heart ...," she said slowly, "I can show you how to take control of the storm itself."

"And if I can command the storm ..."

"You can make it disappear." Constance finished her thought. "You can stop it from bringing the dead to life, if you wish. You will be a necromancer. And who knows what else you may be capable of."

"What do I do?" Lena breathed. She felt the butterfly crawl through her hair, its wings gently opening.

"It's not going to be easy. There's a ritual." Constance was hauling herself to her feet now. "We'll have to go down below, where we won't be disturbed."

"The crypts?"

Constance nodded. She scooped up the cane. "We'll need to go deep enough to ensure we're left alone." She looked down on the people in the courtyard. "Things are changing in Duke's Forest—but I don't think they're ready to see magic like this." Her eyes glinted as she replaced the brass mask over her face.

The two young women hesitated on the steps. If Constance had ever thought to gain control of the people, Lena saw at once that it was not possible. *Chaos has taken over already*, she realized in wonderment. The courtyard was flooded with townsfolk, and some of the guards, who either had witnessed the Justice's fall or assumed he had fled, were flinging down their weapons in surrender; others were running out toward the gardens. Very few were fighting. It was like trying to stand against the sea: the sheer number pressing through the gates was enough to overwhelm every guardsman in the castle, even if they'd all been willing to lay down their lives for . . . well, for what?

"The storm is making it worse," said Constance quietly. "It is born of Chaos and feeds on death. Before, fear largely kept people inside, protected. But now . . . The more they breathe in its vapors, the more they are driven wild."

The dogs had apparently been released but were attacking people indiscriminately—Lena averted her eyes from a body already torn and half-devoured by a pack of the snarling creatures. The houndmaster was nowhere to be seen. The doors to the living quarters had been locked and bolted, but people were breaking in through the windows, and Lena watched as others came out carrying everything from food to candlesticks. The air was alive with screams and howls and tearing flesh and the rumble of the thunder, more thunder than ever before, as if the storm was feasting on the horror and bloodshed.

"It . . . wants this to happen?"

"Yes. And that is why we—you—have to seize control of it. The longer we leave it, the worse it will get. It will whip Duke's Forest into a frenzy of death until the city has destroyed itself. And then ..."

"And then what?"

"Like I said, the spell is born of Chaos. If nobody takes possession of it, it will go wild. A storm such as this roaming the land ..." She shook her head. "It doesn't bear thinking about."

And this thing is part of me? Lena thought, feeling the beat of the spell's heart inside her own.

Constance started down the steps. "Come. We'll go to the great hall—there's not much to loot in there but tapestries and floor reeds, and it's an easy route down into the crypts."

What choice did Lena have? She could carry on as she was, the storm's heart tugging inside her like a child longing to return to its mother, remain ignorant of how to stop it, draw on the scrap of the spell's power to pretend she was a true mage. Or she could die, and the spell would die with her.

Or ... she could learn to command it. She felt a thrill of excitement. It felt right. This was why the butterfly had chosen her. This was her destiny. She watched as the small metal creature landed on her hand. She stroked it as she slipped it back into her pocket, the feel of its filigree wings calming her, as always. Now she would find out who she really was, and where she belonged.

But Emris . . . Worry and disappointment suddenly clouded her certainty. He had been sure that the spell had to be destroyed. Would he accept her choice? Where was he? Had he survived the forest?

"Lena, we have to go," Constance said sharply, reappearing at the top of the steps.

Lena took a deep breath and followed her down into the fray. They skirted the courtyard. People were flooding the castle, their faces ugly and bloodthirsty, and screams started to rise from those discovered hiding inside the buildings. When a man in rough-spun clothing tried to grab Constance around the waist, she dispatched him with a calm flick of her fingers. He lay still on the cobblestones.

"Is he dead?" Lena asked, chilled by how easy it had looked.

Constance shrugged. "Come on, we don't have much time."

Nobody else noticed the two shadowy figures as they slid around the side toward the hall, up the broad steps to the door.

Lena hesitated at the top when she heard a particularly heart-wrenching cry from an upstairs window nearby—it sounded like a child—but Constance pulled her through the doorway, her hand curiously hard and cold beneath its velvet glove. "Come on. You already know how we can help all of them." Her voice was hard too.

Doesn't she care about her people at all?

Lena had never felt much affection for the citizens of Duke's Forest, who had forced her to live in the dark ... But they were still people. She tried not to think about what was happening.

Constance led her into the great hall. Some had already passed through here, and the bodies of two black-clad guards and one woman dressed in plain brown skirts lay among the bloodied floor reeds. The smell of death soaked the air, stale and metallic. She tapped her cane on the floor and the trapdoors to the crypts burst open with a *bang*.

"Constance!" a young man's voice called.

The two women turned. Lena recognized the man on the hall's threshold, and he recognized her too, she realized, his eyes widening fractionally. He was the Duke's son—the late Duchess's son. The son who had watched in horror and grief as his dead mother had grabbed her arm. He had wept silently over the body as Lena was escorted from the funeral. She saw that his longsword was drawn but clean.

"Winton," Constance replied after a moment's awkward hesitation. "What are you doing here? Are you all right?"

"Dr. Thorn and Lord Irvine are in your apartments, guarded by Irvine's remaining men and Barbarus. But I heard the portcullis give and thought I should be with you, to keep you safe."

"Thank you, Brother," Constance said, her voice clipped. "But the Justice is dead, and Lena and I must destroy the storm spell. I would rather you returned to Lord Irvine."

"The Justice is dead?" Winton's eyes shone. "Thank the Ancestors." He stepped forward. "Let me come with you, Sister, to end this once and for all. I don't want to leave you again—I want to help if I can. We have to stop what is happening out there."

"I can't allow it." Her annoyance was obvious now. "Lena and I have to go into the crypts. What you would see down there—"

"Can it be worse than the dead rising, Constance? I've seen that already." His jaw had set determinedly, and Lena could tell there would be no arguing with him.

"Winton—"

"I will not take no for an answer—I can't risk you dying too. Not after all we've lost already."

Lena looked down at the reed-strewn floor, feeling as if she were intruding.

Constance's voice softened a little. "Fine," she said.

He nodded. "Then let's go." And he picked up an oil lantern hanging on the wall, lit it with a flick of the contraption at its base, and led the way toward the trapdoors.

Constance tapped her cane on the ground—a pale purple light emanated from its pommel. "Winton," she said.

He stopped on the top step.

"The spell's heart is inside Lena. The ritual will allow her to control and dispel the storm, but it's not pretty. We'll be going deep inside the crypts—we can't risk being disturbed. And it won't be easy. If you're coming, you have to promise me that whatever happens, you will not interfere. All right?

You will do as I say, guard the door, and make sure nobody stops us. I don't want to put you in any more danger than necessary." Her tone was businesslike, completely uncompromising. Lena wondered with a chill what exactly would be so difficult and secretive about this ritual.

Winton nodded his agreement. "I don't pretend to understand, but I promise not to interfere." He glanced across at Lena, meeting her eyes properly for the first time since she had ruined his mother's Descent. Pain flashed in his expression, but he smiled kindly. "Come, let's go."

Lena took a few steps forward but hesitated on the edge of the staircase. It led into a darkness so deep it swam before her eyes. She hadn't ventured into the crypts since that day when the Duchess had grabbed her arm with hard, white fingers. She shivered. She was an outcast; she had prayed to a foreign god, accepted his presence for a time. But now—she rested her hand over her heart, where the spell lay—now she belonged to no one. Was that better or worse? Would the Ancestors hate her, or would they be indifferent?

"Hurry," said Constance sharply from behind. "We haven't got much time."

Lena began to make her way slowly down the steps. Noises emanated from below—even more horrific than the sounds of fighting and death they were leaving behind— shuffles, the chink of old metal, and hisses like whispers. Lena swore she heard hurried footsteps somewhere in the warren of the tunnels. Cryptlings? Morticians? She hoped so. She wondered what had happened to those trapped down there when the Ancestors had started to stir. Had they been able to escape? Halfway down she stopped again. Her palms prickled with sweat. *Exactly how deep is this terrible mountain? How many Ancestors sleep here?* Even as a cryptling, she had never truly found out. There were passages that had long been abandoned, Ancestors forgotten. Where would Constance take her?

What was she doing?

"We have nowhere else to go, Lena." Constance was standing very close to her, blocking the route back up the staircase, and Lena was painfully aware of her height, of the power emanating from the glowing cane. "Don't you want to save our people? Don't you want to save our home?"

"It'll be all right," said Winton softly from the step below. "Once the spell is gone, the people of Duke's Forest will be saved, and you will be richly rewarded. Right, Constance?"

Constance gave a slight, nearly imperceptible nod.

A scream of terror rang out somewhere outside—the desperate "Please, please!" of a woman. Were the people of Duke's Forest truly her people? They had abandoned her to the dead. This didn't feel like her home—it never had.

But the spell . . . She had a terrible feeling about this—about all of it. But if she didn't go with Constance now, she would never know what she might be capable of. Lena took a deep breath and continued to descend.

The butterfly slipped out of her pocket.

"Hey!" She spun around, tried to catch it—but the creature flew far out of her reach, its little cloud-heart puffing with the effort as it headed back out the trapdoors. Lena tried to follow but Constance caught her arm.

"It's not important," she said firmly. "Come on. We have to go."

They reached the bottom, and Lena's breath caught in her throat as Constance spelled the big trapdoors shut behind them, and the whole space was lit in the steady purplish light of her cane and Winton's lantern.

Lena reached for her pocket, but its emptiness set her heart racing. No butterfly.

No butterfly, for the first time in six years.

She felt completely lost.

She stopped, her attention caught by the horror of the scene confronting her. The sarcophagi were open, the great tomb doors of the dukes hanging on their hinges.

Constance swept her cane in a broad, slow arc, and a series of lamps sprang to life on the far walls, ignited by her magic. The ghastly scene was illuminated further. In the flickering firelight, Lena could see the shapes of skeletal bodies in the gloom—not lying in state on their plinths, but strewn around, fallen, and unraveling. A weird tension hung in the air. It was as if they'd interrupted a drunken gathering. As if, moments ago, a revelry of the dead had been raging under the earth and their stillness was nothing more than a party game. Lena could see the eye gemstones scattered across the stone floor, glinting in the lamplight.

She felt choked up with tears and nausea. She was glad Vigo had not lived to experience such a thing.

Constance misinterpreted her expression. "No time for squeamishness—let's just be grateful they're not attacking us yet."

"Why are they attacking people anyway?" Lena asked as Constance led her farther into the chamber, picking a careful route between the bodies on the floor.

"The spell is fed by death, remember? Hence the Pestilence."

Lena's eyes widened.

"The Pestilence was linked to the spell?" Winton asked from farther behind.

"Of course," Constance said—and despite everything, her voice quickened with enthusiasm as she explained. "Like a child growing in the womb, the spell has various stages of development." And then her voice took on a chanting tone, as if reciting a poem. "'*First year, a vapor, a mist. Second year, a fog, a storm cloud. Then three years in summer, it shall feast on death. In the sixth year, the sickness stops—the quiet before the storm. And then . . .*'" She paused. "Then the contractions start. That's the stage we're in now. In a series of increasingly powerful and frequent contractions, the storm cloud is animating the Ancestors and filling them with its hunger for death. What it needs to reach its full potential, to loose itself on the world, is a lot of deaths very quickly."

Suddenly Constance hesitated beside a particular sarcophagus. The occupant was on the floor, facedown, chestnut hair spilling over the flagstones. Her face was turned slightly to one side, and Lena could see the glint of her gemstone eyes still in place—almost lifelike. Except for the shrunken, skeletal hands, Lena thought, she could have been alive. Her time as a cryptling had taught her to judge the age of an Ancestor—she guessed from the skin that this woman had been around fifteen years dead.

"You see, the spell's not really bringing the dead to life at all," Constance continued in the same tone, but somehow changed. "It's just turning them into tools for its own ends." Her voice sank to a whisper. "Only bringing the spell under a mage's control can change that. Only a necromancer can bring back the dead's very essence."

Turning abruptly from the Ancestor, Constance led them on, Lena and Winton walking side by side behind. Winton flashed her a small, sad smile. "I think that was her mother," he whispered very quietly, and Lena nodded in understanding.

A narrow archway at the far end of the chamber opened onto a spiral staircase leading down. Lena had heard of the chambers beneath, where dukes and duchesses of past centuries—millennia, even—were moved once the main accessible chamber had been filled to capacity. Nobody ventured down there anymore, not even cryptlings—no one would until the main chamber filled again and the older bodies had to be relocated—and the staircase was thick with cobwebs.

Lena heard Winton swallow nervously at her side. "Is this

really necessary? I'm sure with the trapdoors shut and this far into the tombs, no one—"

"You promised, Winton," Constance said firmly.

The torches on the next level sprang to life with another wave of Constance's cane. A small chamber opened out, a honeycomb of doorways leading off into darknesses beyond. The scene here was similar—the open tombs, the corpses on the floor—yet these were in a greater state of decay, barely more than bones and rotted clothes, the skin on the skulls shrunken to a thin, brown film baring yellowed teeth. The preserving potions of morticians could not last forever.

"Lie down here." Constance pointed to an unoccupied plinth set in the center of the floor—the length of a grown man.

Nothing repulsed Lena more than the thought of the cold stone sarcophagus against her back. "Whatever we're doing, I'd rather stand," she said, her voice shaking a little with determination.

"Too bad. You'll have to lie down: I can't restrain you standing up."

"Restrain me?"

Constance nodded slowly. "You'll need it, Lena. I told you this wouldn't be easy."

Lena backed away, fear clenching in her gut. *This feels wrong.* "I . . . I don't know . . ." She felt something within her snap, some instinct springing to life. "I'm sorry, but I've changed my mind," she said, her voice quivering. "There must be another way."

In a flash of purple light, she flew back against the plinth, knocking her head.

"Constance!" Winton stepped forward, his face pale with shock.

As Lena sat on the floor, her head spinning, she watched Constance turn on her brother, her mask glowing gold in the lamplight. "I warned you," she said. "Now, be quiet and watch the doorway."

Lena couldn't see Winton's reaction—but she guessed he assented as she heard no further argument, his footsteps retreating a few paces into the gloom. She felt winded and dizzy, as if she'd been punched in the stomach. Constance stood over her, strands of her long fair hair falling around her shoulders, her dark eyes glowing faintly violet through the eyeholes of the mask.

"I'm sorry, Lena. Would that the spell had stayed where it was. Things would have been so much simpler."

She flicked her cane, and Lena felt herself lifted into the air, her limbs straightened out like a doll's. She was dropped into the empty sarcophagus, a cloud of dust rising from it. Her hair spilled over the ledge of old stone, and she felt the scuttle of some disturbed insect or spider across her brow. She tried to lift her arms, to summon her magic, but Constance was too fast: invisible bindings wrapped around her wrists and ankles, glowing purple in the darkness as the spell took hold.

And suddenly it came to her: Lena remembered the color of the butterfly's magic the first time she had seen it.

Yes, it had been pale—almost white.

But certainly, without a doubt, it had been purple too.

"It was you," said Lena slowly and dimly, as if through a fog. "*You* cast the spell." Her eyes struggled to focus as Constance leaned over her, the mask gleaming in the mage-light.

TWENTY-FOUR
The Truth

Constance smiled beneath her mask. Perhaps . . . at last . . . it was time for the truth.

"What does she mean?" Winton's voice drifted weak and low out of the shadows near the staircase, like the voice of a child. "What does she mean, Constance?"

She turned to face her brother. "She means *I* cast the storm spell. She means *I* am to be the necromancer. And I am here not to destroy it, but to reclaim it."

Winton's face crumpled, and through her anger and annoyance and determination Constance felt a pull of love and guilt, her emotions woven so tightly together they felt inseparable, like the strings of a rope binding her, tugging around her neck.

Cut the rope. You cannot be restrained anymore.

Emotions fought for ownership of Winton's face too—confusion, anger, love, despair. "Why would you do such a thing? I don't understand . . ."

"Listen to me, Winton," she said softly, stepping closer to him. "I was four years old when my mother died, but I remember her. She was a mage too. She told wonderful stories, and she showed me little tricks, little games. She showed me books—atlases, storybooks, picture books... and *other* texts too. Magical books. In secret, of course. In her own chambers. And I loved her, Winton, because she was wonderful, and magical, and she was my mother. She was like nobody else in this dark place—even as a small child, I knew that." Constance felt her eyes sting, and she turned aside. "I know I was young, but I remember everything so clearly. And when she died—so suddenly, even suspiciously—I knew there was a lot more she had to tell me. What stories, what knowledge, had I lost in losing her? What secrets? What... love?" Her voice cracked, and she bowed slightly under the weight of the admission. And then she drew her shoulders back, her spine straight. "As soon as my powers started to manifest, I knew I had to find out how to bring her back."

"Oh, Constance..." Winton shook his head. "I don't know much about magic, but even I know that's not possi—"

"*Who* is to say what is possible?" Constance snapped, interrupting. "What gives *you* the right? People never stop judging. *This* is allowed. *This* is forbidden. And what for? Isn't all magic just a tool to be turned to a purpose?" She stepped toward Winton, challenging him, her whole body alive with fire and energy and purpose. "All I know is that my mother did not deserve to die. I read all her books over the years, scoured them. And there was one with such a spell. And I learned it. Who would have done differently? Can you deny your heart leaped when you saw your dead mother move again?"

A strangled noise emerged from Winton's throat, a note of pure anguish.

"You cast the spell in the crypts that night six years ago, over your mother's body," the girl whispered from behind her.

Constance turned, held her glowing cane over Lena's stuttering heart. She could feel its rhythm—her own spell calling to her, begging to be possessed. "That's right," she said. "But I didn't really understand what I was doing. How could I? I was so young, completely untrained. Spells that complicated take years to master—there are whole text-books and treatises to explain their complexities, explore their possibilities. I had nothing but the spell itself and my own ability. I thought it was a spell to bring one person back from the dead, but it was bigger than that. I didn't know it would create the storm cloud. I didn't know it was a spell to create a necromancer. A spell I should have lodged inside my heart to grow alongside my magic. Instead, released into the wild, it found the nearest vessel: my mother's butterfly." Constance shook her head. "I thought it was a brooch, but it was also a receptacle. Who knows what she originally intended it for? And then . . ."

"The butterfly found me," Lena said. "It *chose* me," she added, her voice suddenly warm.

"Chose you?" Constance stepped closer and peered into the girl's eyes, intrigued. "Yes . . ." Why *had* the spell chosen

Lena, a small, ugly cryptling? Could it not have found its way back to its creator? She turned the idea over. No, it was chance. Constance simply hadn't known how to cast the spell properly—but now she would fix her mistake.

"What?" the girl breathed. "What do you mean, yes?"

"It shouldn't have been possible for it to lodge itself inside a person like that. Its willing creator, yes. An empty receptacle, yes." She pulled the long velvet glove from her left hand, exposing the metal beneath and flexing its fingers, the perfect hinges and wheels whirring, clicking in the half-light. She heard the cryptling inhale sharply. "But a girl?" She shook her head slowly. "No, it doesn't make a jot of sense." She smiled beneath her mask. "But that's what happened, nevertheless. I guess you must've been empty too. Broken somehow. There must have been a space for a spell, right here."

Constance rested her cane over Lena's heart, and the light on the end started to throb and grow brighter, whiter with every heartbeat. Faster and faster. "Perhaps it was because you were so *un*remarkable, so *empty*, that you were chosen," she whispered. "But now . . ." She sent her magic flowing into the girl's heart, searching for the spell. Yes, there it was—a pulse of cloud with its own flickering, rumbling beat, entangled in a prison of flesh and blood. She flexed her fingers again, flicked the cog on the side of her mask, and *saw* it. And then, ever so gently, she started to pull it. Lena gasped in pain and started to struggle against her bindings.

"Constance, what are you doing?" Winton's voice again. "Will she be all right?"

"Shut up," she snapped. The light on her cane flickered and intensified. The spell's heart rose up a few inches, hovered beneath the girl's skin, a swirl of dark cloud, a growl of thunder, a stutter of lightning. She held her metal arm over it as she started to unpick the threads binding it to the girl's quivering heart: she was ready to receive the storm. The spell had grown strong. She shut her eyes. She was so close . . . She unpicked it carefully, so carefully, so as not to damage it . . . The girl was screaming.

Mother, Constance thought, remembering the sensation of her arms around her, the feeling of warmth and safety. *I am coming.*

But Winton's footsteps hurried nearer. "Constance, stop! *Stop!* You're killing her!" He laid a hand on her shoulder, tried to pull her away.

Anger and power flowed through her in an irresistible wave. She turned, raising her palm in a surge of violet light against her brother. He was flung violently through the air, landing hard against a sarcophagus with a resounding *crack*. He slumped sideways onto the floor. Blood ran down his face and into his thickly curled hair. He was quiet.

Constance found she was panting, her breath fast and shallow. He would not disturb her again.

She returned to the girl, whose wide eyes left no doubt she had seen what had occurred.

"Why did you do that?" Lena whispered.

"He is not like us, Lena. He could never understand."

"What?"

"We are not like other people," said Constance softly, her glowing cane hovering over Lena's heart, ready to continue her work. "I cast the greatest spell in the world, and you have held it, grown it for me all these years. Other people are flesh and bone and sinew, and they wander through life like cattle or sheep, aimless and happy. But we are different." She smiled a hidden smile. "We are blood and thunder." She leaned over, feeling the rush of the spell against her face, cool and electric. "We are the heart of the spell." And she started her work again.

TWENTY-FIVE
Wings

The sensation was . . . unbearable. It felt like Constance was reaching into her chest with sharp nails and grappling with her heart. She drifted in and out of consciousness, brief and vivid dreams finding her, dreams where she was running through the forest, in the crypts, even on the steps of the Holy Council, enveloped by the storm cloud. It was calling to her, clinging to her: its thunder was her heartbeat, its lightning her spark of life.

It did *choose me.*

Memories flickered in and out of her vision, punctuated by screams, intense moments of struggling against invisible bindings that pinned her to the unyielding tomb.

She knew it instinctively: if Constance succeeded, this was the end. The spell and Lena were twined together, and she would die without it.

Hot tears ran from her eyes and soaked her hair where it met her temples. And then, through her tears, a faintly glowing speck—like a ghost—slid over her vision, lit by purple mage-light and yellow fire. The butterfly fluttered around her head, spewing puffs of cloud. *Another dream?* It had left her to face the dark alone. And suddenly footsteps sounded on the stairs.

"Lena?"

She felt a stab of pain so deep her vision started to fade, the butterfly wavering before her eyes as if it had been plunged into water. Constance was easing the spell from her like a stubborn weed from hard ground. The blank mask remained focused on its task.

The voice again. "Lena!"

Emris?

"Constance? What are you doing?" His voice was tight with shock.

But it was as if the masked lady hadn't noticed. And that meant Lena was imagining it. *A dream, just a dream.* The spell's heart was tethered to her by a thread, her own heartbeat wild and confused. The butterfly landed on her nose, flapping its wings slowly. She swore she felt the tiny impressions of its legs on her skin.

TWENTY-SIX
Hunting the Storm

The girl had passed, at last. In seconds, Constance knew, she would be in full control of the spell, *her* spell. Expectation flooded her body with a thrill so blissful it was nearly ecstatic. Again, she rested her left arm against the girl's heart—now quiet—and the spell rose up, untethered. She felt the power start to flow inside her metal arm, the empty receptacle for which she had sacrificed her own flesh.

Lena's story was ending.

Hers was just beginning.

"Constance!" A familiar voice pulled her aggressively from her trancelike state, and the magic slipped through her fingers like sand. Her eyes flickered to the doorway.

"Emris?" she managed. She hadn't realized how exhausted she was, but now the thrill had rushed away and left her panting and shaking, a cold sweat on her brow. Emris's scarred face was twisted with rage. He raised a hand, and the power hit her like a hammer. She shot off to the side, landing on a corpse that let off a cloud of desiccated flesh, covering her in a film of greasy gray. She breathed and instantly coughed, choking on the foul dust trapped under her mask.

She pulled it off and saw Emris at Lena's side, shaking her. "Lena? Lena?" The desperation on his face, the . . .

The love.

Constance's vision cleared further as she blinked away the dust, and she saw the spell lingering above the girl. It had manifested as a dark cloud, flickering with green-blue lightning and hovering, curiously still, around two inches above Lena's chest. The power thrumming from it was . . . extraordinary. Longing filled her with a sweetness so terrible it felt like grief. The spell was her creation. It belonged to her. And she had pulled it from Lena but not yet accepted it into her own body. So there was still time . . . but not much.

"Emris," she said quietly, trying not to spit his name like a curse. "I'm sorry, but it's too late for Lena." She tried to sound sorry, but it felt like her voice was dripping with sarcasm. "You have to let me take control of the spell."

"What?" When he turned toward her, his eyes were brimming—it was as if he wasn't seeing her at all.

Her heart twisted, but she forced herself to remain calm.

"If the spell is loosed on its own . . . you know what that means, don't you? It's a Chaos spell, Emris. Without a necromancer to control it, it will go wild."

He shook his head dumbly. "I trusted you," he said. "You said you wanted to destroy the spell, but you're the one who cast it, aren't you? Was anything you told me true?" He looked at her metal arm. "You said Chatham did that to you. You said it was one of his experiments—and I've hated him for it ever since. But you did it to yourself, didn't you?"

She felt a spark of anger—he wasn't the only one who had been disappointed. He had let her down, too. She tried to control her tone. "Yes. I did it. And I cast the spell."

In the cold silence that followed, she buried her face in a shaking hand that smelled of corpse dust. She forced herself to be calm. "Emris, we don't have long. The spell doesn't realize what's happened yet. It's used to Lena, so it's clinging on to her for now. But once it understands it's free—"

The chamber was rent by a groan, a rattling of bones or jewelry. Constance saw movement from the corner of her eye. The dead were stirring.

"The spell has been quickening for some time now—the gaps between the periods of activity are growing shorter." She stood up slowly, dust falling from her hunting gear. "If I accept the spell, I can stop this . . . and . . . I can bring Lena back, if that's what it takes to convince you."

Emris hesitated, shook his head slowly as he lifted his ear from Lena's chest. "She's still breathing," he said, hope brightening his voice. "Her heart is beating."

"What?" She blinked.

"Stand back, Constance."

She stepped forward, instinctively disobeying his command, but was slammed against the wall and bound by invisible bonds. She thought to blast through the spell, but Emris waved his arm in a broad arc and her cane flew from her hand, as if ripped by a strong gust of wind.

"What do you think you're doing?" she said, her voice tight and low.

"As you refuse to, *I'm* going to destroy it," he said, his jaw set.

"Emris, you can't," she said, her eyes widening with fear. "You don't understand."

"It's Chaos, isn't it? Haven't I done this a thousand times before?"

Nearby, an Ancestor started to lift its head, as if waking from a deep sleep. Constance watched, holding her breath, as eye-gems clattered to the floor—but then the head slumped back down and was still once again. How long before the spell untethered itself for good? Everything was slipping from her grasp.

"Emris, it's not the same. And you don't have fifteen other hunters to help you. And, Emris—" But with a sharp movement of his hand, his magic clamped her mouth shut.

She would have said: *If you destroy the spell, Lena will die. If you fail, the spell will destroy you.*

He reached out toward the storm cloud's heart, invisible threads of power suspended between his fingers. He circled his palms around it—and even this simple act brought beads of sweat to his brow, his fingers trembling.

She tried to shout out—but it was useless.

TWENTY-SEVEN
Cloud-Heart

Lena was searching, but the forest was empty. The trees stretched into the distance, cloud curling around their roots. Her boots disappeared into the mulch of the forest floor as she ran.

"Where are you?" she called, but her voice was swallowed in the silence. And what was she looking for anyway?

She felt an aching pain between her lungs, and when she looked down she saw her chest cavity was open. Her heart was fluttering inside, grumbling and flickering with electricity. She frowned. A pair of wings separated from the tangle of blood and thunder, slowly, slowly. A butterfly crawled out. Lena watched with a kind of dispassionate fascination as it perched on her rib cage and flicked its wings.

The butterfly flew from her chest and landed on a branch nearby, brass gleaming and wet with blood, a little cog whirring beneath each of its wings. It fluttered clumsily to the next branch off to the right, and Lena started to follow, pulling her old habit tight to hide her gaping chest.

It felt like forever, but eventually she heard a voice.

"Lena? Lena?" It drifted from far above, like dappled light through the trees.

There was a dead man slumped at the foot of a tree, his face hidden as if he had fallen asleep on his last watch. She knelt beside him—she wasn't afraid. "What do I have to do?" she asked. The storm cloud whirled between the trunks, the dead leaves rustling on the ground.

He raised his head, and though his face was blackened and decayed, she did not turn away. "She who spins the cloud weaves the storm," he whispered, in a voice that smelled of sweetness and rot.

And, at last, she understood.

Lena woke to find the butterfly settled on her forehead, the realization fresh in her mind. The butterfly fluttered out in front of her eyes, flapping and puffing wildly, as if trying to tell her something important. The pain in her heart and throughout her whole body was nearly unbearable—it was like someone had stretched her out, cracked her open.

"Emris?" She turned her head, grimacing at the movement.

He was standing a few feet to her left, and she saw that he was holding a small storm cloud suspended between his hands, and sweat was pouring down his face, his three parallel scars shining in the gloom. The cloud growled and jolted, lashing out with streaks of blue that threw ghastly light across the chamber.

"By the power of Faul, I banish thee, Chaos," Emris said.

The words, the rumbling cloud, spurred a memory. Lena looked down at her chest, expecting her heart to be bared—but of course there was nothing but her gray Faul's uniform, dirtied and scorched by her adventures. The butterfly flapped over her heart and fluttered pointedly toward the storm cloud.

Then she realized. The cloud *was* her heart.

"Emris, no!" She managed to roll off the sarcophagus, landing hard and painfully on her stomach. She raised herself onto her elbows. Constance was unmasked and bound by some power to the wall, her lips apparently sealed, her eyes flashing angrily. Her cane—the pommel glowing—lay abandoned on the ground. The lamps flickered. All around, the dead stirred like restless sleepers.

"By the power of Faul, I bind thee to the void," Emris said. Lena edged onto her hands and knees, her muscles shuddering in protest, and pushed herself into a crouch. She could tell it was a struggle for Emris to force the words from his lips: the storm was restless, strong, flashing and bulging wildly between his hands. Lena staggered unsteadily to her feet. Her body screamed in agony and she felt her vision blur. She gasped, but clung to consciousness. The butterfly had settled on her shoulder, and she felt with sudden certainty that her connection to the creature was the single thread that bound her to the spell, to life.

"Emris!" she cried. "If you destroy it, I will die!" But he couldn't hear her. He could sense nothing beyond his bubble of concentration; she could feel the surge of his power beneath her skin, fighting to master the storm spell. She had to do something—before he finished the incantation.

"By the power of Faul, I bind thee—"

Lena leaped at the storm cloud.

It exploded at her touch, lightning arcing through the chamber in bridges of unstoppable blue-green light. Power surged through her, the pain that racked her body disappearing under a jolt of pure euphoria. A heartbeat sounded in her ears. She felt whole again and breathed in deeply, absorbing the cloud back into her lungs. It settled inside her. And then the chamber cleared, and she was standing over Emris, who lay motionless on the ground, his face frozen into shock, his eyes wide but unseeing.

Constance fell to her knees, panting, the spell that had bound her now broken. "You fool, you stupid fool!" she screamed, her voice faltering as she crawled to Emris's side. She was not crying. If anything, she looked enraged. Lena couldn't tell if she was shouting at her or Emris or herself.

"Oh . . ." Lena's voice broke as tears streamed down her face unbidden. "What have I done?"

But they didn't have time. The dead were rising to their feet, and they had noticed the living in their midst. Lena turned around, quaking with fear at the haggard, fleshless faces, the collection of rattling limbs. The certainty that had filled her when she'd woken up was gone, but the dead man's words still resonated in her ears.

She who spins the cloud weaves the storm.

Didn't that mean . . . didn't it suggest that she had to use the spell, to command it? But . . . how? How did she bring someone back from the dead? She didn't want to animate a corpse—not like the rotting Ancestors who encircled them, closing in slowly like a knot pulled by hesitant hands. That was not life. That was the spell trying to feed itself by killing the living. She wanted Emris back, his smile, his spirit, his very self. She could barely believe she had lost him already.

"Help me, Constance," she said. "I don't know how to do it! Don't you love him too? Please!"

The woman's face might as well have been masked for all it revealed. Doubt flickered across her eyes—and quickly hardened. And then she simply said, "No."

"No?"

Constance rose to her feet, picked up her cane. The mask lay some distance away, surrounded by a clutch of the dead, and with a little quirk of her brow she appeared to accept its loss.

"You have made your choices, all of you," she said, looking at Lena, her brother, and the man she had loved. "There is nothing for me here anymore." And, flitting past the few Ancestors rising in her path, she stalked out the door.

TWENTY-EIGHT
Mother

Constance ran up the spiral staircase and into the main burial chamber. Here the risen Ancestors walked in a slow procession up the steps—the trapdoors to the great hall already flung open. Once more, cries of fear drifted down into the darkness like the ghostly screams of owls. Constance hurried forward as she spied her mother's hair, her long blue gown soiled but recognizable as she walked for the first time in years.

Hope and horror tugged at Constance's heart. Before she quite knew what she was doing, she cried out, "Mother!"

To her surprise, the figure stopped. And when it turned, the last rays of daylight falling through the trapdoors from the great hall illuminated its face. The effect was different from mage-light somehow, as if the distant sun conferred a life of its own, even upon the dead. Constance could see her mother now. Although she looked hollowed out and pale, a ghost of herself, the embalmers had done their work in preserving her likeness. The high cheekbones, the full lips, the skin a shade darker than Constance's, the hair a rich brown. The sapphires in her eyes even glittered a deep blue, lifelike. But it was false. This creature, gazing at her blankly in the semi-light, was not her mother.

Constance cried out in renewed rage. Power drained from her in a torrent of grief. She had failed. And she was weakened: the effort of drawing out the storm spell had nearly brought her to the end of her resources. She held out her cane and pulled on her magic, a loose, churning thing inside her, as insubstantial as the foam on the sea around the islands of her mother's home.

In the moment before it was destroyed, Constance gazed one last time at the thing that had once been her mother. It almost looked as if it were about to speak. She let her magic go, and the Ancestor crumbled to dust—the gemstones of its eyes clinking as they rolled on the stone floor.

Constance hurried across the burial chamber, weaving in and out of the Ancestors and the empty graves. Tears streamed from her eyes, but she didn't care. The masked priestesses had taught her how to lie, and be strong, and to hide her true self—and for what?

Run faster.

She dodged a grasping hand, stumbled, continued. She knew she could not fight every Ancestor in the crypts. She had to escape.

Survive. Live.

Meager firelight from somewhere filtered down through the open trapdoors. The sun had vanished. Dusk had fallen. The Ancestors crowded around the stairs like a funeral procession in reverse, and Constance felt a needle of doubt.

Can I really do this?

But she hardened her determination.

You have no choice.

She spotted a small gap, barreled through, choking as the impact with the corpses threw up foul-smelling dust into her face. She swung her cane at the Ancestor in front, allowing a little magic to weave through, strengthening the blow. The Ancestor fell, and Constance surged up the steps. She was halfway to the top—but the Ancestors ahead of her were turning slowly, disapprovingly, as if she were an unruly child spoiling the sanctity of a funeral.

She scowled, swept her cane, and dispatched another corpse—took another step toward the top. But they had surrounded her now, and they were closing in.

"Get away from me!" she screamed. She had created the spell. She was the necromancer. They should submit to her command. "I command you to stop!"

But they did not. She drew on the last of her reserves as bony hands closed around both arms—the cold, useless metal and the warm flesh. She screamed again. Her cane flashed a brilliant, intense purple.

For a moment, the hands disappeared.

And she fell onto the stairs, her metal arm clanging on the stone. She tried to crawl, but she had used up every last scrap of her energy. Figures blocked out the light ahead. There was nothing left of her, nothing but the beat of her heart, demanding: *Live, live, live.*

TWENTY-NINE
Spinning the Cloud

Lena bowed over Emris's corpse, her forehead resting against his forehead. She was crying. The light had started to flicker out, the chamber lit by a dying torch and a single oil lamp discarded on the ground. Winton's lamp. Winton, who lay prone at Emris's side. Lena sat up, sobbing, and felt Winton's wrist. To her surprise, it was warm, a pulse thrumming, despite the blood running down his face.

But what did it matter? The dead were closing in on them, long shadows following in their wake. If Winton wasn't dead now, he would be soon enough.

"Please . . . please come back, Emris, please," she whispered over and over, blindly reaching for the magic in her heart, trying to understand what it required. But she was fumbling, and although bright electric sparks danced between her hands, nothing happened.

Something touched her hair, an Ancestor shuffling right up close. The stench of death filled her mouth, and panic flooded her.

"Stop!" she shouted. "Stop, stop, stop!"

And . . . weirdly . . . they stopped. The Ancestors surrounded her like an audience waiting for a show to start—the one next to her was reaching down, empty eye sockets fixed on her face. She shut her eyes. She felt suddenly how they were tethered to her, tethered to the spell—how a hundred thousand threads pulled them like a company of marionettes. Her eyes flicked open. The butterfly fluttered around her head excitedly, as if it understood and agreed.

"Step back from me," she commanded, shutting her eyes again and sending the thought along the strings.

And the Ancestors shuffled a few steps backward.

She who spins the cloud weaves the storm.

Threads, spinning, weaving. From all her years as a cryptling, helping to cut open and stitch Ancestors back together, she knew a little about that. She rested her hand over Emris's body, trying to find the threads of him . . . and there . . . there they were. Unlike the threads of the Ancestors—gray and dusty and weak as spiderwebs—his felt strong, a shining string of silver wisping away into the ceiling . . . She tugged, trying to catch it in a needle of her own power, but she couldn't keep hold of it. The effort of sensing it, of controlling it, was like trying to stitch an eyelid while wearing mittens.

Her eyes fell upon the mask Constance had discarded on the floor, and she had a stroke of inspiration. Constance had clearly found it helpful—perhaps she would too. She stood up and moved cautiously through the standing Ancestors to pick it up. When she slipped it on, the room changed abruptly. She could *see* magic. The spiderweb threads connecting the Ancestors to the storm spell in her heart shimmered softly. The remnants of the spell Constance had used to bind her to the central plinth glowed a soft, fading purple. And the ghost of Emris's magic was here too—gray smears like moonlight scattered across the floor where she had forced the cloud from his grasp.

She choked back a sob at the sight of him—because there was no magic in his body now that he was dead.

Focus.

She knelt at his side once more and started to weave the thread of his life back into his body. Sparks flew from her fingers as she held them over his chest, tugging the thread down, down, down . . .

He returned to himself with a gasp so loud it was almost a scream. He opened his eyes.

"Constance?" Fear was written over his face.

She pulled off the mask, and his expression changed, caught somewhere between love and regret.

"What have you done?" he whispered.

And she kissed him on the lips to shut him up. She didn't want to hear what he had to say.

EPILOGUE

One week later

Lena stood on the summit of the east tower, gazing out at the winter horizon. The rising moon was an eerie pinkish-red in the light of the dying sun. In the sky's farthest deepness, stars sputtered to life like tiny candles. She shut her eyes. Opened them again. Somehow the new world remained—no howling hounds, no Justice, no thunder except for the beat in her own heart, no cloud but her own breath in the freezing air.

Emris stood at her side, his huntsman's cloak shifting in the icy breeze. "Look," he said. "That must be the last of them—at least for today."

She turned her eyes to the courtyard far below, where Emris pointed. The cryptlings were arriving through the castle's gates, carrying bulky packs on their shoulders, home from their day's work at the city walls. Lena noticed a few cowls pushed back, timid faces turned toward the sunset—but far more of the cryptlings were hooded, heads bowed, hiding. She tried not to feel impatient. Duke Winton had lifted many of the restrictions on cryptlings, but the people themselves would take time to change.

One memory returned to her again and again—a memory like a joyful song she couldn't wipe from her mind. She thought of it now: the moment she, Emris, and Winton had stepped out from the crypts into a moonlight so bright it had cast shadows, to find the people calm and wondering, and the world washed new in silver. She held on to that feeling, blinked, and returned her attention to the present.

One by one, the cryptlings lowered their burdens onto the ground while someone opened the trapdoors to the warren of tunnels beneath the castle. The bundles of cloth contained the skeletons of those executed under the Justice's tyranny, finally finding a home in the sacred crypts. The evening was so quiet, she swore she could hear the bones rattle as they were set down on the cobblestones. Vigo was there somewhere. If she shut her eyes, she could almost sense him standing at her side, watching along with her. How would he feel about the person she had become?

He would be proud. He always told me I was strong. He always knew that I was important. Now I know it too.

"So many dead, Emris," she said quietly, raising her hand to touch her forehead, lips, and heart as the remains were borne down into the shadows.

A moment's silence. She didn't realize he'd been watching her until he said, "What does that mean? That gesture?"

She wondered for a moment what he was talking

about—then smiled. She'd done it subconsciously; perhaps it was because she'd been thinking of Vigo. "It's like a promise. It says to the Ancestors: you will be alive in our memories"—she touched her head—"in our prayers"—she touched her lips—"and in our hearts"—she rested her fingers lightly against her chest. Then she shook her head, letting her hand drop to her side. "I suppose I'll have to get out of the habit one day."

She turned toward him to share a smile, only to find a flash of discomfort passing across his face. He clutched at the crenellations with one hand, raised the other to his chest. She stepped closer and held his hand tightly. Ever since she'd brought him back, he'd suffered from small fits of weakness and pain.

"Are you all right?" she said as the attack passed, his features relaxing.

"I'm fine. But I'll be glad to leave this place. After all this death, I feel like I need to learn to live again."

He was right. The past week had been dedicated to the dead: the bones of innocents executed under the Justice's orders, the Ancestors who had moved, restless, from their graves—and of course the newly dead: the hundreds who had died in the battle for the castle, nobles and commoners, servants and guards of every livery. The bodies had been scattered in all corners of the castle. Even Constance's apartments in the south tower had not been spared. A man in a physician's brown coat, one of his hands covered by the twin of the Justice's gauntlet device, had been found dead at the foot of a bed. His body had lain twisted on the floor, blood pooling under his nose and strange burn marks streaking down his face. Lena had known instinctively that the lightning with which she had fought and defeated the Justice had been the death of him too. Another man, a nobleman dressed in silks, had been found stone-cold on the bed, a victim of internal injuries.

"Do you think you will get better?" Lena asked.

He squeezed her hand tenderly. "It's thanks to you that I am alive," he said, his voice barely louder than a whisper. "What's a little pain every now and then!"

The sun was sinking farther, and the deeper chill of the night was curling around them. She turned toward the west tower, one final body laid out on its summit, surrounded by sputtering torches sending bright sparks into the evening.

"Are you sure about this?" Emris asked, noticing where she was looking.

"I'm sure."

In the dusk light, from the distance of the east tower, Constance looked serene—a sleeping woman with long fair hair spilling over the wooden platform on which she had been raised, hands folded on her stomach. But Lena had found her body at the top of the steps to the great hall, covered in old corpses and ravaged by cuts, bruises, and vicious gashes—as if the Ancestors really had tried to wreak their revenge on the woman who had broken their eternal sleep. Lena had cleaned Constance herself, dabbing her wounds, helping the other cryptlings dress the Lady Protector in fresh silks from her chest. *We don't judge the dead*, Vigo had always told her. *We simply serve them.*

"I still don't understand. Constance tried to kill you for the spell," Emris said, frowning, his voice tight with the hurt and anger that always touched his voice now when he spoke of the woman he had once loved. "And then she abandoned us both to the dead when she might have helped you bring me back. Why do you pay her body so much respect? Why do you feel you owe her anything?"

Lena didn't know at first. She tried to focus, grasping for the right words. "It's like . . . it's like we're sisters, of a sort. I'm bound to her, whether I like it or not. Without her, I would not be me. It doesn't matter what she did. Who she loved. Who she betrayed." She tilted her face toward his, reached up and traced his three scars with the tips of her fingers. His eyes softened. "There is still so much I don't know about you," she said. "And now I'll have time to find out. I just need to do this one thing. To finish her story—and to start mine."

He kissed her gently. "All right. I'll see you at the feast." He glanced at the sky. "You don't have long before people start to gather."

As Emris descended, Lena gazed down at the empty courtyard, the windows lit up in the towers and the wings, the doors of the great hall flung open and yellow light spilling from inside. Duke Winton had ordered an enormous funeral feast—in remembrance and celebration of the lives lost during the dark years. The storm years. The whole castle was holding its breath, waiting to sigh. Waiting to breathe again.

Night had nearly fallen by the time she saw Emris cross the courtyard and disappear into a doorway, heading for his room, the sun a thin red line on the horizon. Lena gazed across the distance to the body of her enemy, the body of her sister.

I'll give you what you always wanted.

Lena raised her arms and tugged upon the magic inside her heart. The storm responded like a horse left too long in the stables, straining to race across the sky—bolting from her in a motion that pushed her backward against the wall. The rush of it was heady, intoxicating—wonderful. Black clouds rushed from her mouth, spun from her fingers. She felt the cold burn of lightning beneath her lungs, the wild rumble in her blood, the joyous freedom of commanding a power so great it could swallow mountains. The clouds poured into the clear evening sky over Constance's body, weaving around her, spinning tight, and enveloping her in a coiled embrace. The storm cloud was like a hive, a buzzing, contained thing encasing the top of the tower.

Thunder crashed, lightning flickered as the storm intensified, a jet of ice-blue electricity streaking down onto the dry wood of the funeral pyre. A spark caught. Great winds toppled the flaming torches, feeding the fire. Lena breathed deeply and smelled smoke. She felt the urge to fill the sky with clouds . . .

Think of all we could achieve . . . all we could master . . .

She shook her head sharply.

Enough.

As Lena drew the storm cloud back into herself, gasping, she caught a glimpse of Constance's body encased in flames, as if in a tomb of light.

The opposite of the dark tombs honeycombing the mountain.

And then her hair caught fire, and her dress, and Lena could see no more of Constance in the blinding brightness.

The storm had returned to Lena's heart. The sky was clear and calm again, the stars brightening. The glow of the funeral pyre felt suddenly peaceful, like a beacon in the night, promising haven.

ACKNOWLEDGMENTS

Years ago, the beginning of a story popped into my mind: it was an image of a girl who was marked, running for her life through swirling clouds . . . But as yet, I didn't know why. There are so many people who have helped me find out in their own ways.

To Mum and Dad, thank you endlessly for all your love and support over the years—you're the best parents anyone could hope for. And Jeff, thank you for weathering all the storms of married life with a writer, cooking my dinners, and always knowing how to make me smile.

To Natasha Pulley, my very own bestselling author on call and official Font of Writing Knowledge. I would be lost without you! And to Catherine and Tim, my earliest readers— thank you. You're crazy and wonderful and I love you for it.

Thank you, too, to everyone in my writing group. You are invaluable sources of advice, inspiration, fun, and prosecco. Jess Rigby, Jess Rule, Katherine, Maddy, Natasha—you're all so talented. I'm truly lucky to benefit from your intuition and encouragement!

I am fortunate to have a day job that I love as much as writing. The Chicken House team has been so supportive, but a big shout-out to Laura for reading an entire early version of the manuscript. Thank you, Rachel L. and Barry: you're the best of bosses. Esther, Jazz, Lucy, and Sarah: you've all shared every step of the journey with me—this book truly feels like a team effort!

An extra-special thank-you to the two people who together made this dream a reality: my agent, Veronique Baxter, and my editor, Zöe Griffiths. Veronique, I can't thank you enough for your persistence, patience, and general loveliness—you found my story a perfect home. Zöe—with your ever-cheerful and insightful guidance I've written a story I am truly proud of and had the chance to tell it to the world.

There are so many people who contribute to creating a book and making it a success, and I'd like to thank everyone who's been involved at Bloomsbury. To my copyeditor, Helen, my US editors, Hali and Annette, and my proof-readers, Anna in the UK and Emily and Katharine in the US, I'm so grateful for your eagle-eyed attention to detail. And, Fliss, you managed the process so smoothly—I really appreciate it. Bea, my publicist, thank you for introducing my story to the world—and, Jet, thank you for designing my gorgeous UK cover and picking the übertalented Miranda Meeks to draw it. I don't have space to mention everyone who worked on this book by name, but thank you all—I am honored to have such an amazing team behind me!

Last but far from least—thank you, Reader, and I hope we cross paths in the forest again ...